Ian was born in Essex in England, and at the age of 11 became abscessed with writing; it began with poems, then stories – mostly written for his own enjoyment. It wasn't until he emigrated, with his family, to Australia that a chance meeting with a friend, who suggested that he should think of publishing one of his stories; the first being, *Nursery Rhymes,* and then *They Never Saw It Coming*, a sequel. He has now followed it with *Vengeance Is Mine,* a follow on from his two previous novels. His latest book *Titania's Treasure* is awaiting publication.

This novel is dedicated to my loving Shirley, Fiona, Gracey, Joel and Ross.

Ian Smith

VENGEANCE IS MINE

AUSTIN MACAULEY PUBLISHERS™

LONDON * CAMBRIDGE * NEW YORK * SHARJAH

Copyright © Ian Smith 2023

The right of Ian Smith to be identified as author of this work has been asserted by the author in accordance with sections 77 and 78 of the Copyright, Designs and Patents Act 1988.

All rights reserved. No part of this publication may be reproduced, stored in a retrieval system, or transmitted in any form or by any means, electronic, mechanical, photocopying, recording, or otherwise, without the prior permission of the publishers.

Any person who commits any unauthorised act in relation to this publication may be liable to criminal prosecution and civil claims for damages.

This is a work of fiction. Names, characters, businesses, places, events, locales, and incidents are either the products of the author's imagination or used in a fictitious manner. Any resemblance to actual persons, living or dead, or actual events is purely coincidental.

A CIP catalogue record for this title is available from the British Library.

ISBN 9781398497870 (Paperback)
ISBN 9781398497887 (Hardback)
ISBN 9781398497894 (ePub e-book)

www.austinmacauley.com

First Published 2023
Austin Macauley Publishers Ltd®
1 Canada Square
Canary Wharf
London
E14 5AA

Table of Contents

Chapter One	11
Chapter Two	13
Chapter Three	16
Chapter Four	19
Chapter Five	22
Chapter Six	24
Chapter Seven	25
Chapter Eight	27
Chapter Nine	35
Chapter Ten	36
Chapter Eleven	38
Chapter Twelve	41
Chapter Thirteen	43
Chapter Fourteen	49
Chapter Fifteen	53
Chapter Sixteen	55
Chapter Seventeen	57
Chapter Eighteen	61
Chapter Nineteen	63
Chapter Twenty	71

Chapter Twenty-One	73
Chapter Twenty-Two	75
Chapter Twenty-Three	78
Chapter Twenty-Four	80
Chapter Twenty-Five	83
Chapter Twenty-Six	86
Chapter Twenty-Seven	89
Chapter Twenty-Eight	91
Chapter Twenty-Nine	94
Chapter Thirty	99
Chapter Thirty-One	101
Chapter Thirty-Two	105
Chapter Thirty-Three	108
Chapter Thirty-Four	110
Chapter Thirty-Five	115
Chapter Thirty-Six	120
Chapter Thirty Seven	126
Chapter Thirty-Eight	129
Chapter Thirty-Nine	142
Chapter Forty	148
Chapter Forty-One	153
Chapter Forty-Two	156
Chapter Forty-Three	159
Chapter Forty-Four	162
Chapter Forty-Five	165

Chapter Forty-Six	168
Chapter Forty-Seven	171
Chapter Forty-Eight	173
Chapter Forty-Nine	176
Chapter Fifty	179
Chapter Fifty-One	183
Chapter Fifty-Two	185
Chapter Fifty-Three	189
Chapter Fifty-Four	193
Chapter Fifty-Five	196
Chapter Fifty-Six	198
Chapter Fifty-Seven	203
Chapter Fifty-Eight	206
Chapter Fifty-Nine	209
Chapter Sixty	214
Chapter Sixty-One	218
Chapter Sixty-Two	220
Chapter Sixty-Three	223
Chapter Sixty-Four	226
Chapter Sixty-Five	229
Chapter Sixty-Six	232
Chapter Sixty-Seven	235
Chapter Sixty-Eight	240
Chapter Sixty-Nine	243
Chapter Seventy	248

Chapter Seventy-One   251

Chapter Seventy-Two   253

Chapter Seventy-Three   256

Chapter Seventy-Four   264

Chapter Seventy-Five   267

Chapter Seventy-Six   270

Chapter One

"Has he gone?" Bill asked.

Keir, leaning back in his chair smiling, said, "Yes, sunshine," and chuckled. "Our Ex-Superintendent Parker, affectionately known to all and sundry as Nosy, is probably at this very moment, sitting on a Brighton beach, in a deck chair, a handkerchief tied at all four corners stuck on his head, his trousers rolled up to his knees, contemplating whether or not to cover the stony Brighton beach crossing, to dabble his bunions in the bloody freezing cold English Channel."

"So who's replacing him, Tel?" Bill asked.

"Trevor is going to pop down a couple a time a week, just to keep an eye, until Nosy's replacement arrives," Keir replied.

"Any idea who that might be, Tel?" Bill asked.

"Well," Keir began, "Trevor is being very cagey, all he's told me is, it's someone by the name of Jarman and that he's quite a bit younger than Nosy when he became superintendent, and from all accounts very cluey, not Nosy, this Jarman chap," he replied.

"Any idea where he's from?" Bill inquired.

"All I managed to get out of Trevor was that this Jarman chap has been overseas, for quite a few years, but he got to the top the hard way, whatever that is supposed to mean, so he didn't suck his way to the top, from all accounts."

"Well from what you've just told me, he sounds just what the doctor did or didn't order," Bill chuckled.

"Well! Anything is better than Nosy has been for the last month," Keir replied.

"What are you talking about, Tel? He was never here, mind you his golf handicap has dropped." Bill stated grinning.

"Precisely Bill, every time I needed the prick, he was either on the green or in a bunker, bloody load of good that was, anyway more to the point, how's Liam?" Keir asked.

"Don't you mean the Sisco Kid?" came the reply, "He's fine now, poor sod actually thought that he had shot that cafe owner."

"That was a bloody near call, Bill, thank god Trevor's mates were there, why he wanted to go solo, I'll never know."

"I think it was the way the brothers were taken out that made Liam want to pay that priest back," Bill replied.

"And talking about that Irish prick," Keir began, "what's happened to the bastard?"

"Well, that projectile that Trevor's sniper used, took out all eight carpal bones, it's designed that on impact, it opens up into four pieces, whereas an ordinary bullet makes a half inch hole, this bullet opens up to about four inches, so it's a waste of time trying to reattach the hand, all the carpal bones are gone, so all he's going to end up with is a stump," Bill stated.

"I couldn't give a rat's arse, what he's left with Bill, all I want to know is, what's happened to the bastard?"

Bill smiled at his mate. "Well," he began, "thanks to you he won't lose his arm, your quick thinking with that tourniquet, saved it, he's in a room on his own, his left hand handcuffed to the bed, and two local lads sitting outside his room with orders not to allow anyone in, except by Superintendents Woods strict instructions, so you can sleep tonight, or whatever," he chuckled.

"Should have let the bastard bleed to death," Keir retorted.

Chapter Two

Keir had arrived early that morning, two cups of piping hot, strong sweet black coffee sitting on his desk, and a copy of the local rag in his hands, when his office door tentatively opened and a grinning Bill Day stood there, "Your coffee, mate," Keir stated, looking up from the Gray's and Tilbury newspaper. Bill crossed the floor and sat down opposite his mate smiling, Keir folded the local rag, then tossed it into his waste bin, "Well that was a waste of time, unless you're interested in the Thurrock Council and the Exmouth swimming pool," he stated, looking at Bill's smiling face, "get your leg over last night, Bill?" he asked returning Bill's smile.

"Actually no, Tel," Bill replied, still smiling, "so what's the Cheshire Cat routine for?" he asked. Bill picked up his mug of coffee, blew across the top and took a sip, "Saw our new Super this morning, nice set of wheels, looked like a nineteen fifty's Morgan, Liam's going to have his work cut out keeping up with it," he chuckled.

Keir sat up straight, "What's he like?" he asked stern faced.

"About five nine five ten, not in bad shape, nothing like Nosy, even got a smile," Bill replied.

"Did he say anything, Bill?" Keir asked.

"Only good morning," Bill replied. Trying to put on a straight face.

"Well in that case, we'll finish our coffee's and then pay our new leader a visit, shall we Bill?" Keir inquired.

"Love to, mate, but I'm wanted, you go, let me know what you think of our new leader," he said, draining his mug, and placing it back on Keir's desk.

"Be back in a couple of hours, mate," he managed to say as he closed Keir's office door.

"Oh well, here goes," Keir said to his empty office, as he picked up the two empty coffee mugs, and left his office heading for the canteen. Six minutes later

Keir found himself outside the Superintendents door, shrugging his broad shoulders, he knocked, then waited, receiving no reply he knocked again and this time received a 'Yes'.

Keir, turning the doorknob opened the door and entered, the sight that struck him was a female, dressed in jeans, roll neck sweater, and wearing cowboy boots, in her right hand she had a feather duster and her left a cup, she looked to be in her early thirties, shoulder length auburn hair, when she smiled at Keir showing perfect white teeth, Keir returned the smile to this very attractive young woman, "Cleaner," he said to himself.

"Come in please, I won't be a minute, this office hasn't seen a feather duster in ages," she chuckled.

"So where's this new Super?" Keir asked himself.

"And you are?" She enquired smiling. Keir was a bit taken aback by this question, "Why does a cleaner want to know who I am," he thought, as she walked towards him smiling.

"Er! I'm DCI Dickson, why?" he asked, a quizzical look on his face.

"Sorry," she said, placing the feather duster under her left arm, and offering Keir her right hand, "my names Fiona Jarman, and I'm very pleased to meet you Keir, it is Keir isn't it, I may call you Keir, I've been told so much about you, it will be a pleasure working with you."

"I'll bloody well kill that Bill Day when I see him next," he said to himself, as he took Fiona's out stretched hand, and was taken aback by the strength of her handshake, "nice to meet you Ma'am."

"No! Keir, it's not Ma'am, in here, or when we aren't in company, it's Fiona, okay?"

"Yes Ma'am, err, Fiona," he managed to reply, "I know it's not the norm, but neither am I, as you'll find out, I hear you have a great team, and I will work hard to be part of your team, I'm not going to be sitting behind this desk," she said, pointing, "if I can help you in any way, and if you will let me, we'll get on like a house on fire."

"Can I sit down, Ma—Fiona?" Keir asked.

"So, Trevor Woods," she began, "no! He bloody well didn't," Fiona cracked up laughing. "Sorry" she managed to eventually say, as she slumped down in her chair, "well in that case Keir, we'll have to return the complement, won't we, and I know just how to do just that," she chuckled rubbing her hands together.

Keir grinned. "And how are we going to achieve that, M! Fiona?" he asked.
"This has got to be between you and me Keir, Yes?" she asked.
"Mum's the word," he replied grinning.

Chapter Three

The four catholic priests walked slowly towards the two police officers sitting outside Shaun O'Brien's room, on seeing the approaching clergy both police officer stood, "Sorry father, but no one is allowed into this room," the nearest officer to the priests stated. The leading clergy smiled at the two officers and withdrew from his inside pocket a large sealed envelope, "We have been to see your superiors in London, a Mr Trevor Woods, and he would like you to accommodate the holy father's wishes," he said, offering the large envelope to the closest officer.

Both officers gazed at the Logo heading, "Metropolitan Police," then at each other, "I am Mon Signor Alberto from the Vatican, once you have read that letter, you are at liberty to phone your superior, and mention my name, officers," he said, bowing his head and smiling. The police officer holding the envelope removed a small penknife from his trouser pocket, and on opening it, slit open the envelope and removed the Metropolitan headed sheet of paper, the four Priest watched as the two officers read, "To whom it may concern. The prisoner Shaun O'Brien has been Excommunicated from the Catholic Church. Mon Signor Alberto has brought from the Vatican a document that the prisoner has to sign confirming his Excommunication, please allow them the privacy to carry out the Vatican's wishes. Signed, T. Woods."

"If you wish to phone New Scotland Yard and speak to Mr Woods, we will wait on your return officers," Mon Signor said, smiling. Both officers gazed once more at the letter, shrugged their shoulders and opened the door.

"Thank you my son, may god be with you," the Mon Signor stated as the four priest entered the room. Both officers looked at each other, shrugged their shoulder and sat back down. Ten minutes later the door opened and three of the priest began walking down the corridor, Mon Signor stood in the doorway as the three other priest made their way out, he turned closing the door behind him and smiled at the two seated officer. "Thank you both for your consideration my sons, his holy father will be most grateful."

"You're welcome father," came the twin replies.

Ben looked across at his mate who was just about to dose of to sleep, "You want a coffee Jack?" he shouted, bringing his mate wide awake.

"This sitting on your arse for eight hour sucks," he stated standing up, "I'll get them this time, do you want anything to eat Ben?" he asked.

"See if they've got any of those chocolate eclairs left, cheers mate, our reliefs should be here in forty five minutes, so make it quick, Jack."

"Will do mate," Jack replied as he strode away towards the cafeteria.

Allen Oakley, Now! Police Sergeant Allen Oakley, stepped out of the Wolseley police car, and opened the rear door to allow the two brand new W.P.Cs to exit the vehicle.

"This is a doddle of an assignment ladies, all you have to do is sit on your pretty bottoms for eight hours, and under no circumstances let anybody into the prisoners room except for nurses which you will accompany into the room and wait with them until they exit. There's a cafeteria, so one of you can take it in turns getting something to drink, and I do believe that there is a library, but someone has to be outside that room at all times, okay?" he asked smiling, as the trio approached the two seated officers.

"Yes Sarge," came the reply. Allen loved the sound of this new word, when other officers answered his questions or orders, "Yes Sarge, No Sarge, Will do Sarge," would cause a wide grin to spread across his face.

"Your reliefs are here lads," he shouted as the trio approached the two seated police officers.

"All quiet on the western front, I presume?" Allen asked smiling.

"Yes Sarge," That word again.

"Just those four priests a Mon Signors, from the Vatican," the officer called Jack informed him, All four officers watch the blood drain from Allen's face.

"What! Priest?" Allen screamed, rushing forward, "The priest, Superintendent Woods said to let them see the prisoner," Jack said, offering Allen the large envelope, tearing open the package Allen ran his eyes over the headed sheet of paper.

"Do you know Superintendents Woods signature constable, and did you call him to confirm it, and did you check the prisoner after these priests had left?" he asked. As he yanked open the prisoners door.

"No Sarge," came a mumbled reply. Allen yanked back the sheets covering the still body of a man, "Who the fuck is this," he hollered, as the four officers rush into the room, the two male officers white faced, the two WPC grinning.

"When did these so-called priest leave here?" He shouted, the officer named Ben looked at his wrist-watch.

"Just over a hour ago, Sarge," he mumbled.

"You two," he shouted pointing at the two male officers, "back to the yard, and hand in your warrant card, your suspended. On second thoughts, you stay right where you are, DCI Dickson will want to question you both, before he blows what little brains you've got, out through your stupid arses," then pointing at one of the WPCs, "get on the car radio, and tell DCI Dickson to get his arse down here pronto."

"Yes Sarge, what do I tell him?" he was asked. Allen slumped down onto a chair, his head in his hands, "Tell him, the fucking prisoner has escaped," he managed to say.

Chapter Four

The two W.P.C.s shot to attention on hearing running footsteps approaching. As Keir and Bill Day came skidding to a halt outside the room, "At ease, ladies," Keir stated. Leaning against the door jamb trying to get his breath back, Bill Day bending over hyperventilating. Keir pushed back his shoulders and entered, his first sight was Sergeant Allen Oakley bent over on a seat his head in his hands, the second sight was two constables sitting on the floor, "You two outside, and wait, I'll deal with you two later," he ordered.

On hearing Keir's voice, Allen shot up out of his chair, "Sorry Gov," he said.

"What happened, Allen?" Keir asked.

"All I know, Gov," he began, "is what those two have told me," he said, pointing at the door, where the two constables had exited.

"They told me that four priests gave them a letter from Superintendent Woods," he said, offering Keir the sheet of typed paper, "that, O'Brien was being excommunicated from the Catholic Church, and he had to sign some document to confirm it, and the stupid bastards fell for it, when I came in here and pulled back the sheets I found this," he said, pulling the sheet back again.

"Has anybody touched anything, Allen?" Keir asked.

"No Gov, I pulled the sheet back when I rushed in, that's when I realised something was wrong, and covered him up again until you arrived, but whoever he is he's out cold."

"Or dead," they heard Bill say, as he walked towards the prone figure laying on the bed.

"I bloody well hope he's not dead Bill, he's got quite a few questions to answer," Bill walked to the head of the bed, placing his middle and index finger on the man's neck, "sorry Tel, this gentleman won't be answering any of your question, I'm sorry to say."

"Shit," came the reply.

"And what! May I ask is going on here?" Was heard, as a stout looking Matron pushed her way passed the two W.P.C.s and into the room, "This is a crime scene madam, so I would like you to leave, Now!" Keir stated.

"I am not a Madam, I am Matron of this hospital, and this is a private ward, and I would like to know why Mr Lazel is laying in this bed, when he should be in the general ward, and where is the patient that was here?" she asked. Her hands on her hips, her ample bust pushing forward.

"You know this man?" Keir asked.

"And what business is it of yours, young man?" The Matron replied.

Keir extracted his warrant card from his inside pocket and held it up, "DCI Keir Dickson Matron, the person that was in this bed has absconded and this gentleman has taken his place," he said, pointing at the now deceased person.

Bill Day moved forward into the Matrons line of sight, "Hello Alice," he said, smiling, the Matron seeing Bill returned his smile.

"Bill Day," she whispered, "what on earth are you doing here?" She enquired.

"Came to see if you were behaving your young self," he chuckled.

"I'll give you, Young! You old flatterer," she replied smiling.

"Not so much of the old, Alice, if you don't mind. But we have a problem, and it must remain in this room, the man that was in this room is of concern to us, and we don't know who this chap is," he said, pointing at the prone figure.

"That's easy, this is Mr Leonard Lazel, poor fellow, but what he's doing in here, I wouldn't have a clue, when he comes in, it's to the general ward for his treatment."

"What treatment would that be, Alice?" Bill asked.

Matron put her hands to her mouth, "I'm afraid he's terminal Bill, cancer is right through the poor chaps body, he'll be lucky to see another month, all we can do is fill him with pain killing drugs, but they bind him up, so three or four times a week, he comes in for, well you know what," she said.

Bill pulled the sheets all the way back, and looked down at the prone figure laying on its side, easing it over onto its back, Bill pointed to the corpses left arm, "He was helped," he said, taking a plastic bag from his jacket pocket, and removing the hypodermic needle that was embedded in the man's vein.

"He's dead?" Matron whispered, placing both her hands over her mouth, "But why! He only had weeks to live."

Bill placed his arm around her shoulder, and squeezed, "Sorry about this, Alice, but this room is now a crime scene, no hospital personnel in this room, and can you give us all the information you have on your Mr Leonard Lazel, please," he said as he escorted her out of the room.

Chapter Five

Keir was sitting at his desk going over what had happened the day before, Christine had sensed that something was wrong when Keir had returned home that evening, so had Shambuck and Ntombi and despite the trio's best efforts they could not bring a smile to his face.

"It's nothing to do with here my precious," he had said, "it's to do with a problem at the station, but we'll get there," he said, forcing a smile.

"If you want to bounce things off me darling, I'm here," she had said.

Keir was brought back to reality by a knock on his door. "Come," he shouted, as the door inched open, and Superintendent Fiona Jarman's head appeared, "okay to come in Keir?" she asked smiling.

"You never need to ask 'Ma' Fiona, my door is always open," Keir replied, rising from his chair, as a fully uniformed Superintendent walked into his office.

"I'm going to introduce myself to the whole station this morning Keir, then after, could you get your team together and fill me in on what happened yesterday, I know the basics, that the prisoner absconded, but I would like to talk to the people that were there, if that's okay?" she asked.

"Look," Keir began, pointing to a chair, "you are our Superintendent, so you can do whatever you wish," he said, smiling.

As Fiona sat down, "Thank you Keir," Fiona replied straightening her shirt, "but as you have already deduced, this is my first assignment as a Superintendent, and I'm going to need help, your help, Yes I know all the legalities of the position, and I have been informed as to what my predecessor was like."

Keir smiled. "But I want you to know, that that! Will not be happening from now on, do I make myself clear?" she asked. Keir stood up, and leaning over his desk offered Fiona his right hand, a grin spreading across his face, "Crystal," he replied.

"Good! Now can you give me your thoughts on what happened yesterday please?" she asked. As a sharp knock on Keir's door made both Keir and Fiona glance in that direction.

"Have you…" Bill began as he entered, then seeing Fiona stopped, "Ma'am," he stated.

"Come in, sit down, and shut up," Keir stated.

"This is, as you bloody well know, is our new Superintendent, Miss," he stopped and looked at Fiona, who nodded in response, "Fiona Jarman."

"Sorry Tel," came Bill's sheepish reply.

"I was just about to state what happened yesterday, when you barged in, so I'll continued, shall I?" Bill sat down and just nodded his head.

"Well Ma'am," Keir began, "it would appear, that four so-called priests conned two police officer who were supposed to be guarding the prisoner, by showing them a letter from, supposedly Superintendent Trevor Woods, stating that they had a letter from the Vatican, that the prisoner was going to be excommunicated from the Catholic Church, and that the prisoner had to sign this document, confirming his excommunication, and unfortunately the two police officers, didn't follow procedure, and verify the signature, or call him to confirm the enclosed request, it would appear that one of the so-called priests was a gentleman called Leonard Lazel, a terminally ill patient, who we found had had his death brought forward by a syringe in his left arm, which Bill," he said, looking at his mate, "is having examined."

"Cyanide," Bill retorted, "so we have a murder, do we?" Fiona asked.

Keir looked across at Bill and nodded. "Well Ma'am ethically speaking, yes we do, Mr Lazel was alive when they injected him with the cyanide, but he must have known what was going to happen, he knew he was dying and only had a short time to live, and they would have put him out before they injected the cyanide, so it was an assisted death," Bill said.

"We are dealing with some very clever criminals, gentlemen," Fiona stated.

"I assume Mr Lazel was married, so a visit to his wife would be in order, and ask her if her husband spoke with her the last time she saw him, I'll bet her bank balance has improved, he knew he was dying, and this way he would be providing for his wife, and probably children," she said, Bill looked at Keir, they both smiled.

"We've got a good one here," Keir said to himself.

Chapter Six

Fiona strode into the main detectives office smiling, as all assembled rose to their feet, raising her right hand she said, "Please be seated, ladies and gentlemen," as she stood behind the rostrum at the head of the room.

"My name is Fiona Jarman," she began, "and I am very lucky to have been given this station," which received smiles and a round of applause, "I have my ideas how this station should be run, and you have yours, and when we put both our ideas together, this is going to be the most efficient station in the U.K." More smiles and applause plus cheers.

"My door," she continued, "will always be open, if you have a problem, and I can help, I will, but it does have to be a real problem, Not! The toilet paper in the loo is too thin," she said, smiling, which received laughter from all assembled in the room.

"I'm going to have a letter box fitted just outside my door, so that if I'm not available just pop your problem in the box, with your name and rank, any questions?" she asked.

There was silence for a minute, then a voice said, "Where have you been?"

"Hong Kong," Fiona replied smiling, as she turned and left the room, closing the door behind her, but waited for a second listening, to hear a roar and someone say, "God she's fucking gorgeous" Fiona threw back her head smiling, and skipped along the corridor.

Chapter Seven

Fiona sat smiling at the five faces sitting opposite her, "Superintendent Trevor Woods said, that he would try and get here sometime today," she began, "but in the meantime I think we have a lot to talk about, regarding the escaped prisoner, has anybody had any ideas?" she asked.

Liam Smith rose from his chair, "D.S. Liam Smith, Ma'am," he began, "I think we are dealing with a very well organised bunch of criminals, obviously they must have planned this escape down to the last letter, Ma'am."

Fiona smiled. "I won't say that, that is stating the obvious Liam, but DCI Dickson and myself have come to the same view. Yes you are correct, they are very clever, and well organised, and at the moment, are one step or maybe more, ahead of us. I've read the reports on this Shaun O'Brien, I believe his motto is 'Revenge is better served cold', it took him some considerable time to accumulate enough explosives to totally destroy New Scotland Yard, and Aldershot Barracks, so time to him is of little consequence, he leaves it simmering just below the surface."

"The reason I'm bring this up, and not wanting to put the wind up anyone, but a similar situation happened to me in Hong-Kong. This Shaun O'Brien could not full fill his threat to destroy the police or the soldiers, and the people that stopped him accomplishing this task, I'm afraid gentlemen, are you! And my belief is, that his next targets will be, need I say?"

"Shit," Allen Oakley uttered, "precisely Sergeant, so anyone that came into close contact with O'Brien, should be on the lookout for anything that is out of the ordinary, especially you Liam," she said, looking straight her Detective Sergeant.

"As of now, you will be driving an under-cover car whilst you are on duty, your red M.G. Is far too conspicuous, it would appear that we aren't dealing with one individual, due to the fact that four males helped O'Brien escape, well three males, Mr Lazel had his reasons to be part of the conspiracy, and when his wife is being interviewed Keir, if it's okay, I would like to be there, with a women there she might feel that she's not under threat, and be more forthcoming."

"Yes Ma'am," Keir replied.

James Cain, now Detective Constable James Cain, raised his hand, "Ma'am," he stated getting to his feet, "Detective Constable James Cain, Ma'am," he began, "whilst DCI Dickson and Mr Bill Day were at the hospital, I spoke to a couple of porters, it would appear that they were having a quiet smoke at the side of the main entrance, they told me that four men got into a white Jaguar car, one of the porters noticed that one of the passengers at the car was wearing a black robe, but what drew his attention to this man was, that he opened the driver's side passengers door with his left hand, and the right sleeve of the robe was just hanging loose, when I asked him if he could remember the registration, all he came up with was, HOM 2 something, I've ran it through traffic first thing this morning, and no Jag's came up with that rego, so I've told traffic to keep an eye open for it, Ma'am."

"Thank you constable, I don't suppose the porters were able to give you a description of the four men?" she asked.

"Just that they were all dressed in long flowing robes, with coloured skull caps Ma'am."

"Thank you, constable" Fiona said, then turning to Keir asked.

"Keir, the two constables that were supposed to be guarding O'Brien, did they get a good look at the four men, could they make an identification, if so can you get a police artist, and see if they can get some sketches done."

"Yes Ma'am" Keir replied smiling, having received a dig in the ribs by his mate, Bill day.

"I'm not teaching Grandmother how to suck eggs, because having read your files, you all appear to be at the top of your game, but please, in light of what has happened, if you see the same car twice, take note. We know that this O'Brien wouldn't think twice about putting a bullet into you, as D.S. Liam Smith knows only too well, I know I have the best team, and I would like to keep every one of you, so from now on, please! Be extra observant," Fiona stated. Smiling at her five officers.

Chapter Eight

Fiona pulled her Morgan to a stop outside twenty seven Stafford Clay's Road. Keir looked across Fiona at the end terrace house, with its 'Dun Rovin' sign, neat front lawn, the crazy paving path leading to the front door, and the pristine lawns either side of the path displaying four sculptured rose bushes two either side, and flower beds.

"Nice," he exclaimed, as he opened his door, and walked round to open Fiona's door, getting a glimpse of her beautifully shaped calves, as she swung her legs round to exit her Morgan. They both stood at the front gate taking in the neat and tidy house and front garden.

"Someone at the front window, I saw the lace curtain move," Fiona stated as Keir opened the gate, allowing Fiona to enter. They were only yards from the front door, when it was thrown open, and a woman in her late fifties stepped out onto a step, she was wearing a floral dress, and an apron around her waist, thick brown stockings and lambs skin slippers on he feet, she placed both her clenched fists on her ample hips, then throwing out her chest stated.

"I don't want Jehovah's Witnesses on my property, so kindly turn around, get in your car, and go away," she said, and was about to turn when Fiona stepped forward, "we are police, Mrs Lazel, I am Fiona and my colleague here id DCI Keir Dickson, we would just like to have a quick word with you, if you have the time, if you haven't, you could always come down to the station, if it's more convenient, it's about your dear husband Leonard."

Both Keir and Fiona noticed the woman's eyes begin to fill with tears, "Leonard died of cancer," she managed to say, as she turned and entered her front door, which she left open. Keir and Fiona followed the woman into a well laid out front room, a black and white eighteen inches television displaying the B.B.C. News, which she immediately switched off when Fiona and Keir entered her front room.

"Sorry about that," she said, "but last week I couldn't get rid of them, some even turned up with little children. Now! what is it you want to know, Leonard and I knew he didn't have long, but he did say that he wanted to die in his own bed, but obviously he didn't get his wish, it was just as well he was at the hospital, and not driving home when he left us, he could have hurt someone," she said, solemnly.

Fiona looked at Keir who nodded, "What have you been told, Mrs Lazel?" Fiona asked.

"Call me Margaret please, and before we start, would you like a cup of tea, I was just about to make one when you turned up," she said, "that would be lovely Margaret, thank you," Fiona replied.

Mrs Lazel returned seven minutes later with a tray carrying a tea pot, sugar bowl, milk jug, three bone china cups and saucers, and a plate of chocolate digestive biscuits.

"Help yourselves to the biscuits," she said, as she laid the tray down on a coffee table, "I'll be Mum, shall I?" she asked smiling, as she sat down opposite Fiona and Keir.

"So what have I been told," she said, as she picked up the teapot and began to pore, "just that Leonard had passed away peacefully in a hospital bed."

Fiona looked at Keir and raised her eyebrows, "Been married long, Margaret?" Keir asked as he accepted the bone china cup and saucer.

"Help yourself to sugar and milk," Margaret instructed, "All our lives," she whispered, "I fell in love with Leonard at the age of seven."

"Seven!" Fiona gasped.

Mrs Lazel smiled. "Yes seven, Leonard was ten, a bully stole my apple at break, Leonard saw him and got it back for me, but not before punching the boy on the nose, and making it bleed," she chuckled.

"So you had a Knight in Shining Armour, did you, Margaret?" Fiona said, smiling.

"Leonard has been my Shining Knight all our married life," she whispered, as tears streamed down her cheeks, Keir whipped his pocket handkerchief from his top pocket, and putting down his cup, knelt down in front of Margaret, "here," Keir said, Margaret wiped her eyes then blew her nose, "sorry about that," she managed to say.

"Right," Fiona began, as Keir sat down beside her, "can you tell us what happened before Leonard left us, did he have any visitors, did he say anything yesterday before he went to the hospital, anything at all, Margaret."

Margaret sat there looking into her cup, then taking a deep breath began, "Well, about a week or so ago, two men turned up at just after we had had our tea, one was a doctor, I could tell you know, he had a stethoscope in one hand and a medical bag in the other, they were both dressed really nice in suites, Leonard took them into the front room, and told me that they had received some new results, and there was a new treatment out that they wanted to try, and that he would have to strip off, so to go Into the kitchen, and that he would call when they were finished. Anyway, they were only in the front room for about six minutes when Leonard comes out smiling, and ask me to make a pot of tea, when I took the tray in, they were all smiling, they seemed nice gentlemen, I notice the doctor came from abroad, because of his accent."

On hearing this, both Fiona and Keir sat bolt upright. "From abroad?" Keir asked.

"Yes, why?" Margaret replied.

"You didn't manage to catch their names, by any chance?" Fiona asked.

"No I didn't, is there something wrong?" Margaret asked, a concerned look on her face.

"No Margaret, there's nothing wrong, everything is fine as far as we are concerned, we have to ask these questions, one thing Keir and Myself know for a fact, is that your Leonard loved you very much, even in your loss you are a very lucky lady." This statement sent Margaret into floods of tears, causing both Keir and Fiona to rush to her side and embrace her.

It took at least five minutes before Margaret could get her emotions under control, "Sorry about this," she kept saying.

"You have nothing to be sorry about, Margaret, just think how lucky you have been to have had someone who loved you, do you have anyone that can come and sit with you?" Keir asked squeezing her shoulder, "Both our daughters are in Australia, Emma is a barrister in Melbourne, and Matty is an orthopaedic surgeon in Brisbane, so no I don't," she managed to say.

"Did Leonard say or do anything unusual before he went to the hospital yesterday Margaret?" Fiona asked.

At this question, Margaret began to blush, and started to catch her breath, "it's very embarrassing," she whispered, "I'll take these cups and saucers into the kitchen, whilst you two girls have a women's chat, shall I?" Keir said, picking up the tray, Fiona looked up into Keir's face smiling, and winked, mouthing, "Thank you."

"This is very embarrassing," Keir heard as he shut the door, "just take your own sweet time Margaret, it's just us now," Fiona said, squeezing Margaret's shoulder.

"Well," Margaret whispered, "Leonard and I haven't been close, if you know what I mean, with the cancer and all, but yesterday he asked me to take off my nightie and lay with him, I thought it was something to do with the doctor, that he had given Leonard something, we laid on the bed running our hands over each other, but bless him nothing happened, but it was wonderful having him cuddle me. Then he said, "If this treatment doesn't work, and I don't make it, I was to sell the house, there was some money in the bank, and that I was to go and live with either Matty or Emma in Australia, and that I had to promise that I would do as he had asked."

"And I will, but I don't know about any money in the bank, the last time I looked we only had seventy six pounds seven shillings and sixpence, so where that is going to take me I don't know, it will be selling the house that will get me to Australia, I've been plucking up courage to phone the girls about their dad."

Fiona looked at her wrist-watch and seeing ten passed twelve, said, "Well don't ring now, they'll be tucked up in bed, it's only ten passed three in the morning," she chuckled, as Keir knocked on the door, "you girls finish ripping me to bits?" he asked as he walked into Margaret's front room.

"Yep!" Fiona replied smiling, then squeezing Margaret's shoulders said, "I think your Leonard has been very naughty, and that he has a very big surprise in store for you, young lady."

"How?" Fiona was asked.

"Just put it down to women's intuition, us girls have got it, they haven't," she said, pointing at Keir. Keir sat down on Margaret's settee, then leaning forward asked, "You didn't happen to notice when the doctor and his friend turned up, what sort of car they were driving, by any chance?"

"All I can tell you," Margret began, "it was big and it was white."

The three occupants of Margaret's front room were distracted by the sound of the Westminster chimes coming from the hall way, "I'll go," Keir said, rising from the settee, Keir could make out two blurred figures, through the frosted glass as he approached the front door, placing his hand inside his jacket feeling for his warrant card as he opened the door, to be confronted by two armed Securecor guards, "special delivery for a Mrs Margaret Lazel," Keir was told.

"And we need a signature, sir," Keir drew out his warrant card, "DCI Keir Dickson, gents, I'll sign for it," he stated.

"Sorry sir, but the package is addressed to a Mrs Margaret Lazel, and you could be the queen of England, but if I don't go back Mrs Lazel's signature, the package goes back with us, and the lady will have to retrieve it from our main office, and tell the lady to bring identification," Keir was told, Keir stepped through the door partially closing it, as the two men stepped back, "look fellers," he began, "Margaret's husband has been murdered, and she's very upset, my superintendent and myself are trying to help her, you can come in if you like."

"We are very sorry to hear that sir, but unfortunately, we are not allowed to cross the threshold of any domestic property."

"Wait here," Keir said, rolling his eyes. Opening the front room door and leaning in, he said, "Margaret Securecor have a special delivery for you and they need your signature, sorry about this, but they won't accept mine."

"Coming," she said, blowing her nose and wiping her eyes. Keir placed his arm around Margaret's shoulder as he escorted her to the front door, "Yes" Margaret said to the two men, "are you Mrs Margaret Lazel, of," he stopped to read the name and address on his clip board, "of twenty seven Stafford Clays Road."

"Yes," Margaret replied.

"Have you any means of confirming that, madam?"

"Right!" Keir hollered, taking out his notebook and leaning forward, "Clive Shilling, number six one six one six, you!" He said, pointing at the older second man, "Come here," he shouted.

The man stepped forward smiling, "Yes Gov?"

There was silence for a minute, "Do I know you?" Keir asked, a quizzical look on his face, "You probably don't remember me Gov, do you remember that robbery at that jewellers in Pitsea, and you caught the two at Tarpots, well I was first on the scene, you were having a problem with that bus conductor," he chuckled.

"Sorry about Clive, Gov, he's only been with us a couple of months, so if the lady will just sign here," he said, taking the clip board and handing it to Keir, "we're sorry for the lady's loss, Gov, and we'll be on our way."

"Trevor Knight, constable Trevor Knight," Keir beamed, "yes Gov, that fat bloke took some moving, after you had clobbered his prisoner," he said, as Margaret signed her name.

"Thank you, Constable," Keir said smiling.

"Not anymore, Gov," Trevor replied as he handed over the large package, "you're driving," he said, throwing a bunch of keys and scowling at his co-worker, as they turned and walked toward their armoured car.

"Do you know anyone in Jersey, Margaret?" Keir asked looking at the post mark on the large package, as he closed the front door behind them.

"No inspector, I don't, Leonard the girls and myself went there some years ago, for a holiday, but other than that no, why?" she asked.

Keir smiled. "Please call me Keir, Margaret, it's just that the post mark states it began its journey from Jersey in the Channel Islands, that's all."

"Well," she replied. As they walked into the front room, "I haven't got a clue, we did get brochures for a while from the hotel we stayed in, but that stopped years ago."

"Well you'll just have to open the package and see, won't you," Keir said, smiling.

"What happened at the door?" Fiona asked, rising from the settee.

"Securicor special delivery," Keir replied.

"All the way from Jersey in the Channel Islands," he added. Margaret sat down in an armchair, the package on her lap, Keir and Fiona stood looking down, as Margaret removed the wide Cello tape from the end of the package, opening it up, then placing her hand into the end, began sliding the contents out onto her lap. When the room was shattered by a scream, as Margaret stared at an envelope attached to a cardboard box, her hands going to her mouth as she burst into tears. Keir caught the box just before it hit the floor, as Fiona wrapped her arms around the sobbing woman.

Keir looked at the envelope, in copper plate script was written, "My Precious M," he then looked across at Fiona, who had the distraught woman in her arms, and raised his eyebrows.

"What the hell happened there," he said to himself, all they could hear between sobs were, "Leonard, Leonard, Leonard." It took at least five or more minutes, before Margaret could speak coherently, Keir also noticed that Fiona was trying hard to fight back the tears, without much success, then placing his hand on her shoulder, squeezed.

"Margaret," he whispered, "what's wrong?"

Margaret pointed at the envelope, "Leonard," she managed to say, both Fiona and Keir stared at the copper plate statement, "that's Leonard writing," she sobbed, "would you like me to open the letter, Margaret?" Fiona asked.

Margaret just nodded. Keir had removed the letter from the cardboard box and handed it to Fiona, she opened it, and looking at the beautiful handwriting, but she was only able to read a few lines before she too burst into tears, and offered the letter to Keir shaking her head from side to side. Keir took the letter, and after reading its contents, had to fight back the tears as well.

"That husband of yours, Margaret, was quite something," he managed to say, "good job Bills not here, don't want him seeing this side," he said to himself.

"Right," he began, placing the letter back in the envelope, "it would appear that your Leonard has taken out an insurance policy, and he states that he wants you to keep your promise to him that you will sell the house and move to Australia, with your two daughters, and to take the money from the box and place it in the bank" Fiona looked up into Keir's face. "Later," he mouthed.

Keir took a penknife from his trouser pocket and on opening the blade, ran it round all four sides of the box, but when he removed the lid, gasped at its contents. Two neat rows of stacked five pound notes, double banked, Keir did a quick calculation, "Five thousand fucking pounds," he said to himself as he replaced the box lid.

"I think it would be a good idea if you gave Fiona here, your bank book, so she could run this little bit of money to your bank, is it Barclays in Stanford?" he asked.

"Yes it is, but I can catch the bus in the morning, I need some shopping, so I'd be killing two birds with one stone, so to speak," Keir was gazing at Fiona shaking his head, "no Margaret, you're not going on a bus with some money in your bag, either Fiona or myself will quickly run this box to your bank and put it in a safe place, I insist," he stated.

Margaret went over to her writing desk, and pulling down the flap retrieved her bank book, "Here," she said. Fiona placed her hand into her jacket pocket, "My keys, Keir," she said, holding them up to him, "I'll stay with Margaret until you get back, I'll just have to show you the gear shift, it can be a bit sticky," she said, getting to her feet.

Keir placed the box under his arm, and took Fiona's car keys, "Won't be a minute, Margaret," Fiona said, as they exited Margaret's front room. As soon as they closed the front door Fiona grabbed Keir's arm, "What's in the box Keir?" she asked.

He turned and faced her, "You were right, Fiona," he replied, "they paid Leonard five thousand pounds to take O'Brien's place."

"Holy cow," she gasped, as they walked towards her Morgan.

Chapter Nine

"Has Colleen been taken care of?" O'Brien asked.

"Yes, Shaun," came the reply, "so what does Colleen think happened?" O'Brien added, "We told her that the protestants tried to recruit him, but he refused, so they took him out."

"Is Colleen going to continued running Shannan's?" O'Brien asked.

"So she said," came the reply.

"And this Lazel chap?" O'Brien asked.

"Yes Shaun, Securicor has already delivered the package."

"Can it be traced back to us?" the man was asked.

"No Shaun, all there was, was the box with five thousand pounds in it, and a letter to his wife, I read the letter, he just gave his wife instructions to sell their house and move to Australia, plus lovey stuff, we tried to knock him down in price, but he just stuck to the one amount, and time was running out, the only chance we had was whilst you were in hospital, if you had been in prison, we would have had one hell of a job getting you out."

"So how's our bank balance now?" O'Brien asked. The man smiled. "In the Jersey account you have just over six hundred thousand pounds, and in the Zurich account," he said, looking at a notebook he had removed from his jacket pocket, "you have one hundred and seventy seven thousand American dollars, but enough of that," he said, opening his medical bag, "it's time for your injection, you haven't been out of hospital long, and you're open to infection."

"Right," stated O'Brien, as he removed his shirt, wincing as the sleeve ran over the end of his damaged arm, "just one situation that I have to repay, then The West Indies," he said, smiling.

Chapter Ten

Fiona, Bill, and Liam were seated in Keir's office, four cups of steaming hot coffee in their hands, Keir gazing down at the large envelope that was laying on his blotter, "I think we can safely say that there would be an Irish connection somewhere," stated Fiona.

Three heads nodded in agreement, "I know I'm stating the obvious, but we know that the money was sent from Jersey," she added.

"Well," Liam began, "we know Jersey and Guernsey are tax havens, people who work abroad have their salary paid into one of the Channel Island banks, then transfer a smaller amount into a U.K. Bank, so they pay next to nothing in tax, so you are right Ma'am, it's very feasible that this O'Brien chap would choose an off shore bank, but which one, there must be dozens?" he asked.

"Well maybe O'Brien is patriotic," she said, smiling, "so check any banks that have Irish connections," she added.

"And how is Angela, Liam?" she asked smiling.

Liam's eyebrows shot up, "F-fine Ma'am," he managed to say, "why?"

"Have you told your intended what has transpired with this O'Brien chap, Liam?" She enquired.

"No Ma'am, why?" Fiona lent forward and looked straight at him, "I don't know if you remember me saying about an incident that happen to me in Hong Kong, but I lost one of my best detectives. Have you ever heard of the Triads?" she asked.

"There are seven gangs in Hong Kong, my detective was instrumental in bring to justice, one of the top men in the Sun Yee On gang, three months later he didn't turn up for duty, when I sent a constable round to his house, his wife and four children had been burnt alive in their house, and he was found hanging by his feet from a tree in his garden, they had skinned him alive, it took him days to die."

"Jesus Christ!" Bill uttered, "The poor bastard."

"So Liam, please inform your Angela to be on the lookout, if she sees the same car or person more than twice and she doesn't know them, be careful, and that goes for all of you," Fiona said.

"Well," began Keir, "if you wanted to scare the living crap out of all of us, I would say you have succeeded Ma'am, no disrespects meant," he stated.

"That was my intention Keir, this O'Brien nurtured hatred for many years, so he won't forget who stopped him from getting his revenge against the police and the army. I just want you all to be safe, please!" She said.

"Thank you Ma'am," Liam said, "I'll get Angela to move back home, she can wrap Judge Frobisher round her little finger, but I know she won't be happy about the whole situation."

"As soon as we catch O'Brien, and! We will, normal life will return, so can we get our heads together, and excuse my language, catch the bastard," she exclaimed.

Chapter Eleven

"According to the report, this O'Toole chap owned a I in Tilbury, Keir, but his wife ran it, is that correct?" Fiona asked. It was just the two of them, Bill and Liam had left, Bill to check on Jersey and Guernsey banks, with the help of the teams new detective constable James Cain, and Liam to have a discussion with his future wife.

"Yes Fiona," he replied, "she seemed to run the place, I did meet her when we were doing under cover observations, but not to talk to, why?" he asked.

"Does she know what happened to her husband?" Fiona asked.

"I'm not sure, the funny thing is that when she was told that her husband was shot," her reply was, "well I hope you catch the bastard that did it," which rather threw us a bit."

"Well in that case, I think you and I should pay Mrs O'Toole a visit, don't you?" she asked smiling. Keir began to laugh, tears rolling down his face, "What's funny?" Fiona enquired, a serious look on her face.

"Sorry," Keir managed to say, trying to take deep breaths, and shaking his head, to get his humour under control, "when I first met you," he chuckled, "I thought you were a cleaner, what with your feather duster, and cowboy boots, then when you said, your name, my thoughts were, excuse my language, 'Not a bloody woman', but you've dispelled any ideas I've ever had about female commanders, I thank god, you chose this station," he said, a broad grin on his face.

Fiona had turned crimson at Keir's remark, and delved into her shoulder bag, looking for anything, so as not to look at Keir, "That's very nice Keir, but there are times when I still regard myself as a DCI, but shouldn't we be on our way to Icafe," she managed to say.

"Your car or mine?" Keir asked smiling.

Fiona smiled as she approach Keir's Morris one thousand, but stopped when she saw the look on his face. "Never judge a book by its cover," Keir stated as he opened the passenger door, "does that also apply to Police Superintendents Keir?" She chuckled.

"Touché!" Keir replied, a broad grin on his face, as Fiona gave him another glimpse of those feminine calves.

"Wow!" Fiona exclaimed as she fastened her seat belt, "the interior puts the exterior to shame Keir," she added.

"Glad you think so, Police Superintendent Jarman, Ma'am," he chuckled as he fired up, what was now affectionately known to all as 'The Beast'.

Keir put the Beast into reverse and sedately backed out of his reserved spot, "Tilbury here we come," he stated. As his rear wheels tried to make traction with the surface of the Police car park asphalt surface.

"So," Keir began, as he eased onto Corringham Road, "so how did Fiona Jarman become a copper?" he asked.

Fiona chuckled. "Purely by accident, actually," she replied.

"My father was a captain in the army, but was disabled out, so he chose politics and became a British Attaché, his first assignment was in Pretoria, South Africa, that was where I was conceived, I should have been born on the thirty first of July, my parents had worked it out to the day, they never let me forget it," she chuckled.

"It would have been on their wedding anniversary, but I was quite happy where I was, so I waited until they were at a government function in Johannesburg, it was then that I decided to make my entrance into the world, much to my mother's annoyance, they were twenty days out. When I reached the age of eleven, my father was transferred to Hong Kong, I did okay at school so my father sent me over here to stay with his sister, I managed to get into Oxford and studied law, this is where the accident happened, we were in a discussion group, and this idiot who thought he was god's gift to women, because Daddy had a title, started mouthing off about women in the police force, that we were just there to service the male police officers, and the highest rank a women could attain was constable, all us girls turned on him, and Bell, bless her, cut him down to size."

"How come?" Keir asked smiling at this honest outburst, as he turned onto Chadwell Road.

"She said, I quote, 'From what we've been told Simon, there's no point you joining the police force, yours is no bigger than a belly button' unquote, It was then that I decided that I wanted to be, as you put it a copper," she chuckled.

"Thank you, Simon," Keir hollered as he pulled into Dock Road.

Chapter Twelve

Father Patrick O'Connell bowed before the alter, then rising to his feet, walked over to his confessional box, pull the curtain across and sat down. Sliding the hatch way door to the side, he heard, "Forgive me father for I have sinned, it's been two weeks since my last confession," Father O'Connell waited, the silence continued for at least two minutes when, "my boyfriend wants me to have sex with him Father," he was told, "how old are you my child?" he asked. Silence again, then "I'm sixteen and four months, Father."

"Well she's legal," he thought to himself, clearing his throat Patrick asked.

"Have you been together long, my child?"

"Just over three weeks, Father," came the reply, "you do realise that fornication out of wedlock is a mortal sin, my child," he said.

"Yes Father," came the reply, "but when he starts to caress me down there, I want him to make love to me Father," she snivelled.

"Right, my child," he began, "it is a great temptation to satisfy these desires, and these temptation are thrust upon us, but we must fight against such temptations, until we enter the holy sanctuary of wedlock."

Patrick sat there waiting, all he could hear was sobbing, then nothing, except the door to the confessional being shut, and running footsteps, "Another unwanted pregnancy," he said to himself as he heard the door to the confessional open and shut.

"Forgive me Father for I have sinned," Father Patrick O'Connell sat bolt upright, the hairs on the back of his neck standing straight up.

"Shaun! What the devil are you doing here, don't you know everyone is looking for you," he whispered through the partition.

"Yes, Patrick," came the reply, "I'm fully aware, that the police are looking for me, but I managed to walk in here, and nobody recognised me, so don't panic, I need your help," he stated. Father O'Connell sat there in silence, his brain trying to put this situation into context, "You lied to me, Shaun, why?" he asked.

"We had to Patrick, we had to, we didn't want you to get into any trouble."

"Trouble," Father O'Connell shouted, "I was bringing drugs into the country Shaun, not gin as I thought, I thought we were helping the children, but we weren't, were we?" He stated.

"As I've just said, Patrick we didn't want you to get into trouble, it was the only way that my plan would work, you had to be kept innocent of what was going to happen."

"You mean killing as many police and soldiers as you could, Yes?" he asked.

"They shot and killed Michael and Brendon, and tortured me, our dear lord knew my plan, to put things right."

"If as you say, our dear lord knew your plan, how come it failed, and you are now a wanted man?" Father O'Connell asked.

"Because of an interfering policeman and two greedy criminals," he said, "we go back a long way, Patrick, and I'm asking for your help," he added.

"Vengeance is mine, saith our lord, or had you forgotten that Shaun?" Patrick asked.

"They were my young brothers Patrick, they shouldn't have been murdered," he screamed, "maybe you are right Shaun, maybe they shouldn't have been shot, but they were trying to run a road block, the soldiers didn't know they were just mucking about, and they had been given orders. I was there Shaun I saw it all happen, I didn't see the brutality to you, but I have seen the aftermath, and I can except how you must feel. You've asked for my help, I will pray for you Shaun, and I won't say a word to anyone that I have spoken to you, but that is all the help I can give you Shaun, I'm sorry," Patrick sat there waiting for a reply, but nothing came.

Chapter Thirteen

"It's in Calcutta Road, Fiona," Keir stated as he slowed down, "so how do you want to handle it?" he asked.

"Well," Fiona replied, as they pulled into Calcutta Road and came to a halt. "From what you have told me, her reaction when told that her husband had been shot was, 'Well I hope you catch the bastard that shot him'. So I'm thinking that she knew he'd been shot before your police officer notified her of his demise, so let's just play it by ear, and see what she has to say, shall we?" she asked.

"You're the Governor," Keir replied smiling, as they moved off. Four minutes later Keir cruised to a halt, ten yards from the Shamrock Cafe front door, then switching off the ignition, exited his Morris, Fiona hadn't bothered to wait for Keir to be a gentleman, and was standing on the pavement waiting as he came round the rear of his Beast.

"After you, young lady," he stated giving Fiona a Sir Francis Drake bow, "thank you kind Sir," came the smiling reply. Two minutes later Keir push open the door to the Shamrock Cafe, where a smiling Colleen greeted them.

"She doesn't seem too distraught at becoming a widow," Keir whispered as he turned and closed the door.

"And how can I help you two lovely people?" Colleen O'Toole asked smiling. "We would like two coffees, and I'll have your famous Irish Soda Bread bacon sandwich, and my friend will have—" Keir said, turning, and looking at Fiona, "I'll have the same, and could we have a minute of your time, Mrs O'Toole please, we need to talk."

"What do we need to talk about?" Colleen asked.

"Your husband, Mrs O'Toole," Fiona replied.

"Somebody shot him, he's dead, all the talking isn't going to bring him back, is it? I'll get your order," she said, as she turned and went behind the counter. Fiona and Keir sat facing each other at a table overlooking Calcutta Road, "do you think she's upset at losing her husband?" Keir asked.

"She might be hiding it, keeping it inside I don't know," Fiona replied.

"Or she might be rubbing her hands together, now that she owns this," he said, bring his arm around, "but we'll soon find out," he said, as he looked toward the counter, where Colleen O'Toole with a tray and their order was heading there was.

"So what do you want to talk about?" Colleen O'Toole asked, as she placed the tray on their table. Fiona and Keir both rose, "Could we have five minutes of your time, please Mrs O'Toole?"

"Well," Colleen replied looking around at empty cafe, "it's not that I'm rushed off of my feet right now, but if I get busy, we'll have to cut it short, I've got a living to make," she said as she sat down beside Keir.

"Thank you, Mrs O'Toole," Fiona said, as they all sat down, Fiona offered Colleen her right hand, "Mrs O'Toole," she began as Colleen took her hand, "my name is Fiona Jarman," she said, smiling, "and I'm Police Superintendent, my colleague here," she said, pointing at Keir, "is DCI Keir Dickson, and we would like to talk to you about your recent loss."

Colleen smiled. "So you've caught the person that shot him, have you?" she asked smiling.

Fiona looked at Keir, "Mrs O'Toole," Keir began.

"It's Colleen," he was told, "thank you Colleen, could you tell us what you've been told, please," Colleen O'Toole first looked at Keir, then at Fiona, "well," she began, "first there was this doctor, then two of your officers came in and told me that he had been shot, why?" she asked.

Keir took out his notebook and Parker fountain pen, from his inside jacket pocket, and placed them on the Formica tabletop, flipping open his notebook, he asked, "What is the name of this doctor, and do you know where he practises?"

"Why?" he was asked.

"Just routine, Colleen, I have to jot things down, I've got a crap memory, I'm sorry to say, luckily my wife has a brilliant memory, the number of times she tells me, 'You'd forget your head, if it wasn't screwed on'," he chuckled.

"I know exactly what you mean, that stupid husband of mine, had a brain like a sieve, it got that I would have to make out a list for our suppliers, and phone it through, he was useless."

"The doctors name, Colleen?" Keir stated.

"Yes sorry, It's doctor Roberto Porcelli and his practise is in Dagenham, why Shamus went there I will never know, I go to one in Tilbury here, do you want him as well?" she asked. As Keir wrote down this information.

"So can you tell us what he told you Colleen, please?" Fiona asked, as Keir took a bite out of his bacon sandwich.

"Well," Colleen began, as Fiona sipped her coffee, "he told me that Sheamus had been approached by some Irish Protestant to infiltrate the I.R.A., which was stupid because he didn't know anyone in it. Well! I didn't think he did, and he refused, so they shot him, stupid bugger."

Keir looked at Fiona and shook his head, "What?" Colleen asked. A concerned look on her face.

"Colleen," Fiona said, placing her hand across the table, "do you know a Shaun O'Brien by any chance?" she asked.

"Don't you mean, Father Shaun O'Brien?" Colleen asked.

"Yes," Fiona replied.

"Yes I know him, but only to talk to on the phone, Sheamus dealt with him quite a bit, and it was all sort of secret, if he rang I had to leave the room, it got up my nose, and caused arguments," she said. Keir had finished his sandwich, then taking a handkerchief from his trouser pocket, wiped his mouth and hands.

"Colleen," he said, turning, "we have something to tell you, and please can you just listen to what we say and after, we will answer any question that you ask us, okay?"

"Am I in trouble?" she asked, a worried look on her face.

"No Colleen, you are not in any trouble," Keir replied.

"You see that photograph on the wall over there," he said, pointing, "yes" came the reply, "do you know who they are?" he asked.

"It was when the boys were young, and had motor bikes," she answered, "do you know what happened to two of the boys?" Keir asked.

Colleen crossed her arms, and stared at Keir, "I know that two of them were playing silly buggers and got shot, trying to run a road block, Why?" she asked.

"Did you know that the two chaps that were shot, were Shaun O'Brien's brothers?" He enquired.

"Yes," she replied.

"But what's this got to do with Sheamus O'Toole being shot by the Protestants?" she asked.

"Right Colleen, you have been lied to I'm afraid," Keir said, "Shaun O'Brien and your husband had planned to blow up New Scotland Yard and Aldershots Barracks, they were smuggling drugs into England to pay for explosives, they had two vehicles packed nearly ready to go, that would have killed hundreds of innocent people, but we caught wind of it and were able to stop it, both your husband and O'Brien were at a warehouse in West Thurrock, ready to drive the two vehicles, O'Brien had one of our officers at gun point heading for the warehouse, when a Police marksman took O'Brien's gun hand out, your husband hearing the gun shot, drew a German Luger pistol and was about to kill our police officer, when another police marksman shot your husband, so it was nothing to do with either the Protestants or the I.R.A. And Both Fiona and myself are sorry for your loss," he said, placing his hand on Colleens shoulder.

There was silence for at least two minutes, as Fiona and Keir stared at Colleens face, trying hard to see a reaction when, "What a fucking idiot! Serve the stupid bastard right," Colleen said, leaning back and began laughing, "he was going to try and blow up New Scotland Yard, was he?" She chuckled.

"Always thought he was a shilling short of a sixpence," she said, slamming her hands down on the Formica table top and bursting into laughter, Fiona and Keir just stared at each other, "but" Colleen managed to say, "why would Sheamus' doctor tell me it was the Protestants who shot him, and then give me one thousand pounds, from an insurance policy that Sheamus had supposedly taken out?" she asked.

"So this doctor came here and told you about your husband, then gave you a thousand pounds, Colleen?" Fiona asked.

"Yes," she was told. Fiona opened her shoulder bag, and pulled out a folded sheet of paper, "So you had a good look at this doctor person, did you Colleen?" she asked.

"Well I was sitting here, and he was sitting there," she said, pointing at Fiona, "so yes, I would say I had a good look at him, why?" she asked. Fiona unfolded the sheet of paper, and flattened it out, swivelling it round, she pushed it in front of Colleen, "Do you recognise this man?" She said.

Colleen stared at the sketch for over a minute, "Where did you get this?" She enquired, "One of the constables that were guarding a prisoner, gave a description of one of the priest who visited the prisoner to a police artist, and this is what he came up with," Fiona replied.

Colleen giggled, "Well," she said, bring her hand up to her mouth, "get rid of that moustache, and that's a dead ringer for Sheamus' doctor, so who was the prisoner he was visiting?"

"Shaun O'Brien," Keir stated.

"So you've got him in custody?" Colleen asked. There was an embarrassing silence for a while, when Fiona replied, "Not any longer Colleen, with the aid of your doctor friend, he managed to escape."

"He was no friend of mine, I can assure you, he came in here, told me he had some bad news, that he was my husband's Doctor, there had been some shooting by Protestants, and that my husband was dead, then he took out an envelope and handed it to me, saying it was from an insurance company, said, he was sorry for my loss, then left. So no, he was no friend of mine," she stated.

"So how do you know his practise is in Dagenham, Colleen?" Fiona asked.

"Sheamus would say, just nipping up to Dagenham to see my doc, I asked him why he didn't get one local, he replied, "I prefer Roberto." Thought he was stupid going all the way up there, when there's one just up the road. So! I was right, he was stupid, New Scotland Yard, you've got to be bloody joking," she said, slapping the Formica table and bursting into laughter.

Keir and Fiona justlred at the cafe owner bewildered. Colleen looked at both Keir and Fiona and went into hysterics, tears streaming down her face, then shaking her hands in the air, managed to say 'Sorry' it was a good four minutes before she was able to get her feelings under control.

"You both must think me very callous," she stated.

"But it's a long story, there never was any love in our marriage, he made me pregnant when I was seventeen, and my old man told him, 'Marry my daughter or die' so he married me, I lost the baby, but we were married by that time, he told me he didn't love me and that if he fancied someone else, so be it, what he didn't know was, I controlled the money, I bought alle food for the cafe, did all the cooking and cleaning, he spent most of his time at Shannon's, with his mates, we haven't slept together for god knows how many years, and when it used to happen, all those years ago, it was always wam bam thank you mam, so I decided when he bought this place, that I would have a little account stashed away, plus the thousand pounds from that so-called doctor, so I'll be selling up in about a years' time, and moving to somewhere warm like Malta."

"Well damn, good luck to you Colleen," Fiona said, as she offered Colleen her outstretched hand.

"Right ladies," Keir stated.

"This is all very nice, but can we get back to the matter in hand, please," then turning to Colleen he said, "would you regard this O'Brien as a friend, Colleen?"

"Well," she began, "up until an hour ago, I wouldn't have considered him an enemy, why?" she asked.

"He's on the run Colleen, he might ask you for help, and if you refuse he will probably get violent, we know for a fact that he ordered three peoples death, so what I'd like to do," he said, taking a card from his pocket, "that's my private number, it doesn't say police, just K, L, D. enterprises, when someone answers all you say is, 'This is Colleen O'Toole from Shamrocks, the bacon that you sent was off', and hang up, so if O'Brien shows, just call that number, say what I've told you, hang up the phone, then make some excuse that you need the loo, and get to hell out of here, we'll have a squad here in minutes, do you understand?" he asked.

"Why?" Colleen replied, "do you think he will come here."

"Just covering your arse! Young lady, Sorry, your backside," he said, Fiona just smiled.

Chapter Fourteen

Liam left his M.G. engine running as he stepped onto his driveway, and headed towards his garage roller door, placing a key in the door lock and turning it, he began to lift the door to its maximum height. He stood staring into the darkness, whilst the fluorescent overhead light flickered then struck, bathing the interior of his garage in a dim sixty watt illumination.

"Have to move Angela down to the end, or there won't be room," he stated. As he walked towards his second love. Pulling the Triumph Thunder Bird off of its stand and began wheeling it towards the far end of the garage, when the rear door opened, "What are you doing darling?" he was asked.

Liam look round to see Angela leaning against the door jamb smiling, "I'm putting the M.G away, my love," he replied as he pulled his bike back onto its stand, "why?" he was asked, as he walked out to his waiting motor.

"I'll tell you in a minute, precious," he said, over his shoulder, then sitting down behind his steering wheel, put the gear shift into first gear, releasing the clutch, he crept slowly forward into his garage. Switching off his ignition he looked up to see Angela sitting on his Thunder Bird smiling, her red silk dressing gown slightly parting, showing her shapely calves. Liam lifted his six foot plus frame out of the driver's seat and walking to the front of his garage, brought down the roller door, when he turned and looked over the M.G.

At his Thunder Bird, Angela was now laying full length along its seat and tank, her red silk dressing gown now laying either side of the bike, her feet resting on Liam's rear number plate, her knees wide apart, and she was smiling as he walked towards her.

"You are going to make wifey happy darling, aren't you?" She whispered, cupping her breasts. Any thought of O'Brien were long gone, as he approached his naked wife. He stood facing Angela, the sight of her perfect pubic curls, had his Lordship at full attention, as Angela placed her ankles on his shoulders, "Fuck me, my darling please," she whispered.

Liam sat at the kitchen bench, a glass of Saint James French Sautern resting in his hand, Angela sat opposite her man smiling, "So what else can we christen, darling?" She said, pouting and leaning forward, so that her silk dressing gown fell open, revealing her firm breast.

"We have to talk my love," Liam said, as he began sipping his wine, "something has come up."

"Yes my love, I watched as his Lordship came up, it was beautiful," she giggled, "I would love it if he came up again," she said, as she let her dressing gown slip off of her shoulders.

"Angela!" he shouted, trying hard to divert his eyes from her near naked body, "this is serious darling, and we really need to talk," Angela scowled, pulling her dressing gown back on, and tightening the belt around her slim waist, "right," she said, "if you would rather talk, than have your wicked way with me, I suppose I will have to wait, won't I?" She stated.

"But I've waited all day for you to make love to me, so hurry up, her Ladyship is dripping with love juice, so she needs his Lordship."

"Fuck this," Liam shouted, "get that fucking dressing gown off, now!" He said, as he stood up.

"Yes my love," came the reply, as the dressing gown hit the kitchen floor, and a grinning Angela ran round to Liam's side, "I knew you wanted his Lordship inside my Ladyship," she giggled, as she removed Liam's dressing gown belt, as she released the belt his gown parted.

"See," she screamed, running her hand along his swollen shaft, "you did want to fuck me, didn't you?" She said, as she ran her tongue over the end of his Lordship.

"Bend over and hang onto the bench, its Cruffs Show time," Liam stated.

"Thank you my love," Angela whispered, as she snuggled up to Liam, "so what was so important that we have to talk about it?" she asked.

Liam pushed himself up, so that his head was resting on the padded headboard, Angela didn't move, but Liam felt her hand sliding down from his chest, across his stomach, and knew where it was heading, "Nice try darling," he said, as he grabbed her hand, "but I just want to play."

"First we'll talk, and if your still in the mood, we'll play, okay?" He said.

"And why wouldn't I be in the mood?" she asked. Gazing up into Liam's face.

"Do you remember that case, where two chaps were going to blow up New Scotland Yard?" he asked.

"And you thought that you had shot one of them?" She replied.

"Yes," Liam answered, "of course I do, why," she asked.

"Well the so-called priest that had his hand blown off, was in the hospital handcuffed to the bed, four chaps dressed as priests turned up with some bull shit story. They had a letter from supposedly, Trevor Woods saying they were allowed to see the prisoner, and the two constables guarding the priest fell for it. Cutting a long story short, the prisoner escaped and is on the run."

"So what have we got to talk about, Liam?" Angela asked.

"Well my love," he began, "our new Superintendent Fiona Jarman has warned us to be on the lookout, she said, that this priest held a grudge against the police and the army for years, and it was us that stopped him, so now she thinks that he will seek his revenge on us, and because I was the one that arrested him, I'm first in line."

Angela sat bolt upright, "What do you mean, you're the first in line?" She screamed.

Liam placed his arm around Angela's shoulder, but she shook it off, "What do you mean, first in line," she repeated looking Liam straight in the face, "don't get your knickers in a twist darling, we can work something out."

"Firstly, as you are aware of, I don't wear knickers, Well not when I'm at home. And secondly what is it that we have to work out?" she asked. Liam pulled Angela to his chest, and kissed her forehead.

"Well my love," he began, "I would feel much safer if you moved back to your mummy and daddy's house." With that, Angela threw back the bed sheets, turned and squatting on her knees, glared at Liam her hands on her hips, "If you think for one minute that I would go back home Liam Smith, you can have another think coming," she hollered.

Liam gazed at this beautiful spectacle in front of him and sighed, "Please don't sit like that darling, that's not fair," he stated frowning, Angela looked down at her nakedness, and moved her hands to her knees, spreading them wide, "that's even worse," Liam managed to say.

"Well, my love, if you won't to slide in here every night," she said, running her fingers through her curls, "you can forget about me moving back home, so there," she stated, then began to giggle as she watched his Lordship begin to react.

"It would only be, until we caught him, darling," he managed to say, as Angela began to caress her Ladyship, spreading her knees even wider, "I can see that his Lordship would hate for me to move out. So that's two to one, you're out numbered, darling," she said, as she straddled Liam's naked body.

Chapter Fifteen

Fiona and Keir gazed at the James Abbot and Dennis Smith Real Estate sign, that was now in Margaret Lazel's front flowerbed, "Well that didn't take long," Keir said, as he opened the front gate for Fiona, no sooner had he closed the gate, than the front door was thrown open and a smiling Margaret came running down her garden path, and threw her arms around Fiona.

"Thank you, thank you, thank you," she blubbered, "please come in," she managed to say, "I've got so much to tell you," she said, as she put her arm through Fiona's arm. Keir stood behind the two girls as they walked towards Margaret's front door, "The kettles just boiled, so you two wonderful people go and sit in the front room, I'll be with you in a jiffy," she said, as she ran down her hallway into the kitchen. Keir and Fiona sat on Margaret's settee, to the accompaniment of singing coming from the kitchen.

"She seems happy," Fiona commented, "so I wonder what her news is?" She added, as the front room door opened and Margaret made a grand entrance pushing a double decked tea trolley, "For some unknown reason, I knew you two wonderful people would be here today, so I've done some baking, hope you like them," she said, pointing at the bottom shelf of the trolley, "there's Lemon Curd, Apricot, and fresh Strawberry Jam tarts, so please help yourselves," she said, offering Fiona and Keir bone china side plates.

"You shouldn't have gone to so much trouble Margaret," Fiona stated, as Keir demolished a Lemon Curd tart in one swift move.

"Where you two are concerned, nothing is too much trouble," Margaret said, as she poured the tea.

"So what do I own for the pleasure of your company today?" she asked as she sat down. Fiona opened her shoulder bag and withdrew the sketch the police artist had produced, "Have you seen this man before?" Fiona asked, passing the sheet of paper to Margaret, who delving into her house coat pocket, removed a pair of glasses, then slipping them on gazed at the sketch, "Well," she began, "I could be wrong, but without the moustache, I would say that, that was the doctor that came and saw Leonard with another chap, why?" she asked.

"Did he say anything to you, by any chance?" Keir asked, picking up another Lemon Curd tart from the trolley, "Only pleased to meet you, and was Leonard at home, why?"

"Was he English, Margaret?" He continued.

"Now it's funny you should ask that, his English was very good, but I got the impression, he wasn't."

"Thank you, Margaret, and may I say these lemon Curd Tarts are absolutely fabulous," he managed to say, as another tart was consumed, getting a look from Fiona.

"I'll put some in a box for when you leave, shall I?" Margaret asked smiling, Keir looked at Fiona, smiled, shrugged his shoulders, and replied, "That would be wonderful Margaret, thank you," Fiona coughed, "so what's your news?" she asked.

"Well unbeknownst to me, Leonard had taken out a policy some years ago, a chap from The Prudential turned up a few days ago, and told me that the policy had matured, and gave me a cheque for five hundred pounds, so what with the other money that you saw, and selling this house, I should be fine. My daughters can't wait for me to join them, and Emma said, as soon as the house is sold she'll come over and help me sort things out, and fly back with me."

"That's wonderful Margaret, really wonderful," Fiona said, smiling, as Keir devoured another tart, Fiona just shook her head and grinned.

Chapter Sixteen

"Why Shaun, why?" Roberto Boceli asked.

"You know full damn well, why, Robert," O'Brien replied, as he removed the straps holding the artificial hand in place.

"You tried to get revenge for your brothers, and failed, and lost your hand in the bargain, the hatred is eating away at your soul Shaun, so you're not thinking straight anymore."

"And the people that made me fail, will have to pay," O'Brien shouted, "so just leave me alone," he added, "because of you, Sheamus O'Toole was shot and killed, how many more have to die?" he was asked.

"Just one" came the reply.

"I could have all the documents you'll need in a week Shaun, you could be on a plane out of here in ten days, and laying on a beach somewhere warm, you have the money, just think about it please?" Roberto asked.

"That's all I ever think about Roberto, I know I have to take the blame for Sheamus, but he knew what we were doing, and if it hadn't been for that dammed policeman, we would have had our revenge, and I would be out of here," O'Brien stated.

"Did you have any luck with Father O'Connell, Shaun?" Roberto asked.

"Huh!" Came the reply, as O'Brien using his left hand, poured himself a large Bushmills Blackbush Whisky.

"I'll take that as a no then, shall I?" Roberto asked.

"He kept on about that I had lied to him, I tried to tell him that we didn't want him to get into trouble, but all he said, was, that I'd lied, when I asked him for his help, he replied he would pray for me, and that he wouldn't say that I had contacted him, so, that was a complete waste of time."

"But," began Roberto, "you did lie to him."

"Yes I know," O'Brien said, "but if we had told him the plan, he would have tried to stop us, so we had to keep him in the dark," he said, taking a large swallow of his whisky.

"So what's the plan now?" Roberto asked.

"All you need to know is that I need a car, preferably an old one, but mechanically sound and small, something like a ford prefect. Can do?" he asked.

Chapter Seventeen

"I hear that your beautiful wife serves rather Cordon Blue meals at her establishment, is that correct, Keir?" Fiona asked. Standing in Keir's office doorway.

Keir looked up and smiled. "Yes Ma'am," he replied.

"And the cellar is well stocked as well," he added, a broad grin on his face, as Fiona entered and closed the door behind her, "wonderful," she said, as she sat down, "I've invited Trevor Woods and a friend of mine to have dinner tonight at your wife's Swan hotel."

At the name Trevor Woods, Keir's expression changed. "Let bygones be bygones Keir," she said, smiling, "you know the old saying, What goes around, comes around, so you never know what will happen in the future, do you?" she asked.

"So I've booked a table for seven thirty, I was hoping that you will join us, I did say it was for four," she said. Keir thought to himself, "That's all I bloody need" but, smiling said, "I'll try and make it, I don't know what Christine has got lined up for tonight, Fiona."

"Oh! Christine knows all about it Keir, we had quite a long chat, she sounds lovely," she said, smiling.

"Shit," Keir said to himself.

Keir pulled into the 'Swan' car park, and killed the engine, he sat there as Shambuck and Ntombi raced towards their master, then stopped short, and sat waiting for Keir to exit his vehicle. This was the normal routine every night, Shambuck with his head in the air, Ntombi her backside going at a hundred miles an hour. Keir smiled at his two mates and opened the door wide, "Here," he commanded, and within seconds, he was pushed back into his Morris.

"I need you two and that wife of mine," he tried to say as he pushed his way out of his car.

"Your wish is our command, darling," he heard Christine say, at the sound of her voice, both Dobermans turned and bounded towards their Mistress, "thanks very much, you two," he hollered, as he strode towards where the trio were waiting for him.

"Bad day, darling?" he was asked.

"I've got to have dinner with that prick Trevor Woods, Fiona Jarman more or less, made it an order," Christine tried to hide a smile.

"It's not funny Christine, that prick Woods knew all along about Fiona Jarman, I felt a right idiot when I went into her office and thought she was a cleaner," Christine had to cover her mouth to stop herself from laughing, "it's only a meal darling," she managed to say, as she put her arms around him.

"I'm going to get the bastard one of these days," he said, as they walked to the back door.

"Of course you will darling," Christine managed to say.

"You two in there," Keir said, pointing at the garage, "I'll bring your dinner in a minute," he added, two dejected hounds turned, and slumped away.

Keir felt a slap on his back, followed by, "Keir Dickson you old bastard, long time no see."

"Not bloody long enough," Keir said to himself. "Hi Trevor," he replied, trying hard to force a smile.

"What's wrong mate, lost a pound and found a shilling?" Trevor asked, as he sat down beside Keir.

"No Trevor, it's this O'Brien escape," he lied.

"Don't think work mate, not after five o'clock, you'll get an ulcer," he chuckled.

"Your guest," Christine managed to say, as Fiona and her friend walked towards their table. Both men stood and gazed at the two new arrivals, Trevor Woods immediately shot to the other side of the table, pulling out a chair, Keir turned and gasped, Fiona was wearing black leather pant, black leather bomber jacket, six inch black stiletto heels, over her shoulder a black leather shoulder bag, and on her head a N.Y. Cap. But what took Keir's breath away, was the vision standing beside Fiona.

"This is my dear friend Robin," she said, Keir was speechless, whereas, Trevor Woods quickly stepped forward and placing his arm around Robin's slim waist, "call me Trevor," he said, smiling, as he ushered her into the seat beside him. This Robin was wearing a knee length sky blue sequined dress, complimenting her sky blue sequined six inch stiletto shoes, her neck line leaving nothing to the imagination, her blonde hair just touching her bare shoulders, and the face and make up, all Keir could think was, 'Wow!' Fiona sat beside Keir, who just gazed at the vision opposite him, mouth open.

"Are we ready to order?" Christine asked. Looking at Fiona, a sly smile on her face, "We will have a bottle of Dom Perignon thirty nine," Trevor said, smiling.

"Thank you sir," Christine said, "I'll just nip down to the cellar, it's not often that we get called for that particular champagne," she managed to say. Fiona edged her shoulder bag to the edge of the table, then with a sly touch of her little finger, sent her shoulder bag toppling to the floor, "silly me," she said, as she bent down to retrieve it, then looking under the table, smiled.

"Sorry sir," Christine said, as she returned to their table, "we only have the thirty eight, which I believe was quite a good year."

"Not quite as good as the thirty nine, but it will suffice for the time being," Trevor stated.

"Where is the ladies room?" Fiona asked. Rising from her seat, followed by the two males, "If you follow me, madam," Christine said, smiling, "I'll show you."

As Fiona left, both men returned to their seats, Keir had to look away, "No guessing who lover boy will be fucking tonight," he said to himself, as Fiona sat down.

"Sorry about that, too much coffee," she said, as Christine placed an ice bucket at the side of their table, "would you like me to open it for you, sir?" she asked.

"Err, yes please," Trevor managed to say, as he and Robin gazed at each other.

"I'm going to either throw up, or punch his bloody lights out, why doesn't he screw the arse of her right now," Keir said to himself. Christine popped the cork and was about to give Trevor a sample, when she was told, "Just fill the four glasses."

"I would like to make a toast," Trevor said, raising his glass, "to two very beautiful young ladies," he said, as he swallowed the bubbly.

"Sorry," Keir said, rising, "I need the little boys room," trying hard to force a smile.

As Keir went to move, Christine came to the table, "There's a call for Miss Fiona Jarman, you can take it at the desk, if you like," she said, as Fiona began to rise from her chair, "sorry about this," she said, as she followed Christine.

Keir had waited for Fiona to move, before he stepped into the isle, "Won't be a minute," he stated to two people who couldn't have cared less, "bollocks to this," he said to himself, as he watched Fiona and Christine chatting, at the desk, then Fiona picking up the phone from its cradle and began talking. Fiona seeing Keir approaching smiled at him, saying, "Be right there," and replaced the receiver, "sorry about this Keir, but I've got to go," she managed to say, noting the expression on his face, Christine had to turn away.

"Well in that case," Keir stated.

"So am I, I'm not sitting on that table for another minute, with those two."

"So I'll tell them you've been called away, shall I?" Fiona asked. Her hand covering her mouth, "I couldn't give a shit what you tell them," he mumbled, as he pushed his way between the two girl, and stormed into their flat, Fiona gave the thumbs up sign to Christine, who returned the gesture.

Chapter Eighteen

Fiona looked down from her office window, as Superintendent Trevor Woods Land, Rover, roared into the car park, she watched smiling, as he exited his vehicle, slamming the car door, and striding across the asphalt, the expression on his face sent Fiona into hysteric's. She sat back down behind her desk trying hard to get her breath back, and her emotions under control.

"I'll give them four minutes," she said to her empty office, taking her powder compact from her shoulder bag, she examined her face in the small mirror, "oh my God!" she uttered, "your eyes look like footsteps in the snow, or a Panda," she said, as she rushed over to her dressing room.

Three minutes later her makeup was perfect as she left her office and headed for the stairs. As she turned into the corridor that lead to Keir's office, she could see Bill Day eaves dropping to the shouting that was going on inside. Bill looked up as Fiona approached, "I would steer well clear, Ma'am, I was told in no uncertain terms, to 'F' off," he said, pointing, then turned and walked off. Fiona stood there for a while listening, hearing the debacle going on inside.

"You fucking well knew, didn't you?" Keir said, "I haven't got a fucking clue what you're talking about, Sir!" Woods said, "Don't tell fucking lies inspector, you fucking well knew."

Keir said, "You are pissing me right off, Sir! Because I haven't got a clue what's got up your fucking nose, so either tell me, or fuck off."

"Now," Fiona said, as she knocked on Keir's door, to be unceremoniously told, "stay out," by Trevor Woods. Fiona open the door smiling, "I said," began Trevor Woods, but on seeing Fiona stopped.

"Morning gentlemen, and how are we this lovely morning?" she asked, but received no reply, just two faces that looked like thunder.

"Sorry I had to leave last night, but duty calls," she managed to say, a grin spreading across her face.

"Robin is such a great chap and such good company, his wife Debby is even better company, especially when she's had a few drinks."

"Robin is a bloke?" Keir shouted, then pointing at Trevor, "and you thought," was all he was able to say, before he doubled over laughing. Fiona looked at Trevor, "Could have sworn that I told you that Robbin likes to go out dressed as a woman," she said, straight faced.

"But the voice, it was a woman's voice?" Keir just about managed to say, "Oh that's nothing," Fiona replied.

"You want to hear him do Winny's. Well fight them on the beaches," he's absolutely brilliant. Trevor Woods hadn't said, a word, he had his hands stuffed in his pocket, and he was staring at his shoes.

"So you both thought that Robin was a girl friend of mine, did you?" she asked. Looking at Trevor, Trevor just kept staring at the floor.

"You didn't, did you?" she asked. Looking at Trevor.

"Oh! My god, you did," she exclaimed. Trevor turned and pointed at Keir, "You say one word of this, outside this office, and you'll be directing traffic."

"So you feel a bit of a twit, do you Trevor?" she asked. "Your past proceeds you Trevor, even to Hong Kong, you thought to embarrass my DCI Keir Dickson, here," she said, pointing at Keir, "by not divulging that his new Superintendent was a woman, so when we first met, he thought I was a cleaning lady, and was quite embarrassed to find out I was his new boss. And don't you ever threaten any one of my team again, or it won't be my team that makes this known, I'll be the one who will take it all the way to the top. So," she said, smiling.

"You played a joke on Keir, and I played a joke on you, it was nothing to do with Keir, just me. But I still consider you a very dear friend, we've all had a giggle, so can we all be friends again," she said, offering Trevor her right hand. Trevor slumped down onto a chair, "they told me you were good, but they never told me how good," he chuckled.

"Boy! Did you have me fooled," he said, taking her hand, "sorry Keir," he said, "but I would have sworn that you knew," he said, grinning, "well you would have been wrong mate, wouldn't you?"

Keir said, offering his hand, "Yep!" Came the reply.

Chapter Nineteen

Angela closed and locked their front door, placing her keys in her waist belt pouch, then sliding it around to her back began her warmup. This was her ritual three times a week, Monday, Wednesday, and Friday, would see her at her front door exercising, then running on the spot before she took off on her morning six mile run. This morning was fresh, already her breath was coursing a mist as it hit the cold air.

She jogged to the front gate, still running on the spot, until she had closed the gate behind her, it was then that she took off at a run, heading for Corringham Road, as she approached where she would cross and head across the main road, and into Rainbow Lane making her way to the sea wall and the River Thames, she noticed a small white car, parked at the side of the road, its engine running, smoke coming from its exhaust, thinking that the driver was about to pull off, she began to run on the spot staring at the driver, then not receiving any acknowledgement, sprinted across Corringham road and into Rainbow Lane. It was then that Liam's warning, "If you see anything out of the ordinary."

"My imagination is getting the better of me," she said to herself, as she jogged towards Billet Lane, where Cromwell, supposedly billeted his troupes. But when she reached Billet Lane, that small white car was there, parked, still with its engine running, but coming towards her, she spotted farmer Smith on his Ferguson tractor, she smiled and began waving, Farmer Smith recognising the young lady, removed his peek cap and waved back, Angela sprinted across Billet Lane and wait as the Ferguson Tractor came to a halt, "Good morning Angela, off on our morning jog are we?" he asked, as she ran on the spot, "Yes," she replied, looking sideways, to see the small white car leave Billet Lane and turn left, heading for Corringham Road.

"You take care now," she was told, "will do," Angela replied watching the white car move away, "RBB 727, RBB727," she said to herself, as she restarted her six mile run. She ran passed Farmer Smith's huge farm house, across the style and into the paddock heading for the sea wall and the Shell Haven railway line. Some mornings she would cheat, she would wait for the train, and as the last tanker passed her, she would sprint and jump onto the back buffers, and catch a ride to Wharf Road, but this morning she was going to do the full six miles.

She was about two hundred yards from Wharf Road, when she heard the approaching Shell Haven steam train, she was just about to cross the railway lines, so that she wouldn't have to wait for the train to pass before she headed up Wharf Road making for Stanford village, but for some unknown reason she kept to the south side of the railway line, and arrived at Wharf Road just as the train warned pedestrians of its arrival, by giving three blasts on its steam whistle.

Angela was facing up Wharf Road as the steam locomotive passed by her, all of a sudden her eyes shot wide open, she thought she saw that white car again, but had to wait for the first tanker to pass, the gap between the first and second tanker confirmed it, It was the same white car, she crouched down, and watched as the small car drove slowly passed Stanford-LeHope grave yard, she began to tremble, her hand shaking, "Liam," she whispered, her eyes filling with tears.

Then, "No," she screamed, she had always headed up Wharf Road, never down, she turned and looked towards the River Thames, "God!" She screamed as she looked at six terraced houses set back from the road, then still in the crouched position, began to run towards the houses. She knew she had to get to the houses before the Shell Have train cleared the crossing, now she was sprinting as she slammed into the first houses front door, and began hammering on the door, then getting down on her knees, screamed through the letter box flap, "Please! Help me." Then she heard, "Are you alright dear?" she was asked.

Looking to her left, stood an elderly woman, in her hand a grease cover frying pan, "Please help me," she sobbed, "there's a man in a white car," she said, pointing back up Wharf road.

"Well, come indoors dear," she was told, still in the crouched position, she followed the woman into a darkened hallway, as soon as Angela was inside, the woman slammed the door.

"Bert," the woman shouted, "get in here, now!"

"Why Marj?" Came the gruff reply, "There's a lady here that needs our help, so get in here now!" Angela was sitting on her haunches, her arms wrapped around her knees shaking, her sobs racking her body.

"There's a car out there, with a man in it, and this lady is scared," she said, squatting down besides Angela, placing her arm around her shaking shoulder.

"Don't worry dear," the woman's husband said, "I'll sort the bastard out," as he snatch the frying pan out of his wife hands.

"No!" Angela screamed, "he mustn't know I'm in here, please," she sobbed.

"Right Bert, take the lady into the front room, then make us all a nice cup of tea, there's a dear," his wife said, as both the husband and wife helped Angela to her feet.

"I'm just going to sweep the front step," she said, as she opened the front door. The wife heard the car approaching as she began sweeping, but never looked in the direction of the oncoming vehicle.

"Excuse me," she heard, and on turning, was confronted by a white haired man, the driver's window wound all the way down, "yes dear," she replied.

"Where does this road lead to?" she was asked.

"Oh," she said, leaning on her broom, "it leads down to the River Thames, why?" she asked.

"I'm new around here, I just wondered where it went, that's all," he stated.

"We don't get much traffic down here," she said, walking towards the small car, "in fact you're the first car I've seen in days, we might get a few joggers, but that's about it," she said, smiling.

"Any joggers today?" he asked.

"Not so far, and I've been cleaning my windows I usually see one or two, late afternoon," she lied, "thanks for your help madam," he said, smiling, as he put the car in reverse, and backed up to where he could turn round, giving one beep on his hooter, as he sped off.

Marj walked indoors, leaving the broom leaning against their hallway wall.

"Right dear," she said, as she walked into their front room, to see Angela standing at the lace curtained window, staring out, "so what's this all about?" she asked. Patting the thread bare settee, Angela walked across to where Marj was sitting, and sat down beside her.

"My fiancé is a policeman," she began, "he arrested some really nasty people, and he has been told that their friends were out to get him, or anyone close, I didn't take much notice at first, but after today I'm going to take Liam's advice," she said.

Marj placed her hand on Angela's knee, "Well Bert will run you home, after we've had a nice cup of tea" then at the top of her voice screamed, "Bert! Where's that bloody tea."

"Coming," came the reply.

"Sorry," Angela said, forcing a smile, "my names Angela, and I can't thank you enough, for what you just did, I haven't seen that man before, except for today, that was the third time I've seen him."

"Well dear, all I can tell you Angela," Marj began, "is, he comes from Ireland, and has white hair, Oh! And I almost forgot, he wears black leather gloves."

Bert kicked the door fully open, "Tea up," he hollered, as he entered their front room, "yours is the WestHam mug dear," he said, placing the plastic tray down on their Formica coffee table, "it's Angela Bert," he was told.

Angela had to smile, when she remembered her own Chinese Bone China at home, "There's sugar and a bottle of milk," he said, pointing, at the tray, receiving a scowl from his wife, "I didn't know how you like your tea," he added, giving Angela a toothless smile.

"We'll finish these," Marj said, lifting up her chipped mug, and blowing across the surface before she took a slurp, "then we'll run you home dear, won't we Bert?" She said.

"I don't mean to be a nuisance, after all that you have done for me," Angela said, cradling the WestHam mug in both hands, "but could you run me to the police station please?" she asked.

Marj looked up at her husband, "That won't be a problem, will it Bert?" she asked.

Bert was quiet for a minute, "Er! No Marj," came the reply, but the look on his face told Angela that there could be a problem.

"Sorry about the mess" Marj said, as they walked into the kitchen, "I was just about to clear up, when I heard you hammering on next door," she said, an embarrassed expression on her face, as she opened the back door. Angela stopped dead in her tracks, parked in the back garden was a gleaming black, Ford 'V' 8 Pilot, "Wow!" she exclaimed, "she's beautiful."

"That's Bert's pride and joy, sometimes I think he love it, more than he does me," Marj stated with a giggle. It was then that Angela realised why Bert wasn't keen on running her to the police station, instead of a tax disk on the passenger's side windscreen, there was a Guinness Label, she smiled as she walked towards the car.

"You get in the back Angela, and lay down," Bert instructed, "you never know, that white car might be parked up somewhere," he added. Angela lay full length, on the red leather upholstery, as Marj and Bert climbed into the front seats, seconds later she heard the 'V' 8 spring into life, wrapping her arms around her shoulders she squeezed herself and smiled.

"You okay back there Angela?" Marj asked. As Bert backed his Pilot out of their garden, and headed for Wharf Road, "I'll drop you off just outside the station Angela, I've got to get some things, so I can't stop," Bert said, over his shoulder, Angela smiled. "what have you got to get Bert?" Marj asked.

"You never told me," she added. Then Angela heard, "Oh!"

Angela had to cover her mouth, obviously Bert had pointed to the windscreen, "Can't see your white car anywhere Angela," Marj said, as they turned left down Church Hill, then waited at the Railway Tavern, for traffic coming up, before Bert turned his Pilot into Kings Street, "I'll take the Homestead Road, and come up through the Shell Estate Angela, okay?" he asked.

"Fine Bert," she replied.

"And I know why," she said to herself.

It only took about six minutes before Angela heard Bert change down into first gear and cruise to a halt, "There you go dear," Marj said, looking over the front seat, "we're here."

Angela sat up, and looking left, smiled. "Right you two wonderful people, I want you both to wait right here, I'll be back in two minutes," she said, as she began opening her door.

"Sorry," Bert began, "no Bert, you will wait right here, done worry about the Guinness Label," she chuckled.

"After what you two have done, my Liam would let you get away with murder," she said, smiling, then opening her door, sprinted towards the main entrance, bursting through the front door, and taking the steps three at a time, raced down the corridor and burst into Keir's office. Keir, Liam, Bill and detective constable James Cain stared at an out of breath Angela.

"Liam," she screamed, "give me five pounds, and come and meet the two people that probably saved my life," she screamed, grabbing his arm. Liam pulled his arm away, "what the blazes are you talking about, Angela?" he hollered.

"Do you want to meet the two that saved my life, and spoke to the Irish murderer, or sit there?" She screamed.

All four officers leapt to their feet, "Where?" Keir asked, as he came round his desk, Angela had grabbed Liam's arm, "Hurry," she said, as she raced out the door, followed by the foursome.

Bert looked to his left, "Shit," he said, as Angela burst through the station door, followed by four men, his hand going to the ignition switch, "no Bert," Marj stated. Angela wrapped on Marj's window as she crashed into the Pilots door, making the gesture of winding down her window, as the four men arrived.

"Marj," she said, as she grabbed hold of Liam's sleeve and pulled him forward, "this is my fiancé, Liam Smith," she managed to say, Liam thrust out his right hand through the now open window, "please to meet you Marj," he said, "I suppose I'll get the whole story eventually," he said, smiling. Angela and Liam were nudged politely out of the way, as Keir offered Marj his hand.

"Hello young lady," he began, "I'm DCI Dickson, and I have been lead to believe that you spoke to a person in a car with an Irish accent, is that correct?" he asked.

Marj returned his smile, "Yes," she replied.

"Would you be so kind as to come and have a look at some photos, please?" he asked. Marj looked across at Bert, who had delved into his jacket pocket, and removing a set of false dentures, shoved them into his mouth.

"You ready for this, Bert?" she asked smiling, at her husband's embarrassment, "Yes, Marj" came the nervous reply, as he exited his Pilot.

"Two point two?" Keir asked smiling, as Bert came round the front of his car, "No," replied Bert, "she was three point six, but I had the heads skimmed, so she's nearer four now, bit heavy on juice, especially round here," he said.

"She's a real beauty," Keir remarked, as Marj stepped onto the pavement, allowing him to have a quick look inside.

"I think he thinks more of his blinking V8 Pilot than he does of me, at times," Marj stated.

"Would you like a coffee, or maybe something stronger?" Keir said, taking Marj's arm.

"That would be nice," she replied as they walked towards the station door. Angela pulled Liam to one side, "Have you got a five pound note?" She whispered.

"What for?" Came the whispered reply, "Those two," she said, pointing, "saved my life, if it hadn't been for them, I'd be either dead or a hostage."

"Are you going to tell me what happened?" Liam asked taking out his wallet, and pulling out five one pound notes. Angela grabbed the notes and ran to where Bert was just about to enter the station, "Bert," she called, making him turn, "thank you," she said, stuffing the notes in his jacket pocket.

Bert put his hand into his pocket removing the screwed-up notes, "What's this for?" he asked staring at the notes.

"It's a thank you, Bert," Angela said, squeezing his arm.

"What for?" he asked again, "Bert," she said, with her hands on her hips, and a scowl on her face, "just stuff that back in your pocket, and go and do your bloody civic duty, will you," she hollered.

"Better do as she tells you, Bert," Liam chuckled as he drew close to Angela, "she is one lady you don't want to mess with, I can assure you of that," he said, putting his arms around Angela's waist and squeezing. Bert placed the notes back in his jacket pocket, shaking his head, and followed his wife into the station.

"So are you now! going to tell me what happened?" he asked, turning Angela round, and kissing her forehead. Angela threw her arms around Liam and began to sob, he body shaking. Liam crushed her to his chest, "Darling," he whispered, "it's okay, I'm here, just tell me what happened," Angela slumped down onto the station steps.

"I was a bloody fool not to take you seriously, Liam," she managed to say, as Liam sat down beside her, placing his arm around her shoulder.

"I was going for my normal morning run, when I got to Corringham Road, there was a small white car at the curb with its engine running, I thought it was just about to drive off, so I just ran on the spot for a minute, but it just stayed there, I raised my hand to the driver, then sprinted across the road. Didn't think anything about it until I arrived at Billet Lane, and there! with the engine running was this car, it was then that I remembered you saying, "Look for the unusual" it was then that farmer Smith came along On his tractor, he stopped and we chatted for a minute, but I kept looking at this white car, even remembered its number plate, as it turned into Rainbow lane, anyway to cut a long story short, I ran along the railway lines to wharf road, the daft thing is, I normally run on the north side of the tracks so that when I get to Wharf Road I don't have to wait for the Shell Haven train to go by."

"But for some unknown reason, I ran on the south side, I heard the train coming as I approached Wharf Road and slowed down, when I arrived at the level crossing I looked up between the train and the tankers, it was then that I thought that I saw that car again, ducking down, and waiting for the next gap, I knew it was the same car, I started to panic looking for somewhere to hide, it was then that I saw the line of six terraced houses, I sprinted to the first one, but no one answered, but with me screaming and banging on the door, Marj came out and asked me what was wrong, I pointed up the road and said, there was a car after me, so she hassled me in doors, and into their front room."

"Marj got a broom and made out she was sweeping the front step, when this white car pulls up, I know she talked to the driver, because a minute later he backs up and drives off, then Bert and Marj brought me here, I've never been so scared in my life Liam," she managed to say, as she clung to Liam's arm.

Chapter Twenty

Marj and Bert were seated at a table in the station canteen, Keir sat opposite the couple waiting, as Bill walked towards them carrying a loaded tray, "You did say tea?" he asked, as he placed the tray in the middle of the table, "That will be lovely," replied Marg, gazing at the tray and smiling, "the apple tart is quite nice, but I prefer the apricot flan myself, so I brought both, there's cream in the jug, so just help yourselves," Bill stated.

Bert's hand shot forward, but was slapped back by his wife, "Thank you," she said, placing a sweet plate in front of her husband, then using a cake slice, lifted a portion of both pie and flan placing them both on Bert's plate, Bert was just about to pick up the portion of the apple pie with his grubby hand, when he was wrapped across the knuckles by a spoon. Keir and Bill had to look away, if looks could kill, Marj would be dead, "Help yourself to cream dear," Marj instructed her husband.

"Right, Marj," Keir began, "can you tell us what happened, please?" he asked as D.C. Cain placed a file on the table, "Can you nip up and tell Superintendent Jarman to come down constable, please?" he asked.

"Sorry about this, Marj, but I would like you to meet our Superintendent before we go any further, so just help yourself, she won't be a minute," he stated, as Liam and Angela joined them. Bill offered Angela his seat, but Liam had grabbed two vacant seats as he walked towards the foursome, "Cheers Bill," he said, as he placed the two chairs at the table, "coffee darling?" he asked as Angela sat down, receiving a nod.

The eight were all clustered around the table, all introductions had been made, Bert was on his second plate full of apple and apricot flan, smothered in cream.

"Right, Marj," Keir began, "it's all yours," Marj smiled at the group, "well," she said, wiping her mouth on her coat sleeve, "I was indoors when I heard a ruckus coming from next door, when I went out, Angela here," she said, pointing, "was screaming through next doors letter box, she told me that a car was after her."

"Sorry Marjorie," Fiona interrupted, "But did you see the car, and perhaps the driver?" she asked.

"Not only that," Marj grinned, "I spoke to the driver."

"Would you recognise the driver?" Keir asked opening the file D.C. Cain had placed on the table earlier.

"Well seeing as how I was as close to him as I am to you, yes I would," Marj replied. Keir swivelled the file round, then slid it across the table in front of Marj, "Is this the driver Marj?" he asked.

Marj grinned, "Yes that's him, and he's Irish," she stated.

"I don't suppose you notice the type of car, or the number plate, by any chance?" Keir asked.

"It was an old white Ford Prefect, registration RBB 727," Angela said. Fiona immediately turned to D.C. Cain, "Constable," she said, as James shot up out of his seat, "already on it, Ma'am," he said, as he rushed out of the canteen.

"Anything else you can remember Marjorie?" Fiona asked. Marj sat there for a minute, staring at the table, then looking up, said, "Well now you come to mention it," she began, "what seemed peculiar at the time was, he had a glove on his right hand, but his left hand which was on the gear stick, didn't," she said.

James Cain came running back to the table, "That registration Ma'am," he managed to say, taking a deep breath, "belongs to a nineteen forty nine Vauxhall Wyvern, stolen three months ago," he stated as he slumped down in his seat, "and traffic are now on the lookout for it, Ma'am," James said.

"Thank you, constable," Fiona replied.

Chapter Twenty-One

"I sincerely hope that there isn't any conflict between young Liam, and yourself, my dear?" Sebastian Frobisher asked his daughter, as he sipped his Napoleon Brandy, "No father," came the reply.

"Well then my dear, perhaps you can explain to your mother and myself, why our only daughter is blessing us with her company?" He said.

"If Angela wishes to return home, for whatever reason, it is none of our business, Sebastian," his wife informed him, "we are just overjoyed that Angela has come home, aren't we?" she asked the judge.

"Of course my love, it's just that," he began, but was cut off by his wife's, "there are no! It's just that's, it's none of our business, end of conversation," she stated.

"Have you two finished?" Angela asked.

"The reason I'm not living in Stanford-Le-Hope is because my wonderful Liam is worried for my safety," she stated. Sebastian sat bolt upright, as his wife rushed to her daughter's side.

"Your safety," her mother screamed, "why! Angela?" she asked placing her arm around her daughter's shoulder.

"I knew this was going to cause problems," Angela said, as she wriggled free from her mother's embrace.

"Well my dearest daughter," Sebastian began, "would you be so kind as to enlighten your dear mother and father, as to why your wonderful Liam, is worried about your safety?" he asked as he sat back in his armchair, and took another sip of his Napoleon Brandy.

Angela curled her legs up under neath her, and folding her arms, began, "That darling future husband of mine arrested a very nasty person, that person was handcuffed to a bed in a hospital, but someone helped him escape, and Liam's new Superintendent told him to warn me, that if I saw something that looked out of the ordinary, to be careful. I didn't really believe that anyone would try something, but they did, and I was very lucky to get away from the person that they are trying to catch, he must have been watching Liam's and my house, and saw my routine. So Liam has told me to move back home, so that is why I'm here, but if it's going to cause a problem, I'll find somewhere else," she said, staring at her father.

"You will do no such thing, young lady," her father hollered, "and from now on, you will be in my, or your mother's company at all times, do you understand?" he asked.

"Yes father," Angela replied.

"But I'm worried sick about Liam, if anything happened to him, my life would be over," she managed to say, as her eyes filled with tears. Elizabeth Frobisher put her arms around her daughter, "nothing is going to happen to your Liam, my darling," her mother whispered. Angela buried her head on her mother's shoulders and burst into tears.

Chapter Twenty-Two

"Trevor Woods is pulling out all the stops to find this so call Doctor Roberto Bocelli," Fiona said, "traffic has come up empty on the white car, but is still looking, but we now know for sure that you were right Ma'am, O'Brien isn't going away," Keir stated.

"I wish I had been wrong, gentlemen," Fiona replied.

"Now Liam," she began, looking directly at him, "I think it would be a good idea if you had in the meantime, a temporary transfer to somewhere like Southend," she smiled.

"Firstly Ma'am, that's very considerate of you, so thank you," Liam stated.

"And secondly with all due respect Ma'am, I don't think it would be a good idea at all. This O'Brien it would appear, wants me, yes?" he asked.

"Especially after what nearly happened to Angela, so we will have a better chance of catching him if I'm around, at the moment it would appear that I'm his main target, if I wasn't here, god knows what his target would be, so the more I show myself, the better our chances will be of catching him."

There was absolute silence in Keir's office, Fiona, Keir, Bill and detective constable James Cain, all stared at Liam.

"Angela is now with her mother and father, Judge Frobisher, so she is safe, they won't let her out of their sight, her being their only child, so that's one problem solved, so he can't get to me through her." Still no response from his four compatriots.

Seconds went by until Fiona asked, "So you are willing to be the bait Liam?" she asked, a concerned look on her face.

"Well Ma'am, unless O'Brien gets all religious, and walks into the station saying, 'Sorry' I can't think of a better way, can you?" he asked.

More silence, "Well I'm not happy," stated Fiona, "you are putting yourself directly in the cross hairs sergeant."

"Problem solved," Keir said, smiling, all four turned and stared at him, "right," he began, "Christine has a room at the back of her property that Liam could use, it hasn't been used in years, so it might need some T.L.C. But the food is out of this world, or I can move in with him, but my cooking is crap."

Detective Constable James Cain shot his hand into the air, "Back at school are we constable?" Bill chuckled.

"Bill!" Keir hollered.

"Sorry," came the whispered reply.

"Yes James?" Keir asked.

"Well, gov," he began, "my mum's on her own now, so it's just her and me, we've got a three bed roomed house, my sister is married and has her own place now, so her room is empty, and not only that," he said, grinning, "my mum's a bloody good cook, Oh! Sorry Ma'am," he said, the blood rushing to his face.

Liam smiled at the assembled company, "Thank you all," he said, "but I move in with anyone, and I put them in danger, and we don't know as yet what O'Brien can lay his hands on, so I think the best laid plans of mice and men, as Robert Burns once said, is to leave the status quo as it is. But thank you all for your concern."

"Well," Keir said, rising from his chair.

"You will not be living on your own, I have a friend who will keep you company," he said, grinning, "I'll have a word with him, as to what is needed, and you should be as safe as houses."

"But," replied Liam.

"No buts, sergeant, you have met him, and if I remember correctly you got on together quite well," Bill slapped his knee grinning, "shambuck!" He hollered.

"Shambuck?" Fiona asked a quizzical look on her face.

"Yes Ma'am," Keir replied smiling.

"Brilliant, Keir," Bill stated.

"Will somebody enlighten me as to who this Shambuck is, please?" Fiona asked. Looking around the room.

Bill answered first, "Ma'am," he began, "DCI Dickson is the youngest DCI In Essex, and the reason for that is, he has this friend, namely Shambuck, between the two, they have solved move cases than you can poke a stick at," he chuckled.

"Will somebody please put me in the picture!" Fiona stated.

"Sorry Ma'am," Keir interrupted, "but Shambuck is my three year old Doberman."

"And he can talk," Bill chuckled.

"A dog?" she asked.

"No Ma'am, not a dog," Keir replied.

"Shambuck has the honorary title of Detective Constable, and yes, thanks to him, quite a few cases were solved!"

"I would very much like to meet this new member of our team," Fiona said, a smile lighting up her face.

"It was Shambuck that put Keir on the right path for the Nursery Rhyme case, and, sorry about the language Ma'am, Sit for Brains, when they broke into a T.V. store," Bill stated.

"Well in that case, we should put him on the pay roll then, shouldn't we gentlemen?" Fiona chuckled.

Chapter Twenty-Three

"So what did you hope to achieve, by going after that woman?" Roberto asked O'Brien, "I needed Smith to suffer, as I have suffered," he replied, as he poured his Bushmills Whiskey into a small crystal tumbler, "he stopped me revenging my brothers," he added.

"Why leave it at him?" countered Bocelli.

"He was taking orders, then there's the two snipers, one shot and killed O'Toole, the other sniper took away your right hand, then there's the two police officers that dragged you away, and threw you into the back of their paddy wagon, and from what I've heard, a chap from New Scotland Yard, was the one who brought in the two snipers, so there's six that you could seek your revenge on, but let's take it one step further," Roberto continued, "say for arguments sake that you and O'Toole had succeeded with your plan, would you have been satisfied?" he asked, O'Brien just sat there sipping his BushMills.

"Precisely," exclaimed Bocelli, "your hatred for the army and police, would not have diminished, would it?" he asked, O'Brien just sat there, not saying a word.

"Shaun!" Roberto shouted.

"I've heard every word that you have said," O'Brien replied.

"But you haven't suffered the loss of two brothers, or been tortured, have you?" he asked.

"Your two brothers tried to run a road block, the soldiers orders were to shoot anyone that tried to break through the road block, you went crazy and put one policeman in hospital. The police stick together, one or more of them gets hurt, they retaliate, just as you did, so who was in the wrong? Your brothers, the army, the police, you?" he asked.

"You can't understand, unless you had been there," O'Brien replied.

"You're absolutely right Shaun, I don't understand, you are now a wanted man, if you had any brains my friend, you would high tail it out of this country, before they catch you, and catch you, they will, mark my words," Roberto stated.

"I need another car," O'Brien said, "she might have noticed the registration and make of the car?" he asked.

"So get rid of it, and somewhere far away."

"Right Shaun," Roberto began, "we have been friends for many years, and I helped you escape from that hospital and found you a safe house," he said, looking around the room, "I'll get rid of the car, and I'll find you another one, but then you are on your own, this hatred is eating into you like a cancer, take my advice, get your money and get as far away from England as you possibly can, before it's too late," O'Brien just sat there sipping his BushMills Irish Whiskey.

Chapter Twenty-Four

"Got a minute, Gov?" Liam asked as he poked his head through Keir's door.

"Sure Liam," came the reply, "come in and take a seat," he was told.

"We think we have found the bank, Gov, it's in Guernsey, and it's the Angola-Irish Bank Corporation. We found two accounts, one called HEVN1 the other called D. Brite, so it looks as though one was for the brothers, the other one is for O'Brien, and there's been activity on the O'Brien account, a cash transfer of eight thousand pounds, one off five thousand pounds, and one for three thousand pounds, to a bank in Dagenham, but the Dagenham branch are being funny, they won't tell us the name that the account is under."

"Oh! They won't, won't they?" Keir asked, smiling, as he flipped through his roller index. Then picking up his phone, began to dial, Liam heard the other phone ringing, then, "inland Revenue, how can I help you," he heard.

"Malcolm Peabody, please?" Keir asked.

"Who shall I say is calling, sir?" Keir was asked.

"Just tell him, who was caught behind the bike shed smoking?" Keir chuckled.

Laughter was heard from the other end, then, "Keir! You old sod, long time no see, so how are you mate?" he was asked. Liam sat there smiling at the conversation.

"Good Mall, and how are you doing these days?" Keir asked.

"Well," he began, "with four kids, and another on the way, how do you think I'm doing."

"You randy old sod," Keir chucked, "it's not me, it's Angie, I think she's going for eleven aside, and not so much of the old, if you don't mind, and come to think of it," he chuckled.

"If my memory serves me correctly, you're eighteen months older than me."

"Smart arse," Keir managed to say, then burst into laughter.

"So how come I'm getting a phone call from an old! School buddy of mine?" Keir was asked.

"Do you remember that puppet show in the geography storeroom?" Keir joked, "And every boy tried to get a handful of Sylvia Panes tits," came the jovial reply, "and you were first in the cue, weren't you?" He added.

Liam put his hand over his mouth, and began to cough, "Right!" Keir hollered, clearing his voice, "enough of this frivolity, I need a favour," he stated.

"When don't you, so how can I help an old school buddy?"

"You're definitely into this Old! Aren't you, young Mall?" laughter was heard from the other end.

"Right Mall," Keir began, "my team has a problem, some money came over from the Angola-Irish Bank Corporation in Guernsey to a bank in Dagenham, but they won't give us the name of the account. We believe that the person that has this account, planned and executed a prison break from a hospital, the prisoner is still on the loose, and he has tried to harm one of my teams families, so we desperately need to find him, and fast mate," Keir stated.

"Leave it with me Keir, as soon as I know, so will you."

"Cheers, mate," Keir replied.

"Give my love to Angie, and the awesome foursome, and I'll wait for your call," Keir stated.

"So how can your mate get the info and we can't?" Liam asked.

"Because, young Liam, the banks couldn't give a rat's arse about the constabulary, and what they want, but the In-land Revenue, scares the living shit out of them. All Mall has to say is, 'We believe that money is coming from Guernsey to your bank, which has not been disclosed to the Inland Revenue, and they will open every door, we will probably be told what the person who has that account, had for breakfast this morning'," he chuckled.

"So how is Angela coping?" Keir asked.

"She said, that the days are fine, except that she worries about me. That the Judge won't let her out of his sight, which is getting up her nose, then at night her mother keeps popping into her bedroom, to make sure she's okay, they've even put a baby monitor in her room, it wouldn't surprise me if the Judge and her mother take it in shifts sitting up all night" Liam replied with a chuckle.

There was a knock on Keir's door as Bill poked his head in, "Just thought you would like to know Tel, they think they have found the white Prefect, or what's left of it, on Purfleet Marshes, it fits the description that Liam's wife gave us, but they took the number plates, before they torched it. Hi! Liam," Bill said, as he opened the door wide to Keir's office, and seeing D.S. Smith, "hi Bill," Liam replied.

"Liam's traced the money to a bank in Guernsey, and then to a bank in Dagenham, we're just waiting on a phone call from a mate of mine, to find out the name of the account," Keir stated. Keir had only just replaced the handset, when his phone rang.

"Dickson," he said, into the mouthpiece, "is that the gentleman from behind the bike shed?" A female voice chuckled. Keir burst out laughing, and managed to reply, "Yes."

"Putting you through, you naughty boy," she told him.

"Keir my old mate, got something for you," he was told.

"Right! Young Mall, cut out the old bit, and make us here, all very happy, okay?" Keir said, as he switched on the speaker, "The account that you enquired about, belongs to a medical practice on Rainham Road South, quite near Dagenham East Station, I have been informed the practice did have two doctors, but now has only one, if that is of any help," Keir, Bill, and Liam sat there smiling.

"You are an officer and a gentleman, mate," Keir hollered, "I owe you one Mall," he added.

"No you don't, you owe me two! And just to let you know, this conversation never, and I mean never took place, correct?" he asked.

"What! Conversation, Mall? Just rang to ask about your beautiful family, you randy young thing, see ya Mate," Keir said, putting down the phone.

Chapter Twenty-Five

"So how do you want to handle this, Keir?" Fiona asked.

"Well Ma'am," he began, "I thought that D.S. Liam Smith, myself and if you wish, yourself, could pay this Practice a visit tomorrow," he said.

"Would you consider a backup team?" she asked smiling.

"D.S. Smith and myself were discussing just that, on our way up to your office, that it might be best if a few officers accompanied us, D.S. Smith would wait in the waiting room, and you and I interview the doctor, Ma'am," Keir stated.

"Then tomorrow it is, and hopefully moving forward," Fiona replied.

The two cars pulled up outside Rainham Road Clinic, Fiona, Keir, and Liam extricated themselves from Keir's Morris One Thousand and walked back to where sergeant Allen Oakley had parked his nineteen thirty nine Hillman Minx, the trio caught the tail of D.C. Cain stating, had Oakley ever thought of cleaning the inside of his heap of shit, to be answered by Oakley statement, Well next time fucking well walk, as they exited the vehicle.

"Is everything okay?" Fiona asked the two officers.

"Yes Ma'am," came a united reply.

"Right, gentlemen," Fiona stated, addressing D.C. Cain and P.S. Oakley, "could you both cover the back and if there are any windows or doors at the side, keep them covered, please?" she asked, and was greeted with a united, "Yes Ma'am."

"Are we ready gentlemen?" she asked Keir and Liam, as they approached the entrance to the clinic. Liam stepped forward and opened the door for Fiona and Keir, them closed it behind him. Seated at the back of the room behind a metal desk, sat a women of about fifty years of age, all in blue, from head to toe, a blue dress with a white Peter Pan collar, a blue beaded necklace around her thick neck, and to top it all, a blue rinse perm.

"Can I help you?" she asked smiling, her broad Scottish accent, leaving no doubt to her ancestry, "We would like to speak to the doctor," Fiona said, holding up her warrant card for the woman to see.

"The doctor has a patient with him at the moment, but he shouldn't be much longer," the receptionist replied, still smiling.

"Have you worked for the doctor for some time?" Keir asked the receptionist smiled at Keir, then closing a ledger, looked up at all three, "I left school at fifteen, did a night school coarse for a secretarial position, and worked for the Co-op during the day, when I received my diploma, I applied for a position here and was chosen out of six applicants," she beamed.

"So you know the doctor here, quite well?" Keir asked.

"Doctors," she replied.

"Sorry?" Keir enquired.

"You said, doctor, not doctors, we have two at the moment, but Doctor Bocelli is on holiday at the moment."

At this statement, all three officers stepped forward, "So doctor Bocelli isn't here at the moment?" Fiona asked, a concerned look on her face.

"I'm sorry, but no he isn't, and we miss him, he's such a lovely man, especially his patients," she beamed.

"So do you know where he might be on holiday?" Keir asked, returning her smile. The receptionist opened a draw and began searching through papers, "It's here somewhere I know, because I stapled it to the receipt for the car I sold him. Well! When I say I sold him the car that's not quite true, it was my nephew who sold him the car, but the doctor had asked me if I knew of anyone who had a small car for sale, so I called Graham, he's a mechanic, you know, does up cars and advertises them in the Exchange and Mart, so that helped Graham and doctor Bocelli didn't it?" she asked smiling.

"I don't suppose you saw the car, by any chance?" Fiona enquired; her fingers crossed.

"Yes! As a matter of fact I did, because Graham brought the little car here for the doctor to test drive, and sort out the paperwork, it was a nice little Ford something," she said.

"Could I have a look at that holiday address please, young lady?" Keir asked smiling. A crimson face receptionist, handed Keir the receipt, he took one look at the address on the card and gasped, "Thank you young lady for all your help, we needn't bother your doctor," he managed to say, offering her his hand.

As soon as they reached Keir's Morris, Keir leaned on the roof of his car and burst into laughter. Fiona, Liam, and Bill just stared at him, scratching their heads. Liam had walk round to the rear of the building, and told Cain and Oakley that the surveillance was over, and return to their car. When he returned, Keir was now leaning with is back to his car smiling.

"Well two things have been cleared up. One! we now know where the car came from, but the registration on that receipt wasn't RBB727, and second!" He chuckled, "This so-called doctor is staying at your predecessor's sisters boarding house in Brighton Fiona," he managed to say before bursting into laughter again.

"Liam," Fiona stated.

"Could nip back in and ask the receptionist where her nephew's place of work is and his sir name, please?" she asked. Ten minutes later Liam returned shaking his head, "A problem?" Fiona asked.

"Her name is Ethel Brite and her nephew's sir names Brite, he's her brothers son, and Why? Did we need to know, so I had to tell a few porkies, Ma'am," Fiona smiled.

Chapter Twenty-Six

It was a gorgeous July day for the two-hour drive down to Brighton. Fiona and Keir had taken the Tilbury Ferry across the river Thames to Gravesend heading south, Keir driving his Morris, as they hit the outskirts of Patcham.

"According to Liam," Fiona began, "the Boarding house is about one mile east of The Brighton Palace Pier Keir, and we can't miss it, because it's blue and cream, with a couple of plastic Peacocks in the front garden, plus some tables and chairs," she said, as she put the road mat into the Morris's glove box.

Fiona gazed across her driver and colleague at the English Channel, as the waves broke onto the stony Brighton beach, she smiled as snow white bathers shivered on the water's edge, plucking up courage to take the plunge into the chilly waters.

"There it is," Keir said, as he dropped the Morris down into second gear, and coasted to a halt.

They both sat there for a moment, gazing up at the slightly elevated garden, a smile spreading across Keir's face at one of the occupants sitting at a small round table.

"That young lady was your predecessor," he said, pointing.

"And I could be wrong, but the chap who Nosy is chatting to, looks very much like our missing doctor," he said, "shall we go and have a chat with said, doctor?" Fiona asked.

"We could," replied Keir, "but if you were to confirm its him, and signal me, because if we both go up together, Nosy will probably mention that I'm with the police and our doctor could clam up, so if you were to say something like, you were told that a doctor Bocelli was staying here, and that you needed to see a doctor, he might confirm it, if he does, open your handbag, when I see that I'll join you, just keep him chatting for a second, and I'll be there, now please don't take this the wrong way Ma'am! But if you could, maybe undo a couple of button, and lean forward when you talk to him, it would be quite a distraction."

Fiona began to giggle, "I do believe Chief Inspector, that you are blushing," she managed to say.

"So you think he's a boob man, do you?" she asked smiling.

"Well I know Nosy is," Keir replied.

"So what would you advise Chief Inspector, two or three buttons?" She giggled.

"Whatever," came a mumbled reply. Keir watched as Fiona sashayed her way towards the two seated men, it was obvious to him that Fiona, now had their full attention, the expression on both their faces, coursing Keir to smile, "go for it girl," he said to his empty Morris One Thousand. Keir began to chuckle, as Fiona placed both her hand on the men's table and lent forward. The look on both men's faces was a picture of pure lust, "You little beauty," Keir chuckled.

But then Fiona stood erect and opened her hand bag, the smile left Keir's face as he exited his car, and bounded towards the trio.

"What the hell are you doing here Dickson?" Ex Superintendent Parker hollered, "It's Detective Chief Inspector Dickson, Mr Parker, and this," he said, turning, "is Superintendent Fiona Jarman, and we have come here to arrest your companion, doctor Roberto Bocelli, or is it Monsignor Alberto?" Keir asked.

The chair Bocelli was sitting in flew backwards, the doctors right hand sliding into his jackets inside pocket, but then he froze unable to move, due to the fact that Fiona's right hand, was crushing a neck muscle, rendering him paralysed.

"What the hell is going on, Dickson?" Parker hollered, getting to his feet.

"If I were you, Mr Parker," Fiona said, as she released her grip on Bocelli's neck, and brought the doctors right arm up between his shoulder blades, "I would shut up and sit down, or I will arrest you for interfering with police procedure, do I make myself clear?" she asked.

"But why are you arresting Doctor Bocelli?" Parker asked.

"That's none of your business Mr Parker, you are no longer in the police force, so please just sit there and be quiet," Fiona ordered him.

"You can't talk to me like that, Madam," he blustered.

"Yes! She can," Keir shouted, his face only inches away, "so shut your mouth, Nosy, and it's Superintendent Jarman, not Madam," he hollered.

"I'm going to report this," Parker mumbled.

"One more word out of you Mr Parker, and I will arrest you, do you understand?" Fiona stated. Parker just bowed his head, and mumbled something no one could understand. Fiona had taken a pair of handcuff from her jacket pocket and had Doctor Bocelli's hands handcuffed behind his back.

"I'll take him Ma'am, but I think we should remove this," Keir said, as he removed an army revolver from its shoulder holster, inside Bocelli's jacket, then leaning forward whispered, "I'd button up those four buttons if I were you, Fiona," he said, as he dragged Bocelli away to his Morris.

Chapter Twenty-Seven

Interview room number one, now had four occupants, Fiona, Keir, Bocelli, and his legal representative, "Would you like either tea, coffee, or water, before we begin, and I'm letting you know now, that the interview will be recorded, which you will be given a copy of, do you understand?" Fiona asked.

"My name is Pilkinton Smythe, and I am here to represent my client Mr Roberto Bocelli. We thank you for the offer of refreshment, but decline your offer, I'm a very busy man, so can we proceed with this farce, Madam?" He said.

"For your information, Smythe" Keir stated.

"It's Superintendent Fiona Jarman, not Madam, so you will refer to her as Ma'am, do you understand," he scowled, "as you wish," came the reply.

"So how is Mrs Barns enjoying Holloway, Mr Smythe?" Keir asked, receiving a curious expression from his boss.

"What!" The solicitor hollered.

"Surely you remember Mrs Barns, extortion with malice, insurance fraud, you represented her, just can't remember how many years she was given," Keir said, grinning.

"I'm here to represent Mr Bocelli, so can we move forward," he blustered.

"Right, Mr Bocelli," Fiona began, "you do know why you are here, don't you?" she asked.

"No comment," came the reply from Bocelli, as he sat back in his chair his arms folded across his chest. Fiona turn towards Pilkinton Smythe, "Seeing as how you are his representative Mr Smythe, and it would appear that Mr Bocelli does not wish to co-operate, I will now inform you as to why Mr Bocelli is in custody, after which my colleague and I will leave you, so that you can advise your client how to proceed, do you understand?" Fiona asked.

"Yes Ma'am," came the curt reply, "good," she stated.

"Your client, Mr Roberto Bocelli was instrumental and probably planned the escape from custody a Mr Shaun O'Brien, who was waiting on trial for drug smuggling, three murders, a terrorist attack on New Scotland Yard, and Aldershot Army Barracks, killing hundreds of innocent people, he purchase a small white Ford car for Mr O'Brien, for the purpose of kidnapping a wife of one of my officers, which failed, and he was instrumental and involved in the murder of Mr Leonard Lazel who was poisoned with cyanide, at the hospital where O'Brien was being held."

At this statement, Bocelli shot straight up knocking over his chair, "I never touched that syringe, I didn't kill him, he administered it himself," he hollered.

"Gotcha, ya bastard" Keir said to himself.

Fiona and Keir sat back in their chairs, looking up at Bocelli, with both his fists clenched.

"I would sit down Mr Bocelli," Keir instructed, "and listen, because there is more bad news, your account in both your banks has been frozen, both Guernsey and Dagenham, so Mr Smythe might be concerned about who is going to pay your legal bills or he might be kind and represent you, Pro-Bono," he added smiling, "you can't do that," screamed Bocelli, "I think you will find out, that we can," Keir stated.

"Right," Fiona began, "you are going to prison Mr Bocelli, for how long depends on you, if you co-operate with us, we will mention this to the judge, we need to find this O'Brien, and fast. So Mr Bocelli the choice is yours, my colleague and I will leave you to discuss this with your solicitor, but the clock is ticking," she said, as both officers stood, picking up a file, and terminating the recording.

"So what's with this, Mrs Barns Keir?" Fiona asked as Keir closed the door on interview room one, Keir smiled at this question. "It was a case we had, initially we were investigating one murder of a not very nice individual, he was killed, or more to the point murdered by a very poisonous spider, then his partner in crime was found murdered and found under a haystack, but through these murders we found an extortion ring, and armed robbery, run by the wife of his partner in crime, a Mrs Barns. If we had left it until the Monday, she would have been living in luxury on the French Riviera but we didn't, and Mr Pilkinton Smythe tried to get her off and failed miserably, so the woman is now a resident of Holloway Prison," he chuckled.

"So they were the Nursery Rhymes murders, were they?" Fiona asked smiling.

Chapter Twenty-Eight

Shaun O'Brien cautiously strolled along Clarence Road Grays with the aid of a walking cane, he was looking for a car showroom that advertised Channel Island second hand cars, with new registration number plates. He was standing outside Chuck Bursey's bicycle shop, gazing across Clarence Road at a Black Wolseley saloon motor car. O'Brien was dressed in his clergyman's attire, he now sported a black goatee beard, his, now long white hair dyed black, and tied back in an out of fashion ponytail, to finish off his disguise he was wearing horn rimmed glasses, and he had developed a severe limp, accentuated by his walking cane. Waiting for the traffic to clear, O'Brien made a slow crossing of Clarence Road, and approached the Black Wolseley saloon car.

"She's a real beauty, father," O'Brien heard as he drew closer to the vehicle, "very low mileage, and in immaculate condition, care for a test drive father?" he was asked.

"That's very kind you my son, that would be very nice of you, thank you," O'Brien replied.

"I'll just get the keys, father," the salesman beamed. When he returned, he found O'Brien sitting in the driver's seat, "Is it alright if I drive, Mr Er?" O'Brien asked.

"It's Collin father, Collin Friend, and yes of course you can drive," he said, offering O'Brien a set of keys. O'Brien inserted the key into the ignition switch and turned it, the Wolseley's engine immediately sprang into life, O'Brien forced a smile, "she sounds fine," he stated.

"She's only done three thousand four hundred miles father, just about run in," he chuckled. O'Brien slowly move the Wolseley forward off of the pavement and onto Clarence Road heading east.

"I don't know this area very well my son, so you will have to give me directions," he lied, "just keep on Clarence Road, father, you'll come up to a Tee junction, there's a church on your right, if you turn left it will take us passed

Palmer's Boys college and onto Pigs Corner where there are traffic lights, turn right and when we get to Daneholes roundabout take the second exit onto Wood View, and you will be able to open her up a bit," he said, smiling.

"There doesn't seem to be a lot of petrol, are we going far my son?" O'Brien asked, returning a fake smile.

"No problem there, father," Collin replied.

"Daneholes garage is just the other side of the roundabout, so you can pull in and I'll shove a couple of gallons in the Wolseley," he added, "might as well fill her right up my son, just put the price of the fuel on the bill," O'Brien stated.

"So you're going to buy her, father?" A jubilant Collin asked.

"Yes my son, she's just what I've been looking for."

"Thank you father, you've made my day, this is my first week at my new job, and you are my first customer," Collin replied, a grin spreading across his face, "and could you make it Super, please, my son?" O'Brien asked.

"And you've made my day as well," he said to himself.

As they pulled into Daneholes Ford dealership, and coasted up to the petrol pumps, "Don't forget super my son, and could you please get me a bottle of lemonade, whilst you're in there?" O'Brien asked smiling. Collin was out like a shot, as soon as the Wolseley came to a halt, and O'Brien killed the engine. Collin picked up the Super petrol nozzle and showed O'Brien, who gave the thumbs up signal, O'Brien watched the smiling face of Collin, as the petrol gauge showed the tank being filled, when Collin had to jump back as the petrol tank over filled, petrol spilling down the side of the car, Collin quickly removing the nozzle the replacing the petrol cap, took a bucket of water and washed the side of the Wolseley where the petrol had spilt, then taking a dry cloth polished the area.

O'Brien watched Collin give him the thumbs up sign, then ran into the dealership, as Collin entered the building O'Brien turned the ignition switch on and fired up the Wolseley's engine, taking one more backward look at the building, accelerated out onto Wood View, "Sorry Collin," he chuckled as he hit sixty miles per hour, passing Palmer's Girls College.

Six minutes later the Wolseley was parked up behind Shannon's Auto Repair Shop. O'Brien sitting opposite Michel Flanagan, Shannon's new owner, "I need the Wolseley's appearance changed, and also the number plates change Michel, is there a problem?" he asked.

"Well father," Flanagan began, "I want that car miles away from here, this is the first place the police will come sniffing around. Why did you dress as a priest, that sales chap will say an Irish Priest stole the car, so where are they going to come to first, Here!" He said, "So get back in your car, and follow me, I don't want that car on my premises," he added.

O'Brien pulled out onto Calcutta road and began following the Shannon's breakdown truck, they turned left into Feenan Highway, then slowed as they approached St Chads Road, turning right and heading for Chadwell Hill. At the top of the hill, the Shannon Breakdown Truck turned right onto Linford Road heading east. They had travelled about four miles, when the Shannon truck began to slow, O'Brien looked ahead and noticed a derelict looking house, standing back from the road, no other houses in sight, he watched as the truck turned left onto a weed covered drive, and disappeared up the side of the property.

O'Brien followed the truck and smiled as he took in a massive wooden barn. Michael Flanagan had jumped out of his truck, and was swinging back two large wooden doors, beckoning O'Brien to drive the Wolseley into the barn. O'Brien had killed the engine and was standing on the concrete floor, as Flanagan approached him, "You can stay here until the car is finished," he began, "and I'll send a chap up here tomorrow to start work on the Wolseley, you can use the house, it used to belong to friends of mine, a Daphne and Roy Barns, Roy was shot and Daphne ended up in Holloway, she needed the money for legal purposes which turned out to be a waste of time. Anyway it's fully furnished and there's food in the freezer, there's also a phone, you know the number, but! you don't go out, and you don't! switch on any lights, this house is supposed to be deserted, so anyone driving buy and seeing a light on, will know it's not, and start asking question, and I don't want that, especially from the law, do you understand father?" he asked, handing O'Brien a bunch of keys.

"I do," came the reply, "and thank you Michael," O'Brien added.

"Just so we are on the same page father," he began, "I'll fix up your car, you can stay in the house, but when the car is finished."

"Yes my son," O'Brien interrupted, "you will not see or hear of me again, I give you my word on that," he said.

Chapter Twenty-Nine

Fiona stood at the podium, facing a crowded room, which had become silent as she entered, "Right everybody," she began, "this is as far as we have managed to get with the O'Brien case. A Mr Roberto Bocelli who without a solicitor has turned Kings evidence, not that that is much good to us, due to the fact that we already knew most of it. He confessed to helping O'Brien escape, and supplying him with a car, he did tell us that he did try to talk O'Brien into leaving this country, but it would appear that request fell on deaf ears, he is adamant that he does not know where O'Brien is at the moment, but he feels sure that he is still somewhere in the area."

Sergeant Allen Oakley's hand shot into the air, "Yes Sergeant?" Fiona asked.

"Well Ma'am," he began, "I don't know if this has any bearing on our case, but I was talking to a colleague of mine who is stationed in Grays, they had a call, that a car had been stolen from Clarence Road, a black Wolseley. The chap that reported, it is a Mr Collin Friend, and he did say that the person that stole the car was an Irish Priest, Ma'am."

"Thank you Sergeant," Fiona replied.

"I would like you to go down to this Clarence Road and interview this Mr Friend, did he give a description of this priest to your colleague in Grays?" she asked.

"I'll give my colleague a call, Ma'am," Allen replied.

"Better still sergeant, go and interview Mr Friend yourself, plus take the photograph of O'Brien, and now would be a good time, don't you think?" she asked.

"Yes Ma'am," Allen replied as he rose from his seat and left the room.

"Any other suggestions, ladies and gentlemen?" she asked smiling.

Liam shot his hand into the air, and didn't wait for a response, "What about Father Patrick O'Connell over at Romford Ma'am, he knew O'Brien well, they grew up together, and he was there when O'Brien's twin brothers were shot."

"Good point sergeant, can I leave that in your capable hands?" Fiona asked.

"On it, Ma'am," Liam replied, as he followed Oakley's example and left the room.

Allen managed to find a parking space fifty yards away from the Clarence Road car show rooms, and on switching off the ignition turned, "Right, constable," he began, "just leave the talking to me, but take everything that Mr Collin Friend says down, okay?"

"Yes, Gov," came the reply, "how many stripes do you see, constable?" Allen asked.

"Three, Gov," came the reply, "great! So there's nothing wrong with your eyesight, so what do three stripes represent to you constable?" he asked. W.P.C. Kittle looked at Allen, her face turning pink, "Sorry sergeant," she managed to say, "right! So that's that sorted out, got your notebook and pen constable?" he asked.

"Yes, Gov, sorry Sergeant," came the reply. Allen just shook his head as he exited their police car, a grin spreading across his face.

As the pair walked toward the car show room, a rather stout looking gentleman strolled out onto the pavement, he was wearing white flannel trousers, red suede shoes, a brilliant red jacket, over a pure white shirt, and to complete the ensemble a bright red tie, he looked like a Butlins Red Coat as he turned and gazed at the sign which advertised Clarence Road Car Sales, he smiled as Allen and W.P.C. Kittle approached, "Good day to you officers," he beamed, "are we perhaps looking for a newly registered car?" he asked.

"They come with three months warranty, and my mechanic goes over them with a fine-tooth comb, they are as new," he said, smiling.

"Mr Collin Friend?" Allen asked, returning the smile, at the mention of that name the man's expression changed to a scowl.

"No! I am not," he uttered, "he no longer works for me, I take it that you are here about Friend letting someone stealing the Wolseley from under his stupid nose," he stated.

"So you fired him, did you?" Allen asked.

"Damn right, I did," came the reply, "was the vehicle insured sir?" W.P.C. Kittle enquired.

"Of course it was, all my vehicles are insured," he hollered, "what's that got to do with anything," he added, "so you won't be out of pocket sir, so why fire Mr Friend?" She said, Allen had to turn away and smiled.

"We need to speak to Mr Friend and it's urgent, the person that stole your vehicle is a wanted criminal, your Mr Friend is very lucky to have come out of this unscathed and in one piece, we can't tell you what this person has done, all we will say is that when he is arrested, he will never be seen of again, your Mr Friend was conned by a master criminal, and if it had been you! You would have been sucked in as well," Allen stated.

"So can you please tell us where we can contact Mr Friend, and if you have any brains, reemploy him," he added.

"Twenty three Bredford Road, it's just around the corner, and if you see Collin tell him he can start back on Monday," an embarrassed proprietor stated.

It only took Allen and W.P.C. Kittle about four minutes before they were standing on the pavement outside twenty three Bredford Road, Kittle stepping forward and knocking three times on the front door, then stepping back onto the pavement and waiting. Allen was just about to duplicate W.P.C. Kittle's action, when the front door was opened by a very disgruntled Collin Friend, "Yes?" he asked.

In reply, Allen stepped forward his warrant card in his hand, "Mr Collin Friend, I'm Police Sergeant Oakley, and this is W.P.C. Kittle, could we have a minute of your time please?" he asked.

"I suppose it's about that bloody car, isn't it?" He said, then added, "Sorry Miss."

"Whose at the front door, Collin?" They heard a woman holler, "Because we're not heating up the whole of Bredford road," she added.

"It's the police, Mum," he shouted back.

"Well bring them in and shut that dam door, now!" She hollered.

"Yes Mum" Collin replied stepping back.

It was a typical nineteen twenty's middle terraced house, a small open fireplace with ornaments at either end, and a clock taking pride of place in the middle of the surround. There were two small armchairs and a matching settee, the carpet had seen better days, especially the area that lead from the front door to the rear of the home. Collin had closed the front door, "Please have a seat," he said.

"I take it, that it's about that car," he added, "not entirely," Allen replied, as the two officers commandeered the two armchairs, Collin sat down on the vacant settee, a forlorn look on his face, "so what's this all about?" he asked.

"I've already told the police what happened." Allen smiled at the dejected young man. "Firstly Collin, I can call you Collin?" he asked.

The young man just nodded his head, "Well the good news, for you anyway, is that we spoke to your boss."

"He isn't my boss anymore, he fired me," he hollered.

"Wrong! Collin, we explained the situation to him, and the fact that if you had not been there, that he had been approach by the man, he would have reacted exactly the same way, so he wants you back on Monday."

Collin shot off of the settee and grabbed Allen hand, "Thank you," he hollered, then running out of the room screaming, "Mum I've got my job back."

Allen and W.P.C. Kittled smiled at each other, as Collin return to their front room grinning, "Sorry about that," he said, "but it's only Mum and me, I went down to the labour exchange when he fired me, but there's not a lot on offer, and what with losing my old man, mum and I need the money."

"Collin," Allen began, removing an eight by ten photograph from inside his jacket, "was this the man that stole the car?" he asked.

Collin sat back down on the settee, and studied the photo, "Well, the hair is different, but yes that's the bastard, sorry Miss," he said.

"Can you tell us anything else, Collin?" Allen enquired.

"Like what?" He replied.

"Anything at all?" Allen asked.

Collin sat there for a minute deep in thought, "Well," he began, "he limped, had a walking cane, his hair is long and black and in a ponytail, he's got a black goatee, and he was wearing black leather gloves, what I did notice was his right hand didn't move, if that's any help, Oh and he is Irish."

"You didn't happen to notice in which direction he went, by any chance?" Allen asked.

"No I didn't, I came out of the show room with his bottle of lemonade, and he was gone, there was another bloke filling his Ford I asked him if he saw a Wolseley drive off, he told me, it didn't drive off, it shot off, and he pointed towards Wood View, so I ran back into the show room and told the operator to dial nine nine nine, because a bloody priest had stolen my car, sorry Miss," he stated.

"And thanks for putting a good word in with Mr potter for me," he concluded still grinning.

Chapter Thirty

Liam pushed his Triumph Thunder Bird behind the cemetery's stone wall, out of sight from the main road, and pulled the bike up onto its stand, then taking off his helmet and Bellstaff waterproof jacket, placed them in the bike's side panniers. Liam strode toward the church, looking for father O'Connell, it wasn't until he slowly pushed open the church door that he saw Father Patrick O'Connel kneeling in front of the altar, seemingly deep in prayer. Liam waited for what he considered to be a reasonable time, then cleared his throat. Father O'Connell raised his head, crossed himself and stood up, he turned smiling, until he saw Liam, "I know why you are here, my son," he said to himself.

Liam strode toward the priest smiling, his right hand outstretched, "How's the shoulder, father?" Liam asked.

"I have my days, my son," the priest replied.

"It's worst with the cold weather, and getting on in years doesn't help," he said, taking Liam's outstretched hand.

"I guess you know why I'm here, Father?" He said.

"I'm afraid I do my son, but there is little that I can tell you, I'm sorry to say."

"Can we sit father?" Liam asked.

Both men settled into the front pew, and turned to face each other, "You do know that everything that is divulged in the confessional is sacrosanct, my son don't you?" The priest asked.

"So O'Brien has been here to see you father?" Liam stated. Father O'Connell looked away, "I'll take that as a yes, then," Liam said, "I'm not saying he was, or that he wasn't, but if he had come to me, I would tell him that I would only pray for him, my son."

"So O'Brien asked for your help, but you refused, Father?" Liam asked, once again Father O'Connell looked away.

"To bring you up to date father, and this is between you and me, Yes! To get O'Brien out of hospital, a man was killed to take O'Brien's place, four clergy entered and four clergy left, but one of them was now O'Brien. He managed to acquire a car and tried to kidnap my wife, god knows what he would have done, I shiver every time I think about it."

Father O'Connell's hands took hold of Liam's hands and squeezed them, "If I knew where he was or what he had planned, I would tell you my son, I know I'm sworn to secrecy, but I don't know what is wrong with the man, he's obsessed, the devil has captured his soul, and I feel that he is a lost soul," he said, bowing his head and crossing himself, "all I can do, is pray that you find him quickly, before he hurts more people," he concluded.

Chapter Thirty-One

Keir and Bill had travelled down to Shannon's in Keir's Morris One Thousand, Bill's knuckles were white, where he had clung to the passengers door handle.

"You alright?" Keir asked.

"Well seeing as how only fifteen minutes ago we were sitting in your office, with her ladyship, Liam, and young Oakley, I think my stomach is still back in your office," Bill replied white faced.

"Safe as houses, young Bill, safe as houses," Keir chuckled.

"When we get to Shannon's," Keir said, as he slowed down in the built up area, to thirty miles an hour, "I'll get out first, and nobble this Flanagan chap, you give me three minutes, and try and pick up a conversation with one of his chaps, how Fiona managed to get a phone tap so quickly I'll never know, but if I can scare this Flanagan chap to make a call to O'Brien we'll know he's still in the area, I just hope he makes a slip as to where he's shacked up," Keir stated as he pulled his Morris One Thousand onto Shannon's forecourt and killed the engine, hearing a sigh from his passenger, Keir just smiled at his mate.

Keir strolled into Shannon's office, leaving Bill sitting in his car, his warrant card in his hand.

"I would like to speak to the proprietor, young lady," Keir said to a young woman of about twenty five, he estimated, although his attention was drawn to the plunging neck line of her sky blue blouse, leaving nothing to Keir's imagination.

"Can I ask whose calling, Sir?" A broad Belfast accent asked.

"Detective Chief Inspector Keir Dickson, young lady," Keir replied smiling, showing her his warrant card.

"I'll see if Mr Flanagan is available, inspector," she said, getting to her feet. Keir's eyes bulged at the sight, as she stood up, and walked around her desk, in six-inch bright red stiletto heeled shoes, she stood at least six foot six inches tall, and to cap it all, she was nearly wearing a bright red leather mini skirt, which nearly covered her backside, Keir gazed at the young women perfectly shaped exceptionally long legs, "I won't be a minute inspector," she smirked, noticing the look on Keir's face.

"Good job Bills not here, he'd have an orgasm just looking at her," he said to himself smiling.

Keir was gazing at a page three calendar, when he heard a cough, "Mr Flanagan will be with you in a minute inspector," she said, as she sauntered into the office. As she approached her desk, Keir couldn't help seeing her slide a small notebook to the edge of her working surface, where it fell to the floor, Keir went to move forward, but was stopped in his tracks by the view of the young women bending over retrieving the notebook.

"G string," Keir smiled to himself, "and I'll bet my month's salary, that's not the first time, either."

"Sorry to have kept you waiting inspector," he heard, "I hope Jeanette kept you occupied," Keir turned, Michael Flanagan stood about six foot one inches tall, his flaming red hair hanging down to his broad shoulders, he was wearing a dark green overall with Shannon's logo on the breast pocket, and cleaning his hands on a dirty rag.

"Trouble with one of the diagnostic machines," he said, smiling, "now how may I be of assistance inspector," he asked.

"Could we have a chat somewhere private, sir?" Keir asked.

"Follow me inspector, tea or coffee?" he asked.

"Not for me, sir," then turning to his receptionist, Flanagan said, "I'll have my usual Jeanette, in my office."

"I wonder what his usual is," Keir thought.

Keir followed him into a well-kept tidy office, "Please take a seat inspector," Flanagan said, as he sat down in a rather expensive leather swivel chair smiling.

"So how can I help you inspector?" he asked leaning forward and resting both elbows on his Mahogany desk, and cupping his hands together.

"Right sir," Keir began, "we are investigating a theft of a Wholseley motor vehicle, from Clarence Road Car Sales, and we have witnesses that have seen the vehicle in the Tilbury area, would you have happened to have seen this vehicle sir?" Keir asked, taking out his notebook and Parker Fifty One fountain pen from his inside jacket pocket. Flanagan frowned, and began scratching his forehead, "A Wholseley car you say, I would have to ask my staff inspector, but I don't personally remember a car of that description, when was the theft?" he asked.

"It was yesterday, sir," Keir replied.

"And I will level with you, it was stolen by an Irish person masquerading as a priest, he is wanted on several charges, one of which is murder."

"Murder!" Flanagan hollered, "oh my God."

"Yes sir, so if you know anything of this person, now would be a good time to help us, withholding information from the police is a criminal offence sir."

"Oh my God, Murder," Flanagan repeated, running his fingers through his long red hair.

"So can you help us, sir?" Keir asked. Flanagan now had his head in both his hands shaking from side to side.

"God almighty," he whispered.

"Can you help us sir?" Keir asked again, "Sorry inspector," he said, raising his head and staring at Keir, "if I see or hear anything I'll be straight on the phone, have you got a card or a phone number please?" he asked putting out his hand.

Keir removed a card from the back of his notebook and handed it to Michael Flanagan, "Thank you Inspector," he was just able to say as he took the card.

Keir slid into his driver's seat, and looked across at Bill, "Any luck?" he asked.

Bill shook his head, "According to the two chaps I talk to, they haven't see a Wolseley, but on the other hand they might have been told to keep their Irish cake holes shut, what about your end?" he asked.

"Well his secretary is something else," Keir chuckled.

"Well that will really! help the investigation, won't it," Bill snidely replied.

Keir grinned, "The tits were on full display, the Mini skirt was that bloody short, and she made sure that when she bent over, I would see she was only wearing a 'G' string."

"And she told you where we could capture O'Brien, did she, whilst you were getting a hard on?" Bill sarcastically asked.

Keir looked at his mate, "Well," he chuckled.

"It was either her 'G' string and boobs, or a page three calendar, but joking aside, Mr Michael Flanagan, is a brilliant actor, he had me going there for a minute, but I'll bet right this minute he's on the phone, so let's go and listen to what he is saying, shall we?" Keir asked, as he left tyre rubber on Shannon's driveway.

Chapter Thirty-Two

"Jeanette!" Michael Flanagan screamed, "get in here!"

No sooner had he called, that the door was opened, then closed and locked, "Yes Michael," she whispered, smiling as she walked around his desk all the buttons on her blouse now undone, "no Jeanette," he said, gazing at her full breasts, "but Michael Darling, you love me doing this, don't you?" she asked running her right hand up his thigh, whilst her left hand began undoing his fly buttons.

"Fuck it why not, after what I've just been told," he said, laying back in his leather swivel chair, as Jeanette took his erection in her mouth, her tongue driving him crazy as her tongue encircled the head, "do you want to fuck me now Darling," she whispered, as she got up off her knees, and bent over Flanagan's desk pulling the 'G' string to one side.

"Pussy is waiting, darling, for you to fuck my brains out," she giggled. Her mini skirt was up round her waist, her long legs spread wide apart, two round cheeks and a pouting pussy were now all Flanagan could focus on. O'Brien was the last thing he was thinking about, as he rammed his erection all the way into Jeanette's vagina.

"Yes! Darling yes!" She screamed, "Harder my darling harder, please." They could both hear the slapping, as their bodies slammed together over and over, "I'm coming Michael," she screamed, "don't stop fucking me, please," she whimpered.

Michael was thrusting so hard, that his desk was inching its way across the office floor, "Yes," she screamed, as both Flanagan and Jeanette came together, he lent forward cupping both her breasts, then lifting her bodily up and fell backwards into his office chair, they were still coupled together as Jeanette unclipped the middle of her bra, releasing her full firm breasts for him to fondle, leaning her head back onto Flanagan's shoulder as he kissed her neck.

"God," she whispered, "you certainly know how to fuck a girl, Michael," she said, as he caressed her tort nipples.

They had made love two more times, each time with Jeanette laying across Michael's desk, her long legs wrapped around his waist locking them together, before she asked.

"So what did the police want, Michael?"

"Fuck it," he said, taking hold of Jeanette's ankles, then standing up, and pulling out his semi erection, he gazed at her widely spread legs, and his white love juice as it trickled out onto his desk blotter.

"I need to make a couple of phone calls, Jeanette," he said, as Jeanette sat up and re clipped the front of her bra, and buttoned her blouse, then leaning forward she smiled as Flanagan began to try and put his semi erection back into his trousers, "I'll do that Darling," she said, brushing his hands away as she slid of his desk, and placed both her hands around his manhood, "I'll just make sure he is nice and clean," she giggled.

Before he could say anything, Jeanette was sucking the last drops of love juice from his now throbbing erection, "No Jeanette, I've got to make a phone call," he said, trying to pull back, "but he's so hard now darling, just one more time, then you can make your phone call, you know you want to fuck me again, I know he does," she said, running her tongue over Michael's throbbing erection. Michael spun her round and threw her over his desk, lifting her mini skirt above her waist.

"Yes Michael. Yes," she screamed as he rammed his erection all the way home.

On the second ring, it was answered, "Yes." Flanagan heard, "Joe it's me, how far along is the car?" he asked.

"She's all masked up and ready for the first coat, gov," came the reply, "that's all its going to have, then rip off the masking tape, and get back here, make sure you clean and lock up and bring it all back here and burn it, then tell your mate to get out, there's problems, you hear me, Joe?" Flanagan asked.

"You're the boss," came the reply.

Flanagan waited three quarters of an hour, then picking up the phone, looked at Keir's card and began dialling. Keir picked up his phone and began to smile when he heard, "Can I speak to Detective Chief Inspector Keir Dickson, please," recognising the voice immediately.

"Mr Flanagan," Keir began, "how can I help you?" He replied smiling, whilst Fiona and Bill sat listening to the recording of the conversation.

"I'm afraid I haven't been completely honest with you I'm afraid," he began, "oh!" replied Keir still smiling, "in what way?" Keir asked.

"Well," Flanagan began, "I knew, as he was then Father O'Brien, I'd heard rumours about the fact that he was in trouble with the police, but I didn't realise until you told me that he was wanted for murder. Yes he did bring that car to me, I'm sorry I lied, and I know where he is living at the moment, it's a derelict house on the Linford Road."

"So is the car there?" Keir asked.

"It was Inspector," came the reply, "so what was being done to the car, Mr Flanagan?" Keir asked.

"He wanted it a different colour, it's probably white now, but as soon as you left I phone my chap and told him to stop, so I wouldn't know what state it's in, I know I'm in trouble, but it wasn't until you told me how serious his crimes were, that I wished I'd had never set eyes on the dam man, him being Irish and a priest didn't help. You can't miss the house, it's the only house for miles, on the Linford Road, it looks derelict from the outside, and there's a large barn at the back that I use for spraying and repairing crashed vehicles," he stated.

"That house didn't belong to a Mr and Mrs Barns by any chance?" Keir asked grinning, "Yes Inspector it did, Why? Do you know the property?" he asked.

"Yes Mr Flanagan, I most certainly do," Keir replied.

"So," Flanagan began, "do you want me to turn myself in Inspector?" he asked.

Keir looked across at Fiona and shrugged his shoulders, Fiona shook her head, "We'll be in touch Mr Flanagan, but please don't think of going on holiday, will you?" He said.

"No Sir, and if I can be of any help just ask, and once again, I'm sorry I wasn't up front with you."

"Duly noted, Mr Flanagan," Keir said, as he hung up the phone.

Chapter Thirty-Three

Michael Flanagan had just put the phone down when he heard Jeanette talking to a voice he knew well, "Joe!" He shouted, "In here, now!"

"Yes, Gov," came the reply. He was just about to get out of his office chair, when his office door was opened, "Come in and shut the door," he ordered, Joe quickly entered the room, turned and shut the door.

"Yes, Gov," he said, as he stood in front of Flanagan's desk, his head slightly bowed.

"It's okay Joe," Flanagan stated.

"Take a seat and tell me what happened, I've had the Fuzz here, and between you and me, I've balls up big time," he added.

Joe looked up at his boss, "Why, what happened, Gov?" he asked.

"I thought I was helping an Irish colleague I've known for a few years, I knew he was wanted by the police, from rumours I had heard, but I've now been told, he's up for murder."

Joe shot straight up, "Murder! Fucking hell," he uttered, "no wonder you want him gone."

"So we need to get our stories straight, Joe," Flanagan stated.

"Yes, Gov," Joe replied.

"Right," Flanagan began, "you had a twenty gallon drum of old army paint, so you managed to give it one coat, but it looks like crap, because you weren't able to finish off, okay," Joe just nodded his head, and listened to his boss.

"You know nothing about the number plates, and you didn't talk to the priest, he stayed in the house whilst you were working, after I called you, you just ripped off all the masking and came back here, got it?" he asked.

"Yes, Gov," Joe replied smiling, "one coat of a khaki army paint, it looked like crap only having one coat, you called me back here and said, you didn't want anything to do with the car, so I ripped off the masking and came back, okay?" he asked.

Flanagan put both his elbows on his desk, his head in his hands, "That's not going to fucking well work, is it?" he asked, running his fingers through his flaming red hair, "When they catch him, and I'll bet a pound to a pinch of shit they will, they'll know we've been bull shitting them, so what actually did you do to the fucking motor?" he asked.

"I did what I thought you wanted, Gov, the bottom half along the doors is now cream, so it's sort of two tone," Joe replied. Flanagan sat there for over three minutes, then sitting back, smiled.

"So the bottom of the doors are now cream Joe, yeah?" he asked.

"Yes, Gov," came the reply.

"Right! The car had been waxed, so you had to wash all the wax off with meths, Yes?" Joe just nodded, "That took you some time, yes?" Again a nod, "You then began to mask the car, you had just finished masking it up when I phoned you up and told you to get out, Yes?"

"Right Gov, and I know nothing about number plates," Joe stated, a grin spreading across his face.

"So when they catch him, we'll say, he must have done it himself, or got someone else to do it, okay," Flanagan said, leaning back in his leather chair smiling.

"Is that it, then Gov?" Joe asked.

"Yes thanks Joe, this is just between you and me, I was a real cunt letting O'Brien talk me into it, and talking about cunt, tell Jeanette to get her arse in here when you go, okay?" Flanagan asked.

Joe stood up, "A murderer," he mumbled, "fucking hell," as he left Flanagan's office.

"Yes Michael?" Jeanette said, smiling, as she entered, "Shut and lock the fucking door sweet, and get naked," he said, "yes Michael," she whispered, as her red leather mini skirt dropped to the floor.

Chapter Thirty-Four

O'Brien had asked Joe why he was ripping the masking from the car, when he was told that the police had spoken to his boss, and he was told to leave the car, O'Brien had rushed into the house, quickly throwing on a navy blue Duffel coat with a hood, picked up a suitcase that contain the previous owners clothing, checked his wallet and the passport in the name of Sheamus Donahue, that Roberto Bocelli had acquired for him, and thrown them onto the back seat of the Wolseley. Joe had just removed the last piece of masking tape, as O'Brien fired up the engine, and began backing out of the Barn, "Thanks," he hollered through the open window as he accelerated along the weed covered drive and onto the Linford Road.

He had seven hundred and fifty pound in his wallet plus some small change, a passport, and a change of clothes, although the clothing was a bit on the large size, but he knew there was no way that he could go back to his own house, it would probably be under surveillance, "So where the hell can I go," he said to himself as he came up to the 'A' thirteen, and turned right, heading towards Southend-On-Sea.

"A, B and B for the night will have to do for now," he said, out loud to his empty vehicle, as he kept strictly to the speed limit. He was approaching five bells roundabout at Vange, when he spotted a couple walking hand in hand, the man's right hand outstretched, his thumb pointing skywards.

"The police are looking for a single man in a Wolseley car," he said, as he began to slow, the couple smiled as O'Brien pulled up alongside them, and stopped. O'Brien lent across the seat and rolled down the window, "Would you like a lift?" he asked to the smiling couple.

"Yes please," the woman replied opening the front passenger door, and sliding into the passenger seat, her male companion opting for the seat behind her.

"How far are you going?" The woman asked.

"Well, to be honest," O'Brien began, "I've been driving all day, and right now I'm just looking for a B and B for the night, I'm on my way to Harwich," he lied.

"You should have taken the 'A' twelve sir, it's much quicker" the male passenger stated. O'Brien laughed, "I have all the time in the world, young man, and the coast road is much more interesting, all the different towns."

"My name," the woman stated, "is Amanda Welsh and my brother is Andrew, and we might be able to help you, it just so happens that Andrew and I are stay with our aunt Rosie, she has a boarding house just outside of Shoeburyness, it's an old farm house, and I know she has two spare rooms, well she did have this morning," she stated.

"Well Shoeburyness it is then" O'Brien said, smiling, as he pulled away.

"Just pull in here, and at the end of the drive is an old barn, you can park there, just look out for Aunty Rosie's Lambretta, and Uncle Sam's Land Rover, and keep well away from Uncle Sam's diesel tank, it stinks and the tap leaks, I'll pop in and okay it with Aunt Rosie," the young woman said.

O'Brien did as instructed and thinking all the time, "This is perfect," as the young woman ran to the back door of the farm house, three minutes later, she was back grinning, "Auntie Rosie says, you are more than welcome, and the timing is perfect, because she has just started preparing dinner, and from the aroma coming from her kitchen, it's my favourite, Rabbit Pie, and Rhubarb Crumble, you're in luck sir," she said, "it's Sheamus Amanda," O'Brien lied.

O'Brien had the navy-blue Duffel coat wrapped tightly around him, he had to get out of the clerical cloths and into civilian gear, the dog collar would be a complete give away, as he walk into the warm farm house kitchen, "Could I use your bathroom, please madam?" he asked forcing a smile.

"We're all family here, so it's Rosie, and you are?" She enquired, "It's Sheamus, Aunty," Amanda said, "I'll show Sheamus his room first, shall I, you're busy," she added.

"I hope you won't think I'm being rude, Sheamus?" Amanda said, as she opened a bedroom door, "But you were so kind giving Andrew and I a lift, but I noticed that you have a problem with your right hand," she said, a somewhat embarrassed look on her face.

O'Brien forced a smile, "Long time ago Amanda," he began, his brain going ten to the dozen, "I came off of my motor bike, hit a slippery part of the road, and unfortunately there was a large articulated truck coming the other way, it's four tyres crushed my right hand, I was very lucky I didn't lose my arm," he lied.

"Oh! You poor man," she uttered, "how do you cope?" she asked.

"After thirty two years, Amanda, I don't really notice it, but thanks for your concern," he said.

O'Brien had changed out of his clerical cloths and began dressing himself from the suite case, the waist on the trousers were that big, that he had to loop it over at the back, the tartan shirt he chose, he wore outside the trousers and to make sure the trousers could not be seen, he found a fisherman's jersey which came down below his backside.

"That will have to do," he said, looking in a full length mirror.

All four occupants were seated around the large oak kitchen table, O'Brien had just caught himself from saying grace, as Aunt Rosie stated, "Enjoy."

"Do you need a hand, Sheamus?" Amanda asked as O'Brien took the knife in his left hand and inserted the handle into an opening in his prosthetic hand then securing it with a strap, "I'm fine Amanda, been doing this for years," he lied, "Sheamus lost his hand in a motor bike accident," Amanda said to her aunt and Brother, "a big truck ran over it, he was lucky he didn't lose his arm," she added.

Her brother looked across at O'Brien, "So what happened, Sheamus?" Andrew asked.

"Sheamus hit a slippery patch on the road, and came flying off his bike, there was a large truck coming the other way, and all four tyres crushed his hand," Amanda stated. O'Brien just raised his head and smiled at the company.

"What sort of bike was it, Sheamus?" Andrew asked. O'Brien put down his fork, then picking up a napkin, wiped his mouth, "It was a BSA five hundred C.C. B34 Gold Star Andrew, but that was over thirty odd years ago, and I try very hard to forget it," he lied picking up his fork, "sorry" came the reply, "that's alright Andrew, I often get asked but may I say," he said, turning to Aunt Rosie, "this meal is absolutely superb, Aunt Rosie, so how much am I in your debt for this wonderful hospitality?" he asked smiling.

"Would one pound be okay, that would include breakfast of course," she said, blushing.

"Capital Aunt Rosie, Capital," O'Brien replied.

"Now if you don't mind, I'm going to have an early night, the drive up from Dover has taken its toll, but thank you all once again," he said, releasing the knife from his prosthetic hand and placing it on his empty plate, "good night Sheamus, sleep well," he was told, as he left the kitchen.

O'Brien opened the door to the bathroom, and was about to enter when he heard footsteps running up the stair, "Sorry Sheamus," Rosie said, gasping for breath, "I forgot that you might need the bathroom," as she pushed passed him, "My husband will need a clean shirt for tomorrow," she said, smiling, then looking at O'Brien's concerned face, "are you okay Sheamus?" she asked.

O'Brien froze as he glanced at the three 'V' stripes on both sleeves, "Not a problem young lady, so your husband is in the police force I take it," O'Brien managed to say, "yes, Sam's on the late shift this week, but you'll meet him at breakfast, eight o-clock okay?" she asked.

"Perfect," he replied as he closed the bathroom door.

O'Brien sat on the side of the bath hyperventilating, trying to get his nerves under control, "Can I pick them?" He said to himself as he sat there.

Five minutes later he was back in his bedroom, the suite case packed, he looked at the illuminated dial on his wrist-watch, "Eight fifteen," he said to himself, as he walked to the window overlooking the gravel drive.

"He won't be home before ten thirty, so just calm down O'Brien, and wait," he said. He must have dosed off to sleep, but the noise of car tyres on the drive brought him fully awake, crossing to the window he stood back as twin headlights floodlit the front of the house. He could see the sign on the front bumper stating Police, the patrol car had come to a halt, the passenger door had opened and a man of about six foot had stepped out onto the drive, O'Brien heard, "Same time tomorrow George and thanks," as the man stood up straight and slammed the patrol car door shut.

O'Brien watched as the vehicle completed a three point turn, then sped off along the driveway.

O'Brien gazed at his watch, it told him it was twenty past one, it was then that he heard footsteps approaching along the corridor toward his room, he froze as the footsteps stopped outside his room, placing his ear to the door he heard a male voice whisper, "So what's this Irish bloke like," then Rosie replied, "he's a very nice polite man, he gave Amanda and Andrew a lift home, anyway Sam you'll meet him at breakfast, now come to bed," she said.

O'Brien sat on the bed, he was wearing the navy-blue Duffel coat over his borrowed clothing, every few minute gazing at his wrist-watch. At a quarter to three, he stood up and made his way to the bedroom door, on turning the key he unlocked the door and listened as he stuck his head into the corridor. He smiled as the sound of snoring could be heard coming from the far end of the corridor, picking up his suitcase and then locking the bedroom door, he made his way to the head of the stairs, keeping to the side of the stair treads, he made his way down, and into the kitchen and over to the back door, which he found unlocked.

"Why would you bother to lock up living out here?" he asked himself, as he stepped out into the moon lit yard. O'Brien sprinted across the yard and into the barn.

Whilst sitting in his bedroom he had formulated a plan, the Wolseley would have to go, but the Lambretta would be his new means of transport, placing the suite case in front of the Lambretta's seat, he pushed it off of its stand and wheeled it out into the yard, he then went over to the large orange fuel tank, taking the bucket that was under the dripping tap and opened the tap, filling the bucket three quarters full, he then began walking backward trickling a trail of diesel towards the house, arriving at the open back door, he threw the remaining diesel onto the kitchen floor, then ran back into the barn.

Filling the bucket once again, he threw diesel over the Wolseley and the Land Rover, then placing the bucket on its side under the tap, opened the tap halfway. He watched as the diesel began to spread across the barn floor, "Time to go," he said to himself, as he ran into the yard, stopping halfway, he removed a box of matches he had picked up from the kitchen stove, and striking a Swan Vesta dropped it onto the diesel trail.

As soon as the diesel ignited and began travelling towards both the barn and farmhouse, O'Brien ran to the Lambretta pushing it off of its stand and running it down the drive, as he came to the entrance of the property, he heard a Whoosh, and turning, watched as the barn became an inferno.

Chapter Thirty-Five

Bill barged into Keir's office, "Have you read this," he hollered, throwing a copy of The Southend-On-Sea Gazette newspaper onto Keir's desk, "inside the first page, Tel," he added. Keir picked up the newspaper and opened it, the headlines read, "Good Samaritan Dies In House Fire." Then underneath the headline, a photograph depicting two adults and two young adults, standing in front of a burnt out house.

"Okay," Keir said, laying the newspaper on his desk, and looking up at his mate, "so! A house burns down, so what?" he asked. Bill placed both his hands on Keir's desk, and leaning forward whispered, "Read the fucking article Tel." Keir picked the newspaper back up and began reading, "Senior Sergeant Samuel Parsons his wife Rose and their niece and nephew Amanda and Andrew, escaped an inferno as their house burnt to the ground, a guest staying at the farmhouse wasn't so fortunate."

The guest, a Mr Sheamus Donahue perished in the blaze, he had given the niece and nephew a lift home and was staying for the night.

"I tried to wake him, but the door was locked from the inside," Senior Sergeant Parsons stated. His niece a Miss Amanda Welsh cried as she talked about this good Samaritan, "He was such a lovely man," she said, "I felt so sorry for him, because he had lost his right hand in a motor bike accident," Keir stared at the last line.

"I felt so sorry for him, because he had lost his right hand in a motor bike accident," he said, out loud. Bill stood bolt upright, his hands on his hips, "well!" He enquired.

"Nah! can't be," Keir replied.

"How many one handed Irishmen do you know Tel?" Bill asked.

Keir sat there thinking, "Wait," He yelled, as he shot out of his chair, and rushed to his filing cabinet, second later he was sitting at his desk a file laying open, "Mr Roberto Bocelli stated," he said, running his finger down the statement, "That he had acquired a passport for O'Brien in the name of Sheamus Donahue!" He shouted.

Bill stood there a big grin spreading across his face, "So the bastard burned in hell," he said. Keir sat there deep in thought.

"What?" Bill asked, looking puzzled, "The bastard's dead, Tel."

"Is he?" Keir asked looking up at his mate.

"That Sergeant said he tried to save him, but the door was locked."

"If they find a body, and the right hand is missing, I'll go along with you, but knowing O'Brien as we do, I'll lay money this was a set up, he wants us to think that he died in that fire. So I think we should find out where this fire was, and go and have a little chat to this young lady Amanda Welsh," he said. Keir was just about to get out of his chair, when the door was knocked and Fiona entered, "Hope I'm not interrupting anything?" she asked.

"No Ma'am," Keir replied.

"Would you like to cast your eyes over this article," he said, offering Fiona the opened newspaper. Fiona took the paper, and moving over to a vacant chair, sat down crossing her shapely legs, and began reading. Bill and Keir watched as Fiona read the article, she looked up at the two of them and smiled. "So O'Brien wants us to think that he perished in that house fire, does he?" she asked smiling.

"I think it would be of great advantage, if you two gentlemen had a chat to this young lady to confirm if this Sheamus Donahue is in fact O'Brien, and that they can confirm that they have found his body," Bill stood there shaking his head, "I don't believe you two," he said.

Keir flipped open his rollerdex, then picking up his phone, began to dial.

"This is Detective Chief Inspector Dickson, can you put me through to the news desk, please?" He said, looking at Fiona who was smiling, and Bill Day who wasn't.

"Hi there," they heard Keir say, "my name is Keir Dickson, I'm a DCI With the Essex Constabulary, your article regarding Senior Sergeant Sam Parsons and the house fire, can you tell me what station he is stationed at please." There was silence for a minute, whilst Keir listened, "I can appreciate that, young lady," they heard him say, then, "I tell you what, phone Corringham Police Station, and ask to be put through to DCI Keir Dickson, or better still, you could ask for Detective Superintendent Fiona Jarman, she's my Governor," he said, smiling at Fiona.

"Thank you," he said, covering the mouthpiece, "she's seeing if she can divulge," he chuckled taking his hand away from the mouthpiece.

"Thank you, young lady, so he is stationed at Shoeburyness," he said, giving the thumbs up sign, "thank you very much for your help," he said, replacing the receiver.

"Can't see the point of phoning that station," Bill stated.

"If my house had just burnt to the ground, there's no way that I would be at work."

"Point taken Bill, but it's the niece and nephew we need to speak to, it was them that O'Brien gave a lift to," Keir said, picking up his phone.

"Sarge," he began, "can you get Shoeburyness on the phone for us, I need to speak to the Desk Sergeant please?" He said, "Thanks Sarge," he added, holding the phone and waiting.

"Shoeburyness on the line, Gov," he was told. Keir switched on the speaker and waited, "Shoeburyness police station, Sergeant William Parks speaking, how can I help you," they all heard, "this is DCI Keir Dickson here Sergeant, I'm making enquiries about the fire at Senior Sergeant Parson's house."

"Sam's not in today Gov, he's out hiring two caravans, he lost everything, you know," Sergeant Parks stated.

"We really need to speak to his niece and nephew, Sarge?" Keir replied.

"That's why he's looking for two caravans Gov, they're staying with him, there on vacation from uni," they all heard.

"Have they found the body of the guest, Sarge?" Keir asked.

"You'll be lucky," came the reply, then, "sorry Gov."

"From what Sam told us, it's just one big pile of ashes, the old farmhouse was mostly timber, Sam said, that even a hundred yards away the heat was unbearable, the barn is the same, that was all! Timber, as soon as I hear from Sam Gov, I'll get him to call you, he's supposed to call in later on today, I'll tell him it's urgent, okay?"

"Thank you Sergeant, and yes! It is urgent," Keir replied replacing the phone.

Bill had just returned to Keir's office, carrying a tray laden with three bacon sandwiches, and three mugs of steaming hot black coffee, which he placed on Keir's desk, "I think a dash of this will add to the flavour," Keir said, smiling at his two compatriots, as he removed a half bottle of single malt from his desk draw, "only a dash in mine please Keir?" Fiona asked.

"Yes Ma'am," came the reply. Keir had just taken a huge bite of his bacon sandwich when his phone began to ring, Fiona lent across his desk picking up his phone, "Detective Superintendent Jarman," she stated. Then said, "Could you hold the line for a second, Senior Sergeant, DCI Dickson will be with you in a second," as Keir switched his phone to speaker, "sorry about that Sergeant," Keir chuckled.

"You caught me with a mouth full of our canteen's famous bacon sandwich, but thank for call back so quickly," he said, "I was told it was urgent Gov, so how can I help?" Senior Sergeant Parson asked.

"Would it be possible to talk to your niece and nephew about your guest?" Keir asked. There was silence for a while then the three were told, "I tried to wake him Sir, but his door was locked, I hammered on his door but the flames were coming up the stairs, and I needed to get my family out, I was the last one to escape, the flames were up to his door, so I couldn't go back, I'm sorry Sir," he managed to say.

"Did you meet the man, Sergeant?" Keir asked.

"No Sir, I didn't," came the reply, "right Sam, I can call you Sam?" Keir asked.

"Yes Sir," came the reply, "right Sam, my name is Keir, so forget about the Sir, Gov will be fine, so you never met the man, am I right?" Keir enquired.

"No Gov, I was on late shift, arrived home just after ten thirty, my mate dropped me off, when I came indoors Rosie my wife told me we had a guest, we sat round the kitchen table chatting till about twenty past one, and then went to bed, it must have been after three, when I heard a *Whoosh*, when I looked out of the bedroom window I saw the barn on fire, I shook Rosie and told her to wake the kids, but when I opened our bedroom door I could see a glow coming up the stairs, I ran to the spare bedroom and tried the handle, screaming at the top of my voice, but the door was locked, so I hammered on the door, by this time Amanda and Andrew were dressed and with the wife. All four of us ran to the end of the corridor, I ripped the sheets off of our bed and tied them together, the window at the end of the corridor is a sash window, so I opened it all the way up, and with the sheets, lowered my family to the ground, I told them to get as far away as they could, I turned to go back for the man, but opening the sash window brought the flames closer, there was nothing I could do Gov, so I tied the sheets off and lowered myself to the ground, by this time the top of the house was an inferno, the flames were coming out of the window that I had escaped from."

"I'm glad that your family is safe Sam, and I'm sorry you lost your home, but it's your nephew and niece we need to speak to please."

"Yes Gov, but do you mind if I ask why?" Keir looked across at Fiona and mouthed, "Do I tell him?"

Fiona just nodded her head, "Right Sam," Keir began, "this conversation is on speaker, I'm now going to ask my Detective Superintendent Fiona Jarman, and a colleague Mr Bill Day, to let you know that they are present, okay?" Keir asked.

"Yes Gov," came the reply.

"Thank you, Sergeant for your time," Fiona stated.

"I'm Bill Day Sam, sorry about the house."

"Now that we have all been introduce Sam," Keir began, "this conversation is only between us four, do you understand?" he asked.

"Yes Gov," came the reply, "so whatever you are told now, goes no further, I have two witnesses that you have given your word, right?" he asked.

"Well Gov, if you don't mind me saying so, you are scaring the living crap out of me, Sorry Ma'am," Keir smiled.

"You have nothing to worry about Sam. We believe that your guest is an escaped prisoner, and to cover his tracks, he set fire to your house and barn."

"What!" They heard him shout, then, "sorry about that Gov."

"So as I've said, Sam," Keir continued, "they won't find a body, my colleague and I will be out to your property tomorrow, do you happen to know what was in your barn by any chance?" Keir asked.

"Just my Land Rover, Rosie's scooter, and the chaps car," he replied.

"You wouldn't happen to know what make of car it was Sam, would you?"

Keir said, "No Gov, I didn't go into the barn when I arrived home, it was gone ten thirty and pitch black. I only found out we had a guest, when I went indoors," he stated.

"Any luck with the caravans, Sam?" Keir asked.

"As a matter of fact Gov, I should have two Eldis Tornado's on my property in about an hour's time, I've still got electricity and water so we should be able to muddle through, until they clear the site. Mind you, I'm going to miss the old house, it's been in my family for years," the three heard the emotional reply, "see you tomorrow, Sam" Keir said, replacing the receiver.

Chapter Thirty-Six

It was just coming up to ten thirty, as Keir's souped-up Morris Minor One Thousand pulled into Sam Parson's drive.

"Oh my god," Fiona exclaimed at the sight that hit her. Both her and Keir gazed at the hive of activity, two fire engines and three police car were in attendance, firemen were hosing down smouldering embers, the police rummaging through the debris, one of the officer seeing Keir's Morris ran towards them, both his arms raised, Keir slowed as the officer approach taking his warrant card from his inside pocket and winding down the driver's window, the police officer ran towards them, his right hand raised, Keir applied the brakes as the officer came alongside the Morris.

"Sorry," he shouted, "you'll have to t'turn round m'mate, the police are h'here and we are i'investigating," he stated as he looked at Keir, "it's, you'll have to turn round Sir! Constable, and you are addressing DCI Dickson, and Detective Superintendent Fiona Jarman," he said, pushing his warrant card through the car window, and inches away from the officers face.

"Sorry G'gov, s'sorry M'ma'am, please g'go r'right ahead," he managed to say, "and in future constable, you will always address a member of the public as either Sir or Madam, and not as Mate, right constable?" he asked.

"Y'yes G'gov," came the nervous reply, as Keir engaged first gear, and pulled away.

Keir was wearing fawn coloured slacks, a fawn Safari jacket, a cream open necked shirt, and light brown brogue shoes, Fiona on the other hand was in her full Superintendents uniform, complete with epaulettes, as they walked toward two men in suits and two police officer, one of them showing three stripes, "Good morning gentlemen," Fiona said, as they approached the group, but it appeared that she hadn't been heard.

Keir gave a loud cough, "Be with you! in a minute" they were unceremoniously told. Keir threw back his shoulder, and in a town criers voice shouted, "Superintendent Jarman wishes to speak to Senior Sergeant Samuel Parsons, Now!" all four men froze, and on turning, stood to attention, "Sorry Ma'am," they all said, in unison.

One of the suited men stepped forward, an embarrassed look on his face, "D.S. Jones Ma'am," he said, offering his right hand, "and this is D.C. Smith," he said, indicating the other suited officer, "so you two are the notorious Smith and Jones, are you?" she asked smiling.

"Yes Ma'am," Jones replied returning the smile.

"And this gentlemen is DCI Keir Dickson," Fiona stated.

"And we would like to speak to Senior Sergeant Parsons, and in particular his niece and nephew Amanda and Andrew," she added, the officer with three stripes stepped forward, "Sergeant Bill Parks Ma'am, I believe I spoke to DCI Dickson on the phone and gave Sam the message to call, and you'll find Sam and his family over there Ma'am," he said, pointing, "you can't see them from here, the two vans are behind those haystacks, just follow the hose pipe, Ma'am," he said.

Keir raised his right hand, "Excuse me Sergeant," he said, as two officers turned their gaze in his direction, "any ideas yet?" he asked.

D.S. Jones stepped forward, "From what we can ascertain at the moment Gov," he began, "the fuel tank had a dodgy tap, it leaked, Senior Sergeant Parsons knew about it, and as a temporary fix, stuck a bucket under it, he was waiting until the diesel fuel was low before he fitted a new tap, the nearly full bucket must have fallen over, or been knocked over by some animal and the diesel fuel ran across the yard, how it ignited we haven't been able to ascertain as yet Gov, but Sam has lost his Land Rover, and his guest has lost his vehicle as well, plus his life I'm sorry to say," he concluded.

"Thank you Sergeant," Keir stated.

"Over behind those haystacks, you said?" He said, pointing.

"Yes Gov," came the reply.

Fiona and Keir thanked the officers, and began to walk towards the hose that was trailing along the ground from a standpipe, near to where the barn used to stand. As they cleared the haystacks, the two caravans came into view, they were parked side by side twelve feet apart, the doors facing each other, a large dark green canvas tarp had been placed over the two vans, giving shelter.

"Somebody knew what they were doing," Keir remarked, as they came to the opening between the two vans, to be greeted with a domestic scene. A table and six chairs stood between the two vans, a small generator stood to one side, with cables running to both vans, sitting at the table were Mr and Mrs Parsons, deeply engrossed in paperwork, where as their niece and nephew had the table covered in books.

"Good morning, ladies and gentlemen," Fiona said, as she and Keir stepped under the canvas tarp. Sam seeing Fiona's uniform, immediately stood to attention.

"At ease, Sam," Keir said, smiling at Sam's rigid stance, "we would just like to have a word with young Amanda and Andrew, if that's okay?" he asked.

Mrs Parsons stood up, "Tea or coffee?" she asked as she walked towards one of the caravans, "Coffee would be wonderful Mrs Parsons, thank you," Fiona said smiling.

"It's Rosie," came the jovial reply, "black or white, and sugar?" she asked. Fiona had pulled out one of the chairs when she asked.

"Do you need a hand, Rosie?"

"No Ma'am, but thanks for asking," came the reply, "it's Fiona, Rosie," Fiona corrected, "mine black with none, Keir's is black with three," she chuckled.

"Right! Now you two young people," Fiona began, as she sat down, "can you tell Keir and myself what happened from when you were picked up, please."

Amanda looked across at Fiona, her eyes filling with tears, "Well," she managed to say, but that was it, her shoulders began to shake, she stood bolt upright knocking over her chair, and ran to the other caravan sobbing, "sorry," they all heard as she slammed the van door.

"Right! What happened was," Andrew began, "we'd thumbed a lift as far as One Tree Hill, the chap was going to work at one of the refineries, so he had to turn right, heading for Corringham, so we were walking towards Vange, when Sheamus pulls over and asks us where we are going, we tell him Shoeburyness, cutting a long story short, he tells us that he's looking for a B and B, because he's driven up from Dover and he needs a break. We tell him that Aunt Rosie does B and B, and his actual words were, "Shoeburyness here we come," we get home, Aunt Rosie says fine, so he came in, Amanda showed him his room, half an hour later he comes done, mind you his sense of dress left a lot to be desired, he had his evening meal, said, he wanted an early night because he was heading for Harwich, then he went to bed, he did tell Amanda how he lost his hand in a motor bike accident, but that's about it, I'm afraid," he stated.

Rosie place a tray on the table, displaying two bone china cups and saucers, and a plate of homemade scones, which had been cut open, the strawberry jam and cream oozing from the sides, "Help yourselves," she chuckled. Fiona picked up her brief case and placed it on the table, "I would very much appreciate it, if you would have a look at a photograph and say if you recognise this person," she said opening the lid, and removing an eight by ten photograph of O'Brien, and placing it on the table.

Both Rosie and Andrew lent over the table and gazed down at the eight by ten photograph, "Well" began Andrew, "the hairs a different colour, but that's Sheamus all right," he said, sitting back down.

"Rosie?" Fiona asked.

"Yes," Rosie replied.

"That's him, no doubt about it," she said, as she poured Fiona and Keir's coffee. Fiona put the photograph back in her briefcase, then looking up asked.

"Did anything unusual happen whilst he was here," there was silence for a minute, Andrew just sat there shaking his head, Rosie smiled at Fiona.

"Well," she began, "it's probably nothing, and I feel silly saying it. But he had just finished his dinner, and said, he wanted an early night, he very nicely asked me how much he owed for the meal and bed, I told him one pound, he seemed very happy with that as he left the table, we all said, good night, it was then that I remembered that I'd left two of Sam's shirts in the bathroom, and he needed a clean shirt for the morning, I caught Sheamus just as he was about to go into the bathroom, I told him I just had to get Sam's shirts for the morning, as I came out with the shirts on clothes hangers, his face went a ashen colour, I asked if he was okay, and he replied that he was fine, is that of any help?" she asked.

"Were the shirts his uniform shirts Rosie?" Keir asked.

"Yes why?" She replied. Keir and Fiona just smiled at each other.

"Andrew," Fiona said, "can you ask your sister to come out here please?" Andrew got to his feet, walked over to the side of their van and clenching his fist hammered on the van wall, "Sis," he shouted, "get out here now! You're wanted."

"Why?" Came the childlike reply, "just get your arse out here now, the police want you," he hollered.

Fiona got to her feet and walked over to the van's open window, "Amanda," she said, "will you please come out and sit down, Keir and I have something to tell you."

"About that nice man?" Fiona was asked. Fiona was just about to enlighten the young lady, but instead just replied, "Yes Amanda," as she walked back to her seat.

"How many vehicles were in the barn, Sam?" Keir asked, with a mouthful of Rosie's scones.

"Just my Land Rover, Rosie's Lambretta and his car," he said as a caravan door opened and a red eyed Amanda joined them at the table.

"I take it you are insured, Sam?" Keir asked.

Sam grinned and lent back in his chair, "We most certainly are, Gov," he said.

"Good," Keir stated.

"Right," he continued, "Sam has an idea what has happened, but to bring you all up to speed, and for the moment this stay between us, Yes!" He stated. All three nodded. Keir pointed at Fiona's briefcase and nodded, Fiona open the case and withdrew the eight by ten photo of O'Brien, and slid it across the table.

"Amanda," he said, "do you recognise this man?" Keir asked as he put the photo in front of her, through teary eyes she sobbed.

"Yes it's Sheamus," she managed to say, Keir lent over picking up the photo and handed it back to Fiona, "that's what he told you, but his real name is Shaun O'Brien, he is an escaped criminal, he has had three people murdered, and was about to kill hundreds more before we caught him."

Amanda sat there, her mouth open, her eyes staring, "That can't be right," she said, bring her fists to her open mouth.

"I'm afraid it is true, Amanda," Fiona interjected, placing her hand on Amanda's shoulder, "the reason he lost his right hand, had nothing to do with a motor bike accident, he was about to shoot a police officer, but a police marksman took the pistol out of his hand along with his hand, he was in hospital handcuffed to the bed, when he was helped to escape, he stole a car, the one in Sam's barn. We think that as soon he learnt that Sam was a police officer, he panicked and wanted people to believe that he had perished in the fire, which he started. When they clear the barn, either the Land Rover, Rosie's Lambretta, or the stolen Wolseley will be missing, so young lady your nice Irish gentleman, isn't a nice gentleman," Fiona stated. There was silence for a while, then it was broken by Amanda's sobs.

"It's okay Sis, you weren't to know," Andrew said, placing his arm around his Sister's shoulders and giving her a hug.

"How are the scones?" Rosie asked, breaking the sombre atmosphere, Fiona looked across at Keir and smiled, as he took another bite of Rosie's cordon blur creations, "I think my colleague, on a one to ten, rates your creations about fifteen Rosie," she chuckled.

Chapter Thirty Seven

O'Brien had taken all the back roads heading for his destination, the cold night air across his face being the only reason he was barely awake. Twice he had found himself dozing off and on the wrong side of the road. But at this time of the morning, Rosie's scooter was the only vehicle on the road. O'Brien had made it as far as the Plough Public House when his fuel ran out, and the bike spluttered to a halt, fortunately for O'Brien the road from The Plough Public House to St Josephs R.C. Had a slight gradient, so rotating the gear change hand control, putting the bike into neutral, he coasted down the road towards the church, thankful for a full moon, with no engine he had no lights.

The grave yard looked foreboding, with the moonlight casting shadows over the tomb stones, as clouds passed across the face of the moon. O'Brien wheeled the scooter to the rear of the church, then walked over to the maintenance shed, and opening the door, retrieved a small green tarp, walking back to where he had placed the scooter at the rear wall of the church, he covered it and made his way to the main church doors, he had tried the vestry door and found it locked, so he had made his way to the main doors, and on turning the handle, found the door unlocked.

Quietly, he opened the door and entered, closing the door behind him. He had to wait awhile until his eyes became accustomed to the gloom, then picking up two kneeling cushions from the back pew, made his way up to the altar, he didn't bother kneeling, or crossing himself when he stood In front of statue of Christ, he just walked up to the altar, lifted the shroud covering, slid the two kneeling cushions into the space and crawled in, dropping the shroud back into place, within minutes he was fast asleep.

Father Patrick O'Connell had slept in, his arthritis had been giving, him problems, even with one of his parishioners goose fat remedy. It was now eight fifteen as he pulled the Volvo Estate Car into St Josephs car park, and stopped opposite the Vestry door. Removing the bunch of keys from the ignition, killing the engine, he exited the vehicle and made his way to the Vestry door, using the bunch of keys he finally found the appropriate key and unlocked the door, "I must remember to mark this key with something," he said holding up the key, "I do it every time," he muttered, as he entered, then on switching on the light closed the door behind him.

"Right," he said to himself, as he moved behind his desk and scanned a sheet of 'A' four paper, running his finger down the list of activities, his finger stopping halfway down the list, "The challis," he said, "it's still has a dent from where I fell, and the jeweller will be here at ten, to pick it up for repair," he said, rising to his feet.

Father O'Connell unlocked the vestry door with same key, and walked into the church, he crossed the floor and coming to the area in front of the altar stopped, bent down and crossed himself, then kissing the crucifix that hung around his neck, he rose, and walked toward the altar, he was just about to pick up the damaged challis, when he thought he heard a noise, he turned and stared at the vacant church listening, "Must be hearing thing," he said to himself, as he turned back to the altar and finally picked up the challis.

He took three steps, when the sound came again, he stood frozen, "Anybody there," he shouted, the noise came again, but this time it came from behind him, he turned and stared at a foot that was protruding from under the shroud. Placing the challis back on the altar, he lift the shroud, "Sean," he screamed.

O'Brien woke with such a start, that he sat bolt upright, smashing his head on the underside of the Altar Table.

"Damn you, Patrick," he exclaimed as he fell back onto the two kneeling cushions, "thank you, Sean," Patrick replied with a sarcastic tone to his voice.

"People sleep under my Altar all the time, but not usually people that are wanted by the police, so I would very much appreciate it if you left my Church, I kept my promise to you, when I was asked about you, so please return the favour and leave," he said. O'Brien had swung his legs round and was now sitting on the bottom shelf of Father O'Connell's Altar rubbing his forehead that had come into contact with the Altar.

"I now have a headache thanks to you," he stated.

"Not my problem Sean, I have some Aspirin in the Vestry, and a glass of holy water, then you can be on your way," he said, as O'Brien tried to get up. Patrick lent forward taking O'Brien's arm and helped him into a standing position, "Thank you, Patrick," O'Brien said, stifling a yawn, as he stretched his arms, high above his head.

Father Patrick O'Connell never saw it coming as O'Brien's open left palm, and his prosthetic right hand came into contact with both sides of Father O'Connell's neck, with such force that he sank to the Altar floor unconscious. O'Brien lent over the now still body, "Sorry Patrick," he said, "but a Lambretta won't get me to where I want to go."

O'Brien took a cloth from his pocket and shoved it into Father O'Connell's mouth, looking around he spotted two tasselled, gold coloured ropes holding back drapes, removing them from their clips, he bound Father O'Connell's hands and feet behind his back, then removing the scarf from around his neck, gagged the priest, but not before he had gone through the priest's cassock pocket's and removed the bunch of keys.

He stood looking down at his once dear colleague, "Sorry old friend," he said, as he made for to the main doors and locked them, then seeing the holy font took hold of the stone structure and dragged it over to the church doors, he lent against the structure, trying to get his breath back, then returning to the Vestry, walked through and opened the door to the car park, seeing no one in sight, turned and locked the Vestry door, five minutes later he was behind the wheel of the Volvo heading for the 'A' twelve.

Chapter Thirty-Eight

Simon Bradshaw's little white 'A' Thirty Five van pulled into St Joseph's car park at twelve minutes passed ten, looking at his wrist-watch, and seeing no other cars, he slammed his hand down onto the steering wheel, "He could have fucking well waited," he said, as he killed the engine.

"I'll give the old fart another fifteen minutes, I'll lay money he's fucking forgotten," he said, as he opened the door, and exited his van. Simon walked up to the vestry door and tried the handle, "Fuck it," he shouted, then walking to the front of the church tried the main doors, "I thought that the Catholic church doors were supposed to be open all the time," he said, as he tried the handle.

Taking a packet of ten Woodbines and a box of Swan Vesta matches, from his jacket pocket, he sat down in the covered porch, removing one cigarette from his packet and striking a match, lit the Woodbine, inhaling the smoke and exhaling it through his nose. Three cigarette's later he looked at his watch, "Bollocks to this," he said, getting to his feet, and was just about to return to his van, when he was asked.

"What are you doing here young man, and you can't smoke on church property," this statement came from a rather stout lady, wearing a Harris Tweed skirt and jacket, complete with matching hat and brogue shoes.

"I'm waiting for Father O'Connell, I'm supposed to pick up a challis for repair," he said, "but he hasn't turned up yet," he added.

"I know where it is, I'll get it for you, my name is Miss Pike I'm chairperson for this church you know," she said, pushing out her ample bust, as she moved towards the twin doors, "Father O'Connell has probably been delayed," she stated.

"It's locked," she shouted, as she tried to turn the ornate doorknob, "I could have told you that, so is the Vestry door," Simon Bradshaw replied.

"That's most unusual, this door is never locked," she stated, a concerned look on her face.

"Well I can't hang around here all day, when you see him tell him that I was here for the challis, so he'll have to make another appointment," Simon said, as he went to move off.

"But this door is never locked," she said, trying the handle once more, "not my problem, Miss," he said, as he walked away.

"You said, that you tried the Vestry door," she said, as she hurried to catch him up, "try it yourself," he said, over his shoulder.

"Would you please stay with me for a while, I have this horrible feeling that something is wrong, Father O'Connell never locks the main doors," she said, gripping Simon's arm.

"I'll tell you what I'll do Miss Pike," he began, "I'll walk right around your church, and see if there is any way that we can get inside, if we can't, I'm off, okay?" he asked.

"Thank you young man," she said, taking his arm.

They began walking, Simon gazing up at the stain glass windows, "Don't ask me to smash one of those," he stated pointing upwards as they turned the corner of the building, "certainly not," came the stern reply, then, "what's that?" she asked pointing at a green tarp, halfway along the back wall.

"I would say that it is a small green tarpaulin covering something," Simon sarcastically replied.

"I can see that, but what's it doing there," she said, pointing, "it wasn't there yesterday," she added.

"Well let's have a look, shall we?" he asked, taking hold of a loose end and pull it away. They both stared at the now exposed Lambretta, "So Father O'Connell ride a scooter, does he?" Simon remarked.

"No! he does not, he drives a Volvo Estate Car," she rebuked him.

"Well he wouldn't get very far on this little beauty," he said, shaking the bike from side to side, "it's out of petrol, and I'll bet someone has run out of petrol, parked it here, and asked Father O'Connell to run him to a petrol station so he can fill up his scooter," he said, smiling.

"Well if that's the case, why park it here, and why cover it up, you can't see it from the road, and as I've said, Father O'Connell never locks the main doors?" she asked throwing back her shoulders.

"Your guess is as good as mine, but I'll check the other sides, and if I can't get in, I'm afraid to say, the balls in your court, and I have other customers to see," he stated as he strode off.

Miss Pike kept pace with Simon, until they reached the main doors, "Sorry Miss," he said, "but I can't do anymore, so I'm off."

"Could you just run me to the Plough Public House, please young man?" she asked.

"Fancy a pint, do you?" He chuckled.

"No!" She rebuked him, "I'm calling the police," she stated.

Miss Samantha Pike walked into the public bar of the Plough Public House, and straight up to the bar, where a well-endowed Sheila was washing glasses, "Can I help you madam?" she asked smiling and leaning forward, "I need to use the public phone, young lady," Samantha replied.

"She should cover her breasts up," she said to herself.

"The public telephone is at the very end of the private bar madam, just go through those double doors, you can't miss it, it's at the very far end," Sheila stated, pointing at two large half glass doors.

"Thank you young lady, and if you don't mind me saying so, a button up blouse would be a more appropriate attire in this establishment," Samantha said, Sheila grinned, pushing up her abundant breast, "what? And lose customers?" Sheila chuckled.

"No thank you."

"Huh!" Samantha said, as she turned and headed for the two half glass doors.

Not thinking, Samantha placed a shilling into the slot, and dialled nine, nine, nine, she listened and on the second ring was asked. Police, Ambulance, or Fire Brigade, "Police please," she replied, to be told, "putting you through."

Once again she was answered on the second ring, "Police, how can I help you," a male voice stated.

"My name is Samantha Pike," she began, clearing her throat, "I am chairperson at St Joseph's church, near Romford."

"So what can I do for you, Ma'am?" she was asked.

"I think there is something wrong at the church, all the doors are locked, and Father O'Connell never locks the main doors, his car isn't there, and someone has parked a scooter thing at the back of the church that hasn't any petrol in it."

There was silence for a minute, then the male voice said, "Could it be that this Father O'Connell has come to someone's rescue, and is running the person who owns the scooter, to a petrol station?" The officer asked.

"As I have stated officer, I am chairperson at St Josephs, and in all that time, never once have the main doors ever been locked, what's the point of having a church, if you can't get in to worship?" she asked, her face becoming flushed.

"Right Ma'am, will you be at St Josephs?" He replied.

"Yes officer, I will, as soon as we have finished speaking, I will walk back to St Josephs," Samantha stated.

"I'll send a panda car over to St Josephs, as soon as I can Ma'am," she was told, "thank you officer," she replied then she realised that she hadn't pushed button 'A' to get connected, so replacing the handset, pressed button 'B' and smiled as her shilling was returned to her.

Samantha Pike decided to use the rear exit of the private bar, "Displaying her breasts like that. Disgusting!" She said as she pushed the two bars, releasing the door locking mechanism and allowing her to leave the building.

She had cover nearly three quarters of a mile at a very brisk walk, her arms swinging as she hummed Onward Christian Soldiers, when she heard a 'Whee', from an approaching police Panda car. She turned smiling at the two police officers, as the Panda car drew up alongside her, the driver rolled down his window and asked, "Mrs Samantha Pike?"

"It's Miss, Office," she replied.

"Really!" The driver said, raising his eyebrows and smiling.

"Yes officer," she managed to say, her face turning bright red. The passenger door opened and a rather tall police officer got out, "Can we give you a lift, Ma'am?" he asked smiling.

A blushing Samantha walked round to the passenger door, "Thank you officer," she replied as the officer lifted the passenger seat, and squeezed his tall frame into the back seat, then bring the seat back down, he sat side on to accommodate his long legs.

"That's very nice of you, officer," she said, over her shoulder, then closed her door.

"So what seems to be the problem, Ma'am?" The officer driving asked. Samantha pushed down her Harris Tweed skirt that had ridden above her knees as she sat down, the officer driving looked over and smiled. "Both doors to the church are locked, which has never happened before, and someone has parked a scooter behind the church, plus Father O'Connell's Volvo Estate car is missing. Over there!" She hollered, pointing at the Vestry door.

"Thank you Ma'am," the driver stated. As he coasted towards where Samantha was pointing, then coming to a halt, applied the hand break and switched off the ignition. Samantha immediately opened her door, pulling the passenger seat forward as she exited the Panda car, "Thank you Ma'am," the officer sitting in the back seat said, as he slid out feet first, until he was able to sit up straight.

It wasn't until he stood up, that Samantha realised just how tall the officer was, as she gazed up into his face, in reply he looked down at her upturned face and smiling said, "Six foot eleven, Ma'am," Samantha chuckled.

"Oh my god," she uttered.

"Shall we go Ma'am?" he asked taking her arm.

"Err, yes officer," came the reply, "the scooters just round here," she said, as the other officer joined them.

"Right Miss Samantha Pike," the driver said, "I'm Constable Summers, and my colleague here is affectionately known as lofty," he stated.

"It's Constable Symonds Ma'am, not lofty," he said, glaring at his colleague.

"Well I'm very pleased to have met two nice young men," she said, closing the panda car door.

"Now if you would be so kind as to follow me gentlemen," she said, as she move away from the car. They turned the corner of the church, Samantha in the lead, "There," she said, pointing, it was then that Lofty's radio which was attached to his belt came to life, "control to Panda seven, come in please," they all heard, Lofty unclipped the radio from his belt, pressed the call button and stated.

"Panda seven receiving Sarge, over."

"Have you met up with—" Immediately Lofty hit the call button, remembering the comments that had been stated earlier, "Panda seven to control, yes Miss Samantha Pike is with us Sarge, she's just about to show us the Lambretta, over."

"Thank you Panda seven, over and out," came the reply. Lofty inwardly gave a sigh of relief.

"Check the number plate George, see who it belong to," Lofty ordered, as he rocked the bike from side to side, "well she ain't going anywhere," he said, as they heard constable Summers state, "Panda seven to control come in please, over," within seconds the call was answered, "yes Panda seven go ahead, over."

"Can you check a number plate for us Sarge, India, Delta, Hotel, Sierra, nine three nine one, over."

"Okay Panda seven, will do, over and out," came the reply.

"Can we check the doors now please officers?" Samantha asked.

"Certainly, young lady," Lofty replied.

"After you," he said, looking across at his mate George Summers and smiling, as they followed a smiling, blushing Samantha Pike.

Samantha arrive first at the front porch, and noticing the three cigarette buts, quickly kicked them under the left side seat, as the two officers arrived. Samantha was just about to ask them to try the door handle, when George Summers radio came to life, "Control to Panda seven, that registration belong to a Mrs Roslyn Parsons, of Shoeburyness Essex, over."

George looked up at lofty, "Can't be," he said, then, "control, wasn't Senior Sergeant Parson's wife called Rosie, and wasn't he transferred to somewhere out that way, over."

"Yes Panda Seven, Sam's at Shoeburyness, over."

"Well what's Rosie's Lambretta doing near Romford Sarge, over."

"Well Panda seven, I'm here and your there, so find out, over and out."

"I know there is something wrong officers, something has happened to Father O'Connell," Samantha said, a terrified look on her face.

"You remember Sam?" Constable Summers asked.

"When he was made up to Senior Sergeant, he ask for a transfer because the travelling in that Land Rover of his, was getting too much, and I'm sure his wife's name was Rosie?" He added.

"Officer!" Samantha screamed, "we have to get into the church, Now! There's something wrong, I know it," she hollered.

"Bring the Panda round here George, let's see if we can get these doors open," Lofty said, trying the churches doors handles, "and while we're waiting Samantha, why don't you sit down here," he said, patting the porch seat.

"Thank you, constable," she said, as she sat down, "but why have I this terrible feeling that something is wrong?" she asked.

"You must be very close to Father O'Connell, and this situation is out of character, so I can understand your concern," he said, as the Panda car pulled to a halt, constable George Summers, jumping out and going to the back of the vehicle opened the boot lid, "not much in here Pete," he called out over his shoulder.

"Is my naughty bag behind your seat, George," he asked smiling, "what's a naughty bag?" Samantha asked getting up from the porch seat and staring up at Lofty's face.

"Something that young ladies like you, shouldn't know about," he chuckled. Samantha turned a brilliant red colour, and immediately sat back down, gazing at her brogue lace up shoes.

"There you go sunshine," George said, smiling, handing Lofty a black leather doctor's bag, "I'll take a walk shall I, hear no evil see no evil," he said, as he walked over to the Panda car, where he opened both doors wide, then sitting in the driver's seat with his back to the church, and began rolling a cigarette.

Samantha stared at Lofty as he knelt down in front of the door and opened his black leather bag, he looked sideways at Samantha and smiled. "Whatever happens in the next five minutes young lady, you never saw, okay?" he asked. Samantha returned the smile, then turned her head and stared at George who had lit he roll up and was puffing away, but she was attentive to the sound of metal on metal, but curiosity finally won the day as she turned her head, to be confronted by Lofty's broad shoulders obscuring any view of what he was doing.

"Right," she heard as Lofty stood up, then, "George get over here," Lofty hollered, as he closed his black leather back.

"Is the door open, Peter?" Samantha whispered.

"After you, young lady," he said, smiling, performing a Sir Francis Drake bow. Samantha stood up, stepped forward and taking hold of the handle turned it, "it's open," she screamed, and pushed the handle forward, the door only moved an inch and stopped, "there's something stopping it, it won't open," she said, stepping back.

Lofty stepped forward and putting all his weight behind it, tried to push the door open, but only gained about another inch, "Give us a hand, George," he said, as his mate walked into the porch.

"On three," George said, as he stepped to his mates side. Both men lent back in unison, "Three" George shouted, as their shoulder's smashed into the ancient timber door. But the door only moved six inches.

"There's something stopping it," Lofty said, "or someone," replied his mate, "don't say that, please don't say that," Samantha sobbed, "Samantha," Lofty said, putting his hand on her shoulder, "whatever it is, it's really heavy, and it made a grinding sound when George and I moved the door, so it's not somebody, it's something, okay?" he asked smiling down at her upturned face.

"Right George, something stinks, somebody didn't want this door to open, so bring the Panda right up to the porch, I thought I saw some poles at the edge of the car park, I'll see if I can grab one," he said as he sprinted away.

Six minutes later he was back with a twelve foot pole resting on his right shoulder, "Okay George, back up a bit, I need this pole inside the porch," he said, lowering the pole to the ground. George put the Panda into reverse and backed up, "Okay mate," he shouted, raising his right hand. Lofty manoeuvred the pole into the porch, and on seeing two thick phone books under the porch seat beside Samantha, placed them one on top of the other against the church door.

"What's happening sunshine?" he was asked as George entered the porch.

"Whatever is stopping the door from opening, is bloody heavy, Sorry! Samantha, and we are going to stuff up our shoulders if we keep trying, so if we place this pole," he said, pointing, "on top of those phone books, at the base of the door, and the other end of the pole I'll hold it up level with your bumper bar, then you can move forward, and hopefully push open those doors," Lofty stated.

"Who's a clever little copper?" George replied with a grin.

"No George," Samantha stated.

"That is ingenious, truly ingenious."

"Thank you Samantha," Lofty replied.

"But can we finish with the congratulation, and see if it will work."

"It will Peter, I know it will," Samantha said, a smile spreading across her face.

"Ready when you are Lofty," George said, revving the Panda engine. Constable Peter Symonds had placed the end of the pole on top of the two phone books, hard up against the church door, and was now straddling the pole lifting it level with the Panda's approaching front bumper bar, as George inched forward, the bumper bar came in contact with the end of the pole, George felt the impact and heard the engine falter, so bring up the revs and slipping the clutch, he kept the tension on the pole, "Get clear Peter," he shouted, as he slowly released the clutch.

All three watch as the pole took up the pressure and began to move forward, opening the door. Peter was now standing in front of the door as it slowly opened, but with the angle of the door changing, the pole began to slide toward the opening, Peter tried to push his legs against the pole to keep it flat against the door, but suddenly the pole shot forward then stopped.

"Keep pushing, George," he shouted, then suddenly the pole shot into the church, and George had to slam on his brakes, the pole falling to the ground. The door was now open, but only about eighteen inches, Peter pulled the door toward him then pushed it open, to hear it hit something solid. Turning sideways he stuck his head through the gap, then pulled it back, "Your instinct was correct Samantha, somebody didn't want this door opened," he said as George backed the Panda away from the porch, turned off the engine and joined his mate, "what's the score sunshine?" he beamed.

"Someone has stuck a stone font in front of the door, they definitely didn't want this door opening," he said, George stepped forward and copied his mate, pulling his head back, he looked at Samantha, "you'll have to wait until Peter and I have moved the font Samantha."

"Don't worry about me, just make sure Father O'Connell is okay, if he's in there, please," she said, a terrified look on her face.

Lofty was the first to squeeze through the narrow opening, once he was inside he tried to move the stone font, but could only move it an inch or two, which was enough to allow George to squeeze through, "Have a look round first, mate," Peter said, as they moved down the aisle, checking every pew, they were three rows from the front when Lofty looked toward the alter.

"George," he whispered, "look," as he pointed at the altar. Both officers stared at the lifeless form of Father O'Connell's bound and gagged body.

"Get on the radio George, if he's alive we're going to need an ambulance, but do it in there," he said, pointing in the direction of the Vestry, "and don't touch anything, this is a crime scene," he said.

George made his way into the Vestry and was just about to close the door, when he remembered, crime scene. Lofty had removed the gag and rag from the priest's mouth, and checked his breathing, although very shallow, the priest was still breathing.

"Is everything alright, Peter?" He heard Samantha ask.

"Still looking, Samantha," he lied, and received a, "thank you Peter."

"The ambulance is on its way mate, how's the priest?" George asked.

"His breathing is shallow and his pulse could be a bit stronger," Lofty replied.

"So what are we going to do about her ladyship, if we open the door and she comes in here she'll go ape shit?" George asked.

"I'll stay with the priest," he said, picking up the pillows O'Brien had used, placing them under the priests head, and rolling him onto his side, "you go out and keep her company, when the ambulance arrives, we'll move that bloody font and let them in, tell her I'm still looking, or some bull shit, she'll know the truth when the ambulance arrives, if she find out now the St Johns blokes will have two patients to deal with," he said.

"I'll take my time moving the Panda, I'm not too good at bull shitting Pete" George replied.

Samantha was trying to look through the gap when George arrived, "Sorry," she said, as she stepped back, "did you find Father O'Connell?"

"Well," George began rather nervously, "he wasn't in any of the pews, or the Vestry," he replied truthfully, "are you alright George?" she asked.

George moved closer, "I suffer from Ecclesiophobia, but please keep that between us," he whispered, "you suffer from what, George?" she asked, frowning.

"I can't go into a church Samantha, I break out in a hot sweat, my eyes go blurry so I can't see, and I might even faint, that's why Ethel and I were married in a registry office sorry," he lied his hands behind his back his fingers crossed.

"Oh, you poor man," she uttered throwing her rather large arms around his neck, and crushing his body.

George walked toward his Panda car, smiling like a Cheshire Cat, "I can't bullshit, Huh!" He said to himself, as he climbed into his Panda Car. "That was classic Summers, bloody classic, Ethel!" He chuckled.

"Father O'Connell," Lofty whispered at the prone figure, "can you hear me, Sir?" he asked but received no reply. Placing his middle finger on the priest's neck looking for a pulse, and thankfully finding one, even if it was weak, then placing his cheek next to Father O'Connell's open mouth, felt a slight pressure as the priest exhaled. Lofty had his right arm supporting the motionless body, keeping the priest on his side.

"This is killing my knees," he said to himself, "so I think I'll move over to your other side, if you don't mind Father, before my knees cave in," he said to the non-existent congregation.

Keep his hand on the priest's shoulder, Lofty moved to a crouching stance, and straddled the prostrate form, moving his balance over, so he ended up behind Father O'Connell, and sat down, his back supporting the unconscious priest. It seemed to Lofty that he had been sitting supporting the priest for hours, when in actual fact it had only been about twelve minutes, when he heard the distant bells of the approaching ambulance, then George shouting, "They're here, Pete," as he squeezed through the partly opened church door.

Then Samantha shouting, "What's happened?"

George turned to see her face trying to see inside the church, "It's okay Samantha, Lofty has found Father O'Connell, it looks as though he has fainted, he's trying to give him a glass of water, Lofty thought it wisest to call an ambulance, just to be on the safe side, your Father O'Connell is going to be just fine young lady," he lied, "so just sit down, when St John's chaps turn up, Lofty and I will move the font so they can come in and you can be reunited with your friend, but let the St John's chaps check him out first, okay?" he asked.

Then at the top of her voice she screamed, "I'm here Father, it's Samantha Pike, I told the police something was wrong."

"Thanks Samantha," George said, rolling his eyes, "he will appreciate you being here" then ran to where Lofty was sitting supporting the priest.

"How is the old boy, Pete?" He whispered, "No point in whispering George, he can't hear you, he's got a couple of nasty bruises on his neck, I don't think anything is broken, but I'm not prepared to check I'll leave that to the St John's, but he's still breathing thank God."

"Hello," they heard a male voice call out, "St John's but we can't open the door, you have someone who has fainted, we've been told, is that correct?" The male voice asked.

"Thanks Samantha," George said, as he ran to the church door. "Coming through," he shouted as he arrived at the opening, and squeezed through. George looked at the two St John's chaps, "he might get through," he said to himself, then pointing to the younger looking chap he said, "can you come with me please?"

"Why can't I come, officer?" he was asked.

"I need help moving the object that is stopping the door opening Sir, and I'm afraid you wouldn't be able to squeeze through," which caused the older St John's man to immediately pull in his stomach.

"Right," he said, "you go with the office, John, and help him open the door, I'll wait here, this lady has told us the priest has fainted, so just take the smelling salts."

George beckoned the younger Ambo to follow him, as he squeezed through the gap and waited, "I would bring your bag John," George stated.

"Just slide it through the gap, I'll pick it up," he said. With some effort, the young Ambo just managed to make it through the gap, "Boy! That was a bit of a squeeze," he said, as George grabbed his arm, and began dragging him towards the alter, "I thought we were going to move something," he said.

"The priest hasn't fainted, he was hit, bound, and gagged, and he's unconscious, and you're going to need a stretcher, so move it pronto," George said, as they both ran toward where Lofty was sitting holding Father O'Connell.

"Right John, you check out Father O'Connell, Pete and I will try and move that bloody font, so your mate can get in," George stated.

"Will do, officer," came the reply, as Lofty changed places with the Ambo, they watched for a couple of seconds, as the St Johns chap opened his bag removing a stethoscope and slipping it around his neck, then turned and ran to where the font was obstructing the main doors. Lofty had picked up the two ropes that had bound up Father O'Connell's hands and feet, and arriving at the font tied the two ropes together with a reef knot, placing the extended rope around the base of the font, he offered George one end, "When I say pull, put your back into it George, I'm not happy with the way the priest is looking, okay mate?" he asked.

"Okay sunshine," came the reply. Both officers took up the slack, "now!" Lofty shouted, and very slowly the font began to move away from the door, the other St Johns Ambo must have heard the command, and put his excessive weight behind the door, as the font slid and the door opened wide.

"Father," they heard Samantha scream, as both the St Johns Ambo and Samantha tried to make it through the door at the same time, without success.

"No Samantha!" Lofty said, taking her arm, "let the ambulance chaps see to Father O'Connell, go and sit in the ambulance, so you can be with him when he wakes up, you being with him and seeing a familiar face will be good," he said, trying to lead her out of the church, "but he's just fainted, I should be there when he wakes," she persisted.

"Yes," replied Lofty, "but why did Father O'Connell faint, Samantha, let the St John chaps do their job, you can go with them to the hospital so when he wakes, you'll be by his bedside, okay?" he asked as they walked toward the ambulance.

They were only nine feet away from the back doors when the younger Ambo sprinted passed them, flinging open the back doors of the ambulance, and dragging a stretcher out from under a bed, "Can't stop," he managed to say, as he hoisted the stretcher onto his shoulder's.

Samantha tried to pull herself free, "Why do they need a stretcher?" She hollered, "Well they can't very well carry Father O'Connell over their shoulders can they?" Lofty said, pushing Samantha's ample backside into the ambulance, "Now! Samantha, you have been exceptional throughout all of this, if it hadn't been for you Father O'Connell would have laid there for god knows how long, so you have to be there for him when he wakes up, the St Johns will have him out in a minute, so please just sit there, he's going to need you," he said.

"He's such a dear man," she sobbed. Lofty stepped into the ambulance, and sat beside her, placing his arm around her shoulder, he gave her a hug, "he's going to be fine Samantha, so just wait here, Father O'Connell will be with you shortly."

"Thank you, Peter," she managed to say.

Lofty met George and the two St Johns Ambos at the church door, the elderly Ambo out of breath and sweating as he passed the two officer, "Don't ask," stated the younger Ambo, as they trudged towards their vehicle, a worried look on his face.

"We'd better report in George, the Sarge ain't going to believe this, him and his, some stupid woman can't get into her bloody church, I'm going to enjoy this," he chuckled, picking up his radio.

"Panda seven to control over," he said, grinning like a Cheshire cat.

"Control here, Panda seven, where the hell have you been, over?" George and Lofty roared with laughter.

Chapter Thirty-Nine

"Any luck over at Shoeburyness?" Bill asked. Keir rested both his elbows on his desk, his open palms supporting his head, "No Bill, not yet," he stated.

"When the barn collapsed, it buried everything, it's going to take a couple of day before they find anything, so we'll just have to wait, we know O'Brien was there, and I'd lay money, he started the fire, to make us believe he died in the fire."

"So if he's still alive, how did he get away?" Bill enquired. Keir was just about to mull the question over, when his phone buzzed, "Dickson," he said, picking up the handset, "a Senior Sergeant Samuel Parsons, on the line Gov, do you want to take the call?" Keir was asked.

"Thanks Sarge, put him through," Keir said, switching on the speaker and sitting back, "hi Sam," Keir began, "how can I help you, and thank Rosie for those scones," he chuckled.

"Just thought you ought to know, Gov, my old station just called me, they've found Rosie's Lambretta, it was parked behind a church near."

"Romford," Keir said, "yes Gov," Sam replied.

"And they also told me that the old priest was attached, and is in St Georges Hospital in Sutton Lane in Hornchurch, the two young officer had one hell of a job getting into the church, but when they did, they found the old priest bound and gagged and unconscious," he said, "were they able to talk to the priest, Sam?" Keir asked.

"No Gov, from what I was told he was out cold, might pay you to give the Hospital a call," he ventured.

"Cheers Sam, will do, and give our best to your lovely Rosie, okay," Keir said.

"Will do Gov," came the reply.

"So that's how he got away," Bill stated.

"And O'Brien's now driving Father O'Connell's Volvo, he could be anywhere by now," Keir said, as he picked up his phone.

"Sarge," he said, when it was answered, "can you put me through to St George Hospital in Hornchurch, please?" he asked, then covering the mouthpiece said, "I thought they were friends, some bastard of a friend," then, "yes hello, my name is Keir Dickson, I'm a DCI With the Essex police I believe you have a Father Patrick O'Connell that was hurt, would it be at all possible to speak to him?" he asked, and was told to hold the line.

"I.C.U. How can I help you?" he was asked by a female voice, on hearing I.C.U. Bill began to shake his head, "This is DCI Keir Dickson, I'm enquiring about a Father Patrick O'Connell," and was once again asked to hold the line.

"I.C.U." Bill stated shaking his head, "Not a good sign Tel," then Keir was asked by a deep male voice, who was calling, "it's DCI Keir Dickson of the Essex constabulary, would it be possible to speak to Father Patrick O'Connell, with regard to an ongoing case please?" Keir asked.

Bill pointed at Keir's speaker, indicating for him to switch it on, "Father O'Connell is unable to come to the phone, you are speaking to Mr Galbraith, I'm Registrar here."

"Hello Archie," Bill shouted, "so they actually let you near patients now, do they?" He chuckled.

"If that's who I think it is," came the reply, "what the blazes are you doing, helping our boys in blue?"

"Long story Archie," Bill replied.

"We just need to know how Patrick is?" he asked.

"It's not good Bill, he received severe blows to both carotid arteries, which reduced the blood flow to the brain, so we have him in an induced coma, I would like to keep him like that for at least the next seventy two hour, god knows what hit his left carotid, his neck is black."

"It was a prosthetic hand," Keir stated.

"So you know who attached him?" The registrar asked.

"We believe we do Archie, will you please keep us informed on Patrick's progress?" Bill asked.

"I take it that Father O'Connell is a personal friend, Bill."

"Yes he is Archie, and thanks," Bill said, as Keir replaced the receiver.

"You wait until I get my hands on that bastard, I've a good mind to let Shambuck and Ntomi loose on him."

"What! And then have them put down, fat chance," Bill stated.

There was a light knock on Keir's door, followed by Fiona's smiling face, and a greeting, "And how are we today, gentlemen?" she asked.

"O'Brien has escaped again, Ma'am," Bill stated.

"So how do we know that?" she asked the smile disappearing from her face, Keir sat up straight, "Sam Parsons just called," he began, "turns out O'Brien stole Rosie's Lambretta, and made it as far as St Josephs, attacked Father O'Connell bound and gagged him, and stole the Volvo Estate Car, I'm just about to get onto traffic to look for it. Trouble is, which way would he go, my bet would be Ireland, but I could be wrong, he could be anywhere," he said running his hands through his blonde curls.

"How is Father O'Connell?" Fiona asked, a concerned look on her face.

Bill smiled. "He's in St Georges Hospital over at Hornchurch, an old colleague of mine an Archibald Galbraith is registrar over at the hospital, and he's looking after Father O'Connell, Father O'Connell receive two severe blows to his carotid's which reduced the blood flow to his brain, causing him to become unconscious, Archie has him in an induced coma, which will be for at least seventy two hours. Then he will very slowly bring him out of it, Ma'am."

Fiona looked at Bill, "Thank you Bill for the update, and in here," she said, closing Keir's door, "it's Fiona, okay?" She reminded them both, "But I think it's about time that we brought Superintendent Woods back in, New Scotland yard have more resources at their disposal, I'll fax him all the relevant information that we have at the moment, and see what he can come up with. But we know for sure that it was O'Brien that stole the Volvo and attacked Father O'Connell do we?" she asked.

"Well who else could it be, Fiona, O'Brien was staying at Sam's place, Rosie's Lambretta was stolen and found at St Josephs, and to cover his tracks he torched Sam Parsons property."

"True," replied Fiona, "but have Romford C.I.D. Checked out St Josephs and the Lambretta, if O'Brien is alive, which you are probably correct that he is, fine, and they haven't found his remains, but before I contact Trevor Woods, I need to be one hundred percent sure that O'Brien used that scooter, and that he was in actual fact at St Josephs and attacked the priest and stole the Volvo, so until Father Patrick O'Connell can tell us who attacked him, it's all supposition. Yes! I agree with you, it all points towards O'Brien, so can you contact Romford, send them what we've got, and let me know please Keir?" she asked.

"Yes Ma'am," Keir replied, his head in his hands. Fiona smiled at Bill as she turned and opened Keir's door, "Thank you gentlemen," she said, as she closed his door.

"She's right you know," Bill said, with a grin, "just shut to fuck up Bill, I know she is fucking right, that's what's pissing me off, I've put two and two together, and failed my 'O' level maths. Trouble is I know the DCI At Romford, his name is Stanley Pratt, and we get on like a pork chop in a synagogue, they used to call him, Prat by name, and Prat by Nature, so I'm not looking forward to this," he said, picking up his phone.

"Romford police, how can I help you?" Keir was asked.

"Could you put me through to DCI Pratt, please?" Keir stated.

"It's DCI Dickson calling."

"Sorry Sir," came the reply, "but DCI Pratt is off sick, he was rushed to Hornchurch hospital with a suspected stomach ulcer, but D.I. Saunders is running the show in his absence, will he be able to help, Sir?" Keir lent back in his chair, giving Bill the thumbs up sign, a grin spreading across his face, "That will be fine Sergeant, thank you," he replied.

The call was answered on the third ring, "Saunders," Keir was told, "that wouldn't be young Victor Saunders by any chance, who is now a D.I?" Keir asked smiling at Bill, to hear, "Er! Yes, who's calling."

"Nineteen forty six," Keir began, "five thirty, Thursday after noon, Rainham Barclays Bank, Securicor van pulls up."

"Hello! Gov," Keir heard, "long time no see," followed by a chuckle, "so you're running the shop now Vic, so I hear?"

"Yes Gov," came the reply, "I hear your mates in Hornchurch, nothing trivial I hope" Keir chuckled.

"We're all keeping our fingers crossed Gov," came the jovial reply, Bill coughed loudly, and stared at his mate, "yes sorry," Keir said, holding up the palm of his hand.

"The reason I'm calling, Vic," Keir stated, "is, a priest over at St Josephs was attacked, a Lambretta was left there, and a Volvo Estate Car was stolen, we have reason to believe that the perpetrator of the crime is known to us, but we need confirmation, do you know anything about the case?" he asked.

"Yes Gov," came the reply, "do you want the whole story?"

"Only the relevant parts Vic?" Keir said, putting his phone on speaker.

"Right Gov, a woman reported that she couldn't get into St Josephs, a Panda was sent over and constables Summers, and Symonds attended, they found the Lambretta which is registered to a Rosie Parsons, a wife of one of our officers that used to be here, they had one hell of a job getting into the church, and when they did they found the priest unconscious, bound and gagged, so they quickly got him to St Georges, and taped off the church as a crime scene, I've had the forensic lads over there doing their stuff, that's about it for now Gov, I'm waiting on the forensic report," he concluded, "I'm going to send you a set of finger prints of the left hand of someone of interest Vic, plus some police photos, I'm hoping to get a match, okay young man?" Keir asked.

"Just on the off-chance, Gov?" Victor asked.

"And between you and me, you wouldn't have an opening for a D.I. By any chance," Keir burst out laughing, "that bad," he just about managed to say, "you have no idea Gov, when we all heard he was in Hornchurch, the atmosphere in the place shot up to the roof, people are actually smiling, but where we have shit out and we're all of the same opinion, Pratt got his son to marry the Superintendent's daughter, and an uglier bitch you never saw, so we're stuck with him," Saunders replied.

Keir had to cover his mouth, "I'll get those prints and photos over straight away Vic," Keir just about managed to say, "as soon as I get them I'll get our forensic boys onto it Gov, and I wasn't joking about the transfer."

"I'll see what I can do Vic," Keir replied as he replaced the receiver.

"So what's this chap Pratt like?" Bill asked.

Keir sat back in his chair and rolled his eyes, "He's a little shit, when he was on the beat, he would stand back, let his partner do the heavy work, then step in and take the credit, one time his partner got beaten up Stan did nothing to help him, his partner is out for the count, the crim makes a run for it and gets hit by a car, Stan runs over and handcuffs him and gets a bloody commendation, his partner ends up in hospital with brain damage and is retired out. He only looks for the bad in his officers, if they excel on a case, not a word, make one error and he has them in front of the Super, as I said, Pratt by Name, and Pratt by Nature."

"So are you going to do anything about getting this Victor transferred?" Bill asked, "Or was it bull shit," he added.

"I'll have a word with Fiona, one thing that he excels at is languages, he's fluent in French, German, Spanish, Italian, and can get by on a few more, you remember I started the call with, 'Nineteen forty six, Thursday afternoon, yes?'"

Bill nodded, "Well Vic was scanning the wave lengths, when he picked up some Ities rabbiting, turns out they were going to turn over a bank in Rainham, so we were waiting for them, caught them as they threatened the Securicor chaps with sawn off shot guns," he chuckled.

"What we didn't know, but Victor did, was the shot guns were loaded with blanks, so he rushed them, knowing full well he was safe, crafty sod received a commendation for bravery," Keir said, smiling.

Chapter Forty

O'Brien had parked the Volvo in Dacre Road Upton park, between a Pickfords removal truck, and a Bedford Dormabile, far away from any streetlights. Pulling up the hood on his navy-blue Duffel coat, and checking for any pedestrians, he exited the vehicle and locked it, then made his way up Dacre Road to the B165, where he turned right, heading for Bishops Road, he slowed as he approached the telephone box on the corner, taking a quick lock to see if there was any activity happening in Bishops Road. Seeing nothing, he began walking, keeping his head down, but occasionally looking across the road until he came level with his old address, where he stopped, and bending down, pretended to tie his shoelace.

Seeing no one in sight, he sprinted across the road, vaulted the low brick wall and ran down the side of his house. He had to stop to get his breath back as he lent against the side wall, before he lifted his dustbin and smiled as he picked up his back door key. Three minutes later he was inside his house, for six whole minutes he sat on the kitchen floor trembling, "Pull yourself together, Shean," he said to himself, as he began to rise, and made his way to the front room, slowly pushing the door open he entered and made his way over to his drinks cabinet, "have they?" he asked as he opened the doors.

His face scowled at the sight of only a half-bottle of Baileys, his favourite Irish malt whisky bottles were laying empty, "Damn them," he said, as he filled a glass with the Baileys, then moved to one of his upturned armchairs, which had, had the bottom material ripped open, righting the chair he slumped down into it and took his first swallow.

Two hours later he woke startled, it took him several minutes to realise that he was in his own home, the Bailey's glass laying empty in his lap.

"Right," he said, leaning forward, "did they fine it?" he asked rising from his armchair. He was just about to switch on the front room light, his hand only inches away from the wall switch, "You stupid idiot," he exclaimed, as he made his way into his hall, stopping at the under the stairs cupboard. He opened the door and smiled, the four large cardboard boxes were where he had left them, but the two nearest the door had been opened, he lifted the tops of the first cardboard box to reveal twelve small bibles sitting on top of children's clothing.

Pulling it into the hall, he then moved the second box out from under the stairs, when all four boxes were out, he stared at the cupboard floor and smiled. "So you didn't find it," he stated as he bent down, and using his left hand, found the catch and lifted the trapdoor hatch up, revealing a set of step leading down to his cellar and workshop. As O'Brien's head cleared the floor, he pulled the trap door down closing the hatch, then running his good hand along the floor joists, found the light switch and turned on the two fluorescent lights.

He sat down on the third step and smiled at the rooms that he had created, a butlers sink with both hot and cold running water, complete with a timber draining board, housing an electric kettle and toaster, a workshop any craftsman would have been proud of, a small bar fridge, two easy chairs, a small coffee table, a drinks cabinet, two, three kilowatt bar fires, a single bed, and three wall to ceiling cupboards, the painted concrete floor dusty, so as he walked over to the first cupboard he left footprints in his wake.

Opening the two doors of the first cupboard, revealing a row of suits, draws of shirts, socks, underwear, a bar with a selection of ties, and at the bottom, twelve pair of leather shoes.

O'Brien swung back the cupboard door and gazed at his reflection in the full-length mirror, "God Almighty," he stated and began to strip, throwing the clothes from the Linford house, into a dustbin, then walking naked over to the butlers sink, half filled it with warm water, he began to bathe.

Half an hour later, O'Brien was sitting back in one of the easy chairs his feet on a leather parfait, wearing a grey Worsted three-piece suite, white shirt over a white vest, Oxford blue tie, dark brown socks, and on his feet brown brogue shoes, in his left hand, a crystal glass containing his favourite, Bushmills Blackbush whisky.

O'Brien opened a little red book, that had been sitting on the coffee table and started turning the pages, he stopped at Jersey Bank, then looked at his wrist-watch, "No point calling yet," he said to himself, then turned more pages until he came to Charlie Gibbs, he smiled as he gazed at the telephone number, "nice work on the Metropolitan Police letter, Charlie," he said, with a chuckle.

Three hours later he was back in Dacre Road wearing the dark blue Duffel coat with the hood in place, in his coat pocket he carried two tools, a small hand drill, with a one eighth drill in the chuck, and a pop rivet gun, with eight one eighth pop rivets, but down inside his trousers he had Father O'Connell's old Volvo number plates. Two hours later he was back down in his cellar, another crystal glass of Bushmills Blackbush whisky in his hand.

The noise of the crystal glass shattering into a thousand pieces as it hit the concrete floor, brought O'Brien wide awake, "Damn," he exclaimed, as he took his feet off of the pouffe and sat forward, rising from the easy chair, he walked over to the draining board, and bending down remove a small dust pan and brush from the floor, as he began to sweep the shattered glass, cursing himself for falling asleep, he looked at his wrist-watch, "Nine fifteen," he said to himself, "they should be open for business by now," he added, dumping the remains of his crystal glass into the dustbin.

Picking his telephone up off of the coffee table, as he sat back down in his easy chair, placing the phone on his knees, and the handset beside it, using the index finger of his left hand, he began to dial, occasionally looking across at the open red book on the coffee table to ensure he had the correct number. He smiled as he heard the distant telephone begin to ring, after five rings he was informed, "Anglo Irish Bank Corporation, how can I help you?"

O'Brien took a deep breath before he answered, "My name is Sheamus O'Toole, and I would like to know the status of the Shamrock account, please young lady?" He said, and was informed, "Could you hold the line please sir?"

O'Brien waited on hold, beads of perspiration forming on his forehead, when he heard a male voice ask, "Whose calling please?"

"My name is Sheamus O'Toole and I'm enquiring as to the status of the Shamrock account, my wife colleen asked me to find out how we were off financially, as we wish to upgrade our restaurant."

There was silence for at least a minute, when the reply came back, "What!" screamed O'Brien, "I'm sorry sir but we have been told to freeze that particular account until further notice."

"Bastards," O'Brien screamed as he slammed down the receiver.

Pouring himself a large Bushmills Whisky, O'Brien took a large swallow, holding it in his mouth, only letting a small amount trickle down his throat savouring the taste of the amber liquid, as it warmed its way to his stomach.

Placing the crystal glass down, very carefully on the coffee table, he picked up his little red book and began leafing through the pages until he came to 'Z'.

Placing the book on his lap, then picking up the phone, he began to dial, one minute later he was told, "Vantabel, guten morgen, wie kann ich ihnen helfen," clearing his throat O'Brien said, "Guten Morgen, my name is Shaemus O'Toole, and I would like to check my account, please."

"Thank you sir, please hold the line," O'Brien was told, seconds later he heard, "good morning Mr O'Toole, my name is Haans Gruben, how can I help you?" he asked.

"I would like to know the state of my account, Herr Gruben please," O'Brien stated.

"Very good, Mr O'Toole, the account name, please?" he was asked.

"Shamrock," O'Brien replied.

"Thank you," he was told, seconds later he was asked.

"The account number please?"

O'Brien looked down at his little red book and smiled. "SPO19399391," he stated.

"Thank you Mr O'Toole, just one minute please," he was told as the line went silent. O'Brien's left hand and forehead were wet from perspiration as he sat waiting.

"Right Mr O'Toole," he was told, "at the end of business today, you will have at your disposal, $181.867 and 50 cents American, you just caught the interest at 2.75%, if you leave it until close of business today, that is," he was told. O'Brien sat for a while a smile spreading across his face, "That's nearly a hundred and forty thousand pounds," he said to himself. He was brought back to reality when asked.

"Are you there, Mr O'Toole?"

"Yes sorry," O'Brien replied sitting up straight, "So how can I be of help you Mr O'Toole?" O'Brien was asked.

"Well!" O'Brien began, "would it be possible to convert some of the American Dollars into English pounds?" he asked.

"Certainly Sir, how much would you like converted?" Haans Gruben enquired, O'Brien sat there thinking for a moment, "Could you convert some of the American Dollars into, Say! Twelve thousand English pounds please?" he asked.

"Will you give me a minute please Mr O'Toole while I check the amount?" he was asked thirty second later he was told, "That would leave you with a balance of one hundred and sixty five thousand seven hundred and fifty one pounds fourteen pence, English not American Dollars, Mr O'Toole."

"Great," replied O'Brien, "what I would like you to do, if you can? Is parcel the twelve thousand English pounds to an address I will give you, I'm investing in a property, but the vendor will only accept cash and doesn't want it going through his bank, that is why I'm able to purchase it at that price," he lied. There was silence for a moment before Haans replied.

"You do realise the size of this package, so there would be a cost involved, it would have to be hand delivered by two of our couriers, Mr O'Toole, an amount of that size would have to be guarded twenty four hours, and would have to be signed for."

"Yes, I fully appreciate that Mr Gruben and am happy to bear the cost," O'Brien replied.

"Thank you Mr O'Toole, you will be notified at this number when we receive the couriers signed receipt, I will expedite this transaction at close of business today. Now where do you wish this package to be delivered to?" he asked.

Chapter Forty-One

Liam stood beside the bed smiling, as he gazed down at the sleeping figure of Father Patrick O'Connell. He had been informed by Archibald Galbraith the hospital registrar that Father O'Connell was on the mend, he was monitored every four hours, and that the prognosis was good, he should make a full recovery, all he required was rest, and he should be preaching to his flock in no time at all. Liam placed the large bunch of white grapes into a bowl that sat on top of the bed side cabinet, and was just about to turn, when his wrist was grabbed, "Thank you my son," Liam barely heard the response, but taking the priest's hand, smiled. "You're supposed to be asleep Father and resting," he said, pulling over a chair and sitting down. "That's all I've been doing my son, I make Rip-Van-Winkle, look like an insomnia case," he chuckled.

"I have been told that you should be up and about in a few days, all thanks to your Samantha Pike and two police officers, you were very lucky for her persistence, god knows what would have happened if she hadn't called our lads."

"Yes he does, my son, obviously he has more work for me to do," the priest replied.

"Right Father," Liam began, "I can wait until you are fully recovered and back at St Josephs if you like, to let me know about what happened, but if you feel strong enough, perhaps you could tell me now," he said, taking out his notebook.

"I'll do my best my son, but it's still a bit fuzzy," he said, as a petite nurse arrived at the other side of the bed.

"Checking time Father," she said, smiling, as she took his left arm and placed a pressure cuff around it, "mouth open please," she ordered.

"But," came the reply.

"No Buts! Father, open your mouth please," as she stood poised with a thermometer only inches away from Father O'Connell's mouth. Liam smiled as the nurse placed the thermometer under the priest tongue, then placing her stethoscope into her ears began to pump, all the time gazing at her fob watch, three minutes later she had removed the pressure cuff and the thermometer and filled in the results on the chart, then with both hands on her hips, and smiling at the priest she stated.

"You are a fraud Father, you're just in here to look at us young nurses, aren't you?" She chuckled.

"And very beautiful you are my child, why would I be anywhere else to see such beauty," he replied.

"Don't give me your Irish Blarney Father," she said, her face turning bright red, as she hurried away.

"Another conquest Father?" Liam asked smiling, "They have taken such good care of me, and she is correct, I do feel a fraud, my son," the priest replied.

"I beg to differ Father, according to the registrar, if they hadn't got you to the hospital when they did, the story would have been entirely different, you are a very lucky man."

Liam corrected him, "It was god's will, my son," came the reply, "can you recall what happened Father?" Liam asked.

"As I've said," he began, "it's still a bit fuzzy, I remember driving to St Josephs, unlocking the vestry door and going to my desk, it was then that I remembered the challis was damaged and that the jeweller was due to pick it up for repair, I went out into the church, and up to the altar, as I picked up the challis I thought I heard a noise, but turning round the church was empty, then the noise came again, I called out but received no reply. Then a foot came out from under the altar, when I pulled up the altar shroud, I couldn't believe my eyes, Father O'Brien was fast asleep under my Altar, I screamed his name, he shot up banging his head and cursed me, he rolled out from under my altar and stood up, I told him that I wanted him out of my church, he yawned and began to stretch his arms above his head, the next thing I knew was I was in here."

"Did he say anything, Father?" Liam asked. There was silence for a short while, then Father O'Connell said, "It might sound silly, but I thought I heard him say something about a Lambretta, but it wouldn't get him to where he wanted to go, but I could be wrong," the priest stated.

"No Father you're not, that's probably what he did say, we found a Lambretta at the rear of your church, plus the fact that your Volvo was taken, we have traffic looking for it as we speak. The Lambretta was stolen from a B&B in Shoeburyness, then he set fire to a barn and the house, to cover his tracks, hoping that we would think that he had perished in the fire, he had no concern for the other four people that had taken him in, who luckily managed to escape, but they have lost everything."

Father O'Connell lay there, his face a mask, all the colour had drained away, he laid there shaking his head from side to side, "The devil has captured his soul," he kept whispering over and over to himself. Liam placed his hand onto Father O'Connell's shoulder, "It's not your problem Father, you have a flock who need you, you must put O'Brien out of your mind, your flock are more important and they will need you, so you have to stop being a fraud, as the nurse said, and get better quickly," Liam said, smiling at the priest.

"Thank you my son, you are correct, my flock is more important, and I'm afraid that he is a lost soul, and there is nothing that I can do about it, I'm afraid," he concluded.

Chapter Forty-Two

"Now! You do know what to say, don't you?" O'Brien asked.

"Yes Shaun," replied Charlie Gibbs, "I know exactly what I've got to say, we've been over it a dozen bloody time," he said, scowling.

"Will you get it through your thick head! It's not Shaun it's Shaemus, Shaemus Donahue," O'Brien fumed.

"Okay! Okay! Keep your hair on," came the reply, as he picked up the telephone and began to dial.

"It's ringing," he told O'Brien, followed by hearing, "Shannon Auto Service, how can we help you?"

Charlie cleared his throat, "I wish to speak to Michael Flanagan" Charlie stated.

"And who may I say is calling, sir?" he was asked. There was silence for a minute, then Charlie stated, "A friend."

"Putting you through! Sir!" Came the hostile reply.

Second later Charlie heard, "Yes!"

"Mr Michael Flanagan?" Charlie asked.

"Yes, whose calling?" came the reply.

"I wouldn't worry about who's calling, Michael, I would just listen, okay?"

"Well mate, you either tell me your fucking name, or I put this phone down," Michael hollered.

"I wouldn't advise you to do that Michael, it would be to your detriment."

"And why would it be to my fucking detriment you little shit," Michael's temper rising by the second.

"Have you ever heard of Krayleigh Enterprises, it's a company in the East End of London, it is run and owned by twin brothers, Reggy and Ronnie, two lovely chaps, and very successful at what they do, if they like you, your made, cross them," there was silence for over a minute, "do you hear what I'm saying Michael?" Charlie asked.

"I'm listening," came the reply.

"Thank you Michael, I can see that we're going to get along like a house on fire," Charlie stated.

"Right Michael, this is what is going to happen, two legitimate foreign couriers will arrive at your establishment with a parcel, you will have to sign for it. You will keep it in safe custody until someone comes to pick it up, and to put your mind at rest, it is totally legal, if and when someone comes to pick it up. If it is as it was when delivered to you, you will be handsomely rewarded, if on the other hand it has been tampered with, which you would be ill advised to do, Krayleigh Enterprise would! I'm afraid! Pay you a call, do I make myself clear Michael?" Charlie asked.

There was complete silence for over a minute, as Michael absorbed these instructions, "So all you want me to do is take delivery of a parcel, and hold it until someone picks it up, right?" he asked.

"Correct," replied Charlie.

"But how will I know that the person picking up the parcel is the correct person?" he asked.

"There are only four, sorry five people that know of the parcel, you, me, who it is for, and the two couriers, nobody else, okay?" he asked.

"So when can I expect this parcel?" Flanagan enquired.

"In a few days, you'll be contacted," came the reply, then his line went dead.

Michael Flanagan sat in his leather chair, sweat pouring down his body as his office door burst open and Jeanette rushed in, "What the blazes was that all about?" she screamed.

Michael sat bolt upright, "What do you mean?" He hollered, "This parcel thing, and Kray something," she replied.

"Were you listening in," he shouted, dropping her head she mumbled, "he sounded horrible and I was worried about you."

"Do you listen to all my calls?" he asked a furious look on his face, "No! I bloody well don't," she replied, placing her hand on her hips, and returning the look.

"So what are you going to do?" she asked.

"I'm going to wait until this parcel turns up, when it does I'm going to put it in my safe and lock it, when someone turns up for it I'll unlock the safe and give to them, okay?" he asked.

"But shouldn't we tell the police?" She said, as she said as she sat on Michael's desk, "Jeanette," he began, "you have beautiful tits, a gorgeous fanny, and your one hell of a fuck, but brains? I notify the police, and we get a visit from the East End, they'll make you watch them torturing me then blowing my brains out, then they will take it in turns fucking you, they will probably cut of your tits with a cutthroat razor, and let you bleed to death, I'll already be dead, so I won't be able to help you, so I'm going to do exactly what I've been told to do, okay?"

Jeanette threw herself at Michael sobbing, "Oh Michael, what are we going to do?" She sobbed clinging to her boss. Placing his arms around her shaking body, he whispered in her ear, "We will act as if nothing has happened, and until the parcel arrives, we will do our usual, I'll call you in, you'll lock the door, you'll take all your clothes off, and I'll fuck your brains out, okay?" he asked smiling, Jeanette smiled up his face.

"I'll lock the door, shall I?" She giggled.

Chapter Forty-Three

"I had better get dressed," Jeanette said, sliding off of Michael desk, "you should get a nice big settee in here, your desk isn't doing my back any good," she giggled.

"I've got a better idea," Michael said, buttoning up his flies.

"What! A bed, whoopee," Jeanette exclaimed.

"No sweet," he began, "it was you saying about calling the police."

"But about this parcel and this Kray thing, and what they would do to us?" she asked. A worried look on her face.

"How do you fancy a holiday for say, ten days to a fortnight," he asked smiling as he tighten his belt.

"What! On earth are you talking about?" she asked buttoning up her blouse, "Right," he stated.

"I give this Keir Dickson a call, tell him about the phone call, because I think it's dodgy, then you and I go on holiday, I'll tell Alfie that someone will call to pick up a parcel from my safe, and that I've had to go back to Ireland because of a funeral, so I'll be away for a week or so, but you and I won't be here," he said, placing his arms around her and crushing their bodies together, and kissing her, "you want me to take my clothes off again, don't you?" She giggled.

"No darling, where we're going, we won't be wearing any clothes, well! Only if we need shopping, but the rest of the time I'll be gazing at your beautiful naked body."

"And what about you?" she asked smiling, "Just a smile sweet I'll be wearing just a smile," he chuckled.

"So where's this holiday?" she asked. Pushing her hips forward feeling his erection begin, as she rotated her hips.

"Malta," he replied.

"A mate of mine has a small villa in Mellieha Bay, overlooking the sea, it has high walls surrounding it so we can't be seen, plus it has a pool with a spar, how does that sound," She was forcing her hips into him and rotating he hips.

"Fuck me one more time Michael. Please," she whispered.

"Can I speak to DCI Keir Dickson, please?" Michael asked.

"Whose calling?" he was asked.

"Michael Flanagan," he replied.

Keir picked up his phone, "Yes Sarge," he answered, "there's a Mr Michael Flanagan on the line for you Gov, do you want to take the call?" he was asked.

"Thanks Sarge, put him through," Keir replied, as Bill knocked and entered his office, covering the mouthpiece Keir whispered, "Flanagan," as he switched the phone onto speaker. Bill sat down leaning forward, his elbows on his knees and waited.

"Chief Inspector," he heard, "Mr Flanagan, how can I help you Sir?" he asked.

"I'm not sure if this is of any consequence Chief," he began, "but I've just had a very disturbing telephone call."

"In what way, Mr Flanagan?" Keir asked.

"It was abusive and threatening, I was told that a parcel would be delivered here, that I was to lock it up in my safe and wait for it to be picked, if it was tampered with I would get a visit from a company called KrayLeigh Enterprises," he never mentioned a reward. At the mention of KrayLeigh, both Keir and Bill sat bolt upright.

"Did you just say KrayLeigh, Mr Flanagan?" Keir asked.

"Yes," came the reply, "I won't go into the whole conversation," he continued, "but I was told that a parcel would be delivered, I was to lock it up and wait for someone to collect it, if it was untouched there would be no repercussions, the thing is, that I have to go over to Belfast in a couple of days for a funeral, and will be away for a while, you know what our Irish Wakes are like they go on for weeks, and I could be wrong, but I think it might be something to do with that so-called priest, O'Brien."

Keir looked at Bill, who brought both his hands up in the air, a quizzical look on his face, "Why do you think that Mr Flanagan?" Keir asked.

"Two couriers are bringing this parcel in a day or two, to me, that means from abroad, couriers are employed for thing of value, jewellery, money, and why two? It must be something worth a fair bit, to have two couriers and not only that! There not English," he stated.

"Why do you say there not English?" he was asked.

"Because this bloke that called said, 'two foreign couriers' not just couriers, maybe O'Brien had money offshore, I don't know? But I thought you should know, I'm leaving Alfie in charge, he'll get a call first, and when these couriers turn up he'll take this parcel and lock it away, I'll be in Belfast, just thought that you should know Inspector, especially after my stuff up last time," he said.

"Thank you Mr Flanagan, that's food for thought, when do you intend going to Belfast?" Keir asked.

"In a few days," came the reply, "I'll be in touch Mr Flanagan," Keir said, putting down the phone.

"So what do you think?" Bill asked. Looking at his mate, Keir ran his hands through his hair, "Roberto," he said. "What about him?" Bill asked.

"A?" Keir asked.

"Where is the prick, and 'B' we only found one account, O'Brien's out there and he has friends helping him, maybe this is the break we need Bill, because at the moment we're just kicking balls about, and Roberto will know if O'Brien has money."

"Well," Bill began, "he's over at Romford nick, so I guess that's where we're going, right?"

Chapter Forty-Four

"Right, Roberto," Keir said, as two police officers escorted Roberto Docelli into the interview room, and sat him down opposite Bill and himself, "thank you officers," Keir said, looking up, and waited until they had closed the interview room door.

"We think you might be able to help us, and in doing so, we will be able to help you," Keir stated.

Docelli brought his head up and stared at the two officers, "How?" he asked.

"The account in the Channel Islands, wasn't the only account, was it Roberto?" Keir asked smiling, "No comment," came the reply.

"Not the answer we need Roberto, what you don't seem to understand is, O'Brien is out there having a ball, whilst you are stuck in here facing," Keir lifted up his left hand and spread his fingers, "one, obstructing the law, Two, helping a murder escape, Three, aiding and abetting a known criminal, Four, perverting the course of justice, and Five, injecting a poison into Leonard Lazel's arm, and killing him," at this, Bocelli slammed his hand down on the Formica table, "I didn't inject him, he injected himself, he was dying and we paid him five thousand pounds," he hollered.

"Well, your finger print were on the hypodermic syringe," Keir lied.

Bocelli lent back in his chair, folding his arms and smiled. "Now both you and I know this is not true Inspector, don't we, because Leonard Lazel had it in his pocket all the time, from when he was given it," he said, smugly, Keir leant forward placing both his elbows on the Formica table, resting his chin on the palm of his hands, and smiled.

"But who gave Leonard the syringe Robert," he asked. The blood drained from Bocelli's face as he slumped forward in his chair.

Keir sat back smiling and folded his arms, "Now here's the deal Roberto," he began, "you answer my questions, and assisting the death of Leonard Lazel goes off the table, but there's nothing I can do about you helping O'Brien escape, also we will forget about you purchasing him that car, which he was going to use to kidnap one of my officers wife, I'll tell the judge how helpful you have been, and recommend a lenient sentence, okay?" he asked.

Bill was just staring at his mate, his jaw dropped. Becelli slowly raised his head, "You can do that," he mumble, "look Roberto, it's O'Brien we want, he had three people killed, he stole a car, stayed with a young family in Shoeburryness and in the middle of the night set fire to their house and barn, and stole a Lambretta, the four occupants of the house were lucky to get out alive, then he put Father Patrick in hospital and stole his Volvo."

There was silence for over a minute, as Keir and Bill studied Bocelli's face, "What do you want to know?" They were asked.

Both Keir and Bill began breathing normally, "Do you know anything about a company called KrayLiegh Enterprises."

At the mention of this company, Bocelli sat bolt upright, "No way," he stated.

"You have to be joking," he added, "did O'Brien have any dealings with them?" Keir asked.

Bocelli sat for a minute, "I have known Shaun for many years, and never once was that company ever mentioned, they are very bad people," he stated.

"And you and O'Brien aren't," Keir said to himself.

"Why do you ask?" Bocelli inquired.

"Just interested," Keir replied.

"So now about accounts!" He added.

Bocelli lent forward placing both his elbows on the Formica tabletop, "Well," he began, "yes, O'Brien has two accounts, but the one in Switzerland you won't be able to touch, the Swiss are rather particular about their clients, especially if the account is healthy."

"So how healthy is this Swiss account?" Keir asked.

Bocelli sat for a second, "Between one hundred and seventy and one hundred and eighty thousand American dollars, depending on the interest rate at the time, but that's what was in the account the last time I spoke to him," he stated.

Both Keir and Bill stared at Bocelli, "That's about Six hundred thousand quid," Bill whispered.

"And," Bocelli continued, "you would have to know the name of the account password, plus the account number, Shaun kept all those details," he lied, "I think the bank was called Vantoble or Vantable, it's Van something anyway," he said, sitting back, "I hope that's been of help, Inspector," he added, "and you're positive, O'Brien had not had any dealings with this KrayLiegh company, Roberto?" Keir asked.

"Not to my knowledge, Inspector, they are very bad people," he stated. As Bill and Keir both stood up, "Well thank you Roberto," Keir said, offering him his hand, "we'll be in touch."

"Thank you, Inspector," Bocelli said, gripping Keir's hand tight. Bill had walked out, the look on his face, telling a thousand stories, as Keir closed the interview door, Bill's face was only inches away, "so what the fucking hell was that all about, you'll have a word with the judge, and we'll knock this off of the table, you have to be fucking joking, thanks to that cunt," he said, pointing at the interview room door, "O'Brien is on the run, a family have lost their home, and nearly their lives, and Father O'Connell is in hospital and you shook the bastard's hand."

A large grin spread across Keir's face, "Fancy a game of Poker, Bill?" he chuckled as he walked off.

"Fuck you, Keir Dickson," Bill said, as he slid into Keir's Morris One Thousand, Keir was cracking up laughing holding onto his leather covered, sports steering wheel shaking, then turning and looking at Bill's face, slammed his head against the steering wheel, laughing.

Keir had to shake his head several time, to try and bring his breathing under control, "Sorry mate," he managed to say, "but I didn't know how else to get him to talk, it seemed obvious that the name of KrayLiegh, scared the living shit out of him, so how does that connect, all I can think of is, that O'Brien has contacted someone about the money, and to scare Flanagan, threatened him with the name, because that is one family you do not mess with, but I think it's about time Fiona and Trevor Woods should be brought in, Trevor's in the smoke, and I don't know enough about Swiss banks."

Chapter Forty-Five

Fiona and Trevor sat reading Keir's report that had been typed up that morning, Keir and Bill sat there waiting, until Trevor looked up, "Well," he said, "you're right about the Swiss, unless you know the name of the account's password and number, you might as well whistle, Dixy."

Fiona put down the report onto her writing pad and smiled. "Thank you Mr Flanagan," she said, six pairs of eyes focused on her smiling face, "right," she began, "O'Brien we now thinks he has access to a lot of money, but it's more than he dare do, to have it transferred to a English Bank, so he's having it couriered, he can't afford to have it delivered to somewhere that might be under surveillance, so obviously he's contacted someone who put the fear of god into Flanagan with this KrayLiegh crowd, that could be just a ploy, to make sure that he does as he is told, according to this," she said, pointing at Keir's report, "Bocelli doesn't think that O'Brien has any dealing with this KrayLiegh crowd, so I suggest that a little chat with our Mr Flanagan is in order, he's going away for a while, so I think someone should take up residence at Shannon's, to be there when they are contacted, and when the couriers arrive."

"And that person," Trevor stated.

"Should be me," he said, grinning.

"Why?" three voices said, in harmony.

"Because," he began, "I have on file! KrayLiegh associates, so if they are involved I will recognise who comes to pick up the parcel, and fingers crossed it won't be anything to do with that crowd, then who ever picks up the parcel, should lead us to O'Brien," he said, smiling.

"But surely," Bill stated, raising his right hand, "whoever comes to pick up the parcel, will be looking for a tail?" he asked.

"Not if they're not driving a car, they won't," Keir stated. The six pairs of eyes were now focused on him, "Remember how we found out when O'Brien was heading down to the Shamrock to meet up with O'Toole, D.C. Cain tailed him on his six hundred C.C. Panther Combination, and we have two keen bikers, Liam's Thunder Bird and Cain's Panther, it's either that or at least four under cover cars, and depending where this chap takes the parcel, if it's in the city, there's every chance we could lose him, where as a bike, won't," he said.

"So unless anyone else has a better idea?" he asked.

"Right," Trevor stated.

"Whose going to have a word with this Michel Flanagan?" he asked. Keir grinned, "Well one things for sure, you're not going down on your own," he chuckled.

"Why!" Came the response from Trevor Woods, "Because when I went to interview him, his secretary made it perfectly obvious that she was more than just an office ornament, and knowing the situation, we don't need distractions." Trevor had been leaning forward smiling at the mention of Flanagan's secretary, but now sat back his arms folded across his chest, a stern look on his face, the other occupants sat there smiling.

It was then that Keir's phone began to ring, "Sorry about this," he said, picking up the phone, "I did say no call," then into the mouthpiece said, "yes!"

"Sorry Gov" came the reply, "what is it Sarge?" Keir demanded, "Sorry Gov but the Chief Constable says he needs to speak to you and it's urgent," Keir smiled.

"I think I know what this is about," he said, covering the mouthpiece, and switching on the speaker, "put him through Sarge," Keir state. There was a click on the line, then, "Dickson," Keir grinned.

"Good morning Sir and how may I help you?" There was silence for a minute then a cough, "I've had a serious complaint made against you," the Chief Constable stated.

"May I ask who made this serious complaint Sir and what it involved?" Keir asked.

"You were insubordinate to a senior officer, and humiliated him in front of a guest, this conduct I did not expect from one of my senior officers Dickson," Fiona went to get up, but Keir raised his left hand, indicating for her to remain seated, "would that be by any chance, Ex DCS Parker Sir?" he asked, to be told, "Yes Dickson it would."

"Thank you Sir, but to put you in the picture, DCS Fiona Jarman and myself, were informed that a criminal that we needed to question, with regards to assisting a Shaun O'Brien who was in custody for three murders, drug importation, terrorist attack on New Scotland Yard, and Aldershot, plus arson, in escaping from custody, that he was in residence in a B and B in Brighton. It turned out that Ex DCS Parker's guest was the person we wished to question, Mr Parker was under the impression that he was still in the police force, and I can put you through to our new DCS Jarman to corroborate this if you wish, and Mr Parker's guest is now in custody, and by the way the individual was armed with a revolver Sir!"

There was silence for over a minute, all three occupants raising their thumbs and smiling, "Would you like me to put you through to DCS Jarman, Sir?" Keir asked.

"That won't be necessary, Dickson, did Parker know this individual?" Keir was asked.

"I wouldn't know, Sir, but I doubt it," he replied.

"Thank you Keir, I couldn't believe that one of my senior officers would act in this manner, so how is your new DCS Jarman coping?" Keir was asked.

Fiona glared at Keir, pointing her finger, he had to stop himself bursting into laughter, "She's fitted in beautifully Sir, and thank you for asking," he managed to say, "good to hear Keir, keep in touch," the line went dead. The room was shattered with laughter, Fiona turning bright red.

Chapter Forty-Six

"So what's this secretary like?" Trevor Woods asked as he pulled his Land Rover out of the station yard, Keir looked across at his companion, shaking his head and smiling, "One of these days, you're going to come unstuck mate," Keir replied.

"As I said, before I don't believe that she is totally used in a clerical capacity, she made it quite obvious what she was wearing, or more to the point, what she wasn't wearing, so I would say that Michael Flanagan doesn't go short, if you catch my drift," Trevor Woods was grinning all over his face, as his right foot pressed down hard on the Land Rover's accelerator.

Trevor pulled his vehicle onto Shannon's fore court and killed the engine, his eyes scanning the surrounding personnel, just as Jeanette came out of the office and spoke to one of the mechanics, all Keir heard, was a sharp intake of air, "Jesus Christ! Look at the body on that," Trevor said, pointing, "that's got to be her, yes!" He exclaimed.

"That most certainly is, and if I'm not mistaken the chap standing in the doorway is our Michael Flanagan," they watch as Jeanette bent down to speak to the mechanic and the look on Flanagan's face, "she's not wearing any knickers," Trevor gasped.

"Why do you think Flanagan's smiling?" Keir asked. They both sat there watching as Jeanette stood up and sauntered toward the office door, Flanagan turning sideways to let her pass, Trevor had to swallow, as they watched her sidle past her boss, her hand going to his crotch, and lingering, "Is she asking for it, or what!" Trevor exclaimed.

"No mate he's asking, and she's giving, but we'd better get in there now, before they lock the door," Keir stated looking at his mate, who was looking in his rear-view mirror, straightening his tie, and running his fingers through his hair and removing his wedding ring from the third finger on his left hand and sliding it onto the index finger of his right hand, Keir just shook his head.

He had just made it through the reception door as the inner office door closed and was locked, "Hello Police," Keir shouted, ten second later he heard the lock being turned, and a red-faced Jeanette walked out.

"Can I help you officer?" she managed to say, as she walked towards her desk.

"We would like to speak to Mr Flanagan, please," Keir stated.

"I was just about to take dictation, but that will have to wait, I'll see if he is available shall I?" she asked. Trevor walked over to her desk, and placing both his hands on her desk lent forward, smiling, "That won't be necessary, young lady, we'll introduce ourselves, you just sit here and look beautiful," he said, smiling. Jeanette lent forward giving Trevor a full view of her ample cleavage, "Thank you," she whispered.

"You're more than welcome young lady, my name is Trevor," he said, his eyes fixed on her heaving breasts as he offered her his hand.

"You can call me Jeanette," she whispered taking it.

Keir watched as Trevor took her hand and kissed it, "I don't fucking believe this shit," Keir said to himself, as he walked into Michael Flanagan's office.

Michael Flanagan looked up from his desk and smiled. "How can I help you, Chief Inspector?" he asked.

"We need your help, Mr Flanagan."

"Michael! Please, Inspector," came the reply, "right Michael, when you receive the parcel, and when you are told that someone will pick it up, I would like you to call me, here's my card," he said, handing it to him, "I understand you are going over to Ireland for a funeral, when will that be?" he asked.

"When the parcel arrives inspector, I've got to be here to put it in the safe, Alfie my foreman is the only one, other than myself that knows the combination of the safe, so he will be here to give it to whoever turns up, and yes! As soon as I know, so will you," he said, smiling.

"Thanks Michael, it's much appreciated," Keir said, offering him his hand.

"Please don't kiss it," he said to himself, as he walked out of Michael Flanagan's office, to find Trevor sitting on Jeanette's desk holding her hand.

"We're out of here," he stated. As he strode towards the main reception door, "catch you later then," he heard Trevor say, then Keir heard, "looking forward to it Trevor."

Keir sat in the Land Rover passenger seat seething, as a smiling Trevor Woods positioned himself behind his steering wheel, and looked across at his passenger, "What!" He exclaimed.

Keir turned his head and glared at his superior, "You're fucking cunt struck," he said, and turned his head back, staring out of the windscreen, there was silence for a second, then Trevor returning the glare, "do you know who your talking to Chief Inspector?" he asked.

"Sorry," Keir replied.

"Your fucking cunt struck, Sir!" he hollered, "we came down here to do a job, you see that secretary, you've got a hard on up to your fucking eyeballs, when it comes down to it, the job comes second when you see a pair of tits, doesn't it, Sir!"

Trevor began to smile, "Look Keir," he began, "I knew you had everything under control, what was the point of me going in with you, obviously you told Flanagan to contact us when the parcel arrives, and when it was going to be collected, it wouldn't take two of us to tell him that would it?" he asked smiling, "What is it with you Trevor?" Keir asked.

"You're on the ball one minute, then crumpet comes into view and?"

"Yes I know, Keir," interrupted Trevor, "it's been like that from day one, I don't know how, but they seem to send out a signal, it's either 'yes' or 'no' and that Jeanette was a definite 'yes', but it works both ways, I might see a beautiful women and think wow! But the signal comes back 'NO', your boss Fiona, she's gorgeous, Christine your intended she's gorgeous, but they are both big 'No's', Fiona will find her soul mate, and Christine has found hers, other women are still looking, and I'm there to help them," he chuckled. Keir just shook his head, as Trevor fired up his Land Rover.

Chapter Forty-Seven

"So what do I get out of all this crap?" Charlie Gibbs asked, taking a mouth full of Charringtons Stout, then wiping his mouth on the back of his sleeve, "You get the same as Flanagan, five hundred pounds," O'Brien replied.

"You have got to be fucking joking, I drive down to Tilbury to pick up your cash, all he's got to do is give it to me, and he gets five hundred quid, I'm the one that's taking all the fucking risks, so my cut should be more," he said, taking another swig of his stout. There was silence for a minute, then O'Brien replied.

"Okay! Make it seven hundred and fifty."

"No! We'll make it a nice round, one thousand pounds," O'Brien knew Gibbs had him on the back foot, he knew he couldn't collect the money himself, and he was running out of cash, "pour me a Bushmans Charlie and you can have your grand, there's a good chap," he said, forcing a smile.

"So what's the plan Shean?" Charlie asked.

O'Brien sat bolt upright, "How! Many times do I have to tell you," he shouted, "it's Shaemus Donahue not Shean O'Brien, someone calls out Shean, and I turn, I'll be back inside, okay?" He said.

"Okay, keep your shirt on, but by the time I've finished with your face, your own mother wouldn't recognise you, and that's something else Flanagan couldn't do for you, remember that!" Charlie replied pointing at O'Brien.

"That conversation you had with Flanagan?" O'Brien asked.

"You said, something about a KrayLiegh company or someone," he added, Charlie Gibbs smiled.

"What about it?" he answered O'Brien, "Why did you mention them?"

"To scare the living shit out of him, that is one crowd you do not upset, and he would know that," Gibbs replied smiling.

"So you know them do you Charlie?" O'Brien asked.

"I know of them, but I steer well clear of them, a chap I knew got on the wrong side of them, purely by accident, and was found floating in the Thames, so No! I don't know them personally."

"Do you think they might be able to help me?" O'Brien asked.

Gibbs began to roar with laughter, "Fucking right they would," he managed to say, "but it would cost you every fucking penny you have, you're not from the East End of London and your Irish, so forget it, and if you did try, you wouldn't see me for dust," he concluded. O'Brien sat quietly sipping his Bushmills thinking, "Okay Charlie, you're the boss, and thanks," he said.

Chapter Forty-Eight

"We're just waiting for a phone call from Flanagan Ma'am, then Superintendent Woods will go down to Shannon's and wait for whoever comes to pick up the parcel, D.S. Liam Smith will be parked up, when he sees Superintendent Woods give the signal, he'll follow whoever it is, hopefully to where O'Brien is holed up," Keir stated.

"So we're," Fiona began, when Keir's office door was thrown open, and an irate Trevor Woods strode in, "okay," he said, his clenched fists on his hips, "who told her I was married."

Keir, Fiona, and Bill, just stared at him, speechless, "Come on," he hollered, "who told her, was it you?" He said, pointing at Keir.

Keir leant back in his chair, a grin spreading across his face, "Can I assume that a certain young lady refuse your romantic advances?" he asked.

"So it was you," Trevor Woods stated. Placing both his hands on Keir's desk and leaning forward. Keir shot up and mimicked Trevor's stance, "No! It was not," he stated.

Well someone did, I received a phone call, all she said, was, "Don't bother, you're married," then she hung up, so somebody told her." Fiona, Bill, and Keir began to chuckle, Trevor Woods face turning red.

"Would you mind doing what you did when you first saw the young lady?" Keir asked.

Trevor stood up straight, "What the devil are you talking about?" he asked scowling, "Well!" Keir began, "we were sitting in your Land Rover, when a certain young lady came out of the office and bending over spoke to a mechanic, showing certain items, you made a comment, then did something, can you remember what you did?" Keir asked. Trevor stepped back from Keir's desk, "I checked my tie in my rear-view mirror and got out, why?"

"And?" Keir asked.

"And what?" Came the reply, "You straightened your tie, ran your fingers through your hair, then," he said, pointing at Trevor's right hand, Trevor looked at his right hand, "what?" he asked.

"So when we walked into her office what were you wearing on your index finger," Trevor gazed at his right hand, "My wedding ring," he mumbled, "correct! Then you walked over to her desk, placing both your hands on her desk, and told her not to bother, just sit there and—"

"Yes! Okay," interrupted Trevor, Fiona and Bill could see what was coming, and smiled.

"Would you mind taking your wedding ring off now, Trevor, and all will become crystal clear," Keir stated. Trevor looked at all three, a scowl on his face as he removed his wedding ring from his left hand, and placed it on Keir's desk.

"Now place your hands as you did on Jeanette's desk, please?" He said. Trevor did as he was asked, and gazed down at his hands, it took at least two minutes, before the silence was broken, "Shit," Trevor exclaimed, as he looked at the third finger of his left hand, to see the white skin where the ring had been.

All three occupants began to applaud, "Sorry chaps," he said, turning bright red, "what an idiot," he exclaimed, then burst into laughter. All four were laughing when Keir's phone began to ring, and on picking the receiver up, raised his left hand silencing the humour, "Yes Sarge," they heard him say, "put him through."

"It's Flanagan," he mouthed as he switched on the speaker phone.

"Mr Flanagan," Keir said, "how can I help you?" he asked.

"Good morning Inspector, you asked me to let you know when the parcel was due, and when it was going to be picked up," Flanagan stated.

"Yes Michael," Keir replied, smiling at his three companions, "well the parcel will arrive tomorrow morning, and will be picked up late that afternoon, I hope that's helpful, as soon as it arrives I'll put it in my safe, Alf will sort it out, because I'll be off to the wake," Flanagan said.

"Thank you Michael," Keir replied.

"Safe journey to Ireland," he added, "thanks" came the reply, then the line went dead.

"Right everyone," Fiona began, "so now it starts, have you organised with Liam about the tail, Keir?" she asked.

"Yes Ma'am," came the reply, "and D.C. Cain has taken the side car off of his Panther, so that if they get into traffic he can manoeuvre easily, the side car would restrict his ability to tail whoever comes to pick up the parcel, so we will have D.S Smith on his Thunder Bird and D.C. Cain on his six hundred c.c. Panther."

"Thank you Keir," Fiona said, "and Trevor," she said, smiling at him, "I'll be waiting for the parcel to arrive, and I'll wait until who ever turns up, and radio Smith and Cain as to what vehicle to tail, okay?" he asked.

"I think that about covers everything, unless anyone has any questions?" she asked. There was silence for a minute, "Well gentlemen here's to a successful day tomorrow," she said, smiling.

Chapter Forty-Nine

"Thank you, so that's two economy class return flights to Malta, departing at three forty five from Gatwick for a Mr and Mrs Flanagan, Yes?" he asked.

"Thank you," he said, smiling, then at the top of his voice hollered, "Jeanette!" seconds later the door burst open as Jeanette rushed in, her blouse buttons all undone, "Yes Michael," she said, as she closed and locked the office door.

"Yes Jeanette, you have beautiful tits, but what I want you to do right this minute is, do up your blouse, tidy up your desk, then go home and pack, I'll pick you up tomorrow about twelve, we're off to Malta," he said, smiling.

"Do I have to go right now?" she asked as she unclipped the front of her bra, and cupping her ample breasts sidled over to his desk, "Just let me show you what is in store for you in Malta," she whispered as she rounded his desk.

"Why not?" He said, as he swivelled his chair round.

Michael Flanagan pulled up outside twenty seven Feenan Highway Tilbury, and stared at the young woman standing at the roadside, at first he thought he was seeing thing, until Jeanette waved, she was wearing a jet black full length wig, down to her waist, instead of her minute mini skirt, she was wearing a knee length floral dress, and complementary jacket, with pale green heeled shoes. Jeanette stared in amazement as Michael leant over the lush leather passenger seat and opened the passenger door of a Rolls Royce Phantom.

"Whose car is this Michael?" she screamed, picking up her small suite case, and rushing to the open door, "Just get in sweet, we have to be at Gatwick by two, so throw your case in the back, and get your arse in here," he said.

Jeanette stood up and sauntered to the back door, making sure that the neighbours had a good look at her transport.

"Jeanette!" Flanagan shouted, "get your arse in here, Now!"

"Yes darling," came the reply, as she slid in besides him, having closed the rear door.

"So whose car is this?" she asked, leaning across and kissing his cheek, as Michael gunned the engine.

"It belongs to a client of mine, Allen's flying into Gatwick tomorrow and has asked me to leave it in the long-term car park, so I'm killing two birds with one Rolls Royce," he chuckled.

Michael had picked up the tickets from the British Airways counter, and had joined Jeanette in the duty free shop, "Have you seen these prices," she giggled, squeezing Michael's arm.

"Those two piece swim suits are a giveaway," she whispered.

"You won't be wearing a swim suit darling," he whispered back, squeezing her bottom, "but what if we go down to a beach, you want everyone to see what I give you," she said, running her hand along his flies and smiling at him.

"Okay," he said, as over the P.A. system they heard, "British Airways announces flight BA 277 to Malta is now boarding."

"That's us," Michael said, "so I'm going naked then, am I?" Jeanette asked. Michael just smiled.

"This is the bit I love," Michael said, as the aircraft accelerated down the runway, "reminds me of when I first opened up my six fifty BSA Super Rocket, and took her up to the ton," he chuckled. But when he looked across at Jeanette, she had her eyes tightly shut, her head pressed against the headrest, and her knuckles pure white as they gripped the arm rest. He quickly took hold of her right hand and kissed it, then whispered in her ear, "When we get to flying altitude, would you like to join the Mile High Club?"

Jeanette's eyes shot wide open, then turning to look at his smiling face, "What's the Mile High Club?" she asked. A bewildered look on her face.

Michael placed his mouth next to Jeanette's right ear and whispered, "When the Captain states, 'We are at over thirty thousand feet', that means we are over a mile in the air, you get up and go to the toilet and lock the door, I wait two minutes, then I'll knock twice on the toilet door, you unlock the door and…"

"And you'll fuck me at over a mile in the air?" She giggled, "You had better make it four minutes, so I can get naked Darling," she whispered.

"This is your Captain speaking," was all Jeanette heard before her seat belt was undone and she was out of her seat, heading for the toilet, which was only a few feet away, from where she and Michael were seated, she was in such a hurry she didn't notice an air hostess pushing a trolley towards her, "I need the toilet, sorry!" She whispered as they came together.

"Can you squeeze through?" The air hostesses asked smiling, pushing the trolley to the side.

"I'll be fine," Jeanette replied. As she squeezed passed.

"Can I get you anything Sir?" Michael was asked. As the trolley stopped next to him, "Thank you young lady, but I'm fine at the moment, maybe later," he replied. Michael waited until the air hostess had moved far enough down the cabin and seeing a women passenger begin to rise, quickly rose from his seat and knocked twice on the toilet door.

The two air hostesses sat side by side as the aircraft approached Malt's Luqa Airport, "They hold the record in my book, the flying time to Luqa is about just over three hours, and they've spent nearly a quarter of the time in there," the senior hostess said, pointing, "they're either on honey moon, or the randiest couple ever to fly British Airways," she added, as the aircraft made a smooth landing, and taxied to the terminal.

Being right at the back of the aircraft, Michael had told Jeanette to wait until the majority of the passengers had disembarked before they made a move. As Jeanette stood up to disembark, the senior air hostess and her companion walked forward, "We hope you enjoyed your flight?"

She said, "And on behalf of British Airway, please accept this, with our complements," she said, handing Jeanette a rolled-up scroll, with a red, white and blue ribbon wrapped around it with a bow.

"Thank you," Jeanette said, smiling, as she began to undo the ribbon.

"No!" exclaimed the hostess, "wait until you're in the terminal, and collected your luggage, and we hope you will fly with us again," she concluded.

"We most certainly will," Jeanette giggled, as she and Michael left the aircraft.

"So what did she give you?" Michael asked as they waited for the carousel to deliver their luggage.

"Just this," she said, offering Michael the scroll. He smiled as he rolled it out and read the inscription. "We are now full members of the Mile High Club, with five-star rating," he chuckled.

Chapter Fifty

Trevor Woods had parked his Land Rover in one of the maintenance bays and was looking out of the office window when a two-tone Ford Zephyr Six pulled onto the forecourt and stopped, as the driver stepped out, Trevor smiled to himself as the six foot two inch tall driver went to the boot and on opening it, removed a trolley case with wheels. Picking up his handset, Trevor pressed the call button, and said, "Two tone Zephyr Six," Trevor then turned and picking up a motoring magazine sat down on a settee and waited.

Three minutes later the office door opened and the driver plus his case walked in, "Shop!" The driver hollered. Trevor put down the magazine and smiling said, "Hello Charlie what brings you down to this neck of the woods?"

The driver came to a halt, then turning, stared at Trevor, "Mr Woods," he eventually was able to say, "no! Charlie, it's D.C.S. Woods now, and as I just asked you, what brings you down to this neck of the woods."

There was silence for a minute as Charlie Gibbs turned to face Trevor, "Thought I might get some business down this way, Mr Woods," he replied forcing a smile, "what?" Trevor asked.

"You thought someone might need something forged did you, Charlie?" he asked.

"No Mr Woods, I gave that up a long time ago, prison life and me, just don't get on, so I've been going straight, got me self a nice little business going, in fact it's your lucky day Mr Woods," he said, smiling, as he walked over to the settee, and sat down, "why would today be my lucky day Charlie?" Trevor asked, moving to the end of the settee.

"Do you know where your name came from, of course you don't," Charlie chuckled.

"It comes from Scotland, the old English name Wood, also Wod, Vod, Wode, Woode, and Woods, may well come from the Norman French de Vosco, meaning of the Wood, you've even have a coat of arms, quite flash it is, and seeing how it's you, for fifty quid I'll knock one up for you, if you like, I normally charge a ton," he said, opening up his case.

Trevor lent forward as Gibbs pulled the lid of the case back, "That," he said, pointing, "is the coat of arms of Purkins they were keepers of the Royal Hunt, their motto, Simplex Vigilum Veri, not sure what it means, I looked up your Motto, Tutus in Undis, it translates to 'Safe on The Waves'. So what do you recon Mr Woods?" Charlie asked.

Trevor picked up the Purkins parchment and studied it, "You did this?" he asked.

"Yes Mr Woods," came the smiling reply, "it's really good Charlie."

"Thank you," came the reply, "how can I get in touch with you Charlie?" Trevor asked. Putting the parchment back into the case, "I've a little shop in Poplar High Street Mr Woods, Tower Hamlets, I'm there most of the time, pop in anytime and I'll be able to show you my workshop," he said, closing his case and getting to his feet, "and don't forget, only fifty quid," he said, as he opened the office door and walked out.

Trevor picked up his radio, and pressing the call button, as he watched Charlie Gibbs put the case in the boot of the two-tone Ford Zephyr Six said, "He's on the move you two, now don't lose him and let me know if he makes any stops," he said, as the Zephyr pulled out onto Calcutta Road, Trevor then walked over to Jeanette's desk, and on picking up the phone, began to dial.

"Dickson," he heard and smiled.

"I was right," Trevor began, "the person that came down, is someone I nicked some years ago for forgery, and we can forget the KrayLiegh firm, this chap wouldn't touch them with a barge pole, his name is Charlie Gibbs, he was a brilliant forger his white fivers, Wow! But according to him, he's given up the life of crime, he reckons he has a little shop in Poplar High street, doing Heraldry, when I asked him what he was doing here he stated."

"Drumming up business," he then went on to show me some of his work, he even offered to do my coat of arms for fifty quid, so I don't know if it was him that was supposed to pick up the money or not, "Smith and Cain are tailing him, but I'll wait here just in case."

"Did he have a bag or case with him, Trevor?" Keir asked.

"Yes he did," came the reply, "but he opened it up, right next to me and showed me some of the parchment he had made, and between you and me Keir, they were excellent."

It was then that Trevor's radio came to life, "Hold! On Keir," he said, "I've got a call coming in," as he activated the switch, "Woods," he said, and was told that the driver had stopped, and entered the Shamrock Cafe.

"He's just made his first mistake Keir, he's just gone into that Shamrock Cafe, and I'll bet my pension he's not having a meal, he had me going there for a while, I genuinely thought he was straight, so my next call will be Shamrocks," he said, and received a 'Good luck' as his radio fired up, and was told, "he's on the move again, Gov."

"Don't lose him lads," Trevor replied as he left the office, and made his way to where he had parked his Land Rover, giving Alfie the thumbs up sign.

"Colleen," Trevor said, as he approached the counter, holding up his warrant card, "my name is Trevor Woods, I believe a man came in here a few minutes ago, can you tell me what he wanted, please?" he asked smiling.

Colleen came round the counter, wiping her hands on her skirt, "How do you know my name?" she asked, returning his smile, "Fiona and Keir told me all about you," he replied.

"Not everything, I hope," she said, coyly, as she walked passed him, and getting to the door, turned the open sign over and locked the door, "I was just locking up anyway," she said, as she walked towards Trevor, who just happened to notice that three of the buttons of her blouse were now open, "so how can I help you Trevor?" she seductively asked.

Trevor swallowed and looking down at a cleavage asked, "Can you tell me what the chap wanted, that just left here," "Oh! That all?" She said, "He just wanted to use the phone, he placed a one pound note on the counter, and asked if it was okay if he phoned his wife."

"Did you happened to hear what he said, Colleen?" he asked as she took his hand.

"Well this is the phone," she said, pulling him behind the counter, "I was standing here, and he was standing just there," she said, pushing Trevor against the wall, "so yes! I heard every word Trevor," she said, smiling, "so what did you hear him say?" He managed to say.

"Wouldn't you be more comfortable upstairs, I have a bottle of single malt, we can sit and chat, and I can tell you what he said," she said, taking his right hand and placing it on her left breast. Trevor smiled to himself. "This is a turn up for the books, it's usually me," he said to himself.

"Right Colleen," he began, "you tell me what he said, then depending on the answer I'll make a phone call, then we'll go upstairs, and if you would like I will take all your clothes off, lay you on your bed, and make love to you all night," immediately Colleen blurted out, "all he said, was, go to the place I told you about, and I'll call you."

"Thank you Colleen," Trevor said, picking up the phone and dialling, before the phone rang twice Colleen was pushing her hips against Trevor's crotch, and feeling his erection begin to grow, ran her hands down the front of his trousers.

"Oh my god," she whispered, her eyes staring at his massive erection pushing against his clothing. All Trevor was able to say when the phone was eventually answered was, "Keir! Charlie has told O'Brien to get out, I'm off." Because Colleen now had his erection out of his pants and in her hand, and was moving away from the phone, "Upstairs or here?" she asked, ripping off her blouse and bra.

"Both," Trevor managed to reply, as Colleen's skirt fell to the floor.

Chapter Fifty-One

"Did you get the package?" O'Brien nervously asked.

"And why did you tell me to go to your home address," he added.

"A: no I didn't get your fucking money, and B: I'm going to have to stay above my shop, because I could be wrong, but I think I was followed," Gibbs replied.

"Why?" he was asked.

"Because when I arrived at Shannon's, whose sitting in the waiting reception room, none other than fucking DCS Trevor Woods, who put me away for two years, so there was no fucking way that I was going to try and pick up your bleeding money," Charlie shouted down the phone.

"So what happened, what did you say?" O'Brien asked.

"Oh! I just said, 'Hi Mr Woods, I've just popped in to pick up O'Brien's fucking cash'." What do you think I fucking said."

"Just tell me, and can you tone down the profanity, please?" he was asked.

Charlie Gibbs took a deep breath, "I told him I was drumming up business, he asked if I was back doing forging, I told him No! That I had a legitimate business doing peoples coats of arms, and as luck would have it, I knew that I had a couple of parchments in my case, which I showed him, even told him I'd do his for half price," he chuckled.

"So why do you think you were being followed?" O'Brien asked.

"I've been in this game for quite a few years," he began, "so the hairs on the back of my neck, tell me something ain't right, but each time I looked in my rear-view mirror I didn't spot any cars, even did a detour through the Blackwall Tunnel, took me bleeding ages to get to me shop."

"So why do you think you were being followed, if you didn't spot any cars following you?" O'Brien asked again.

"I just had this feeling, and it's never let me down, so! Until something happens you stay where you are, okay?" Gibbs asked.

"But what about the parcel?" O'Brien stated.

"You'll have to leave it with me, I'll leave it for a few days, and sort something out, but the first sign of trouble, you're on your own. No way am I going back inside."

"Forget the one thousand pounds Charlie, you get me that parcel, you get double, okay?"

"Leave it with me," Charlie replied. Putting down the phone.

Chapter Fifty-Two

D.S. Liam Smith, and D.C. James Cain stood facing Keir's desk, "So what happened lads?" he asked.

Liam and James looked at each other, until James said, "After you, Sarge."

"Well Gov," Liam began, "the driver was very good, because he must have thought that he was being followed, we even ended up going through the Blackwall Tunnel, until we eventually ended up in Poplar High Street, it would appear that he has a small shop, James here," he said, looking at D.C. Cain, "parked his Panther a distance from the shop and walked along the pavement looking in shops windows, and it would appear that the owner does Heraldry and coats of arms, and from what D.C. Cain said, they look genuine parchments Gov, I was parked some way away, but it looks as if there is a flat above the shop, because I saw the curtains move and a man looked down into the street, the shops called Charles Gibson's Heraldr."

"Thanks lads," Keir replied.

"According to D.C.S. Woods he was going to nip into O'Toole's I and talk to the owner, he told me she said, he wanted to phone his wife, but all he said, when he got on the phone was, 'Go to the place I told you about, and I'll call you'. I suppose you might say that to your wife, but we'll have to wait until D.C.S Woods gets here, because what he said, was, that he put this Charlie Gibbs away for forgery, so he will know him," Keir stated, as his office door opened, and a grinning Bill Day walked in, followed by a distraught D.C.S. Trevor Woods.

"For Christ sake, Keir, open that bottle, I desperately need a drink," Trevor Woods ordered, as he collapsed onto a vacant chair, and buried his head in his hands. All four occupants stared at D.C.S. Woods in complete wonder, the normally suave immaculate D.C.S. Trevor Woods was a complete wreck, "What the devil happened to you?" Keir asked, pouring a large tot of single malt.

"Don't ask," Trevor said, grabbing the glass and downing the liquid in one gulp, before handing the glass back to Keir for a refill.

"So what happened when you went into Shamrocks?" Keir asked, refilling the glass, "I've told you, Don't ask!" Trevor hollered grabbing the glass and emptying it in one gulp. There was silence for a moment, then a smile began to spread across Keir's face, turning to Bill he winked, "I reckon Bill," he began, "that a certain officer, made a play for a young Irish lady, and came unstuck," he chuckled.

"Well Mr Keir Dickson," Trevor said, sitting up, and indicating a refill, "you couldn't be more wrong, I didn't make a play for her, She made a play for me, if you must know," he said.

"And?" Keir asked, trying to hold back a chuckle.

"She finally fell asleep at five thirty this morning, I left her snoring," he said, placing his head in his hands. The room burst into laughter, as they all heard a knock on Keir's door, and Fiona Jarman's smiling face appeared.

"Good afternoon gentlemen, it's nice to see my team in such good humour," she said, "may I ask the reason for this frivolity?" she asked.

The room went completely silent, everyone staring at Trevor woods, until Bill, who was standing next to Fiona whispered, "Trevor has met his match, Ma'am."

"Oh!" Came her reply.

"Right gentlemen," Fiona began, "will somebody bring me up to speed, Please?" she asked. Trevor sat bolt upright, and on clearing his throat, stated.

"I arrived at Shannon's and waited, until a two tone Zephyr six pulled onto its forecourt, the driver exited the vehicle and ongoing to the boot remove a case, when he turned I recognised the driver, he was someone I had put away for forgery, when he came into the reception I asked him what he was doing there, his reply was 'Drumming up business'.

Turns out he has a small shop that does heraldry, in Poplar High Street, which was confirmed by D.C. Cain and D.S. Smith. The only mistake I could see, was that when he left Shannon's, he made straight for the Shamrock Cafe, I then went to the cafe and interviewed the owner." All four officer had to put their hands over their mouths, "She told me that the man, Gibbs, put a one pound note on the counter and asked if he could call his wife, she said, that when he got through," all he said, was, "go to the place I told you about, and I'll call you." Then he left, that's about it," Trevor said, slouching back in his chair.

"You can corroborate this shop, can't you, constable?" she asked, looking at James, "Yes Ma'am," he replied.

"I looked in the window of the shop, there must have been at least a dozen parchment on display, all different coats of arms, there was also an advertisement for family trees, price on application, Ma'am."

"Thank you constable, so it would appear that this Gibbs chap, runs a legitimate business."

"Yes, it would appear so," interrupted Trevor Woods, "but it looks a bit suss, him turning up on cue, and he can think on his feet. When I put him away, I had to have all my I's dotted and my T's crossed, he's a brilliant forger, and as cunning as a fox, he nearly had me fooled, until he called into that I, so if it was up to me, I'd be getting a warrant to search that shop of his," he stated.

"Already on the cards Trevor," Fiona replied.

D.S. Liam Smith coughed and partially raised his hand, "Yes Sergeant?" Fiona asked.

"Sorry to interrupt Ma'am, but both constable Cain and myself, came to the opinion, that this chap Gibbs was under the impression that he was being followed, because the route that he took to get to Poplar High Street, was to say the least, evasive, and if as D.C.S Woods has said, that he's as cunning as a fox, all traces of O'Brien will be gone from that flat above Gibbs shop, the phone call he made from Shamrocks, saying, 'Go to the place I told you about'." "To me means that this chap Gibbs has another address, and that might be where O'Brien is hold up, if the shops phone was tapped maybe that would give us a lead, Ma'am."

"I'll get that sorted, now," Trevor said, as he rose from his chair and made for the door, "as soon as it's set I'll give you a call, and to put the screws on Gibbs, I'd still search his shop, if he thinks he's in trouble with us he'll turn, I know him," he said, as he left the room. There was an embarrassing silence for over a minute, then the male company burst out laughing.

Fiona stood there gaping, "Sorry Ma'am," Keir managed to say, "okay I give up, what's so funny?" she asked.

"You remember D.C.S Woods mentioned that he interviewed Colleen at the Shamrock Cafe, we should have told him that she told us that she hadn't slept with her husband for years, because he left her snoring at five thirty this morning, and it wasn't him that initiated it," Keir managed to say, "so he called you when?" Fiona asked.

"Yesterday afternoon about three," Keir answered.

Fiona stood there smiling for a while, "I suppose that is what's called stamina," she chuckled, "thirteen hours, my!"

Chapter Fifty-Three

Charlie Gibbs had gone through his upstairs two-bedroom flat with a fine tooth comb, the two beds were stripped and remade, the used bedding thrown into his Hoover washing machine, the bath, toilet and wash hand basin scrubbed, every surface had been dusted and polished, every article and ornament had been cleaned with alcohol, his flat was spotless, not one trace of O'Brien anywhere to be found.

"That Trevor Woods is no fool, but how did he know about that package, unless that bastard Irish git opened his fucking mouth," he said, as he walked down his stairs, and into his workshop.

"That will be the next thing," he said, pointing at his workshop phone, "and if that cunt O'Brien thinks I'll settle for two grand, he's got another fucking think coming, I don't need this shit," he stated as he looked out of his shop front window. Poplar High Street looked its normal self, no one trying to make themselves look inconspicuous, so taking his keys out of his trouser pocket, unlocked the shops front door and stepped out onto the pavement, then giving a quick glance up and down the street, he lock the door and headed towards 'The Troubadour' his local pub.

"Shirley, my love," he called, as he walked up to the bar, "my usual sweat heart, and one for your gorgeous self," he said, as he sat down on one of the bar stools, "coming up, you old flatterer," came the reply.

Charlie grinned, "Not so much of the old, young lady," he chuckled.

"If I was twenty years younger, you'd have to fight me off with a stick," he added, "I wouldn't put up much of a fight Charlie, honest," she giggled as she place his G and T in front of him.

"So what's new, Charlie?" she asked. Then leaning across the bar, Charlie whispered, "How would you like fifty quid, sweat heart" Shirley mirrored his movement, displaying her cleavage, and replied.

"It wouldn't cost you a farthing, Charlie," she whispered.

"I'll take you up on that precious, but this is something else that I need your help with," he said.

Shirley smiled as she moved back. "I get a fifteen minute break in five minutes," she stated smiling, "take your G and T over to that alcove," she said, pointing, "and I'll be with you in a jiffy."

Charlie picked up his drink and walk over to the alcove that Shirley had indicated, and sat down and waited, he watched as Shirley approached the head barman, and said, something to him, the barman looked around the bar, then nodded his head, Shirley kissed him on the cheek, picked up two glasses and after filling them, came round the bar and sauntered over to the alcove putting down the two glasses and sat down beside Charlie, placing her left hand on Charlies right thigh, "Did you mean that, about taking me up on that offer," she whispered in his ear and kissing his cheek.

"Is the Pope Catholic?" Charlie asked smiling, "When?" he was asked, running her hand up his thigh. Charlie took hold of her hand and kissed it, then taking a sip of his G and T said, "I need your help Shirley," he stated.

"I'm trying to help a friend of mine, but it turns out that the constabulary would like to talk to him, I made a phone call to warn him, and I have a feeling that the police might be listening in on my phone, all I said, was, 'Go to where I told you, and I'll call you', I told the woman in the shop where I phoned from, I was calling my wife."

"This is where you come in, in a couple of days I'll pick up my phone, if I hear a click, I'll know, I'll call you and ask how you are, your reply will be," "thank you Charlie, I went where you told me to go, and the people here are really nice to me," I'll say, "as long as your happy now, take care," and hang up. That will be your signal, for a candle lit supper and a passionate night, "Don't bother with the candle lit supper Charlie, I'll just have the passionate night," she giggled, her hand now caressing his upper thigh.

"So what do you say when I phone?" he asked taking her hand, "Spoil sport," she scoffed, "all I say is, Thank you Charlie, I went where you told me to go, and the people here are really nice to me, you'll say take care, I'll hang up the phone, then I'll pop round to your flat, and you'll have your wicked way with me, Yes?" she asked.

"Exactly," replied Charlie, as Shirley's hand once again found its mark, "Shirley! Will you cut it out," he whispered.

"But he's getting so hard," she whispered in his ear, "look!" she said, squeezing his crotch, "just to make sure I get it right, I finish work tonight at eight, I'll pop round to your flat, and we can go over it one more time, okay?" She said, imploringly.

"See you just after eight," he said, as he emptied his glass, put a one pound note on the table, kissed Shirley on the lips, and stood up, "you won't forget tonight Charlie, it's going to be wonderful," she whispered, giving his crotch one last squeeze. Charlie had to push his erection down as he left the pub, it was too obvious that Shirley had wound him up, he smiled to himself as he walked along Poplar High Street, in search of a phone box, anticipating an evening with Shirley.

He had to wait, as the Red G.P.O. Phone box was occupied by an elderly gent of about seventy plus, by Gibbs calculations, so Charlie moved round so that the elderly gent could see that he was waiting to use the phone, giving the old gent the thumbs up sign, and receiving a smile in recognition, "I won't be a minute young man," the gentleman said, pushing open the heavy door, "just calling the hospital to find out how my Betty is," he said.

Charlie smiled. "No problem Gov, you take as long as you like, and give Betty my best," Charlie stated.

"Thank you young man," came the reply, as the old gent closed the door. Seven minutes later Charlie watched as the elderly gentleman replace the receiver, and picked up a pile of coins from the shelf, Charlie took hold of the cup handle and pulled open the heavy door, "So how's your Betty, Gov?" he asked.

"She's out of I.C.U. And they're taking her to a ward," he managed to say, his eyes glistening, "we've been married fifty-six years, met at school, she was the only one for me, and happily I was the only one for her," he said, smiling, as tears trickled down his wrinkled face.

"You're a very lucky man, Gov, hope you get another fifty six years," Charlie said, as he stepped into the phone box, "thank you young man," he heard, as the door closed. Charlie delved into his trouser pocket, and withdrew a hand full of coins, picking up a shilling piece he dropped it in the shilling slot and began to dial, he stood there listening to the distant phone begin to ring.

"Come on O'Brien, pick up the fucking phone," he yelled into the mouthpiece. The phone rang at least twelve time, and Gibbs was just about to slam the phone down, when it was picked up, pressing button 'A', he yelled,

"Don't say a fucking word, just listen," there was silence from the other end, "good!" Charlie said, "now! whatever you do, do not! And I mean do not! Phone the shop, I don't care if my house is on fire, you do not phone the shop, I'll call you from a phone box, I'll get your parcel to you, but the price has gone up," he heard, "why?"

"I said, don't say a fucking word, I'm not going back inside for a cunt like you, I'll get your money to you, then I want you out of my life, when the law is sniffing around, I'm not happy, and thanks to you, I'm going to get a visit, and they're going to go over my place with a fine tooth comb, but to the best of my knowledge there's no trace of you at the flat, and I've organised a few things, but you're going to have to wait until things quieten down, by that I mean, when the plod have gone over my place, when they have, I'll call you, so you'll have to wait, I'll be in touch" Charlie said, and put down the phone and exited the phone box.

Chapter Fifty-Four

Keir and Bill were sitting in his office, Keir had just poured them both a single malt when the door of Keir's office was opened and Trevor Woods walked in, "I'll have one of those," he stated as he sat down, a grin spreading across his face. Keir opened a draw and removing a half empty bottle of whisky, poured the amber liquid into a lead crystal tumbler.

"Keep going," Trevor said, as Keir began to lift the bottle, "do you know how much a bottle of this costs?" he asked, lifting it up into the air, "Yes," came the reply, "but my wife doesn't own a pub, so fill the bloody glass up."

"So what happened with young Colleen," Bill asked smirking.

"None of your bloody business," Trevor said, reaching for the crystal tumbler, Keir pulled the tumbler back, "not until you answer Bills question," he said, smiling, "and we want it verbatim, or no single malt," he said, holding the tumbler away, "you two are a pair of shits, but if you must know, I slept with her, so now can I have my drink?" he asked, holding out his right hand.

"Right," Keir said, still holding the tumbler away, "you walked into Shamrock's, you showed Colleen your warrant card, and said, you were D.C.S. Trevor Woods, we would like a blow-by-blow account of what happened next, before this single malt evaporates," Keir said, grinning. Trevor Woods sat back and folded his arms.

"Right! You two, eat your hearts out," he began, "yes your right, I did just that, then she walked passed me and turned the open sign over and locked the door, telling me she was closing up anyway, when she turned I noticed that the three top buttons on her blouse were now undone, you can guess what was going through my mind."

Bill and Keir just nodded, "Can I have my drink now?" he asked, holding out his hand, "Just as long as the story isn't finish," Keir stated.

"It isn't," Trevor said, taking the tumbler and draining it, "fill please," he said, placing the tumbler on Keir's desk.

"Colleen took my hand and more or less pulled me behind the counter, I asked her what did the man do when he entered, she said, that he put a pound note on the counter and said, could he call his wife, so I asked her, did she hear what he said, it was then that she took my hand and placed it on her breast, saying would I like to go upstairs and she would tell me what he said, I told her if she wanted me to make love to her to tell me now, so she garbled what Charlie said, and got his Lordship out, how I phoned you I'll never know, with her working his Lordship, by this time she was practically naked, and Yes! It was Her that fucked my! brains out until five in the morning, Now! where's my second single malt, you two perverts?" he asked, as Keir's shaking hand managed to fill Trevor's tumbler to the top.

"You're a better man than I am, Trevor," Bill chuckled, as Trevor raised his full tumbler into the air, and at the top of his voice stated.

"To all the young virgins out there."

"There aren't any," they heard, as Fiona walked into Keir's office, "I sincerely hope this has something to do with the case! We are all working on," she said, glaring at the three men.

"Trevor was just relating a toast at a stag night he once attended, Ma'am," Bill said, staring at the floor, "nice try Bill," Fiona sarcastically replied.

"So will somebody kindly inform me as to what progress has been made," she said, taking a seat. Trevor stood up and walked over to the door, "Right Fiona," he began, closing the door, "I should have the search warrant for Charlie Gibbs shop in a couple of days, or even earlier, the phone tap goes on tomorrow morning, so we will be able to hear any incoming and outgoing calls, then it's just a case of waiting for either O'Brien or Gibbs to make a call, when that happens, we bring Gibbs in and grill him," he concluded.

"So it's a waiting game, is it?" she asked.

"Unless you can think of anything else, I'm afraid we have to wait," Trevor replied.

"Has anyone checked that the money is in actual fact at Shannon's?" she asked.

Trevor walked back to his seat and sat down, "If it wasn't! Why would Charlie Gibbs turn up with a suitcase?" he asked.

"Michael Flanagan said, it had been delivered, that's why I was down there," he said.

"But it's He said, They said, I think we should check with this Alfie chap, and make sure the money is in actual fact in Flanagan's safe, and if it is, have someone in situ, keeping an eye on it, don't you?" she asked.

All three men looked at each other, before Keir picked up the phone and began to dial, second later he asked.

"Can I speak to Alfie please, this is Detective Chief Inspector Dickson, thank you?" They all heard him say, after only two minutes Keir smiled. "Hi Alfred," he said, "just a quick question, is the package safely locked up in Michael's safe?" he asked then smiled. "Cheers Alfred," he said, putting the phone down, "yes Ma'am, Alfie says it's all locked up safe and sound."

"Thank you Keir, now get someone down there to keep an eye on it," she said, rising and walking to the door, "thank you gentlemen for the update," she said, as she stormed out.

Chapter Fifty-Five

The address was twenty seven Ambassador Drive, Kingston upon Thames, O'Brien was seated in Charlie Gibbs workshop at the end of a secluded garden, where Charlie's none legal work would be carried out. When O'Brien's taxi had dropped him off at the end of the road, at nine that evening, O'Brien had walked to the alley way between twenty six and twenty seven Ambassador Drive, and finding the back door key where Charlie had told him, let himself into the four bedroom detached house, and as per instructions, closed all the curtains, if he wished to watch the Murphy television, to have the sound turned right down, and if he needed to go out, only do so in the evening, and exit the house from the back door, and use the alley way between the houses.

    Charlie's rear garden was over one hundred yards long, and fifty yards wide, with an abundance of fruit trees, coxes orange pipping, granny smith apples, victorian plums, the whole garden being enclosed by a twelve foot high brick wall, making the area very secluded, down one side of the garden, next to the brick wall, was a crazy paved path that lead down to Charlies workshop, and a gate that lead to an alley way between the houses. When O'Brien first explored the garden and found the twenty by fifteen foot square brick built workshop, he gazed in wonder at how the workshop had been set up, and the mass of tools and equipment at Charlie's disposal. This had set his mind working as he gazed at his prosthetic hand.

    It had taken only a little time for him to come up with an idea to turn his prosthetic hand into a working hand. He had found a brown leather jacket in Charlie's wardrobe, which now had four fine wires woven up the left sleeve, across the back, and down the right sleeve, the three prosthetic fingers and thumb, were now hinged, the four fine wires going down the left sleeve to a black glove, when O'Brien put the jacket on and slipped his good hand into the black leather glove, whatever his left hand did, his prosthetic hand reacted the same, it took quite some time to perfect, but now he could grip cups, plates, a glass of whisky, "I doubt I'll be able to play the piano," he chuckled as he made his way back to the house, but then his mood changed, "so how much of my money is this Gibbs going to take," he said to himself, then smiled, remembering he would still have five hundred and eighty eight thousand pounds at his disposal.

"If I can't get my revenge for Brendan and Michael here, I'll go to where it happened, the Garda and the British army have to pay," he said, as he climbed the stairs to the second level, and walking into the bedroom, and fell into bed.

Chapter Fifty-Six

Charlie Gibbs picked up his workshop phone and listened, when he heard the metallic click he smiled, and began to dial, he waited until he heard, "Anton's Pizza Parlour."

"Anton," Charlie said, "can Brian drop off my usual please?"

"Charlie!" Came the jovial reply, "one sea food pizza with double prawns, of course, Brian's out on a delivery at the moment, but as soon as he gets back, your pizza will be ready, thank you for your order, Charlie."

"Well seeing as how your pizzas are the best, why would I go anywhere else?" Charlie chuckled.

"You're a smooth one Charlie, okay! Heavy on the prawns, be with you in fifteen minutes," came the reply.

Charlie put down the receiver and smiled. "Right Mr Trevor Woods now Mr D.C.S. Trevor Woods, so you are now going to listen into all my telephone conversations are you, well! The best of British luck," Charlie hollered.

Charlie was looking out his shop window as the little white Ford Escort Van pulled up to the curb, displaying, "Anton's Supreme Pizza's," he watched as the driver exited the van, and going to the back, opened the double door, then leaning in withdrew a cardboard carton, Charlie had opened the door and was waiting as the driver walked towards him smiling.

"Brian my friend, come in," Charlie stated standing to the side, to allow Brian to pass, "your usual Charlie with extra prawns," Brian said, as he placed the warm cardboard carton on Charlie's counter.

Charlie lifted the lid of the box, and breathed in the aroma, "Bloody brilliant," Charlie chuckled.

"You say that every time," Brian said, smiling, "and why wouldn't I?" Charlie replied, placing two quid on the counter, "Keep the change, Brian," he said, "boy! Thanks Charlie," Brian replied grinning.

Charlie put his hand on Brian's shoulder, "Do you think you could do me a favour Brian?" he asked. Brian immediately pulled away, a worried look on his face, Charlie burst out laughing.

"I prefer women Brian, sorry about that," he chuckled. Brian's face relaxed, "you had me worried there for a minute Charlie, because I do get some queer bastards, and I do mean queer," he said, smiling, "so what's this favour?" he asked.

"Right," Charlie began, "I'll give you fifty quid if you deliver this letter," he said, giving Brian an envelope, "and four pizzas to a garage called Shannon's down in Tilbury, make it about lunch time, ask for a chap called Alfie he's the foreman, once he's read the letter he'll give you a parcel, you tell him the pizzas are from Mike Flanagan, as a thank you, when you get the parcel, you call this number and ask, 'This is Simon Schultz, is my coat of arms ready', I'll say, 'No but it won't be long', you'll say, 'thank you', and hang up. You hold onto the parcel until I order my next sea food pizza, and if your asked who asked you to deliver the pizzas you say some Irish bloke okay?" Charlie asked.

"This is legal, Charlie isn't it, it won't get me into trouble will it?" Brian asked a concerned look on his face.

"I'll let you into a little secret, Brian," Charlie stated.

"Many years ago I crossed over to the wrong side with the law, nothing serious, I was caught with forged five pound notes that I was looking after for a mate, but I went away for two years. I could have dobbed my mate in, but I didn't, he had kids, so I don't want my name mentioned, I'm doing another mate a favour and I don't want the same thing to happen to me again, surely you can understand that," he said.

Brian smiled. "So all you want me to do is take this letter," he said, holding it up, "take four pizzas down to a garage called Shannon's in Tilbury, give the letter to a bloke called Archie."

"No Brian Alfie! Not Archie," Charlie corrected him.

"Sorry," he replied.

"Alfie, and he'll give me a parcel, I'm to say the pizzas are a thank you from…"

"Mike Flanagan," Charlie said, "yes! Mike Flanagan, I call this number, say I'm Simon Schultz and ask if my coat of arms are ready, you say no but it won't be long, I say thank you and hang up, I hold on to the parcel until you order your next pizza, Right!" He said, beaming.

"Exactly Brian, and when you drop the parcel off here, there will be a little bonus, okay son?" Charlie asked slapping him on the shoulder, "Easy Peasy," Brian said, grinning, as he picked up the two quid.

"So when do you want me to pick up this parcel, Charlie?" he asked.

"I'll call Anton's and tell him, 'Tell the delivery chap his coat of arms are ready to pick up', when he tells you that, you take the four pizza's down to Tilbury, and make sure you get Alfie on his own when you give him the letter, okay?" Charlie replied.

"Gotcha!" Brian said, as he turned and walked out of Charlie's shop whistling.

Charlie had just made his first cup of espresso coffee, with four sugars, and taken a bite out of a slice of Hovis toast, when he heard a squeal of tyres, going to the window overlooking Poplar High Street, he smiled, as a Land Rover skidded to a halt, followed by two Panda cars. Putting down the coffee and half eaten toast on the kitchen bench, he threw on his dressing gown and hurried down the stairs, as Trevor Woods began to hammer on Charlie's glass door, "I'm coming," he shouted, as he ran towards the door, waving his arms.

"Good morning Superintendent," Charlie said, smiling, as he opened the door, "you are a bit early, I was just having my breakfast, would you care for a cup of coffee?" he asked still smiling.

"I have a search warrant to search these premises, so will you kindly step aside and let my officers in," Trevor stated.

"Certainly Superintendent, all I would ask is, if you and your fellow officers would please leave these premises as you have found them, I'm rather fussy about it being neat and tidy, you see."

Trevor just glared at him, "Right lads," he shouted, as eight police officers made their way into Charlie's shop.

"And don't forget officers," Charlie stated.

"Please leave it as you found it, Thank you, so what are you looking for Superintendent, maybe I can save you some time?" he asked.

Trevor just looked at him and smiled. "We know what's going on Mr Gibbs, and when we nail you, you're going away again."

Charlie put on a bewildered face, "I'm sorry Mr Woods, but you've lost me," he said, "don't give me that crap Charlie, I know why you were down at Shannon's, so why don't you save us all, a load of fucking about and admit why you were down there," he said.

When Trevor Woods heard, "Gov, over here," Trevor walked over to where a police officer was looking down and smiling, "what?" he asked.

"Take a look Gov," he was told, Trevor moved to where the officer was standing and following the officer's finger, smiled. "Gotcha," he said to himself, "I take it you have a firearms certificate, Mr Gibbs," he said, addressing Charlie.

"Why on earth would I need a firearms certificate, Mr Woods?" Charlie asked, a grin spreading across his face.

"Because it would appear that you have a gun," Trevor said, pointing at what appeared to be a handgun. Charlie chuckled.

"So you found Jessie, did you Mr Woods, she does look realistic, doesn't she?" Charlie said, as he joined the two officers and looked into the open draw, "Guilty as charged Gov, I'll come quietly," he chuckled. Trevor first stared at the gun and then at Charlie, "You'll go away for this Gibbs, you do realise that, don't you?" Trevor stated, stern faced.

"I didn't realise a water pistol was regarded as a firearm Mr Wood, has that law just come in?" Charlie asked smiling.

"Go ahead and try it Superintendent, just don't point it at me, it's filled with blue ink and methylated spirits, anyone comes into my shop with the intent of taking anything, gets a face full of blue ink and stinging eyes, all I do then is call you boys in blue, and tell them to look out for a robber with a blue face and can't see, it's my civil duty to help your lads," Charlie concluded.

Trevor heard a snigger, and turning shouted, "Get back to the search, every nook and cranny, Now!" He hollered.

"I'm glad you turned up today Mr Woods, come this way," Charlie stated as he walked behind his counter, and pulled out a two foot by one foot folder, and on opening it up, said, "yours Mr Woods, and as I respect you, it's yours for only fifty quid."

Trevor gazed at the parchment, "It's your coat of arms Mr Woods, and that's your motto," he said, pointing at the scroll across the bottom. Two of the officers had heard the conversation, and had manoeuvred over to the counter, to look at the parchment. "Jesus Christ," Trevor heard, tearing his eyes away from the parchment, he shouted, "get back to what you're supposed to be doing."

"Yes Gov," came the reply.

"So what do you think, Mr Woods?" Charlie said, grinning, "I don't have fifty quid on me at the moment," he sheepishly whispered.

"If I can't trust you, Mr Woods, who can I trust, you being a Superintendent and all," Charlie stated.

"That reminds me," he said, picking up the phone and dialling, "tell the delivery driver his coat of arms is ready, thank you," he said, into the mouthpiece, and hung up the phone, "that's the third one this week, Mr Woods, if this keeps going, I'll be thinking about retiring," he chuckled.

Chapter Fifty-Seven

"What the bloody hell has got into you lately Shirley, every time the phone goes off, you're the first one there?" the Barman asked.

"Sorry Bert," Shirley replied.

"But a girlfriend of mine is about to give birth, and she's asked me to be a God mother, and I've given her this number," she lied.

Bert smiled. "Can't see you as a God mother Shirley," he chuckled. Just as the phone rang once more, Bert rolled his eyes and nodded towards the phone. Shirley grabbed the phone and listened, Bert heard, "Yes thank you Charlie, I went to where you told me, and the people are very nice to me, thanks so much."

Bert looked at Shirley's beaming face as she put the phone down, "Everything okay Shirley?" he asked.

"Couldn't be better," she replied hugging herself.

Wearing a full duffel coat with the hood up and carrying a Tesco shopping bag, Shirley pushed the doorbell at Charlies shop door. Charlie had been watching from his front room window, the giveaway beside the six inch stiletto heeled red shoes, was the fact that the air temperature outside was about seventy five degrees Fahrenheit, so although the coat was a good disguise, Shirley would be sweating bucket, Charlie was chuckling as he opened the door, and let Shirley rush in.

"Quick," she said, as she threw off the coat, "my mate let me borrow this dress, it will be ruined if I don't get these sweat stains out," she said, placing her hand behind her back, "start the zip Charlie please, and there's something in the Tesco bag for you," she giggled. Charlie took the bag with one hand, and using his other hand brought the zip down to the waist.

"Thanks Charlie, you're a treasure," she said, as the zip came all the way down, and she stepped out of the dress, "God that's better," she sighed.

Charlie gazed at this young body transfixed, Shirley stood there smiling, the bright red silk bra and knicker plus the red stiletto had Charlie spell bound, "You like Charlie," she asked smiling, he couldn't answer.

"Right," she said, picking up the dress, "where's your bathroom, I need to soak this dress before the stains mark," Charlie just pointed, "after you," he just managed to say.

"So that you can goggle at my backside as I go up your stairs," she giggled, "and don't forget the bag, you're going to need it" as she took the stairs two at a time. Charlie followed gazing at this vision, as Shirley reached the top of the stairs, she turned, "Come on Charlie," she said, bending forward, "I want to show you something, I've had done especially for you," she said, and disappeared into Charlie's flat, "found it," he heard Shirley call, "now get stuck into that Tesco bag, and I'll be out in a minute," she added.

Charlie opened the bag, and on looking inside, smiled, at least a dozen oysters. Emptying them into a glass bowl, he took a knife from a kitchen draw, and began to open them, letting the oysters slide down his throat, he closed his eyes, flavouring the succulent taste. When he opened his eyes, he had to close them again, shake his head and slowly open them again. Shirley was now standing in front of him completely naked, except for the stiletto shoes, her arms held straight in front of her, her hands closed.

"I did this for you Charlie," she said, opening her hands, then placing her hands on her slender hips, Charlie stared speechless, not one single pubic hair on her young body, but just above her vagina was a tattoo of a heart, and just below it, at the beginning of her lips was the word, "Charlie."

"I had this done especially for you Charlie," she whispered, as she walked towards him, "so get those oysters down you and take me to bed, I'm going to have you all night, all to myself," she whispered.

Charlie was laid back, looking up at Shirley's smiling face, her head tilted back and her eyes closed, as she slowly raised and lowered her youthful body. Charlie's fingers and thumbs rotating Shirley's tort pink nipples, "Yes Charlie," she whispered, as her movements became faster and faster, then, "now! Charlie, Now!," she screamed, as both their orgasms shook their bodies.

Shirley fell forward onto Charlie's hairy chest, and began to sob, her arms crushing their moist bodies together, "Charlie, Charlie, Charlie," she sobbed. Charlie took both his hands, and cradling Shirley's face, tenderly kissed her, "now what's this all about?" He whispered, "I know I'm going to stuff things up

Charlie," she replied. Pushing herself up, and sitting astride Charlie's body, wiping her eyes, "You might as well know Charlie," she began, "but do you remember the first time you came into the Troubadour, what happened?" she asked. Charlie chuckled.

"You mean me ordering my G and T, and thinking, 'The lights are on but nobody is home, so I had to ask you again'," he chuckled.

"Yes Charlie," she blushed, "the first time I saw you, I knew I was going to fall in love with you, I spoke to my flat mate about you, she advised me to be a bit provocative when serving you, so that's why you saw a cleavage, no one else did, only you, you have no idea how long I've yearned for this moment," she said, using her pelvic muscles to squeeze Charlie's love shaft inside her.

"I don't expect you to love me Charlie," she whispered, her eyes filling with tears, "but if we could maybe, spend a little time together, I know you might say there's an age difference, but I don't care. Have I stuffed things up Charlie?" She managed to say, tears trickling down her cheeks.

"You most certainly have, young Lady," Charlie stated. A stern look on his face.

"Oh Charlie I'm sorry," she sobbed, trying to get up, but Charlie grabbed her shoulders and pushed her back down, "I'm not happy about this, 'Spending a little time together, business', 'I was thinking more on the lines of you telling your flat mate, you were moving out and moving in with me, but if your happy with a little time'," but before he could finish, Shirley's lips and tongue were inside his mouth.

They laid together naked, Shirley wrapped around her man, "We'll have to get a bigger bed darling," she whispered, "already on the list precious, I've got one small bit of business to take care of, which will take a couple of days, so I'll be away for maybe one or two days, if you want, you can move in now, or wait until I get back."

"I'll wait Charlie, being here without you would drive me nuts, and I'll ask Bert to alter my hour, so I'm here when you finish work, and just to let you know," she giggled, "I've been told, I'm rather a good cook, my flat mate is something with chips, so I do most of the cooking, and seeing as how it will be just you and me up here," she said, running her hand down Charlies body, "I'll always be naked just for you, so you can have your wicked way with me, whenever you want, my precious Charlie," she whispered.

Chapter Fifty-Eight

Brian's Ford Escort van had been adapted, so that the four warming ovens had heater coils that were fed hot water from the vans engine, keeping the pizzas really hot. Brian had chosen four different flavours, Hawaiian, Seafood, All Meat, and a new pizza, Anton had named The New Yorker. Brian had timed it to perfection, as he drove into Calcutta Road, "It's along here somewhere," he said, passing the Shamrock café, and looking at his wrist-watch, "just coming up for twelve, right on time," he chuckled.

He had only driven another five hundred yards, when he spotted the sign, "Shannon's Tyre and Auto Service," turning his left-hand indicator on, he slowed down, and pulled onto the fore court, parking his van next to the office building. Leaving the engine running he exited his vehicle and knocked on the office door, and waited. Not receiving a reply, he open the office door and shouted, "Shop!"

He had just started walking back to his van to switch off the engine when he heard, "Can I help you?" Brian turned to see a man dressed in a green boiler suit, the name Shannon embroidered on his breast pocket, "I've four pizza's courtesy of a Mr Flanagan, who says, 'Thank You', and I need to speak to a chap called Alfred," Brian said.

"Well son," the man said, smiling, "it's your lucky day, that's me," he said, putting out his hand, "pleased to meet you Gov" Brian said, taking his hand.

"The lads are all in the rest room, so your pizza's will go down a treat, perfect timing son," Alfred said, smiling, "can you give me a hand Gov?" Brian asked as he walked to the back of his van, and opened the double doors, "Sure can" came the reply.

Brian opened the two nearest ovens and pulled out the piping hot pizza cartons, picking up two pair of thick mittens, handed them to Alfred, "There very hot Gov," he said, put on his mittens.

"This way son" Alfred said, as he walked into the end bay and turned right, heading to where Brian could hear voices. Alfred came up to a door, and using his industrial boot, kicked it twice, which was immediately opened, Alfred strode into the rest room, a big grin across his face, "Right you lot," he hollered, "this is courtesy of our boss, Mr Michael Flanagan," he said, placing the two carton down on a table, "and keep your bloody hand off 'em, until I get back," he shouted, as Brian placed the other two cartons on the table.

"Right son," he said, turning towards Brian, "what do you want to see me about?" he asked.

"I was given a letter for you, to pick something up, it's in my van Gov," Brian said, walking out of the work bay toward his van.

"So what have you got to pick up, son?" Alfred asked. As Brian leant into his van, removing the envelope from his inside pocket, and on standing up said, "Some parcel, Gov," handing Alfred the envelope.

Alfred studied the heading, "New Scotland Yard," he read, then sliding his finger into the edge ran his finger to the end. Taking out the headed sheet of paper he read, "Dear Alfred, please supply the driver with the parcel that is in Michael's safe, he will be transporting it up to my office at New Scotland Yard, Many thanks for your help, Your Sincerely Trevor Woods, P.S. I'll be dropping my motor in again."

"I wondered when someone was going to come and pick it up," he said, as he opened the office door and walked in, "I'll bring it out son, you wait there," Alfred said, over his shoulder. Five minutes later Brian was turning into Dock Road, a suite case in the back of his van.

Brian didn't know what was in the suite case, and he didn't want to know, the conversation about Charlie doing time had worried him, yes! He was doing a friend a favour, and that friend had kids, so Charlie took the fall, which said a lot for Charlie. But why put yourself in the same boat, he asked himself, as he pulled up outside his mum's house. Brian switched off the engine and sat there thinking until he heard, "You all right Brian?" Turning to his left, he smiled.

"Yes Mum, I'm fine, thanks, just want to drop something off for a mate, and use the phone," he said, getting out of his van. Brian walked to the back of his van, and on opening the two doors picked up Charlies suite case.

"What's that Brian?" his mother asked. As she held the front door open for him, as he walk up the garden path, "Just a suitcase Mum," he said, "I'll stick it in my shed, it belongs to a friend of mine, he's waiting until his flat is finished, and he doesn't want to leave it in the empty flat so he asked me to look after it."

"Why don't you just put it in your bedroom Brian, it'll be quite safe there," she said, "no it won't," he said to himself, knowing his mother, "I thought about that Mum, but he said, he wanted it under lock and key, because some of the things were really valuable, and been in his family for absolute years," he lied.

"Okay dear, you know best" his mother replied as he walked in doors, placing the suitcase down on the floor, picked up the phone and began dialling, "who are you calling Brian?" His mother asked.

Brian rolled his eyes, "Just going to tell my friend I've picked up his suite case, Mum, that's all," he replied.

"Any chance of your famous cup of tea, Mum," he added forcing a smile.

"But you're driving Brian," she said, giving her son a stern look, "one shot won't hurt Mum, anyway! I'm just popping back to Anton's to give him today's takings, and it's only down the road."

"Huh!" He heard, as his mother strode into her kitchen. Brian dialled the number, and hearing, "Yes," whispered, "Simon Schultz hear is my coat of arms ready" Brian wait for 'No sir' then hung up.

"Your tea's ready, Brian," his mother hollered, "cheers Mum, I'll just pop this case in my shed, won't be a minute," he replied picking up the suitcase, "well don't be long, or it will get cold," his mother shouted, as Brian opened the back door.

Brian put the case down, then taking a bunch of key from his trouser pocket, lifted the Yale padlock and smiled. "Nice try Mum," he said, looking at the key I. Knowing his mother as he did, Brian had place a small strip of cello tape across the opening, and sure enough, the tape had been broken. Inserting his key, he unlocked the Yale lock, and opened the shed door, picking up the suitcase, Brian entered his shed, and switched on the fluorescent light, getting a small pair of steps, Brian lifted the suitcase and reaching up as far as he could, placed the case on the top shelf, then collapsing the steps, slid them in between his work bench and tool cupboard, then rummaging through a box of old spanner smiled, as he found a brand new combination lock.

"See if you can work out the combination to this one Mum," he chuckled.

Chapter Fifty-Nine

"One step forward, and three steps back," Trevor Wood stated despondently, "but I'd bet my pension Charlie Gibbs could tell us where O'Brien is hold up," he added, "so what happened?" Fiona asked.

"Huh!" Trevor said, "I was made to look like a complete idiot, we arrive early, he was even in his jimjams and dressing gown when we arrived, I told him we had a search warrant to search his establishment, he replies he's just having his breakfast, and would I like a cup of coffee," Keir, Bill and Fiona smiled.

"Then one of the search team opens a draw and says 'Gov', I go over, and laying in the draw is a revolver, I think, 'Gotcha' then I make myself look a complete idiot by asking Gibbs if he's got a firearms license, he says, 'No! that It's a fair cop, and he would come quietly'." Then I'm told It's water pistol filled with methylated spirits and blue ink, so that if anyone tries to rob him, they end up with stinging eyes, and a blue face. The lads taped every surface for a left handed print, and found nothing, so it was a complete waste of time, and his phone tap revealed absolutely nothing, the call he made saying, "Go to where I told you, and I'll call you later." Turned out to be some women. So we're back to square one, I'm afraid" Trevor stated. Looking very dejected.

"Well at least we know that the parcel is still in Flanagan's safe, otherwise the constable that we had under cover would have reported in," Fiona said, "he hasn't reported in, has he?" she asked.

"Not to my knowledge," Keir replied. Picking up his phone and began dialling, switching on the speaker.

"Alf," they heard Keir say, "Keir Dickson here mate, can I speak to constable Peterson please."

"Just a minute Inspector, I'll get him," came the reply, two minute later a breathless voice stated, "P.C. Peterson here Gov."

"Right constable," Keir began, "has anybody called to pick up the parcel yet?" he asked to be told, "Not to my knowledge Gov, I haven't seen anyone, but

I'm only here from eight in the morning until they close at five, and Alf hasn't said, anything, but I can ask him if anyone came after hour, if you like?" he asked.

"Please Constable," Keir replied. A concerned look on his face.

They then heard P.C. Peterson shout, "Alfie!" two minutes later they heard, "what!"

"Detective Chief Inspector Dickson wants to know if the package is still in the safe?" Peterson asked.

"Well tell him, to ask Trevor Woods where it is, because the driver was taking it to New Scotland Yard," came the reply. Trevor shot out of his seat, and shouted, "Put Alf on the phone Constable," Peterson shouted.

"Alf! Phone," they all waited and heard, "fuck this I've got work to do," followed by, "Alf here, what's the problem?"

"You just said, ask Trevor Woods where it is, because the driver was taking it to New Scotland Yard, why did you say that?" Keir asked.

"Because a chap turned up with four pizzas from our gov, as a thank you, and a letter from Mr Trevor Woods telling me to give the parcel to the driver, who was going to deliver it to New Scotland Yard, the letter's on Jeanette's desk, why?" Alf asked.

"Why didn't you tell Constable Peterson that it had been picked up?" Keir asked.

"Well, when I went into the rest room everyone was getting stuck into the pizza's and it went right out of my head, not only that, the letter was from New Scotland Yard, addressed to me."

"I don't suppose you remember the vehicle or the chap, by any chance?" Keir asked.

"Sorry, all I remember is he was young, and the van was white, why?" Alfred replied.

"Because Alfred," Trevor shouted, "I know nothing about pizza's or a letter from me, so the fucking money has gone, Sorry!" He said, looking at Fiona, "Shit," they all heard from the speaker.

"Tell Peterson to report back to the station Alfred, will you?" a dejected Keir said, as he put the phone down.

"Well gentlemen," Fiona began, "with the statement, one step forward and three back, I don't think we've even taken one step forward have we, the money has gone, and we don't have a clue where O'Brien is, do we?" she asked. There was complete silence in Keir's office, as nobody was prepared to put their hand up, "Any ideas?" Fiona asked, still silence.

"Right," she began, "there have been two letters, one fooled the officers at the hospital, where O'Brien was handcuffed to a bed, now one has fooled the foreman at Shannon's in letting the parcel to be picked up."

"Charlie Gibbs," Trevor said, "but you said, you came up with nothing," Fiona added, "if you want something forged that will pass scrutiny, you can't go passed Charlie Gibbs," Trevor stated.

"I put him away for forged fivers, it took a chap at the Bank of England to pick up the minute floor, even he said, they were brilliant, because it took him a time to spot the floor."

"So you are saying that this Charlie Gibbs, forged the two letters, and has O'Brien holed up somewhere, but not at his place of business, because you found no trace of O'Brien at his residence. So when you add it all up, our only link to O'Brien is this Charlie Gibbs, Yes?" she asked.

"Yes," Trevor replied.

"Well in that case Trevor," Fiona said, smiling, "you can finance a twenty-four seven, surveillance, on our Mr Gibbs, right?" she asked.

"Shit," came a mumbled reply, "I'll take that as a yes then, shall I?" She said, smiling, "Thank you gentlemen, and I would go down to Shannon's and see if Alfred is more forthcoming," she added as she rose from her seat and left Keir's office.

They all waited until Fiona had closed Keir's door, and they heard footsteps reseeding along the corridor before Trevor Woods spoke, "That cunt Gibbs is making me look like a right fucking idiot," he said, Bill and Keir smiled. "Well I'm glad you think it's funny, because I'm fucking sure I don't," he added, the blood rushing to his face.

"Calm down Trevor," Keir said, "you'll give yourself a bloody heart attack, but Fiona's right, our only lead is this chap Gibbs, so I'm afraid our Mr Gibbs has to be watched twenty four seven, if we've got any chance of catching him and O'Brien."

"But it's going to cost me a fucking fortune," he said, burying his head in his hands. Bill and Keir looked at each other and smiled.

"I'll go down to Shannon's tomorrow, and see if I can get any more info from Alf, if you want to come to Trevor, we could pop into the Shamrock for a chat and a cuppa," he said, grinning, and was greeted with, "fuck off Dickson, I need you like a fucking hole in the head."

"Sorry mate, couldn't resist that one," Keir chuckled.

"Yer right," came the reply.

Keir had pulled his Morris One Thousand onto the Shannon's forecourt, and killed the engine, as a tall red headed operator, wearing a green boiler suite walk over to where Keir had parked, and in a broad Irish accent, told Keir to pull into the far bay, and leave the keys in the ignition, "We're here to talk to Alfred," Keir said, holding up his warrant card, as both he and Bill, exited the vehicle.

"Alf's out on a breakdown," they were told, "but you can wait in the office, if you like," the mechanic added, and walked away.

On entering the office, Keir went straight over to the secretaries desk, to find the letter that Alf had said told him to hand over the parcel, picking it up and reading it, he turned to Bill smiling, "I would have believed this," he said, handing the letter to Bill, Bill ran his eyes over the letter, "me too," he replied.

"It looks to be just the same headed paper as the so-called priests had at the hospital, when O'Brien escaped," he added.

"Morning gents, I understand you wanted to see me," Alfred said, as he walked into the office, finding Keir sitting behind the desk, and Bill sitting on a settee, reading a motoring magazine.

"Yes Alf," Keir replied. Getting up and offering his hand, "Just wanted to have a chat about what happened yesterday," he said, "but I've already told that Woods bloke what happened," Alf replied.

"Yes, I know Alf, and Bill and I have read the letter, but if you could just run us through what actually happened again, I can take notes," Keir stated.

"This is a bloody waste of time, as far as I'm concerned," Alf said, sitting on the edge of Jeanette's desk, "right," he began, "it was lunch time, we had just gone into the rest room, when I hears 'Shop' I goes back out onto the forecourt and there's this young bloke, he tells me he's got four pizza's from Mr Flanagan, saying it's a 'Thank you, from Mr Flanagan'. I helped him in with the pizzas, then he tells me he has a letter for me, and gets it from his van, I reads the letter, which tells me to give the driver the parcel in Mr Flanagan's safe, because he's going to take it to New Scotland Yard, so that's what I did, then the chap drives off," he stated.

"Can you describe the van, Alf?" Keir asked.

"It was white," came the reply, "any markings on the side of the van, Alf."

"Didn't take any notice, sorry."

"What about the driver Alf?"

"What about him?"

"Tall, short, fat, thin, English, Irish, Scottish?" Keir asked.

Alf sat for a moment, "Hm," he began, "about my height, five six, five seven, looked about nineteen, maybe twenty, blonde crew cut, that's about it," he said, sliding off of Jeanette's desk.

"Cheers Alf," Keir replied.

"We'll take the letter, and the envelope, okay."

"Help yourselves," Alf replied as he headed for the door, "I've got work to do, and blokes to run," he added as he left the office, and walked out.

"So we've got a nineteen stroke twenty year old with a blonde crew cut, at about five foot six or seven, driving a white van, do we?" Bill asked, putting down the magazine and standing up.

"Well that certainly narrows it down, doesn't it," he said, grinning, "well it's more than we had yesterday Bill, which is something," Keir replied, heading for the door.

Chapter Sixty

Charlie Gibbs was just about to pick up his phone and order his seafood pizza with extra prawns, when he looked out of his lounge window, Poplar High Street was its usual self, no one skulking around looking conspicuous, he had just begun to dial, when a flash of light caught his attention, putting down the phone, he looked across the street at the premises opposite. Charlie wasn't sure at what he had seen, but he was sure that the flash of light had come from the upstairs window of the premises opposite, standing well back from his window, Charlie picked up his Zeiss binoculars, and focused on the window opposite. It wasn't long before the lace curtain moved, and Charlie zoomed in on a telephoto lens the afternoon sun reflecting off of the surface.

"So Mr Woods," he chuckled.

"The game is still on, is it?" He said, "Well we'll just have to go to plan 'B' won't we," he added smiling. Putting on his jacket, Charlie walked down his stairs and into his shop, turning the open sign over, opened the door, and stepped out on the pavement, greeting a passer-by, he then turned and locked the door, and strode in the direction of The Troubadour and Shirley.

"Hi gorgeous," he shouted as he entered, "Charlie" Shirley screamed as he walked to the bar, "my usual please darling," he said, as he sat down on a bar stool, "coming up Charlie" Shirley replied. Shirley placed Charlie's G and T on the bar and leaning forward, whispered, "Can I come round tonight, please Charlie," Charlie smiled, and on picking up his glass whispered, "what would you like me to do to you, my love?"

Shirley giggled, "You know full well, Charlie."

"So you want me to take all your clothes off, caress your body, suck your nipples."

"Stop it Charlie," she whispered, "that's not fair."

"Then when I've driven you crazy, I'll make love to you all night," he said, smiling.

"Oh my god," she whispered, her body shaking, "you've made me come Charlie, my knickers are all creamy and hot."

"Shirley! Customer!" They both heard. Shirley turned, red-faced, "Sorry Bert," she said, and moved down the bar. Charlie put down his G and T on the bar and went to the back wall, where the public telephone was situated, taking a shilling from his trouser pocket and feeding the machine, dialled the number, on hearing the phone being picked up, pressed button 'A' and stated.

"Your money's safe, but the police are watching my shop, so I'm going to have to leave it a few days, just stay where you are, and I'll be in touch" then he hung up the phone, and walked back to the bar and picked up his G and T. As soon as Shirley had finished serving, she was back leaning on the bar in front of Charlie, "I've had to take my nickers off, there a mess, and it's all your fault, Charlie," she whispered, "well don't bother wearing them tonight, my love," he replied.

"I love it when you talk dirty to me Charlie, you turn me on, you naughty man," she whispered, Charlie emptied his glass, and placed it on the bar, "fill this up precious, and I'll fuck your pussy all night," he whispered, "oh! Charlie," she said, picking up his glass, and with shaking hands placed the glass under the Gin optic and pushed up twice, she was shaking as she placed Charlies drink in front of him, "See what you've done to me Charlie," she said, "only because I love you precious, and you are going to give me two sons and two beautiful daughters like their mother," he replied smiling, "Charlie" Shirley whispered, tears streaming down her face.

"Well Mr Woods," he said to himself, as he headed home, "tonight I'll give your mates something to photograph, and we are consenting adults in a private dwelling, Enjoy!" he chuckled.

It was four minutes passed eight, when Charlie heard his shop door open, then close, "Make sure you lock the door darling," he shouted from the top of his stairs, "yes Charlie" Shirley replied, looking up at him.

"I'm waiting," he said, opening his silk dressing gown. Shirley screamed as she gazed at Charlies naked body, his love shaft at full erection.

"Oh my god, but your beautiful Charlie," she managed to say, rushing to the front door, and turning the key, locked the shop door. Shirley took the stairs three at a time, bursting into Charlies front sitting room to find him standing in front of the window, his dressing gown wrapped around his tall body.

"I much prefer it open darling," she whispered, pulling the belt loose, "and I prefer you naked, my love," he said, running Shirley's zip all the way down, Shirley shrugged her shoulders, the dress falling to the floor, "see my love," she said, pushing Charlies silk dressing gown of his shoulders, it joining her dress, "no knickers or bra, now please fuck my brains out darling, make me come," she said, putting her arms around him and crushing his lips, as Charlies hands caressed her breasts.

"Yes my darling," she whispered spreading her legs, as Charlie's love shaft entered her body, sliding all the way till their bodies fused together, "yes my love, now make me come, Charlie," she moaned.

They were still fused together, laying on the bed, Shirley laying on top of Charlie's naked body. Raising her head, she looked up at Charlies smiling face, "Are you happy Charlie?" She whispered.

"And why wouldn't I be my love," he replied, thinking, "I'll have to ask that prick Woods for some of those shots."

"Charlie?" Shirley asked.

"Did you mean what you said, about two boys, and two girls," she whispered.

"Bloody right, I did! Just as long as the boys look like me and the girls look like you, my precious," he chuckled. Shirley crushed their two bodies together, and sighed.

"I'll be just as happy if you want us just to live together Charlie, we don't have to get married, I love you Charlie, I always have, and I always will, as long as we are together, I'll be the happiest girl in the world."

"So you don't want me to make an honest women of you then?" he asked smiling.

"What I want my love," she said, squeezing her virginal muscle, "is for you to make me pregnant, I want a little you inside me, please."

"Oh! Okay," he said, smiling, "but it's only because I'm in love with you Shirley," he whispered.

"Oh! Charlie," she sobbed as she fell onto his chest, "you mean that?" she asked sobbing, "What I can't understand darling," he said, "is why a young gorgeous creature like you, is in love with an old fart like me," he chuckled.

Shirley sat bolt upright, her hand on her hips, and a scowl on her face. "Now! listen here Charlie Gibbs, don't you dare! Call the man I'm in love with, and always will be, an old fart. You hear me," she hollered.

Charlie smiled up at the face. "Did you know when you sit up like that, your tits go all hard, and your nipples bright red," he chuckled.

"Don't try and change the subject Charlie," she tried to say, then added, "do they?" As they both burst out laughing.

Chapter Sixty-One

Trevor Woods picked up his phone and began to dial, as he sat behind his desk, "Come on," he said, after the fifth ring, "yes," he heard, "this is D.C.S. Woods," he replied.

"What's the status at the moment," he added. There was silence for a minute, then a cough, "D.S. Briggs here Gov," came the reply, "nothing much happening at the moment, he's had four customers, I only took over at eight this morning, took a shot of a young female leaving the premises, at eight ten Gov, there was a couple arrived at nine o five, they looked like husband and wife, then an elderly gentleman at ten o nine, and finally an elderly woman at ten thirty five, other than that it's been dead quiet, Gov."

"And you have them all on film Sergeant?" Trevor asked.

"Yes Gov," came the reply, "any photos of the suspect Sergeant?" he asked.

"Only him having his breakfast Gov," Trevor was told, "what about the officers on nights Sergeant, did they have anything to report?" Trevor asked. There was silence for over a minute, "I asked if the officers on nights had anything to report, Sergeant."

"Yes Gov, I heard you," came the reply, "well did they!" Trevor asked, his temper rising.

"Yes Gov, but it might be better if you asked them," came the reply.

"Why! Sergeant," he shouted, "because Gov, the young female I saw leaving this morning, spent the night there."

"And!" Trevor hollered, "they were seen in the window, with no cloths on Gov." Trevor took the phone away from his ear, "Fuck it," he said, then putting the phone to his ear, and lowering his voice said, "no one sees that film Sergeant, but me, got it."

"Yes Gov," came the reply, "thank you Sergeant" Trevor answered, and put the phone down.

"That's all I fucking need," he said, "photos of that bastard Gibbs getting his fucking leg over, shit!"

"He couldn't have seen the surveillance chaps surely?" he said to himself, running his hands through his hair.

Chapter Sixty-Two

Trevor Woods opened the door to Charlie's Heraldry Shop, the small doorbell signifying a customer. Charlie looked up from his counter and smiled. "I wondered how long it would take him to pay me a visit," he said to himself.

"Mr Woods," he hollered smiling, "sorry! Detective Chief Superintendent Woods, how can I help you Sir?" Charlie asked.

"Just popped in to settle up Charlie, I hate owing money," Trevor replied.

"Very commendable of you Sir." Charlie smiled. "I was just about to have my afternoon cuppa, would you care to join me, tea or coffee," he said.

"Coffee will be fine, Charlie."

"It's only instant, I'm afraid," Charlie said, making for his stairs, "he wants to see if his mates across the road can be seen," he said to himself, as he climbed the stairs, "sugar, milk, weak, strong?" Charlie asked. Smiling to himself.

"Strong, white and sweet, please Charlie," Trevor replied.

"Just like the women we want, Mr Woods," Charlie chuckled.

"Whilst we're on our own Charlie, forget the Mr, it's Trevor, okay."

"Whatever tickles your fancy, Trevor, if you go into the front room I'll get the coffee, won't be a minute," Charlie said, as he walked into his small kitchen.

Charlie filled the kettle with water and turning on the gas hob top, took the battery lighter, lit the burner, placing the kettle down. Then taking a bottle of milk from the small fridge, a bottle of Camp coffee and sugar bowl from a cupboard, placed them all on the kitchen bench, "Just waiting for the kettle to boil Mr Woods," he shouted, but receiving no reply, poked his head around the kitchen door, then quickly dived back into his kitchen smiling. Trevor Woods was standing at Charlie's window, his hands crossing and uncrossing.

"Won't be long," he shouted again, picking up a tin of biscuits and placing them on a tray, just as the whistling kettle began to scream.

"There you go," Charlie said, as he walked into his front room, to find Trevor Woods sitting on his settee.

"Nice little set up, you've got here, Charlie," Trevor commented.

"Thanks Mr Woods, it does me," Charlie replied.

"I did say whilst we are on our own Charlie, you could dispense with the Mr Woods, didn't I?" Trevor asked.

"Yes you did," Charlie replied smiling, "but out of respect, and the fact that you are now a Superintendent, I feel uncomfortable calling you by your first name, Mr Woods, sorry!" Charlie stated.

"One strong, white, sweet coffee," he said, offering Trevor a cup and saucer, "thanks Charlie, so you live here on your own, do you?" Trevor asked. Taking a sip of his coffee. Charlie grinned, "Used to Mr Woods, but not anymore, I'm wrapped to say."

"How come Charlie?" Trevor asked. Forcing a smile.

"Well," Charlie began, "to cut a long story short, I've met someone, and we're going to live together, I never thought it would happen, but it would appear that she's loved me for some time, but wouldn't make the first move, plus she says she's a great cook, and I thought I was too old for her, so I never made a move either, but it would seem age doesn't matter," Charlie said, grinning, "and you've got the snapshots to prove it," he said to himself.

"So are you going to stay here Charlie?" Trevor asked same forced smile, "and why wouldn't I? Nice little business, got two bedrooms, if kids come along, don't have to travel to work, just walk downstairs, only time I go out is to drum up business, like the other day when I saw you at Shannon's, I'll show you the Flanagan's coat of arms, when we're finished here, definitely Irish, it's practically all green," he chuckled.

"But surely it's noisy, and there's no views?" Trevor asked picking up a biscuit and taking a bite. "During the day there's traffic but it gets quiet about six, you get the occasional bus, and the bedrooms are at the back, so sleeping is no problem, and the view Ha! Some of the thing that young couples get up to in doorways Mr Woods," Charlie chuckled.

"They would be a right turn on. When Akiva lived over the road, I'd be sitting over there," he said, pointing, "if a couple were using his doorway, I would get my Aldis Lamp and flash dot dot dot, dash dash dash, dot dot dot, at his window, he'd come down and tell them to piss off, and take their French letters with them, but since he's gone, there everywhere, randy little bastards," Charlie chuckled.

"Akiva?" Trevor asked.

"Yes Mr Woods, Akiva Goldman, he was a little Jewish tailor, lovely little bloke, brilliant bespoke tailor, but he's gone back to Jerusalem, something to do with his family, the shops been up for sale for ages, so his doorway is probably chocking a block full of French letters, not a very good selling point, Ay?" Charlie said, smiling.

"Well thanks for the coffee Charlie, and here's the fifty quid I owe you," he said, getting up from the settee, and taking out an envelope from his inside jacket pocket, "thanks Mr Woods, but please have this one on me, I've got Michael Flanagan's to deliver, and I picked up two more when I left you," Charlie lied.

"No Charlie, I insist, I could have you up for trying to bribe a police officer," he chuckled.

"But my coat of arms is now framed and hanging in my office, so thank you," he said, giving Charlie the envelope, "if you put any business my way Mr Woods" Charlie said, smiling, "I won't forget it, I'll show you Mike Flanagan's when we go downstairs."

"Maybe another time, Charlie, but I'm in a bit of a hurry, but thanks," Trevor replied, offering Charlie his hand. Charlie picked up the tray and took it into his kitchen, placing it in the kitchen bench, "cosy," Charlie heard, as Trevor Woods stood in the kitchen doorway, "as I said, Mr Woods, it does me."

"Well thanks again for the coffee and chat, and it's nice to hear you've found someone Charlie, hope it works out for you."

"It will Mr Woods, it will," Charlie said, smiling, as he opened his shop door, and watched as his visitor walk towards a Land Rover.

Chapter Sixty-Three

"You've got a visitor Brian," his mother said, as he walked through the front door, "a Mr Smith, he's in the front room, I offered him a cup of tea, but he said, he didn't want one."

"So what does he want Mum?" Brian asked, as he walked down their hall, "don't ask me," came the reply. Brian opened the front room door and froze, sitting on their settee was Charlie Gibbs, Brian immediately put his finger to his lips, and mouthed, "don't say a word."

"Mr Smith," he shouted, "sorry I haven't got back to you earlier, but it took me a long time to find that engine part you were looking for, but I was able to get one just the other day, it's in my shed," he said, loudly, and beckoned Charlie.

Charlie seeing Brian's mother at the door stood up, "Thank you Brian," was all he said, as he followed Brian into the back garden, and headed for Brian's shed.

"Do you need any help Brian?" He heard his mother asked.

"No Mum, but I'd love a cup of your special tea, thanks, and can you make it two tots, please," he said, over his shoulder, as he turned the combination lock.

"What are you doing here Charlie," he whispered, "come to check on the parcel, have you?" he asked.

"No Brian, I haven't, but I need to speak to you, that's all" Charlie said, as Brian opened the door, and looked back at the house to see his mother still standing there.

"Well! We can't talk here" Brian whispered, "Mum thinks you've come to pick something up, so I'll give you a small cardboard box, we'll walk back to the house, you'll say, 'Thank you Brian' and leave, okay?" he asked switching on the fluorescent light.

"You know my shop Brian don't you?" Charlie asked. Brian looked at Charlie, "Er! You could say that Charlie, seeing as how your one of our most regular customer, bit of a stupid question if you ask me," Brian replied.

"Yes okay, it was stupid, but are you doing anything tonight?" Charlie asked.

"Well I was going to the Odeon Cinema, why," Brian stated.

"Do you know the alley way at the back of the shops?" Charlie asked.

"I know it's there, but I've never had the need to use it" came the reply.

"At the back of my shop, there's a small yard, at the bottom is a double garage, the only way into the yard is through the garage, I'll leave the door open, you drive your van in next to my ford, press the button on the door remote, and the door will close, I'll know you've arrived because the security light will go out, I'll come down and meet you, okay?" Brian stood there for a minute thinking, "This sounds a bit suss to me Charlie, all this cloak and dagger stuff."

"Right Brian," Charlie began, "you come round tonight, and I'll explain everything to you, you've had fifty quid for picking up the parcel, and when we get rid of it, you'll get another one hundred quid, and as far as your concerned, it's all legal, I know you might think it's all cloak and dagger, but I'm keeping you out of it, once the package has gone, along with the individual, I can relax, I should have told the bloke to 'Fuck off' in the first place, but I felt sorry for the poor sod, so will I see you tonight?" Charlie asked.

"So I'm not doing anything illegal Charlie?" he was asked.

"No son, you are not, you picked something up, and you'll drop something off, and you'll be one hundred and fifty quid richer, with no ties, okay."

"See you tonight Charlie" Brian said, handing him an empty shoe box.

Charlie looked at his wrist-watch, it was five past seven, when his security light, flickered and went out, "Thanks Brian," he said, as he made his way down his stairs, and into his workshop. Opening his back door to see a smiling Brian quickly walking up his garden path.

"Glad you could make it son," Charlie said, as Brian climbed the three concrete steps and entered Charlie's workshop.

"We'll stay down here, so take a pew mate," Brian was told.

"So this is where you work Charlie?" Brian said, looking around, "Nice set up," he added, as he sat down, "right! You ready?" he was asked.

"I was born ready Charlie," Brian chuckled.

"The bloke I'm helping out, is or was something to do with the church."

"Like a vicar you mean," Brian chipped in, "yes! Something like that Brian, anyway, the package contains religious stuff, a gold cross, and challis, some very old parchments and bibles," he lied, "and people are after it, so they've brought in the law."

"But you said," Brian exclaimed, Charlie raised his hand, "hang on a minute," he said, seeing the concern on Brian's face, "the package belongs to a church in Ireland, it was stolen from them some years ago, but this chap has found it, and is taking it back, the church that stole it have told the police, so now they are involved, I've had them round my shop asking me if I know anything about it, and of course I said, no, so one evening this week, all I want you to do is bring the package into my garage in your van, I'll put it in my car, then you drive the car to an address, you put the keys under the mat, and make your way back here, leaving the car."

"Why didn't the Irish church tell the police?" Brian asked.

"Because it was southern Ireland, not northern Ireland, so the English police weren't interested Brian."

"Oh!" Came the reply.

"And if anyone asks you, this is what you tell them," Charlie said.

Two nights later, Charlie sat staring at his security light then his wrist-watch, "Come on Brian," he said to himself, then smiled as the light went out, Charlie was down his stairs like a flash, the back door was flung open, and he ran down his garden path, as Brian opened the exit garage door, "get into the Ford Brian and wait, I'll sort everything out, then you can be off, okay?" He said, slightly out of breath.

"You sure Charlie?" he was asked.

"Yes mate," Charlie replied. As he opened the vans back doors, and removed the suite case, then moving over to his Zephyr, popped the boot. Taking a penknife from his trouser pocket, jemmied both suite case locks, and lifted the lid. His eyes bulged at the sight before him, rows and rows of neatly wrapped five pound notes, taking a holdall from inside his boot, he began filling it, "Four thousand one hundred and fifty pounds, thank you very much, Shaun," he said to himself, as he closed the suite case lid and engaged the locks, slamming down the boot and picking up his holdall, he walked to the driver's window.

"You have the address Brian, so just put the keys under the mat, and make your way back here, leave the car at the address, okay, and no! Speeding."

"Okay Charlie," Brian replied firing up the Zephyr Six, "and come in the back way when you get back, here's five quid for a taxi," Charlie said, putting the brand new note through the drivers open window.

"Thanks Charlie," came the reply, as Brian backed the Zephyr out of Charlies garage, and drove off.

Chapter Sixty-Four

"Well the only new info I was able to get from Alf," Keir began, "was the van driver was young, and had a blonde crew cut, the rest we knew," he said. Trevor Woods took a large envelope from his briefcase, and throwing it onto Keir's desk said, "Don't say a word and don't let Fiona see these."

"Why?" Bill asked standing up, and walking over to where Keir was sitting behind his desk.

"You'll see," came the reply, Keir opened the envelope and withdrew, twenty four colour photographs, "what's wrong with these?" Keir asked, as he looked at a couple going into Charlie Gibbs' shop.

"Keep going," he was told, "a single bloke, now an elderly woman, So?" he asked again, "Keep going," he was told, "another couple, Jesus! Christ!" both Keir and Bill hollered in unison, "precisely," Trevor stated.

"Well one things for sure," Bill chuckled.

"Your mate's well hung."

"He's not a fucking mate of mine Bill, and I'm bloody sure he knew we were watching him, in front of a window, with the lights on, give me a break fellers."

"You could sell these Trevor, make a bloody fortune, especially this one," Keir said, holding up an eight by ten, "never tried it that way," he chuckled.

"Never tried what that way?" They all heard, as Fiona knocked and entered Keir's office, all three men looked at each other, until Keir stated.

"Well Ma'am it would appear that surveillance had been organised for Charlie Gibbs' establishment, unbeknown to the officers doing the surveillance, Gibbs had a female companion, and would appear that the two had sex in open view, which was recorded on film, Ma'am," Keir sheepishly stated.

"And what does that tell us, gentlemen?" she asked. Snatching the eight by ten from Keir's grip, "Um!" she said, smiling, "interesting," she added, looking at the photograph, "I would say," she said, her hand going to her chin, "that Mr Charles Gibbs, is taking us for complete idiots, 'A', he knows nothing of

O'Brien, and is enjoying the notoriety of making us look like complete idiots where we should be looking for O'Brien, so he's leading us on a wild goose chase, or 'B', he is a very exceptional and clever criminal, any ideas?" she asked.

"Well," Trevor Woods began, "I went round to his shop on the pretext of paying for a Woods Coat of arms, that he had done, not by my request, I might add. He invited me to partake of a cup of coffee, I could believe my luck, when he invited me up into his flat, I needed to see if my lads were obvious, so I jumped at the chance, whilst Gibbs was making the coffee I went to the window, and for all intense and purposes, all I could see in the flat opposite was a lace curtain, I tried to question him, he told me that he had met someone, who was going to move in with him, and he sounded serious, and by the photos they certainly have a thing going. Either I'm losing it, or he's as you said, a very clever criminal, because he had me believing him, Fiona," Trevor said.

"So the premises has been under twenty four hour surveillance, has it?" Fiona asked.

"Yes," Trevor replied.

"Front and back?" she asked. There was silence, all eyes looking at Trevor, "Well," he sheepishly replied.

"There's only an alley way at the back of the property, so there's nowhere that an officer could conceal himself," he said, looking at the floor.

"So after allowing your lads to take pornographic photos, all he has to do is nip out the back, open a gate, or whatever, and go his merry way, yes?" she asked.

"Well I'm glad it's on your patch, Trevor, and not on ours," she said, and stormed out of Keir's office, slamming the door behind her.

"I've fucked up, haven't I?" he asked no one answered his question, "He told me about an old Jewish Tailor that lived in the flat opposite, that if Gibbs was looking out of his front window at night, and saw some bloke getting his leg over in the doorway, he would get some sort of lamp and flash a signal, because the old Jew boy was fed up getting rid of used French letters," Bill and Keir couldn't hold it back any longer, and doubled over laughing.

"Fuck you two," Trevor shouted, and stormed out of Keir's office.

"I feel sorry for the poor bloke" Keir just managed to say, before bursting into laughter again.

"But our brilliant new Super was right Tel," Bill stated.

"I'm glad it's not on our patch mate. How the fuck, did he become a superintendent?" he asked.

Keir was quiet for over four minutes, and Bill could see by the expression on Keir's face not to invade his thoughts, Keir was not on this planet, he was somewhere else, he always did this when he tried to solve a problem, so Bill just stood there and waited. Then as if he was coming out of a trance, Keir shot up straight, his first words were, "Fuck it."

"Yes Tel, I would go along with that sentiment myself" Bill remarked, "I can't understand Trevor," Keir began, "what info have we got, 'A' the money has gone, Who took it, a blonde headed young lad, what was he doing picking up the parcel, he was delivering pizzas. So where would you be looking first? And what would you ask?" "Have you delivered pizza's to a garage in Tilbury."

"No we haven't."

"Yes we did."

"Do you have a driver with a blonde crew cut?"

"Yes we do, It's not fucking rocket science, Bill," but as Fiona said, "it's not our patch, is it?" he asked, putting his head in his hands.

"You could run that scenario passed our leader Tel, let her make the decision," Bill stated.

"You're right, mate," Keir said, as he stood up.

Chapter Sixty-Five

Brian sat opposite Charlie smiling, "Easy Peasy," he chuckled.

"Did as you said, pulled up outside that flash house, put the keys under the mat, got out, silently shut the door, walked to the end of the road, found a phone box, called a taxi, and here I am, Charlie," he said, grinning.

"You didn't see anybody?" Charlie asked.

"At that time of night, quiet as the grave, Charlie," came the reply.

"This is for you Brian," Charlie said, handing him a bulging envelope, "there's one hundred and fifty quid in there, and my thanks, and you know exactly what to say if anyone ask you about picking up that religious stuff, Yes?" Charlie asked.

"Yes Charlie, a vicar asked me to drop of some pizza's at a garage in Tilbury, and pick up a case and meet him at Waterloo Station, and he gave me fifty quid for doing it" Brian said, smiling, "great Brian, and thanks again, you've helped me out of a jam, so what's the thing with your mum?" he asked.

Brian cracked up laughing, "That's why my old man pissed off," he managed to say, "she has to know everything, and talk about nosy, the number of locks I've put on my shed, but she somehow managed to open them, but I bought a really expensive combination lock with eight tumblers, I know she's tried it, because I always leave it on all zero's, and when I unlock it the numbers are all over the place," he chuckled.

"I got the third degree on what I'd supposedly got you, so whatever you do, don't ever come round my place again," he added.

Charlie had two things to do today as he locked his shop door, and began a brisk walk down Poplar High street. First was a phone box, second would be The Troubadour and Shirley. This time the phone box was vacant, no elderly gentleman phoning a hospital about his ailing wife, as Charlie tool hold of the half cup handle and pulled open the heavy red door and entered. Taking a shilling and placing it into the slot provided, he began to dial, on the second ring Charlie heard the phone being picked up, pressing button.

"A," he said, "listen" not getting a reply, he smiled, "there's a Ford Zephyr Six parked at the curb, the keys are under the driver's mat, your money is in the boot of the car, the logbook is in the glove box, the registered owner is a Shaemus Donahue. Take the car and get out of my house, I've had the law crawling all over me, and I'm not going down for you, so wait until tonight and I don't want to see or hear from you ever again, tap the phone twice in reply," Charlie waited only seconds before he heard two taps, and the word, "thanks," before the line went dead.

Putting the phone down, Charlie screamed, "Yes!" and opened the heavy door a broad grin on his face, "the Troubadour, here we come," he said to himself.

Charlie walked into the Public House, and stood at the doorway, watching Shirley, as she ran from one end of the bar to the other, serving customers. Then at the top of his voice called, "I'll have my usual, gorgeous," this stopped Shirley in her tracks, "coming right up, Charlie," she called back beaming, as Charlie walked toward the bar.

The bar was about half full, as Charlie sat down on a bar stool, "Here you are my love," she whispered, placing Charlie's G and T on the bar, "have you got a minute precious?" Charlie asked, taking a sip of his drink.

"I've got all the time in the world, for you," she whispered leaning over the bar, "good," replied Charlie, "because I want to ask you something," he said, taking her left hand, "the only time I will get down on my knees for you, is when I kiss that little heart."

"Charlie!" She said, turning bright red, and tried to pull away, "So I thought maybe you would consider wearing this," he said, flicking open a small square blue box, exposing a row of, three, light blue, one point five, carrot diamonds, encased in a twenty-four carat gold ring.

"Charlie," she screamed, throwing her arms around Charlie's neck and kissing him. Everyone in the pub were now looking at Shirley's beaming face, including Bert, "about bloody time too Charlie," he hollered, giving the thumbs up sign.

"Cheers Bert!" Charlie replied. Returning the gesture, as Shirley placed the ring on her left hand, and burst into tears.

"The drinks are on the house," Bert hollered, a grin spreading across his face, "thanks Bert, but this is Shirley's and my day, so the drinks are on me.]," Charlie hollered back.

Chapter Sixty-Six

O'Brien walked up the stairs, and into the front bedroom, pulling the lace curtain to one side, looked up and down Ambassador drive, he noticed about a dozen cars parked at the curb, including the Zephyr Six parked right outside number twenty-seven, but no pedestrians, "I'll give it maybe another hour," he said to himself, as he let go of the lace curtain.

O'Brien walked back downstairs and into the chef's kitchen, picking up the key Charlie had hidden, opened the back door and placed the key in its Hidey-hole, next, taking the house key, locked the back door, placing the key on the stainless steel bench top. Looking out of the kitchen window at Charlie's garden, he thought back to his childhood, and his twin brothers, Brendon and Michael, "Sorry Lads," he whispered. Physically shaking himself, he walked out of the kitchen, and into the hall, making for the stained glass front door, using his gloved left hand, he turned the doorknob and slowly opened the door, stepping out of the entrance porch, he glanced up and down Ambassador Drive, even with night coming on, the area seemed clear, O'Brien quietly closed the door, hearing the Yale Lock click locking the front door, ran up the front path, opened the gate, and strode to the Zephyr Six, opening the driver's door, bent down and retrieved the key that Brian had placed there, sliding into the driver's seat, and now being able to use his mechanical hand, pulled the door shut.

Switching on the ignition, he fired up the straight six, and let it idle for a moment, "I'll need a full tank," he said, looking at the fuel gauge, as he slowly eased the Ford into first gear, and pulled away from the curb, making for the 'A' three owe eight and Staines Road. O'Brien had reached Upper Sunbury Road, heading for Staines Road, when up ahead a yellow 'Shell' service station sign, glowed against the night sky.

Turning onto the forecourt, and driving over the pressured airline, letting the attendant know a customer had arrived, O'Brien coasted to a pump, displaying, "Shell Super." Switching off the engine, O'Brien opened the driver's door and exited the vehicle, looking toward the office, began to smile as the attendant opened the door and began walking towards him, then O'Brien froze, as two police officers came out of the building, and began walking toward where O'Brien was standing.

"How much Gov?" The attendant asked smiling, "Er! Fill it up please, young man" O'Brien managed to say.

"Nice set of wheels Sir, it's a six isn't it?" The elderly officer asked.

"Yes sergeant," O'Brien said, noting the three stripes, "going far sir, or just going for a joy ride?" The Sergeant asked.

O'Brien began to relax, "They're not looking for me," he said to himself, and began to smile at the two officers.

"Afraid not Sergeant, I'm headed for Holyhead, just received a phone call from my sister in law, my brother has been in a hit and run accident, and is in a critical condition in I.C.U. So I need to catch the first ferry to Dublin," he lied, "did they catch the driver Sir?" The constable asked.

"I don't know officer, all my sister-in-law said was, 'Shaun's been hit by a car, and is in I.C.U. And to get here quickly'."

"Sorry to hear that Sir," The sergeant said, "if it would help, we could help you get out of the built-up area, rather quickly," he added. O'Brien put his left hand to his eyes and clearing his throat, softly replied.

"It's only a five-hour drive Sergeant, but thank you so much for your kind offer."

"Are you sure Sir?" he was asked. O'Brien just nodded his head, and taking a handkerchief from his pocket, and dabbed his eyes.

"That will be three pounds seven shilling and six pence, sir," the attendant said, replacing the petrol cap, "poor bastard," O'Brien heard the constable say, as the two officers walked away.

O'Brien had made good time as he hit the outskirts of Liverpool, then turning onto the 'A' fifty five, he switched on the Zephyr's interior light and looked at his Timex wrist-watch, "Might just make the night ferry," he said, taking the Zephyr up to seventy miles an hour. He had passed Colwym Bay, Liandudno, and was approaching Bangor, when he switched on the interior light once again, and looked at his wrist-watch, "I'll be cutting it fine," he said, taking the Zephyr up to eighty miles an hour.

O'Brien followed the 'HolyHead Ferry' road signs at a more sedate speed, but as he turned into the embarkation area, he was confronted by a police officer closing the pair of steel gates, accelerating up to thirty miles an hour he shot forward, breaking only feet away from the now closed steel gates. Jumping out of the Zephyr, he shouted, "I have to get on that ferry officer."

The police officer had seen the approaching Ford, and began walking towards O'Brien, "Sorry sir," he said, "they're lifting the ramp, so you'll have to wait for the morning ferry," he stated.

"But I need to get to Dublin as quickly as possible officer, my brother could be dying, he was in a hit and run accident," O'Brien lied.

"Sorry to hear that Sir," the officer replied.

"But the ferry ramp is up, and she's pulling away, so as I just told you, you'll have to catch the morning ferry," he said, walking away, leaving O'Brien standing there.

"Damn," O'Brien cursed, as he walked back to the Zephyr, sliding into the driver's seat, put the car in reverse and backed up, finding the Ferry parking area, pulled in and killed the ignition, he sat there looking at the locked gates, "Sorry Brendon, sorry Michael," he said, then getting out of the driver's seat, opened the back door and laid across the back seat, pulling the door shut, five minutes later he was fast asleep.

Chapter Sixty-Seven

"Dickson," Keir said, picking up his phone, "good afternoon Inspector, Alf here," came the reply, "hi Alf, how can I help you?" Keir asked.

"Do you remember asking me about the white van that delivered those Pizza's, and I said, I hadn't taken any notice?" Alfred asked.

"Yes Alf," Keir replied, sitting bolt upright, "well," Alf began, "we just finished lunch, and one of the lads asks me, "any chance of ringing up that Anton's Pizza Parlour for more of his sea food Pizzas." I asked him how he knew the name, he said, it was on the boxes that the pizza's came in. Hope that might help Inspector, sorry I didn't pick up on it before," he said.

A broad grin spread across Keir's face, "Alf," he yelled into the mouthpiece, "you are a diamond mate, thank you," he said, as Fiona knocked and walked into Keir's office.

"Good news, I hope?" she asked smiling, "The pizza's came from Anton's Pizza Parlour, one of Alf's mechanics asked him if he could order a sea food pizza from this Anton's, his name was on the boxes the pizza's came in," Keir said, grinning, "and they say there's no justice in the world," Fiona chuckled.

"Call Trevor Wood, Keir," she added, "and put it on speaker, I'm going to enjoy this," she said, as she slid onto Keir's desk. The two of them heard the phone ringing, then a male voice answered, "Woods."

"Trevor! How are we today?" Fiona stated.

"Hi Fiona," came the reply, "so how's it going?" she asked there was silence for a moment, then Fiona was asked.

"Do you know how many pizza placed there are in the London area, it's like living in bloody Naples, Ities everywhere," he said.

"Perhaps you might like to try Anton's Pizza Parlour, because that was where the pizza's came from," she said, covering her mouth.

"How! The blazes did you come by that information?" he asked.

"Two ways Trevor, one! Luck, and two! Good Detective work," a gruff "thanks Fiona," was heard, before the phone went dead.

"Nothing quite like a bit of appreciation, and that was Nothing! Like a bit of appreciation," she said, smiling.

Trevor Woods Land Rover screamed to a halt outside Anton's shop, the driver's door was thrown open, and Trevor Woods stormed into the Parlour, his warrant card in his hand, "Yes officer," a smiling Anton, greeted him, "did you deliver four pizzas to a garage in Tilbury?" He shouted.

Anton put his finger to his lips, "There is no need to raise your voice sir, we are more than happy to answer all your questions."

"Sorry," Trevor replied.

"Having a bad day," he added, "so what was it you asked did we deliver a pizza to where?" Anton asked.

"Tilbury, and it was four pizza's," Trevor replied.

"Can you wait a minute officer?" Anton asked.

"I'll just go and ask the lads, I can't remember where the lads go, we cover such a large area," three minutes later Anton returned, "Brian here," Anton said, pointing, "remembers taking four pizzas down to a garage in Tilbury, officer."

"Hi," Brian said, smiling, "can I help you?" He added.

"Is there somewhere we can talk in private?" Trevor asked.

"Well there's the rest room, I'll tell Cyril to piss off if you like," Brian replied.

"You can use my office, officer," Anton said, smiling, then turning to Brian, asked.

"You haven't been speeding Brian, have you?"

"No he hasn't," Trevor stated walking towards Anton's office. Once inside he said, "Close the door Brian and sit down, please."

"Certainly officer, was there something wrong with the pizzas?" Brian asked knowing full well why this copper was there.

"I wouldn't know Brian, I just want you to tell me why you delivered four pizza's to a garage in Tilbury, and who asked you to do it?" Trevor asked.

"And do you mind if I record your reply?" He added, taking a small tape recorder from his jacket pocket and placing it on Anton's desk.

"No problem" Brian replied smiling, "so who told you to take those pizza's down to Tilbury?" Trevor asked switching on the tape recorder.

"Oh! That would have been the vicar," Brian said, still smiling.

"What do you mean, Vicar?" Trevor asked.

"Well I knew he was a vicar or something, coz when I delivered a pizza to his place in Bishops Road, he would always give me a shilling tip, and say 'Thank you, and bless you my son', so he must be something to do with a church," he said.

"So how come he asked you to take four pizza's down to Tilbury?" Trevor asked.

"Yeah," Brian said, screwing up his face, "I pulls in one day, and there's this old geezer standing there, I didn't recognise him at first, not until he came out with this 'My son' stuff. Then he tells me he'll give me fifty quid, if I drop off four pizza's and a letter, and pick up a parcel with church stuff in it, and take it to the left luggage at Waterloo Station, where he'll give me the fifty quid. So that's what I did."

"Why?" Brian asked.

"How do you know the parcel was church stuff?" Trevor asked.

"Coz! He told me, he said, someone had nicked a gold cross and a challis thing, and some old bibles, he'd found them and nicked them back, and was taking then back to where they had been nicked from."

"So you picked up the parcel and then what?" Trevor asked.

"As I said, he told me to meet him at Waterloo Station and give him the parcel, well, it wasn't a parcel it was a suitcase, so that's what I did, and he gave me the fifty quid."

"Then what did you do?" Trevor asked.

"I got in me van and drove back home."

"Why?" Brian asked.

"Did you see which way he went, Brian?" Trevor stated.

"Didn't take any notice, snot every day someone drops you fifty quid for delivering pizzas, is it?" He chuckled. Then straight faced asked.

"Do you mind telling me what's this all about, he is a Vicar, for Christ sake, what's he been doing, mucking about with Choir boys, has he?"

"Thank you Brian, by the way do you know Charlie Gibbs?" Trevor asked.

Brian smiled. "Charlie Gibbs, Akiva Goldman, Clive Dunn, Cyril Shepard, Percy Whittle, Bert Newberry, do you want me to go on, they're all my regulars," he said, smiling.

"Thank you Brian," Trevor said, rising, and switching off the tape recorder, then putting his face only inches away from Brian's nose, whispered, "you do realise, lying to a police officer, is a criminal offence Brian, don't you?"

"Look," Brian said, "I helped a vicar get some stuff back that had been nicked, okay he gave me fifty quid, if that's against the law, I'm guilty, and seeing as how you're a copper I can't tell you to 'F' off can I," he said.

Trevor smiled. "Don't ever cross me Brian" Trevor said, as he opened Anton's office door and walked out.

Trevor knocked twice, and opened Keir's office door, to find the room empty, "Fuck it," he said to himself, then making his way back down to reception, he walked over to the desk Sergeant, and producing his warrant card asked.

"Excuse me Sergeant, do you know where I can find, DCI Dickson, by any chance?" Sergeant Jeffery Frost looked up from the local Thurrock Gazette, and seeing the warrant card quickly slid the local newspaper into an open draw, "I think you will find them all in Superintendent Jarman's office Sir," he managed to say.

"Thank you Sergeant," Trevor replied smiling, "anything of interest?" he asked, pointing at the open draw.

"Not really Sir," Jeffery replied, using his right knee to close the draw.

Trevor knocked twice and waited, "Come," he heard Fiona say, on entering he was greeted with, "you look happy Trevor," as Fiona stood up and came round her desk, all four occupants stood as Trevor entered.

"Just thought you would like to listen to this," he said, taking a small tape recorder from his jacket pocket, "and I owe you a token of my gratitude," he added. Fiona took his outstretched hand, "No you don't Trevor, we were lucky, one of Alf's mechanics remembered the name on the pizza boxes, so Alf phone Keir and told him, so we told you," she said, smiling.

"Well thanks to you, I was able to talk to the driver, and I recorded the interview, see what you can make of it," he said, switching on the recorder. Keir, Bill, Liam, and Fiona sat and listened to the conversation.

"Well?" he asked, as the tape came to an end, there was silence for a moment when Liam asked.

"How old do you think the driver is Sir?"

"Why Sergeant?" Trevor asked.

"Well Sir," Liam began, "he sound quite young, it didn't sound rehearsed, and he seemed to answer your question without hesitation, and it's the information that he gave you, I think him saying that he went to Waterloo Station was informative. If I was O'Brien, I would tell him to meet me at Waterloo, knowing, if he was questioned, he would say Waterloo, making us believe he was heading south to Portsmouth, when in actual fact he's probably heading north or back to Ireland, my bet would be Ireland, Sir."

"Why do you think he's going back to Ireland Sergeant?" Trevor asked.

Liam smiled. "An Irish accent in London, would stick out like a sore thumb Sir, how would you hide a piece of straw, Sir?" Liam asked.

"In a haystack Sergeant," Trevor replied. Keir, Bill, and Fiona, smiled. "Why would he go back to Ireland?" Trevor asked.

"That's where it all started Trevor," Keir stated.

"That's where his two twin brothers were shot and killed, and where O'Brien was tortured by the Garda, he tried taking out all your mates at New Scotland Yard, and the Army at Adlershot, and failed, so I think Liam could be right, he's not giving up on payback," he said.

Chapter Sixty-Eight

"I'll teach you! You fenian bastard, you don' fuck with us protestant police, you hear!" As another live cigarette was screwed into O'Brien's back. O'Brien woke screaming, he could still feel his skin burn as the Garda officer, stubbed out a live cigarette on his back, even though years had passed, the memory was as clear today, as it was those years ago. O'Brien began to sit up, when he heard someone knocking on the window, the temperature outside must have been low, because all O'Brien's windows were misted up, all he could see was a shadow of a man tapping on his window with a torch.

Winding down the window, he was confronted by a young police officer, "The cue for the ferry will be starting soon, Sir, if you would like to go over to the kiosk and purchase your ticket, you will be first onto the ferry," O'Brien was told, "thank you officer," he said, yawning.

"You're welcome Sir, it should be an easy crossing today, the Irish Sea is as flat as a board," came the reply. O'Brien was the first one onto the ferry at Holyhead, and the first to disembark at Dublin's Terminal One, three hours and forty minutes later. Easing the Zephyr onto Terminal Road South, and adhering to the speed limit, made his way to twenty three, O'Connell Street and the Hotel Rui Plaza, The Gresham, this luxury hotel had stood on this location since eighteen seventy, and was one of the prides, of this beautiful city of Dublin.

O'Brien pulled to a stop at the entrance to the hotel, and killed the engine, as a full liveried door man walked down the main steps towards the Zephyr, "Good morning Sir, are we booking in?" O'Brien was asked, as he exited his vehicle.

Turning to face the doorman, O'Brien smiled. "That is my intention, I take it that there is accommodation available?" O'Brien asked.

"Most certainly Sir, I'll authorise someone to take your luggage, shall I," he said, walking to the rear of the Ford.

"That won't be necessary," O'Brien replied.

"But thank you, I only have one case," he said, popping the boot, and lifting out the case, "but if you could have my car parked under cover, I would be most grateful," he said, offering the door man the ignition keys, "very well Sir, I shall get a valet to move it immediately, enjoy your stay at The Gresham," he said, closing the driver's door, and ascending the Gresham steps.

O'Brien followed the doorman, who held open the door, as he arrived, "Reception's over there Sir," he said, pointing.

"Thank you," O'Brien replied as he strode toward an enormous ornate mahogany reception desk.

"Good morning Sir, and how may we help you?" he was asked by a very attractive, smiling young lady, she was wearing a white silk frilly collared blouse, buttoned up to her slender throat, over this, she wore an emerald green jacket, with the Gresham monogram embroidered over her left breast pocket.

"I would like a room please, young lady," O'Brien replied.

"And are they still serving breakfast?" he asked.

"How long do you anticipate staying at the Gresham, Sir," she asked, picking up the phone.

"About a week, to begin with, it will depend on how thing progress," O'Brien replied.

"Sorry about that Sir," she said, putting down the phone.

"The restaurant is still serving breakfast, but if you would prefer, you could have it delivered to your room Sir," she said, smiling.

"Now would you prefer any particular floor Sir?" she asked.

"And could I have your passport please," that smile again. O'Brien took out the passport, and handed it over to an outstretched hand, "any floor will be fine young lady, I've been travelling for over sixteen hours, so I'm hungry and very tired, so if I could have a full English breakfast sent to my room, I'll be able to catch up on both my problems," O'Brien stated.

Looking at the passport, the receptionist smiled. "Right Mr Donahue," she began, handing him a key, "your in room two two seven on the second floor, your full English breakfast will be with you in minutes, If you would be kind enough to sign here Sir," she said, rotating a large ledger to face him, "enjoy your stay with us Sir," she said, as O'Brien, just in time wrote Shaemus Donahue, and not Shaun O'Brien. By the time O'Brien had climbed the third wide stair case, he was breathing heavy, on reaching the second floor, he lent against the wall, then cursed himself, for not taking the lift, as the lift door opened, a maid wheeled out a covered trolley, she looked up as she pushed the trolley into the corridor, seeing O'Brien leaning against the wall asked.

"Are you all right, Sir?"

"Just getting my breath back, should have taken the lift," he replied.

"Are you the gentleman in two two seven, Sir?" she asked.

Pushing himself off of the wall, O'Brien replied, "Yes young lady."

"If you give me your key Sir, I'll open your door and set up your meal for you," she said.

"I'm fine thanks, young lady, just lead the way," he said, smiling.

"Just a few doors down, this way Sir," she said, as she push the trolley along the plush green carpet, then came to a stop and waited for O'Brien, "are you sure you're all right Sir," she asked again, as he came to a stop beside her.

"I've been travelling for over sixteen hour, I'm hungry and I'm tired, I'll have something to eat, and then sleep for a week, and I'll be fine," he said, unlocking the door.

"If you say so Sir, there is a bar fridge in your rocm, and a medicine cabinet in your bathroom," she said, wheeling the trolley into the room.

"Thank you Miss," O'Brien said, putting his left hand in his trouser pocket, and finding a note, handed it to the maid, "thank you Sir," she said, smiling, as she took the English one pound note, and began to uncover the trolley, "I can do that," O'Brien stated.

"It's no problem Sir," she replied.

"It's part of my job," as O'Brien laid down on the double bed, and sank into the soft mattress.

"Enjoy your meal Sir," she said, as she closed O'Brien's door, but O'Brien never heard her, he was fast asleep.

Chapter Sixty-Nine

"Morning Gov," Liam said, as Keir stepped out of his Morris One Thousand, and closed and locked the driver's door.

"Been on to a mate of mine in Belfast, to be on the lookout for O'Brien, he's asked if we can fax him all the info that we've got," Liam added.

"Not a problem, Liam," replied Keir, "but when you weigh it up, what! Have we got?" He said, as they both walked toward the stations doors, "He won't be travelling under the name of O'Brien, so you can pick any Irish name you like, he'll have gotten rid of the dog collar, so he'll look just like Joe Soap, the only thing we have got, is his left hand prints, and we're not sure if its Belfast, it could be Dublin, so as you told Trevor Woods, we're looking for an Irish Man, in Ireland," he said.

"But we do have his mug shots Gov, he can change his hair colour, grow a beard, or shave his head, our police artist could alter his mug shots, surely?" Liam stated.

"Yes he could Liam," Keir replied.

"It's worth a try," he added, as Liam held the door open for his boss, "I'll get onto it straight away Gov," he said, taking the stairs three at a time.

Keir had only just sat down at his desk when his door burst open, "Sorry to bother you Gov," an out of breath Liam stated. As he entered, "It's just an idea, but would it be okay if I popped over to Romford, and had a word with Father Patrick O'Connell?" he asked.

Keir smiled. "So what's going through that head of yours, Liam?" he asked.

"Well Gov," Liam began, "Father O'Connell grew up with O'Brien, they went to school together, although Father O'Connell is older, they both worked for Harland and Wolff, so maybe he can give us some background on O'Brien, because at the present moment we haven't got a hell of a lot, have we?" he asked.

"Have you had a word with the police artist, yet Liam?" Keir asked.

"I was just talking to constable Brett Grover, when the idea came to me Gov," Keir sat back in his chair smiling.

"Finish with the police artist, Liam then go and have a chat with Father O'Connell, okay?"

"Will do Gov," Liam said, as he sprinted from Keir's office.

"What the hell's got into young, Liam?" Bill asked as he walked into Keir's office, "He couldn't have travelled any faster if he'd been driving his M.G. As he shot passed me," he said, sitting down.

"Have we got a team, or! Have we got a team, Bill?" Keir chuckled. Bill just looked at his mate smiling, "So am I in the loop?" he asked.

"Liam's got a bee in his bonnet, so he's going over to Romford, to have a chat with Father Patrick O'Connell, to get as much low down on O'Brien as he can."

"If I were you Tel, I'd seriously think about a Superintendent job, because if you don't watch it, Liam's going to be sitting there," he chuckled pointing at Keir's chair.

Liam pulled his Red M.G. T.A. onto the 'A' twelve, and headed for Saint Joseph's Catholic Church Romford, "Might even pop into the plough and check out Sheila's tits," he chuckled to himself. Liam swung onto the gravel drive, and parked at the stone perimeter wall, expecting to see the two brothers pop their heads over it, but knew they never would, thanks to O'Brien and O'Toole. Liam extricated himself from his M.G and stretched his six foot plus frame, then leaning over and picking up his brief case from his passenger seat, strode through the ancient arch, and headed for Father Patrick's church. He was just about to enter the church porch when Father Patrick O'Connell and an elderly lady opened the ancient oak doors to the church, the two were in deep conversation and hadn't notice Liam's arrival, until Liam putting his right fist to his mouth, coughed loudly.

"Liam!" Father O'Connell shouted, making the lady jump.

"Hello Father," Liam replied smiling.

"Samantha," Patrick said, offering his hand in Liam's direction, "this is a very dear friend of mine, Detective Sergeant Liam Smith, Samantha, Liam, Liam, Samantha," he chuckled.

"Pleased to meet you sergeant," the lady said, offering Liam her hand.

"Likewise Ma'am," Liam replied taking her hand, and immediately regretting it, as she nearly crushed his hand.

"So what do I owe the pleasure of this call my son?" Father O'Connell asked.

"Just popped over to see how you were going Father, and I've got just a couple of questions that you might be able to help me with," Liam stated, rubbing the circulation back into his hand, "right Samantha," he said, turning, "I'll see you tomorrow evening at choir practice, yes?" he asked.

"Samantha has the most beautiful contralto voice, Liam, you must come and hear her sing, you truly must," he said, as a red-faced Samantha scurried away.

"There's coffee in the vestry Liam, why don't we go in there and I'll try and answer your questions," Father O'Connell said.

They were both sitting in Father O'Connell's vestry, a cup of instant coffee in their hands, when Father O'Connell asked, "So how can I help you Liam?"

Liam put his cup of coffee down on the vestry desk, and smiled. "I don't want to upset you Father, and I know it's a subject you would rather not talk about. But I need to know as much as possible about O'Brien, we've hit a brick wall, any help you can give us would be most appreciated."

Father O'Connell put his cup of coffee down on his vestry table, "Your right my son," he began, "and I appreciate you not referring to him as Father, so what do you want to know?" he asked, picking up his cup of coffee, and taking a sip.

"Everything Father, does he have a family, are his parents alive, everything Father?" Liam asked.

Father O'Connell leaned back in his chair, running his hands over his chin, "Hmm!" he began, as Liam took out his notebook, and Parker Fountain pen, "his father is dead, not a very nice person a drunk and a bully, his three sons took after him, how! Or even why! Shaun took holy orders I will never know, I put it down to his brothers being shot that made him see the light, obviously I was wrong, regarding his two sisters, they were also twins, they were just like their mother, tall, clever, and beautiful, I didn't know what happened with the girls, but their mother took them away, there were rumours that the father had tried to molest the girls, and the three boys watched, the mother tried to stop it and was beaten up, the next day whilst the men were at work, Mrs Kiara O'Brien, took Maeve and Niamh away."

"I don't know if the mother is still alive, the father was drunk at work, and fell into a ships hold, broke his neck and smashed his head on a metal girder on the way down, fell over one hundred feet, so I was told, every bone in his useless body was broken. Some years later I did meet Kiara, she had remarried, with her useless husband dying, and being a staunch Catholic divorce was out of the question, she told me the girls were doing well, one is a doctor, I think that was Maeve, and Niamh is a barrister, and the funny thing is, they married twins, Sean and Brendan O'Rourke, and I do believe according to Kiara they live in a very exclusive area of Belfast, I think it's called Malone Road, South Belfast. That's about it, I'm afraid Liam, so you haven't been able to apprehend O'Brien yet, I take it?" Father O'Connell asked.

"No father we haven't, but with this information, we might get lucky, so thank you, and I must say you look your old, young self again, compared to the last time I saw you, you were out cold when I saw you in Hornchurch Hospital," Liam said, smiling.

"Thank you Liam, I would never have believed a brother priest could have acted that way."

"I don't think O'Brien took his holy orders seriously Father," Liam said, as they both stood, shook hands and walked into the church.

"Take care my son, and may the almighty help you in your quest," Father O'Connell said, as they reach the church doors.

Liam fired up his M.G and backed out onto the main road, looking at his wrist-watch he smiled. "A late lunch," he said, and headed towards The Plough.

"This is going to be a giggle," he chuckled as he walked into the practically empty Plough's public bar, and sure enough, behind the bar, polishing her nails was Sheila, the only other occupants were two elderly gentlemen, playing dominoes.

"I'll have a half larger and lime, and a ham salad roll, please Sheila," he said, as he sat on a bar stool at the very end of the bar, "hello stranger," she said, smiling, as she sauntered towards him, "long time no see, so what would you like?" she asked, leaning on the bar, making doubly sure Liam had a perfect view of her magnificent breasts.

"I'll have a half larger and lime, and a ham salad roll, please Sheila," Liam replied.

"Would you care for anything else?" She seductively asked.

"Your being naughty Sheila," he chuckled.

"Well a girl can try, can't she?" She giggled, as she walked off. Four minutes later, Sheila was back, in one hand a china plate with a ham salad roll, in the other hand a half pint glass. What Liam also noticed now was, where Sheila's red silk blouse had once been tucked into her skirt, it was no longer tucked into her skirt, and the only button holding it closed, was at the bottom.

"There you are, young man," she said, smiling, placing the plate and glass in front of Liam, then standing back, her blouse falling open, Sheila was not wearing a bra, only her nipples were covered. She smiled at Liam, knowing the effect she was having on him, "So what are you doing in this neck of the woods?" she asked leaning forward, now her nipples came into view.

"I had to see Father O'Connell," Liam managed to say.

"So where are the two nice chaps that worked for him?" she asked.

Liam shook his head, "There no longer with us Sheila, I'm afraid," he replied.

"That's a pity," she said, "we had lots of fun together," she giggled, "yes Sheila, I know," Liam replied.

"What do you mean, you know?" she asked, pulling her blouse together.

Liam leaned across the bar and whispered, "They told me you love being on top, and they said, you give the best blow job ever, plus when they come, you aim it at your tits, and smother them," he said, smiling.

Sheila stood there for a minute, a grin spreading across her face, "We did have fun," she giggled, "and they were wrong about me being on top was my favourite, I just love sex, anyway anyhow anyone, and I like them coming over my breast, I rub it over them, it makes my skin smooth," she said, opening her blouse, "you can feel if you like," she said, moving closer to Liam and smiling.

Liam leaned over the bar, as Sheila came closer, and whispered, "Thank you sweet, I'd love to, but I'm now going home, and I'm going to fuck my beautiful wife's brains out, thanks to you," he chuckled as he slid of his bar stool.

Then to Liam's surprise, Sheila smiled and leaning over the bar, beckoned him, "When you've fucked her brains out, come back, I've got a caravan out back, and I'll show you how to fuck my brains out, you won't be sorry, ask your two mates, I had them on their knees," she giggled, buttoning up her blouse, "see ya," she said, as she walked away.

Chapter Seventy

O'Brien woke screaming, his left arm thrashing from one side to the other, then seeing no handcuffs, fell back onto the bed, sweat soaking his body. He sat up and looked at the trolley containing a stone cold, full English breakfast, his right arm making him wince in pain, as he tried to stand, holding onto the post of his four poster bed.

He managed to make his way to a small bar fridge, and on opening the door, retrieved a miniature bottle of whisky, then staggering into the bathroom, opened the medicine cabinet door and taking a bottle of Aspirin off of a glass shelf, managed to open it by holding the cap with his teeth, poured out four white tablets, doing the same ritual with the miniature whisky bottle, swallowed the four tablet, washing them down with the whisky.

Staggering back to the bed, he laid down and waited until the Aspirin had taken effect. Twenty minutes later he was standing under an ice cold shower, trying to clear his head, then opening the hot tap, began bringing his body back to life. Putting on a Gresham's towelling dressing gown, he walk over to the bed side cabinet, and picked up the phone, and was immediately asked.

"Yes Sir."

"I would like a pot of coffee and something to eat, please?" he asked.

"What would you like to eat Sir, there is a menu in the rack on the back of the door that you can order from?" he was asked.

"Just a toasted ham sandwich, with a little hot mustard, will be fine, thank you," O'Brien replied.

"And do you do in house dry cleaning?" he asked, and was told, "Yes Sir we do, the maid will bring your meal, and collect your dry cleaning."

"Thank you," O'Brien replied and replaced the receiver.

Ten minutes later O'Brien heard a knock on his door, and a voice stating, "Room service," as the door was unlocked, "okay to come in Sir?" he was asked.

"Come in," he answered. The door was opened by a tall young lady, dressed all in a black and white maids outfit, "Good morning Sir," she said, smiling, "we hope you slept well," she added, looking at the unused bed, "your coffee and sandwich, and I believe you need some dry cleaning done."

"Thank you," O'Brien replied pointing at a pair of trousers, vest and shirt, on the end of the bed.

"Be back in an hour Sir, and I'll take this trolley, shall I?" she asked.

"Thank you," O'Brien said, again, as the maid pushed the breakfast trolley towards the door.

True to her words, one hour later, O'Brien heard, "Room service, your dry-cleaning Sir," He went to the door, and on opening it was confronted by the tall young lady, "Your dry cleaning Sir," she said, offering O'Brien three coat hangers.

O'Brien instinctively raised his right arm to take the cloths, then quickly lowered it, "I'll lay them on the bed for you Sir, or shall I hang them in your closet?"

she asked blushing, "The bed will be fine Miss," he said, going to the bed side cabinet and retrieving a one pound note, "thank you Miss," he said, offering the maid the tip, "thank you! Sir," she said, curtsying, and backing out of the room.

One hour later, O'Brien walked down the last flight of lush green carpeted stair, to be confronted by at least fifty immaculately dressed men and women. Feeling rather out of place in their company he hurried over to reception to hand in his key, "Good morning Sir, going to take in the sites of our beautiful city, are we?" he was asked.

O'Brien place his room key on the counter, "What's the occasion?" he asked placing his room key on the counter and looking at the crowd of immaculately dressed men and women. The receptionist smiled. "That would be The Irish Law Society Sir, they hold a convention here every year, so the restaurant can get quite noisy at times," she said, smiling.

O'Brien walked out onto O'Connell Street and headed for Terminal Road South and the docks, as a well-dressed woman walked over to the reception desk, and looking at the key asked, "Who is the gentleman in room two-two-seven?"

To be told it was a gentleman by the name of Shaemus Donahue, "Thank you," she replied and re-joined her colleagues. O'Brien had been told of a public house called The Liffey Arms, after the river that runs through Dublin, and into

Dublin Bay. It took him over one and a half hours of asking, but finally he found himself outside the establishment, pushing open the door he found himself in a dimly lit bar, as he entered seven men turned and stared at him as he approached the bar, "Yes?" he was asked as he sat down on an ancient bar stool, by the man behind the bar, "What do you want?"

"I'll have a pint of Guinness, and a chat," O'Brien said, putting on a broad Irish accent, "the Guinness I can help you with, but we're right out of chats," the barman said, a scowl on his face.

O'Brien lent over the bar, and placed his prosthetic arm on the counter, "*Tiocfaidh a'r l'a*," he said, in a very low voice, "I have to repay a debt," he added.

There was silence for a minute, then the barman picked up a pint mug, and going over to the pump handle pulled the jet-black nectar up from the cellar below, and nodded towards the seven men, he waited until the head had settled, and topped the pint beer mug up to the brim, placing the pint beer mug in front of O'Brien he said, "*Sla'i'nte* friend," then walked down to the other end of the bar.

O'Brien lifted the pint beer mug to his mouth, and emptied the glass in three swallows, "The same again friend," he said, slamming the mug down on the bar. Two of the men that were at the table, were now at the bar talking to the barman, "be with you in a minute friend," O'Brien was told by the barman.

"Right friend," the barman said, as he walked towards O'Brien, "the same again, you say, and what do you want to chat about?" he asked, as he took O'Brien's pint beer mug, and walked back to the pump, placing the now, full pint mug on the bar.

O'Brien was told, "Start chatting friend," clearing his throat and taking a mouth full of Guinness, O'Brien began, "it's a long story, but I have a debt to repay, my twin younger brothers were murdered by British soldiers, and I was tortured by the northern Garda, that's all I'm prepared to say at the moment, but I need help, can you help me?" he asked, the barman stood there for a moment.

"Wait here," he said, and walked to the other end of the bar, where the two men were waiting. Three minutes later he returned, "Be back here at eight thirty tonight, and come alone, you'll be watched," was all he said, as he walked away.

Chapter Seventy-One

Liam was grinning like a Cheshire cat as he walked toward the station, "Thanks Sheila," he said to himself smiling, the memory of the previous night with Angela still vivid.

"Morning Sarge," he hollered, as he entered the station, taking the stairs three at a time, heading for his office. One hour later he knocked on Keir's door, and hearing, "Yo!" opened the door and walked in.

"Morning Gov," he said, as he walked up to Keir's desk grinning.

"Well," Keir stated smiling, "we either have some good news, or we got our leg over last night Liam, which is it?" he asked, as Bill walked through the door and sat down, "So what's happening?" he asked.

"We are going to find out if Liam here, has some good news, or that he got lucky last night," Keir stated.

"I'm always lucky Gov," Liam began, "but my visit to Father O'Connell was an eye opener. Turns out that O'Brien was one of five children, him, twin boys, who were shot, for being stupid, and twin girls, turns out their old man was a complete bastard, used to get drunk, come home and knock seven bells of shit out of his wife. Father O'Connell said, the three boys were like their old man, but he said, the twin girls were like their mother, tall, beautiful, and clever, then one night the old man comes home pissed, knocks his wife about, but when he went for the girls, the mother went for him, unfortunately he knocked her out and tried to mess with the girls but was too pissed, the three boys just stood there laughing, the next day whilst the old man and the boys were at work, the mother packs suitcases, grabs the girls and legs it.

Sometime later the old man gets pissed, and falls down a ships hold and kills himself, the mum remarried, and the girls have done very well for themselves, ones a doctor, and the other ones a barrister, and they live in Belfast, Father O'Connell has given me their names, so this morning I phoned my mate in Belfast, sent him those mug shots of O'Brien and filled him in on the whole case, plus the names of the girls, and he's going to try and talk to them, funny thing is, the twin girls married twin boys named O'Rourke, and they live in a place called Malone Road, South Belfast, Gov."

Bill began to chuckle, Keir sat back in his chair smiling, Liam just stared at the two of them, "What?" he asked.

"Just a memory came flooding back, Liam," Bill managed to say.

"This mate of yours, Liam?" Keir asked. Sitting forward, "What's his name?"

"Hamish Gov, Hamish McFarland, he's a D.I. Over in Belfast, we were at Oxford together, great bloke," Liam replied.

"So what have you told him?" Keir asked.

"Well Gov, Haggis knew most of it, because we chat quite often, and when O'Brien had that Army Pistol stuck in my back, and what happened afterwards, Haggis couldn't believe my luck."

"Neither could we," Bill stated. Shaking his head.

"So your mate's a D.I. Liam?" Keir asked.

"Yes Gov, and it won't be long before he's a DCI," he chuckled.

"So he's good, Liam."

"No Gov he's not good, he's bloody brilliant," Liam replied.

"I'll lay money, as soon as he put his phone down, after I'd told him the whole story, he's taken off like a rocket, it wouldn't surprise me, if I get a phone call from him today Gov, he's like a terrier, once he get his teeth into something he won't let it go," With this last comment, Bill doubled over laughing, pointing at his mate, leaving Liam with a quizzical look on his face.

"I think we should all go and bring our illustrious leader up to speed on this new development, well done Liam, a brilliant piece of police work," Keir said, rising from his chair.

Chapter Seventy-Two

O'Brien stood at the curb, looking across at the Liffey Arms, it was dead quiet, only the occasional car, he could hear an Irish band, somewhere in the distance, as he looked at his left wrist, "Eight twenty five," he said to himself, as he stepped off of the pavement and into the road. He was only yards away from the Liffey Arms front door, when a Black Ford 'V' Eight Pilot, screeched to a halt, the door to the pub opened and the barman pointed at O'Brien. The doors to the Ford were flung open, four huge men grabbed O'Brien and bundled him into the back of the Pilot, one of the men ramming a ruff sack over his head.

"What the devil," was all he was able to say. Before he felt a needle rammed into his shoulder.

He could hear people talking in the distance, but he couldn't see anything, he began shaking his head, trying to clear his brain, he remembered crossing the road outside the Liffey Arms, then a car screeching to a halt, the barman pointing at him, then nothing.

"He's coming round," a broad Irish accent stated. As the ruff sack was yanked from his head, O'Brien tried to move, but found that his arms and legs were bound to the chair he was sitting on, as the sack was removed O'Brien was blinded by two ark lights, "What gives you the right to say, *Tiocfaifh A'r L'a?*" he was asked.

"Can you switch off those lights, I can't see?" O'Brien asked. For which, he received a fist to the back of his head, "Answer the question," he was told.

O'Brien shook his head, "I need help," he replied.

"Why would we want to help you?" he was asked.

"Because if you are, who I think you are, we want the same thing," O'Brien replied.

"And what is it that we want?" he was asked.

"Right!" O'Brien screamed, sitting bolt upright, "You want to know why?" He screamed.

"I'll Tell you why, the British soldiers murdered my twin brothers, and the Garda tortured me, and if you don't believe me, take a look at my back," he screamed, "I tried to pay them back in England, but failed, so I'll pay them back where it started, so you can either help me, or stick that stupid sack back on my head and take me back to that pub, and you can tell that barman, his days are numbered."

"What happened to your hand?" he was asked.

"A police sniper took it, are you satisfied now?" He screamed. O'Brien could hear low voices talking, then the two flood lights were switch off, and the room was bathed in a low light, he was able to make out six men all dressed in black wearing ski masks, sitting behind where the ark lights stood.

"Why did a Police sniper take your hand out?" he was asked.

"Because Michael O'Toole and I were on our way to blow up New Scotland Yard and Aldershots Baracks, and they didn't want us to do it," O'Brien sarcastically replied.

"That was you?" he was asked.

"Yes! Believe or not, it was me."

"Cut him loose," he heard.

"So you are Shaun O'Brien are you?" he was asked.

"At one time a priest."

"Not any longer," O'Brien replied.

"I'm just the run of the mill civilian now."

"Sorry about the treatment, but we're not very popular in some circles, so we have to take precautions," he was told.

"I quite understand," O'Brien said, standing up and stretching.

"So what is it that you think we could help you with Shaun?" he was asked.

"It's now Shaemus, Shaemus Donahue, and what I need is an Enfield Sten gun, with six clips of ammunition, and eight hand grenades, I want them delivered to the Gresham Hotel, there's a Ford Zephyr six in the underground car park with English number plates, the boot will be open, if someone comes with me now, I'll give him five hundred English pounds, when they are delivered and in the boot, I'll drop another five hundred into the Liffey Pub," he said, "make it one thousand now, and one thousand on delivery, and you have a deal," he was told.

"What the hell!" O'Brien said, smiling, "Deal! When you deliver them, call the Gresham and leave a message saying, 'Tell Mr Donahue the novel is ready for collection'. I'll check the boot, and if you have come up with the equipment as asked for, there will be another thousand pound waiting for you at the Liffey, okay?" he asked, offering the man doing the negotiations his left hand.

"Just to let you Shaemus, if the thousand isn't delivered to the Liffey, we'll come after you, and it will be a slow and painful experience, we'll leave you alive, but you'll have wished we hadn't, because you won't be able to walk, talk, or see, do you understand?" he was asked.

"Understood," O'Brien replied.

Chapter Seventy-Three

O'Brien awoke smiling, "Not long now Brendan and Michael," he said, as he climbed out of his four-poster bed, and made his way to the bathroom. Standing naked under the ice-cold shower, he lathered up his body, then slowly opening the hot tap, brought his body temperature up, turning both taps off and stepping out of the shower, he ran his hand over the steamed up shaving mirror.

"Um!" He stated.

"Can't have this," he said, running his left hand over his chin. Twenty minutes later he was showered, shaved, and dressed, "I think it's about time you bought yourself some new cloths, Shaemus," he said, looking at himself in the full-length mirror, "so we'll make that priority one today shall we?" He said, smiling at his reflection.

Then making his way to the door, unlocked it and stepped into the corridor, descending the last flight of stairs into the foyer, he walked over to the reception desk and placing his room key on the counter was greeted with 'Good morning, I trust we slept well?'

"Thank you, yes," O'Brien replied.

"I'm expecting a message, I've ordered a new novel, and I asked the shop to call here when it comes in, so could you let me know of any messages for me, I'll be in the restaurant for the next hour?" O'Brien stated.

"Certainly sir, but there haven't been any messages so far, except for a lady asking who was in room two two seven" the young receptionist replied.

"What did she want?" O'Brien asked.

"Nothing sir," she just asked.

"Who is the gentleman in room two two seven," "I told her a Mr Shaemus Donahue, she just said, 'Oh!' And walked off."

"Thank you Miss," O'Brien replied as he walked away, "you're welcome Sir," he heard, as he headed for his morning repast.

"Good morning Sir, table for one?" he was asked. As he entered the lavish dining room, "Mr Donahue room two two seven, this way please Sir," he was told, as the waiter picked up a gilt-edged menu, and made his way over to a two seated table by the full length window, overlooking the street below.

"Your seat Sir," the waiter said, pulling the plush chair away from the perfectly set table.

"Could I have today's Irish Independent, please Charles?" he asked, noting the waiter's name embroidered on his green jacket, "Certainly Sir" came the reply, as he handed O'Brien, the gilt-edged menu, and hurried away.

Four minutes later he had return, "Your Irish Independent Sir," he said, laying the newspaper beside O'Brien left hand, "and are we ready to order?" he asked.

O'Brien studied the cordon blur dishes available to him, and smiling up at Charles stated, "Right Charles, we will begin with the grapefruit segments, followed by an Arbroath Smokey, and finally a mushroom and garlic omelette."

"Toast and coffee to finish, Sir?" he was asked.

"Thank you, Charles," O'Brien replied, taking a five-pound note from his left trouser pocket, and placing it on top of the newspaper.

"No! Thank you, Sir," Charles replied smiling, as he retrieved the English five pound note and hurried away.

O'Brien immediately picked up the newspaper, and turning to the sports page, scanned the football results, "Huh!" he uttered when he read that in the Scottish Division, Glasgow Rangers had thrashed Celtic United, four one. Looking up from his Irish Independent, he watched as twelve well-dressed guest entered the restaurant and began talking to Charles, some of them turning and looking at the guests already enjoying their breakfast, picking the newspaper back up, became engrossed in a story about an argument between two Irish politicians in the Seanad Eireann, (The upper House of the Irish Parliament). When the chair at the other side of his table was pulled out.

"Good morning Shaun," he heard a woman's voice say, but he didn't look up, "I said, good morning! Shaun," she repeated.

O'Brien put down the newspaper, and looked at the women, who now sat opposite him, "Sorry," he said, smiling, "were you talking to me?" he asked.

"Yes Shaun, I was talking to you," she replied.

"Well madam I don't know you, and my name is Shaemus, Shaemus Donahue, not Shaun," he stated.

"Yes," she replied.

"The receptionist at the desk said, that the gentleman in room two two seven, was a Mr Shaemus Donahue, well if that is the case, I must be Vera Lynn singing, 'We'll meet Again', at McGonagles Crystal Ballroom, mustn't I," she said, leaning across the table.

"Look!" O'Brien began, "I don't know who you are, or what you want, so will you please leave my table, or I'll call the Maître D and have you removed," he stated. The young woman sat back and smiled at O'Brien.

"You really don't remember me Shaun, do you?" She chuckled.

"No! I do not!" He replied.

"Now will you kindly leave my table."

"Let me refresh your memory, Shaun," she replied smiling, "it's Shaemus!" O'Brien corrected her, sitting back and folding his arms.

"Okay have it your way, Shaemus!" She said, emphasising the name.

"There was this family, comprising of a husband and wife, and five children, an elder boy, then twin boys, and finally twin girls, ring any bells yet?" she asked.

"The pig of a father would get drunk and beat his wife, then one night he tried to assault his two daughters whilst his sons stood there laughing, but their mother tried to protect her daughters, and was knocked unconscious by her so-called husband, How am I doing so far?" she asked.

"Maeve," O'Brien whispered, "sorry Shaun, wrong again, it's Niamh," she said, smiling.

"What do you want, Niamh?" He whispered leaning forward.

"They do say Vengeance is mine sayeth the Lord, and both Maeve and I really wanted vengeance against that pig of a father and his sons, for what they did. But Vengeance isn't ours, I was talking to Maeve last night, and it would appear that you have been a very naughty boy," she chuckled.

"She told me that she had a visit from a friend of mine, a Hamish McFarland, he wanted to know if we knew your wear a bouts, which obviously we didn't, then he went on to tell Maeve why he would like to talk to you, she couldn't believe it at first, but he had too many facts. When I saw you coming down the stairs into the foyer, I could believe my eyes, so I went and asked the receptionist, when she said, your name was Donahue, I thought I'd made a mistake, but when Maeve told me how you lost your hand, I knew I was right."

"What do you want Niamh?" he asked scowling, "Money, is it, I'll give you five thousand pounds, if you get up now and walk away," he said, rising.

"You have the money here?" she asked smiling.

"It's in my room," he replied.

"Let's go, Shaun," she said, getting to her feet and taking his arm. As they approached the restaurant desk, O'Brien beckoned towards Charles.

"Yes Sir?" Charles asked smiling, "Can you hold my breakfast for a while Charles, I shan't be long," O'Brien stated.

"Oh! Yes you will" Niamh said to herself, as they walked out of the restaurant, they were crossing the foyer heading for the stairs, when four men that had been sitting on one of the foyer luxury leather sofas, rose and walked towards them.

"Hello Hamish," she said, smiling, "this is my brother, Shaun O'Brien, I believe you wish to speak to him," she said, as two of the men grabbed O'Brien by the arms, and forced him face down onto the Italian Marble floor.

"You Bitch!" O'Brien screamed.

Niamh knelt down beside the thrashing body, "Vengeance is mine Shaun, Mine!" She whispered.

Niamh walked over to the reception desk. As the three special officers dragged O'Brien screaming out of the Luxury Gresham Hotel, "Yes Madam?" She was nervously asked.

"Mr Shaemus Donahue, has just checked out, so I would like the key to room two two seven, please?" She said, holding out her hand.

"I'll have to check with management Madam, Mr Donahue hasn't paid his bill," the receptionist stated.

"Give me the key, and make up his bill, I will return and settle his bill, okay? If you wish to see my credentials I'm a barrister attending this convention, young lady," she said, as the key was handed to her.

Niamh's eyes shot wide open as she flipped back the lid of the suitcase, and viewed its contents, closing the case, she exited and locked the door of room, two two seven, and took the lift down to the foyer, as she approached the reception desk, there were now two green jacketed men plus the receptionist standing behind the desk, placing the case on the desk she asked.

"Do you have Donahue's bill made up?" What appeared to be the hotel manager stepped forward and asked.

"May I ask who you are Madam and why you require the key to room two two seven, which was allocated to Mr Shaemus Donahue?"

"Yes you may," Niamh replied smiling, "my name is Niamh O'Rourke, I am a barrister, and I am attending a conference here, the man the police have just taken away isn't Shaemus Donahue, his name is Shaun O'Brien, he is an escaped criminal, and is wanted by the police in England. So if you would kindly let me know how much he is in your debt, I'll settle his bill."

"But he has a two-tone Zephyr six car parked in our underground car park, Madam," Niamh was told, "the police will tow it away," she replied.

"Yes, but when?" The manager asked. A concerned look on his face, "We can't have police traipsing all over this hotel, we have our reputation to consider Madam," he stated pushing out his chest.

"Right Mr?"

"Bartholomew Madam."

"Right Mr Bartholomew, give me the keys to his car, I'll take it to the local police station, make out the bill for his room and parking, I have a conference to attend," she said.

Niamh began walking down the ramp, when a black Ford 'V' eight Pilot coasted passed her, she watched as the driver's window was lowered, and a voice shouted, "There" a finger pointing at the two-tone Zephyr, bringing the Pilot to a halt, the driver opened his door and lifting a heavy sack, began walking towards the Ford. Niamh began to run, and screaming at the top of her voice, "Get away from that car," she shouted. The driver turned, and seeing Niamh running towards him, ran back to the Pilot, throwing the sack into the car, jumped in, slamming the door and driving off, leaving tyre marks on the concrete floor.

Niamh was breathless by the time she reached the Zephyr, she stood there leaning on the boot gasping for breath, as the 'V' eight pilot roared out of the underground car park.

"What the blazes was that all about," she shouted. Finally getting her breath back, she took the keys and unlocked the driver's door, sliding into the driver's seat, she had to lift the seat handle and move the seat forward slightly so that her feet could reach the pedals, inserting the key into the ignition, she fired up the six cylinders, and sat there, letting the engine idle for a moment, pushing the clutch to the floor, she engaged reverse, and slowly backed out of the parking space, then putting the car in first gear, drove up the ramp to join the traffic on O'Connell Street.

She waited until it was clear for her to pull onto the main road, and head towards Pearse Street Garda Station. She had only travelled three hundred yards, when she looked into her rear-view mirror, and there, two cars back she could see the Black 'V' Eight Pilot, "Don't panic," she screamed, gripping the steering wheel, her knuckles turning white.

As she approached a set of green traffic light, the car in front turning left, Niamh hit the accelerator, as the traffic lights turned to amber, the Zephyr leaving rubber on the road as the car shot across the intersection, the car behind her hadn't tried to beat the lights and had come to a stop, the 'V' Eight behind it, unable to follow.

Niamh looked up ahead and smiled, far in the distance she could make out the large building at 1–6 Pearse Street, but the smile vanish when she looked in her rear-view mirror and spotted the 'V' Eight coming up fast, her foot hitting the accelerator again she shot forward, swerving into the outside lane then back, the 'V' Eight gaining on her, just as the Garda forecourt came into view, Niamh jumped the curb just missing a pedestrian, and skidded to a halt in the parking area of the police station, as the Black car shot passed.

Niamh knocked the car out of gear and yanked up the hand brake, then throwing open the car door, ran into the police station, once inside, she leant against the wall, her eyes closed, taking deep breaths, trying hard to bring her heart rate back to normal. Pushing herself off of the wall she ran to the reception desk, "Sergeant," she called as she came to a halt, addressing an elderly officer who was talking into a telephone, he looked up and raised his left hand.

"Be with you in a minute Madam," he said, then turned away, and carried on talking, "but Sergeant," Niamh screamed, to receive the left hand again. Four minutes later, the Sergeant replaced the receiver, then smiling at Niamh asked.

"What seems to be the problem Madam?" Niamh, took a deep breath and tried to relate the whole episode, and receive a, "Woe Madam," as he opened a large ledger, "you are staying at the Gresham, the police arrested a man, you were going to bring a car here but a black car chased you, is that correct?" he asked.

"Yes Sergeant?"

"Did you happen to get the registration of this Black car, Madam?" he asked, to which Niamh replied, "No Sergeant I didn't, but if you would like to come outside, the car I was delivering here, is on your forecourt."

"So why would you bring a car here Madam?" she was asked.

By this time, Niamh's blood pressure had begun to rise, taking out her wallet from her jacket inside pocket, she laid it open in front of the police officer, "Right

Sergeant," she began, "do you see that?" she asked pointing, "I am a Barrister for the high court of Belfast, I would like you to come outside, and take possession of a two tone Ford car, the management at The Gresham do not wish police officer crawling over their car park, they informed me, they have a reputation to uphold, do you understand?"

"Yes Ma'am, but what's this thing about a black car?" he asked.

"As I've already stated Sergeant, I was walking down the ramp of the Greshams underground car park to retrieve the two tone car, when this black car drove passed me and stopped at the Ford, a man got out with a sack and was heading for the Ford, I screamed at him, he ran back to his car and drove off at speed, I was on my way here and noticed he was following me, and I have no Idea why, now can we go and you can take possession of the car, please?"

Her blood pressure returning to nearly normal. The sergeant closed the ledger, and opened the counter hatch, as Niamh walked toward the station door.

"It's gone," she screamed, as the sergeant joined her.

"Where did you park this car Ma'am?" he asked, a cynical look on his face.

"Just there," she screamed pointing.

"You do know wasting police time is an offence Ma'am," he said, Niamh placed both her fist on her hips and lent forward, her nose only inches away from the Sergeant's a scowl on her face, "don't quote the law to me Sergeant, I've forgotten more than you will ever know, and if you had acted immediately to my request, and not those stupid questions you asked. The car would still be here, wouldn't it?" She hollered.

"If you say so Ma'am," he replied. A supercilious grin spreading across his face.

"All right Sarge," they both heard, turning, they watched as two constables approached them, the sergeant pushing out his chest smiled, "this lady," he said, pointing at Niamh and grinning, "seems to have mislaid a car, you wouldn't, by any chance have seen one parked here, would you?" he asked, pointing at the forecourt.

The two constables looked at each other, then back at Niamh and their Sergeant, "That wouldn't be a two-tone Zephyr Six, by any chance, Sarge, would it?" he was asked.

"Yes constable," Niamh shouted.

"Well! In that case yes! Ma'am, Constable Price and myself were over there," he said, pointing to the other side of the busy road, "waiting to cross, when a black 'V' Eight pulls up, the passenger door opens and a man runs over to this two-tone Zephyr that had the driver's door open, gets in, slams the door, then both the 'V' Eight and the Zephyr, high tail it up the road, Ma'am," Niamh turned and glared at the now demurred Sergeant.

"Your name, Sergeant," she shouted, "sorry Ma'am, but—"

"Your name!" Niamh screamed.

"Price, Ma'am, Sergeant Colin Price," he replied. Looking at her shoes, "not for much longer! Constable! You won't be."

Chapter Seventy-Four

"Come," Keir called out in reply to a knock on his door.

"Only me Gov," Liam stated as he entered, and walked towards Keir's desk, "just thought you would like to know, I had a long chat with Haggis last night, Gov."

"And?" Keir asked, pointing at a vacant chair.

Liam sat down and crossed his legs, "Do you remember me saying, "I bet as soon as he puts the phone down, he'll be off like a rocket, Gov," Keir nodded his head, "well I was right, he's found one of the twin sisters, but Father O'Connell was wrong, the one named Maeve is not a doctor, she's a top Orthopaedic Surgeon in Belfast, has her own private practice, anyway Maeve, the surgeon, said, that if O'Brien tried to contact her she would let Haggis know, her twin sister who is a Barrister, is down in Dublin at a convention, something to do with the Irish Law Society, so she was going to call Niamh and tell her about O'Brien, the funny thing is Niamh is a prosecuting attorney, and has worked with Haggis on a few cases, so I've told Haggis if he has any luck, to ask to be put through to your phone Gov, hope that's alright?" Liam asked.

Keir smiled at his sergeant. "Fingers crossed Liam, because at the present moment, we're trying to push, shit up hill, and getting nowhere fast," he said.

"Well Gov, if we're right about Ireland, and Haggis is on it, if O'Brien is over there, Haggis will find him. There was one time, he was after a chap that had disposed of his wife, Haggis new he had gotten rid of her body, but couldn't get enough evidence to prove it, no body was found, turns out this chaps father had just died, and was laying in state, at a funeral parlour, Haggis looks at this ornate coffin," Liam chuckled.

"And thinks to himself, that for the size of the corpse, it seemed a bit on the big size, so he gets the funeral director in, tells him to lift the body, and guess what they found?"

"You're joking!" Keir replied grinning.

"No Gov, once Haggis gets even the slightest sniff, he won't let go."

"Well Liam, let's hope that your mate nostrils are in excellent working order," Keir said, smiling.

"Yes Gov," Liam replied. Just as Keir's phone began to ring, picking up his hand-set Keir stated, "Dickson." Seconds later switched his phone to speaker, as a broad Scottish accent was heard asking to speak to someone called 'Lollop', Keir raised his eyebrows, and asked, "Who?"

"Me, Gov," Liam replied grinning, "Haggis, you old reprobate," Liam hollered.

"I am neither, old or a reprobate, Lollop, so cut it out," they heard him chuckle.

"I take it you have some good new, my friend?" Liam asked.

"Maybe," came the reply, "don't stuff around Hamish, have you, or haven't you?" Liam asked.

"So! It's Hamish now, is it," they heard, "will you stop pissing about, Haggis" Liam said, in exacerbation, "watch it Sergeant," they heard him chuckle, "I outrank you."

"And I outrank you D.I. McFarland, so as my good colleague here has just said, and this is DCI Keir Dickson speaking, Stop pissing about," Keir stated.

"Hi Gov," came the jovial reply.

"Liam! Or as he was affectionately known at Oxford as 'Lollop' has told me you can walk on water, so it's an honour to speak to you Sir, but enough of this frivolity, I might have some good news for you, and I say, Might! It turns out that a dear friend of mine, who I have worked with on several cases, is in Dublin at a conference something to do with The Irish Law Society, her sister Maeve O'Roake phoned her after I called round to see her, to tell her about her eldest brother, and that we needed to speak with him. Niamh O'Roake is a barrister and I've just got off the phone from her."

"After Niamh had spoken to her sister and related what I had told Maeve. Well! Niamh thinks she has seen her brother who is staying at the very posh Gresham Hotel, but she's not sure, because, when she asked at reception about the man, she was told it was a gentle man by the name of Shaemus Donahue, so she's going to check him out. So I'm driving down to Dublin tomorrow with my lads, it might be a wild goose chase, but I've got a gut feeling it's him." Hamish said.

Liam sat back in his chair and roared with laughter, "If you've got that famous gut feeling of yours," he managed to say, "we can just put our feet up and wait," he chuckled.

"I'll be in touch Lollop, and it's been nice speaking with you Sir."

"Thanks, Haggis," they both said, in unison, as the phone went dead, they sat back, and grinned at each other, "here's hoping, Liam," Keir said, sliding open his bottom draw.

Chapter Seventy-Five

Hamish McFarland stood up smiling, "Lollop," he chuckled. Shaking his head, then opening his office door made his way to the operation room, and DCI James Faulkner's office, knocking quietly on the door, and turning the handle, found the room empty, "Oh well," he said to himself, as he turned and walked into the op's room, to be greeted by twenty-four smiling faces grinning at him, as DCI James Faulkner standing at a podium hollered, "Now!"

Hamish stood there speechless, as the whole room broke into, "Happy Birthday to You." Hamish stood there listening to their rendition, a broad grin on his face, he had completely forgotten this particular date, when the cheering had stopped, he raised both his hands into the air, "As coppers," he shouted, "your all brilliant, but as a choir you all suck," he chuckled.

To which he received boo's and jeers, until DCI Faulkner bent down and from under the podium produce a Haggis with one lit candle stuck into the top, "Happy Birthday Haggis!" the whole room echoed.

Taking his DCI To one side he asked, "Do you remember me talking about an English case, where a murderer escaped, Gov?" The DCI just nodded his head, "Well Gov," he continued, "I have it on good authority by Councillor Niamh O'Rourke, that the person the police need to speak to, is in Dublin, she thinks she recognised the man, because she knew him years ago, but he's travelling under another name, so she's going to confront him tomorrow, I would like to be there when she does Gov, if that's okay?" He stated.

"Where is Councillor O'Rourke staying, Hamish?" he was asked.

Hamish grinned, "At the Gresham Gov," he replied.

"And the suspect?" he was asked.

"At the Gresham Gov," he answered smiling.

"Take three of the lads with you Hamish, I suppose we'll have to get our brother, law enforcement chaps, over in England out of a jam," he chuckled.

"Keep me informed," he added as he walked off.

"So what's happening, Gov?" Hamish was asked. As he and three detectives drove out of Musgrove Police Station, heading south on the 'A1'.

"We're headed for The Gresham Luxury Hotel, in Dublin, to assist Councillor O'Rourke, in apprehending a known villain." he replied.

"Shouldn't we be wearing tuxedo's Gov," came the jovial reply. Two and a half hours later, Hamish pulled his undercover police car onto the forecourt of the Prestigious Hotel, switching off the engine, all four officers clambered out of the vehicle, to be greeted with, "Sorry Gentlemen, but unless you are guests here, you can't park your vehicle there," the livery dressed doorman stated pointing.

All four officers produced their warrant cards, "Oh " they all heard, "I need to speak to the manager immediately," Hamish stated. And was told, "This way Sir."

The three officers stood in the foyer, mesmerised at the palatial surroundings, "Sit over there lads," Hamish said, pointing at a four-seater luxurious leather settee, "I'll be back in a minute," he said, as he walk toward the ornate reception desk.

"Yes Sir, and how may we help you?" he was asked. By a very attractive young lady, "I wish to speak to the manager, please," Hamish replied holding up his warrant card.

"Certainly Sir I'll call Mr Hogan straight away," she said, picking up the phone. In less than a minute, a door opened and a tall gentleman wearing grey striped trouser, and a black tailed morning coat, with matching waist coat, black shoes that shone, starched white shirt and company tie, strode toward him, "And how may I be of assistance constable?" Hamish was asked.

"It's Inspector sir, not constable," Hamish replied.

Bowing low, the manager said, "I do apologise Inspector, all I was told was that a policeman wished to see me."

"Apology accepted sir, now if I could have a word with you?" Hamish said, moving away from the reception desk.

"Certainly Inspector," the manager replied, hurrying to join Hamish, "now how can I be of assistance?" he asked as they came together.

"Actually Sir, nothing," he began, the manager raising his eye browse, "my colleagues and myself have reason to believe that one of your guests, isn't who he says he is, and is wanted in England, for several different serious crimes, a Barrister friend of the police phoned us and told us she believes he is staying here, she hopes to confirm this, and if she does, we will escort the gentleman from this hotel, as quietly as possible. But I felt it my duty to inform you of what we intend to do, Sir," Hamish stated.

"Thank you inspector, that's very considerate of you, I shall inform my staff of your intent," he replied bowing, then walked back to the reception desk, and picked up the phone.

"What now, Gov?" he was asked. As he sat down, "We wait" Hamish replied. Fifteen minutes later Hamish smiled, as a couple left the restaurant and headed for the stairs, "Show time!" He stated grinning, and getting to his feet, followed by his three colleagues.

"Good morning Hamish," Niamh said, smiling, as the couple stopped in front of him, "this is my Brother Shaun O'Brien."

Chapter Seventy-Six

The Westminter Chiming Clocks, minute hand moved to the twelve noon, Fiona, Keir, Bill, and Liam heard the mechanism begin to operate, as the clock struck twice. All four gazed at the ornate Mahogany encased wall clock, as Fiona's phone began to ring, "Excuse me gentlemen," she said, smiling, as she lifted the handset, and stated.

"Superintendent Fiona Jarman," then immediately switched the phone to speaker, "good morning Ma'am," a broad Scottish accent stated.

"This is D.I. Hamish McFarland, calling from Belfast, would it be possible to speak to D.S. Liam Smith?" he asked.

"Told you," Liam whispered, giving the thumbs up sign, and elbowing Bill in the ribs.

"We are all here, inspector, Keir, Bill Day, and D.S. Smith, I take it you have some news for us?" she asked smiling.

"Morning Lollop," they all heard, "morning Haggis" Liam timidly replied.

"Right Ma'am," Hamish began, "because we're on the phone Hamish, It's—" Fiona tried to say, before Hamish stated.

"Yes Ma'am, I know, Liam has already told me all about you, this conversation is being recorded," he said.

"Thank you Inspector," Fiona replied blushing.

"No! Thank you Ma'am. Right! To put you all in the picture," Hamish began, "three colleagues and myself drove down to Belfast and entered the Gresham Hotel, I spoke to the manager, a Mr Hogan, and told him why we were there, as a courtesy, for which he was appreciative. When Mrs Niamh O'Rourke, a friend and colleague of mine, entered the foyer and approached us, she said, "Good morning Hamish, this is my brother, Shaun O'Brien," my colleagues immediately, man handled him to the floor, but O'Brien began to retaliate causing a scene, unfortunately for O'Brien, D.S. Webb is light heavyweight champion for our station, so we were able to take an unconscious O'Brien and place him in our car.

"He was then transported back to Musgrove Police Station, he became very violent on the journey back, to the extent that D.S. Webb had to restrain him again. When we arrived back here, he was stripped and dressed in a prisoner's boiler suite, and was dragged screaming down to the cells, he kept screaming, "Not again, not again please." When the cell door was closed, he started banging on the door, he was told to be quiet, that he would be transported back to England to stand trial the next day, but he just kept screaming, and the banging continued. "Now comes the bad news, I'm afraid," Hamish sighed.

All four colleagues lent forward, "The banging eventually stopped," Hamish continued, "after about twenty minutes, the Sergeant went to check on him, when he slid open the viewing hatch he couldn't see O'Brien, so he called for assistance before he would open the door. When he did, they found O'Brien laying on the cell floor, his head covered in blood, and froth coming from his mouth, they immediately called the doc, who rushed him off to the local hospital, O'Brien had used his head as a battering ram on the door. Not his fists."

"Are your police officers in attendance at the hospital, Inspector, because we have had this scenario before?" Fiona asked, a concerned look on her face.

"Yes Ma'am I know," Hamish replied.

"But yes, an officer is with him twenty four seven, but O'Brien won't be going anywhere soon Ma'am, according to the hospital, with him using his head as a battering ram, he now has severe brain damage, he just lays there mumbling, 'Sorry Brendon, sorry Michael', over and over and over again. So it won't be Dartmoor, he'll be going to, It'll be Broadmoor near Reading Ma'am," Hamish concluded.

"Well! Thank you Inspector, it's not the outcome we would have wished for, but it's a result, and I would like to thank you personally for all your hard work, it's very much appreciated," Fiona said.

"Don't thank me Ma'am," they heard him chuckle, "it's Lollop you should be thanking, if he hadn't given me the names of the twin sisters and where they lived, I wouldn't have had a clue where to start, and it won't be long before he'll be wearing pips on his shoulder, but you can tell him from me, there's no way I'll call him Sir," they all heard him laughing, as the line went dead.

All three turned smiling, and stared at Liam, who was now gazing at the carpet.

"What's with the name Lollop, Liam?" Fiona asked a grin spreading her face. Liam looked up, his face rather pink.

"Haggis or Hamish and I, were at Oxford together, Ma'am, Professor Ferd, was one of our tutors, he spotted me one day in the gymnasium working out, and told me to stop lolloping about, because I should be studying for my finals, and Hamish being Scottish, Well! Professor Ferdy called every Scotsman Haggis," he said.

"It would appear that Haggis or Hamish," Fiona chuckled.

"Has a very high opinion of you, Liam."

"The feeling is mutual Ma'am, I knew that if O'Brien was in Ireland, Hamish would find him, I told the Gov here" Liam said, looking at Keir, "once Hamish gets his teeth into a case, he won't let go until it's finished, that's probably why he's a D.I. Ma'am," Liam concluded.

"And that's why you should consider going for DI, Liam," Keir said, slapping him on the back.

"And then DCI, Liam," Fiona said, smiling.

Liam sat up straight, "There's no way I would go for DCI. Ma'am, no way!" Liam stated stone-faced.

All three stared at him, "Why on earth not?" Fiona asked.

Liam smiled. "You can only have one DCI at a station, Ma'am," he chuckled.

Keir lent over and placing his arm around Liam's shoulder, "We're a team, Liam."

"Yes Gov," Liam replied. "We're a team."

"So O'Brien was never able to get his revenge for his twin brothers," Bill said, breaking the spell.

Liam stood up and smiled at him. "As our dear friend Father Patrick O'Connell who suffered at the hands or hand of O'Brien would say, Bill, Deuteronomy, Chapter Thirty-Two, Verse Thirty-Five, *Vengeance is Mine*."